BATTLE OF BLOOD

Riley held his position in some brush, trying not to be too scared. He had been in battle before, but this was something a little different, considering the number of Indians they faced. The warriors' tactics also were unnerving, what with them popping up individually from behind a rock or bush or tree. He was certain one of them would do so right next to him and carve his scalp off before he even knew the man was there.

Suddenly the Indians charged, rushing through the brush, seeking to overwhelm the mountain men through sheer numbers.

Riley fired his rifle, knocking a warrior down. Then he heard Fraeb's thick, guttural curses and swung his head that way. Three Sioux surrounded the tough German, who was defending himself with a knife in one hand and a tomahawk in the other. Then one warrior slipped in and shoved his knife to the hilt into Fraeb's lower back.

Riley began running, seeing one of the warriors swing his war club at Fraeb's head. He missed, but the stone ball broke Fraeb's shoulder. One-handed, the old mountain man slashed wildly, but hit nothing.

Just as the other warrior cracked Fraeb's skull with his tomahawk, Riley smashed into the one with the war club, who had fallen onto his back. It was but a few seconds before he had gutted the Sioux. He pushed himself up and turned.

The pain that suddenly hit his left eye was more staggering than anything he had ever experienced before . . .

*The Forts of Freedom Series by John Legg
from St. Martin's Paperbacks*

WAR AT BENT'S FORT
TREATY AT FORT LARAMIE
SIEGE AT FORT DEFIANCE
BLOOD AT FORT BRIDGER

BLOOD AT FORT BRIDGER

JOHN LEGG

ST. MARTIN'S PAPERBACKS

BLOOD AT FORT BRIDGER

Copyright © 1995 by Siegel and Siegel Ltd.

The Forts of Freedom series is a creation of Siegel and Siegel Ltd.

ISBN: 0-312-95447-6

Printed in the United States of America

St. Martin's Paperbacks edition/March 1995

10 9 8 7 6 5 4 3 2 1

For Wendy, Cheryl, Jim, Mary
and all the others
at Apacheland.
And for Debbie
at Book Exchange Plus.
Many thanks
for all your help,
your appreciation
and your friendship.

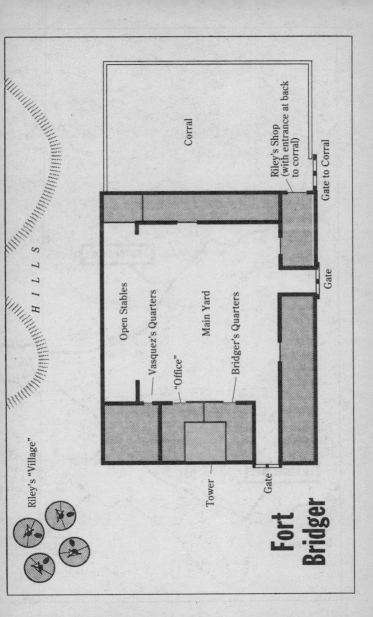

HILLS

Riley's "Village"

Open Stables

Vasquez's Quarters

"Office"

Main Yard

Bridger's Quarters

Tower

Gate

Corral

Riley's Shop
(with entrance at back
to corral)

Gate to Corral

Gate

Fort Bridger

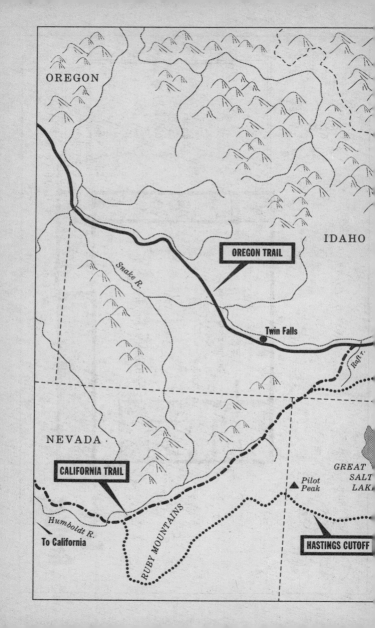

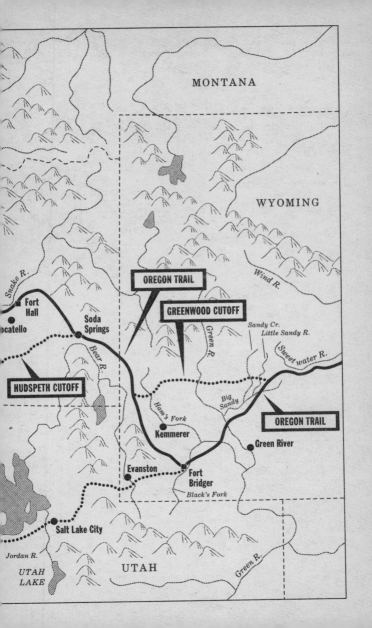

PART 1

One-Eye Pete Riley slammed his eight-pound cross-peen hammer down on the white-hot horseshoe, smashing flat a spot several inches across. "Damn," he muttered angrily as he tossed the useless piece of metal into the bucket of water nearby. He glanced askance at the tall, hard man leaning against the wall of Riley's blacksmith shop.

Riley was the blacksmith at Fort Bridger, and as such was kept plenty busy with work for the army as well as for the many travelers on the California and Mormon Trails. By the time the emigrants reached this point—on Black's Fork of the Green River—they were suffering, and many were in poor humor. Riley, a generally outgoing man, usually dealt with them decently, knowing the hardships they had been through. Occasionally, though, someone who had left his sense back on the trail somewhere would give Riley a hard time. In such cases, often to the chagrin of the fort's commander, Riley—a big, gruff, powerful man—would bounce the offender off the shop walls a bit, before sending him on his way with a good kick in the pants.

Riley hadn't encountered such a troublesome, mouthy emigrant in quite some time. The man, who in his rantings had disclosed that his name was Carter Halsey, had been baiting him for more than fifteen minutes. Riley figured Halsey was trying to get a rise out of him. The big blacksmith decided he had finally succeeded at his mission.

Riley affixed Halsey with the stern, one-eyed glare that kept most fools in line. "You're wearin' on my patience, Mister Halsey," he said in a deep rumble that was his usual voice.

"That so?" Halsey responded, sounding unconcerned. Carter Halsey was a tall, rawboned man with a hard cast to his razor-sharp, hawk-like face. His mien denoted plenty of self-confidence, to the point of arrogance. He was, like most of the travelers, poorly dressed, his clothes having taken a harsh beating on the long trek.

"It is," Riley said in a low growl. It wasn't bad enough that Halsey had just walked into the shop and begun reviling former mountain men, especially Old Jim Bridger and Riley himself, and Shoshonis; no, he had to be a Mormon and one who thought that any Gentile was not worth the mud on the bottom of a Mormon's boots. The latter was what got to Riley the most. He had no liking for Mormons, not since that day back in '47 when the first Mormon wagon train—led by Brigham Young —had arrived at the old wooden trading post. The intervening years had only deepened Riley's dislike for those people.

For his part, Halsey was a longtime Mormon, an elder whose religious fervor had not dimmed one iota over the years. He knew that Riley had had a large hand in the "Mormon War" of two years ago, as well as in the events that had led up to it. Such actions were a terrible affront to any faithful member of the Church of Jesus Christ of Latter-Day Saints. Hearing that Riley was married to a Shoshoni and had several half-breed children only solidified Halsey's hatred for Riley. It wasn't that Halsey disliked Indians, it was just that he had been told by church officials that Riley had had a major role in the Shoshonis' rejection of his church's missionary efforts. Halsey also had personal reasons for hating Riley.

"Your objections mean little—no, less than that—to

me," Halsey said with something of a sneer. Carter Halsey had an extremely high opinion of himself, thinking he was better than other men. He was a veteran of the Mormon struggles in the East, including the troubles at Nauvoo that had ended in the death of Joseph Smith, the church's founder. Because of that, he was more than capable of handling himself in a fight. He also thought himself blessed, both because he was a Mormon and because he had overcome such great adversity.

Besides, he had an extremely low opinion of those who had been mountain men. He thought them lazy, rank-smelling, generally foul and entirely godless. So he had no fear of Riley, despite the blacksmith's size and fierce look.

Riley set his hammer on the anvil and pulled off his heavy leather gloves, which he tossed atop the hammer. He deliberately undid the long, black, tool-stuffed leather apron and dropped it on the shop's dirt floor. Then he moved slowly toward Halsey.

Waiting warily, Halsey took stock of Riley. The blacksmith was about six-foot-tall, Halsey estimated, but had to weigh a good two hundred forty pounds. While Riley had a broad stomach, he carried little fat on the big frame. His face was creased and used by hard living, weather and his looming fortieth birthday. A leather patch covered one eye—and few were fool enough to have the temerity to ask him about it. The eye that could be seen was hard and dark, looking out over a wide nose that had been battered and flattened several times. Riley had thin lips under a thick, wild mustache; his chin and cheeks were coated with stubble. His shoulders were wide and gently sloped down to a chest, back and biceps that strained the calico shirt he wore.

As Riley closed in, Halsey began to wonder if perhaps he had made a mistake in baiting Riley on his own. Throwing caution to the winds, Halsey suddenly launched himself at Riley—and clanged up against a wall of iron. Or so it seemed to him as he staggered backward a few steps. He stopped and shook his head groggily. He had come up against some hard men in his time, but none like this one.

Then Halsey went down on the worn seat of his pants as he was hit by what he could only assume was one of the Wasatch Mountains. "Sweet Jesus," he muttered. Or at least *thought* he muttered; he could not be sure.

The mountain suddenly loomed over him, glaring at him with one bright eye. And then it spoke!

"I'd advise ye to watch your goddamn mouth when you're in my shop, ye scabrous son of a bitch," Riley said angrily. "Next time ye bring your foulness in here, I'll cut your goddamn tongue off for ye and shove it up your ass, where your head is. Ye clear on that, shit pile?"

Halsey tried to nod, not sure that he had accomplished it. Moments later he figured he must have been successful, since Riley hauled him to his feet.

"Best go git yourself some rest, boy," Riley said, not too ungently. His anger was fading some, and so he felt a little more benevolent. Not that he had suddenly taken a liking to Halsey. He still couldn't stand the emigrant or what he stood for. But he tried to be as gentlemanly as he possibly could in any given situation.

Riley guided—well, mostly dragged—Halsey to the wide door of his blacksmith shop and propelled him outside. "Mind what I told ye, boy," Riley said by way of farewell. As Halsey stumbled dazedly a few feet and grabbed onto his saddled horse to keep himself upright, Riley turned back inside and went back to work.

Not that all his anger had dissipated. He still found it hard to believe—as he always had—how someone could act like Halsey had. He had seen it plenty of times, but never once did he figure out what possessed a man to behave so. He sighed. If Halsey had not been a Mormon, it might've been easier to forgive him, but that was not the case.

Riley wondered if perhaps he should have killed Halsey. It wouldn't have been the first time he had killed a man just over words. *Who knows?* he thought, *it might avoid trouble later.* On the other hand, such an act could cause even more trouble. With the way things had been around here the past few years, that'd be the more likely case, Riley figured. That's all he needed was to bring the wrath of a whole wagon train of Mormons—and by extension possibly the entire LDS Church—down on the fort. Brigham Young certainly could raise an army if he so chose. He had done so before.

Now that would be something, Riley thought. He almost smiled. The fort commander, Major Edward Canby, would really appreciate facing a Mormon army.

Riley was in a rather foul mood when he was called into Canby's office. This happened every time he had a run-in with an emigrant. It had been almost comical at first, but these meetings had quickly lost whatever little humor they might have had. Now they only caused Riley annoyance. He had to pretend to be sorry while Canby had to make like he was outraged at the blacksmith's behavior, even when both knew that the emigrant was at fault.

But Riley was furious enough this time to not want to play the game. He entered the office, grunted a greeting at Canby, glowered a moment at Halsey, and then stuffed his bulk into a chair.

"Mister Halsey here tells me you assaulted him, One-Eye," Canby started off, trying to look sternly at Riley. He liked the blacksmith, despite Riley's penchant for getting into trouble.

"He's a lyin' sack of shit, Major, if that's what he says," Riley growled. He felt a touch of joy at the shocked look that appeared on Canby's face and then almost as quickly slipped off again.

"Well, Mister Halsey?" Canby asked, looking at the emigrant. He had decided in that instant to stand behind his blacksmith. Riley had played the apologetic minion often enough.

"My nature doesn't allow lyin'," Halsey responded, the touch of anger in his voice tempered by a bit of hurt.

"Mister Riley's not given over to lying much, or so has been my experience with him. I must admit to you, sir, that this is not the first time a wagon train traveler has accused Mister Riley of attacking him. Generally they are shown to be the fools they are." He paused, leaning forward onto his desk. "Now, sir, are you certain Mister Riley attacked you?" He glared at Halsey.

"Look at my face," Halsey said adamantly.

"It is rather colorful," Canby said dryly. "But that could've come from a lot of things. Maybe you got kicked by one of your mules. Maybe you fell off a wagon. Maybe you had a fight with one of your fellow Saints." He paused, then added flatly, "Or maybe you attacked Mister Riley and he whupped the tar out of you."

"The only way he could whup me, Major," Halsey snarled, "is if he caught me by surprise, which is what he done. I went into his shop to see about having some wagon traces repaired. I turned my back for a moment, and the next I knew, I was flat on the ground."

"So, you had turned away from him when you were attacked?" Canby asked.

"Yep. That's right."

"Then how'd your face get so mucked up?" Canby asked with a touch of harshness in his voice.

Halsey glowered at the fort commander, then said lamely, "I hit the wall after that bastard slugged me." He pointed at Riley, though there was really no reason to.

"Mister Halsey," Canby said with an annoyed sigh, "you are a hell of a poor liar, and I'm not so sure the principals of your church would like you lying. Nor, I think, would they appreciate you trying to stir up trouble here at the fort. We've had more than enough conflict between the army and the Saints."

"I resent such an implication, sir," Halsey sputtered, rage coursing through him.

"Resentment be damned," Canby snapped. He was not one for taking anyone's guff, least of all some bedraggled emigrant. "This is my fort, and I won't listen to false accusations against my men, whether they're my soldiers or the civilians who work here.''

"But I . . .''

Canby loudly slammed a palm on his desk top. "Get the hell out of my office, damn you,'' he said quietly, though with undeniable force. "And don't step foot on this post again. Stay with the wagons.''

Halsey was livid. As he rose, he shook a long, bony finger at Canby. "Brigham Young'll hear about this, damn your hide,'' he snarled. "And when he hears of how this Saint—and others—have been treated here, his retribution will be swift and sure.''

"Mister Young isn't that damned stupid. He's had enough trouble with the army and the government. He won't go looking for more just because one of his Saints was foolish enough to get his ass whupped by some tough old bastard you were dumb enough to challenge. Now get.'' Canby leaned back in his chair and lit a cigar.

Halsey stood there a few moments, fuming. Then he turned and stormed out.

"Lord save me from idiots,'' Canby muttered, blowing smoke toward the ceiling. He looked at Riley. "No way you could've avoided this, One-Eye?'' he asked.

"Sure.'' Riley reached across the desk and picked up one of Canby's cigars. He lit it. "If I wanted him to keep ridiculin' the old mountain boys, ye and everyone else he didn't take a shine to.''

"Damn,'' Canby carped. Then he sighed. "Christ, One-Eye, next time try to have a little more patience, will you?''

Riley grinned and stood. "I'll consider it.'' He left, puffing joyfully on his cigar.

A knock on his cabin door startled Riley only a little. He was used to it. Most of the soldiers, including the fort commander, knew that Riley had his supper about this time every day. This must be important, he figured, as he nodded to his wife to see who it was.

Spirit Grass shoved back her chair and headed for the door. She had been with Riley so long now that she was as at ease with chairs and the white woman's simple calico dress as she was with the lodges and buckskin of her Shoshoni people. She only wished she could get as comfortable with white people in general. None of the few women at the fort—even the lower-class wives of the enlisted men—treated her with any respect at all. She was often lonely, pining for her people. Riley, though, despite his gruff exterior and his harshness with other men, loved her and understood her needs. He took her to her village as often as he could so that she could visit with her people. And she got to spend some time with the Shoshonis when they came to the fort to trade at Judge Carter's store.

Spirit Grass opened the door carefully, then grinned widely when she saw her brother, Sharp Hawk, and four other Shoshoni warriors standing there. Her smile dropped fast at the look on Sharp Hawk's face. The five warriors moved brusquely inside.

Riley saw Sharp Hawk's determined look and shoved

aside his plate of salt beef and beans. With a sharp word in Shoshoni, Riley told his three children—Flat Nose, Arrives with Trouble and Laughing Swan—to leave the table.

They did so immediately, and the five Shoshoni warriors sat. Spirit Grass quietly doled out plates of food and cups of coffee as the men began talking.

"So?" Riley asked, looking straight at Sharp Hawk.

"Several white men attacked one of our bands," Sharp Hawk said in Shoshoni. He paused, anger creasing his hard, handsome face. "They killed three of the People, one of them an infant."

"Damn," Riley growled, in English. Then, in Shoshoni, he asked, "Where'd this happen?"

"Between here and the Bear River. Not too far."

"What were ye doing over there?"

"Hunting. Some of the People had decided to go visit our friends the Utes."

Riley nodded. It was a common enough thing. He did not think to question the veracity of his brother-in-law's story. The Shoshonis had almost invariably been friendly toward whites. He could see no reason that they would have invited an attack; not when there were women and children in the band. "Ye get a good look at any of the attackers?" he asked.

"One was a short man with a scarred face," Sharp Hawk said.

Riley shook his head.

"The only other I saw seemed to be the leader," Sharp Hawk continued. "He was a tall man with a face like a hawk. His face also was colored up."

Riley's eyes widened. "Like he'd been beaten?" he asked in Shoshoni.

Sharp Hawk nodded.

"Damn again," Riley swore.

"You know this man?" Black Dog, one of the other warriors asked.

"I do," Riley said in English, sure that the others would understand. "The name is Carter Halsey. He come through here a couple days ago with a train of Mormon emigrants. Dumb fool started sassin' me somethin' awful, so I pounded him a couple times. I never thought he'd pull some foolishness like this afterward.''

"Maybe it didn't have nothin' to do with you," a warrior named Running Bull said in English.

"Could be," Riley said. He was fighting to control his anger. For once it wasn't too much trouble, since the story seemed somehow unreal, almost as if he were dreaming it.

"What're you gonna do about it?" Sharp Hawk demanded in English.

"I ain't sure there's much I can do," Riley said slowly. "But I'll damn sure try somethin'." He shoved himself up and grabbed his hat from a peg on the wall. "Y'all stay here so's there'll be no trouble whilst I go talk to Major Canby." He slapped on the wide-brimmed hat with the front part folded up against the low crown, and headed out.

Canby was no more happy about having his meal interrupted than Riley had been, but he relented in the face of Riley's persistence in talking to him immediately. "This better be damned good, One-Eye," Canby snapped as Riley sat.

"I don't know as if I'd call it good, Major."

"Important, then. You know what the hell I mean."

Riley pulled off his hat and set it on the table. He nodded thanks as a black servant woman placed a cup of coffee in front of him. "Sharp Hawk and some of the other Shoshonis just rode in," Riley said after a sip of coffee. "They told me some whites attacked a small band of the People who were headin' down toward Ute country for a visit. Killed three of 'em, includin' a babe."

"Damn," Canby snapped. "Any ideas who did it?"

"Halsey was one of 'em," Riley said flatly.

Canby suddenly looked more annoyed than angry. "Jesus Christ, One-Eye, give it up. You thumped the snot out of Halsey. You don't need to go on persecutin' him."

"I thought ye knew me better'n that, Major. Sharp Hawk described two of the attackers. One of 'em was Halsey. I got no idea who the other was, but I'd bet my last dollar all of 'em was with Halsey's train."

Canby almost smiled. "You ain't got a first dollar, let alone a last," he said quietly. After a short pause, he added, "It's still kind of hard to believe they'd do such a thing, One-Eye. The Mormons've always been mostly up-front in their dealings with us here at the fort. At least once we retook control of Utah Territory and showed them who was running things, they have been."

"Dammit, Ed," Riley snapped.

Canby cut him off. "Look, One-Eye," Canby said, "I know how much you dislike the Mormons from the old days, but that's no reason to make such accusations."

"Have I ever pulled such shit, Ed?" Riley asked angrily.

"No, can't say as you have," Canby conceded. "Still, there is the matter of your feelings about those people in general."

"Hell, that ain't no secret to anyone around here. But if I was gonna pull some nonsense like this I would've done it long before now."

"That's probably true," Canby acknowledged. Then he paused to ponder the matter. One-Eye Riley was certainly a volatile man at times, and could hold a grudge as well as anyone. On the other hand, he wasn't known for causing unnecessary trouble. Not trouble of this magnitude anyway. Riley would know full well what this could mean if it got out of hand. The entire region could explode in flames and death with a three-sided war.

Canby did not dislike the Saints in general, though he would admit to himself that he disliked the air of superiority so many of them wore as naturally as shirt and pants. He did not know them all that well, either. He supposed no one but their brethren did, so he was not sure they were not capable of such duplicity. They certainly seemed straightforward, at least where official business was concerned. Yet he could not forget the guerrilla war the Saints had fought against the army as it approached Fort Bridger a couple of years ago. They had certainly been sneaky enough then, though Canby figured he would have been the same had he been in the Mormons' position.

There were also the Shoshonis to consider. They could be making up the story. That, too, seemed unlikely, since they had always been peaceable enough toward the white man, but Canby could not be sure. It was entirely possible that a few hot-blooded warriors had tried to attack a hunting party from the wagon train and gotten in deeper than they had suspected. Then maybe they concocted the story about having been attacked, so as to throw off suspicion on themselves and to have the army help them get revenge. It was far-fetched, yes, but not out of possibility's realm.

Canby sighed. No good was going to come of this, he figured, no matter what he did in the matter. But he also knew he would have to do something.

While Canby was thinking, Riley had gotten a bottle of whiskey and two glasses off a table along one wall. He brought them to the desk, set them down and poured two long drinks. He stuck one in front of the major and then downed his own in one sweet, swift gulp. He poured himself a second and sat back, filling and lighting a pipe. Then he waited.

"Just what do you propose I do about all this, One-Eye?" Canby asked, picking up his glass.

"Send a patrol out after that wagon train and arrest those sons of bitches. Then haul 'em back here, try 'em and hang 'em."

"Jumping the gun a little aren't you?" Canby finished off his drink and reached for the bottle.

Riley shrugged, unconcerned. "If'n ye and the army weren't here, I'd jist git up a few of the ol' mountain boys and take care of things ourselves. But ye been drillin' me since ye got here with the necessity for the niceties, as ye like to call 'em.''

"The niceties are important in a civilized society," Canby said seriously. He leaned back and looked through his whiskey at the fading sunlight easing in through the window. It cast a warm, comforting glow on things, he thought. "And that, by God, is what we're trying to bring to this godforsaken country, One-Eye.''

"Sure ye are," Riley said with a slight grin. "These parts had more than enough civilization—and civility—before the damned Mormons moved in. And then the army and all the other goddamn emigrants.''

"I'm not going to sit here and argue the merits of Shoshoni civilization with you, One-Eye. Nor that of the Saints. I have a job to do and . . .''

"And it ain't bringin' civilization to the Shoshonis or the Utes,'' Riley snapped.

Canby nodded. "No, that isn't my job. My job is keeping the peace between all the fractious parties out here. And it's getting harder and harder all the time, especially when situations like this crop up.''

"Well, if we didn't allow all those goddamn Mormons . . .'' He clapped his mouth shut when Canby raised his hand.

"That's neither here nor there, One-Eye, and you damn well know it," Canby said. "There's no way you or I or the whole United States government can stop them or all the other damnfool emigrants who wander through this way.''

"Yeah," Riley said sadly. He finished off his second drink and set the glass down on the desk. "So, Ed, are ye plannin' to do anything about this?'' He paused, then added pointedly, "Or should I jist round up some boys and take care of it the way we used to?''

"Well," Canby offered thoughtfully, "I just can't order them arrested. Not on just the word of several Indians—and your friends or relatives to boot. Still, I can't just let it pass either. Tell you what, I'll send out a small detachment to find the wagon train and question the

people there. It'll be up to the detachment's commander whether to arrest anyone or not.''

"I'm goin' along.''

"Never thought you wouldn't. But the decision is up
to the detachment's commander. Keep that to mind.''

"I will,'' Riley agreed. "And who's it going to be?''

"Lieutenant Keyes.''

"Jesus, Ed, not that *shit pile*. Ye know how he feels
about Indians. There's no way he's going to come down
on those Mormons when it was 'just' a few Shoshonis
who were killed. Can't ye send Lieutenant Browning
instead?''

"No. Browning's still too inexperienced. I'll send him
along as second in command, if you like. But Lieutenant
Keyes will be in command. He's the only one I can
afford to send out now.''

Riley was not happy with Canby's decision, but he also
knew there was nothing he could do about it. He did
vow silently, though, to see that things were made right
for the Shoshonis, even if he had to do it himself.

"You can leave at first light.''

"I'll be ready,'' Riley said sourly. He stomped out. At
his small cabin, he outlined the plan for Sharp Hawk
and the others, leaving out what he knew of Keyes's
attitude toward Indians. He finished up with, "Ye boys
are welcome to stay the night here.''

Sharp Hawk shook his head. "We don't feel safe here
at the fort,'' he said in Shoshoni. "We'll meet you on
the trail, a mile or so from here.''

The five warriors filed silently out, mounted their ponies and galloped off into the growing night.

3

Lieutenant Irwin Keyes was a tall, slim, aristocratic-looking man with a sneer permanently branded on his thin lips and a wellspring of condescension in his flat brown eyes. He had a pencil-thin mustache under a long, sharp nose, and carried an air of superiority about him. He hated being stationed at this outpost at the rear end of nowhere. He hated this land, with its dryness, its deserts, its sagebrush, harsh terrain and wicked mountains. He hated the searing heat of the summers and the bitter cold and snow of the winters. He hated that he had been in the army more than ten years now and still had not achieved a rank higher than first lieutenant.

Most of all, though, he hated Indians. All Indians. Tribal affiliation didn't mean anything to him, nor did the presence of some white blood. An Indian was an Indian as far as he was concerned. To Lieutenant Irwin Keyes, all Indians were dirty, savage, uncivilized, lazy and useless except for causing trouble. He would as soon see them all exterminated and this entire country opened to the uses of civilization.

Keyes was incensed that Riley's Shoshoni wife and three half-breed children lived in the fort, in a cabin no less, as if they were the equals of the other women and children. He was repulsed by it and complained often to Canby, hoping that the fort commander would throw Riley and his family off the post. But Canby remained unswayed, arguing that Riley was the best interpreter in all of Utah Territory.

For all those reasons, though mostly for the last, Riley had never gotten along with Keyes. He dealt with the officer when he had to, treating him with the barest respect, and that only because Canby had asked him to. He knew that under the swagger and bravado, Keyes was afraid of him, and the thought pleased him. He figured he would use that to his advantage one day, but he was waiting for the right moment.

Riley was a lot friendlier with Second Lieutenant Dwight Browning. The fresh-faced officer was fairly new at the fort, this being his first time in the West. He was tall and reedy, with a face that looked impossibly young for an army officer. His hair was lank and unmanageable, a dirty shade of blond, and he could hardly raise a faint wisp of beard. Browning had been unfortunate enough to be assigned to Keyes's Tenth Infantry. Keyes had seen it as his role to take the young man under his tutelage and indoctrinate him into the way of things in the West. Those lessons included Keyes's overbearing hatred for Indians, and his method of treating the fort's civilian workers as poorly as he treated his enlisted men.

Browning fell into the role, not sure what else to do. But in the ensuing few months at Fort Bridger, he began to see things differently. After a few rather lengthy conversations with Riley, the two had become friends. Listening to the former mountain man's tales and stories, Browning began to change some of his thinking, especially toward Indians. Indeed, he seemed to have become something of a disciple of Riley's.

Because of that, Keyes had found another reason to hate Riley, though he didn't really dare say anything about it. Not to Riley anyway. He did everything to make Browning's life as difficult as he could without crossing the line into mistreatment of a fellow officer.

The small group—Riley, Keyes, Browning, a corporal and three privates—rode out just as dawn was breaking.

Once they were a hundred yards out or so, they broke their tight formation and rode more loosely, not in any real hurry. At that time, too, Browning dropped back to ride alongside Riley, where they chatted about things of little consequence.

When they were about a mile from the fort, Riley suddenly grinned and winked at Browning. "We'll be havin' company soon," he said quietly.

"Who?" Browning asked, surprised.

"Ye jist wait and see. But I'll tell ye one thing, Keyes is gonna shit adobe when they arrive."

Browning was a man of easy humor despite his rather owl-like, serious face. He laughed, then asked, "Shoshonis?"

Riley nodded. "Five of 'em. Sharp Hawk, Running Bull, Black Dog, Empty Horn and Crow Lance. They're the ones who come to the cabin last night to tell me what happened."

"You believe them?"

Riley looked askance at the officer. "What the hell do ye think?"

"I expect you do." He paused. "I don't think this expedition is going to be very useful, though, at least from the Shoshoni standpoint."

"I figure you're right," Riley said, his humor overwhelmed by a sudden anger. "But I aim to try to figure somethin' out that'll help. If not . . ." He shrugged.

"Don't do anything crazy, Pete," Browning said. Even though he and Riley were friends, he could not bring himself to call him One-Eye.

"I ain't plannin' on it, but ye got to keep an open mind to see how things go. That way ye can do what ye need to."

"Just remember you have a wife and children, Pete. You do something too stupid and get thrown in the guardhouse—or killed—what's going to happen to them? You need to keep that in mind."

"Goddamn, boy, ye're worse'n my ol' mam was with yer naggin'," Riley said, a little of his humor returning.

Browning laughed shyly. "Someone has to do it, Pete. You're too damn stupid to do it for yourself."

"Listen to ye," Riley said with a chuckle. "Ye been out here all of five, six months and suddenly ye think ye know everything. Goddamn, if ye ain't got gall, boy. I'll give ye that."

"All I got of it, I got from you."

The two rode on in silence then, trying to ignore the heat pounding on their heads and necks. Riley pulled down the front brim of his hat so it would shade his eyes.

Minutes later, the five Indians suddenly appeared on the horizon to their left. Keyes shouted orders, and the men began forming a battle line.

"Relax, Lieutenant," Riley said sarcastically as he rode up alongside Keyes.

"Those are hostiles, Riley," Keyes said nastily.

"Like hell. They're Shoshonis, and they're goin' with us the rest of the way."

"They are not," Keyes said flatly.

"Then they will become hostile."

"Let them." Keyes seemed almost to relish the thought. "My men'll drop them without a thought."

"Could be, but I wouldn't wager anything of value on that. Besides," Riley added, "ye won't be around to see it." When Keyes looked at him inquisitively, Riley tapped the butts of the two Colt revolving pistols. "You'll be dead long before your men start the fracas."

In a voice tight with rage, Keyes called his men back into order. Moments later the Shoshonis rode up. Without a word, Keyes jerked his horse's head around and trotted off. His soldiers—except for Browning—followed, looking almost as angry as Keyes did. Finally Riley and Browning pulled out, followed by the five warriors.

It was late afternoon before they spotted the wagon train in the distance. They had heard the snapping of whips, the shouts of people and the creak of ungreased wheels long before they even spotted the dust from the wagons.

Keyes halted the small procession. "We'll rest the horses a bit," he ordered. "They should be stopping for the night soon. We'll close in on the wagons then." He looked back at Riley, almost as if challenging him.

Riley leaned over and spit into the dust. He would not give Keyes any satisfaction, even though he figured the officer had the right idea.

An hour later, the men tightened their saddles and moved on. It was still an hour or so before dark when the soldiers and Shoshonis encountered the rearmost of the wagons. Keyes stopped at the first one he came to and asked where the wagon master was.

The Mormon, busy with some task, looked up and grunted, "Up near the front." From his expression, he seemed to think Keyes was an idiot.

They moved up the line of wagons, some formed in small groups to make camp; others in pairs; still others lined up single file. Most of the travelers paid them no mind at all, other than a cursory glance. A few seemed to find some interest in a group of soldiers traveling with a small band of Indians. Two or three fearfully held their children close to them.

They finally found the wagon master, a man named Augustus Gudde. He was a short, fat fellow who had left his native Germany more than a dozen years ago when he had converted to Mormonism. He was red-faced from obesity and enthusiasm, and wheezed a lot as air struggled to wend its way past the lard-laced neck and into his lungs. Despite his having been in the United States and its territories for so long, he still had a fairly thick accent.

"What can I do for you, Lieutenant?" he asked, voice breathless.

"I need to ask you and a few of your fellows some questions, Mister Gudde. Nothing major, I'd say. Just some annoying things to clear up. I hope to bother you as little as possible."

"Yah, I haff no problem with dot. Ask avay these questions."

"Well, since it's getting late, and your people are preparing their evening meal and such, why don't my men and I make camp a little way off. We'll be back to talk to you after a bit."

"Yah."

Keyes smugly led his troop a few hundred yards south and ordered a camp set up. Ignoring him, Riley and the Shoshonis moved off from the army camp and put together their own. There wasn't much to it. A fire was started, some antelope meat the warriors had brought with them was set to cooking, a pot of coffee was put on the fire, and their sleeping robes or blankets were laid out. It was too hot to need the robes, but they would be comfortable to sleep on.

The six men ate slowly, talking softly. It was evident to Riley that his Shoshoni friends were anxious about the meeting. They had dealt with the white man long enough to know that most whites thought little of them. They were sure that they would not be believed, but they didn't know what else to do, so they were trusting in Riley to see that they got justice.

Riley knew what the Shoshonis were thinking, and he had the same fears. During the long ride that day, he had become pretty well convinced that this journey would be futile. He also knew that the warriors were counting on him, and that made him all the angrier. It was difficult, but he hoped he could keep his rage in check until he knew for sure that nothing would be done. He could then decide what action he would take.

When Riley heard the soldiers preparing to move off, he rose. "Ye and the others stay here, Sharp Hawk," he said in Shoshoni. "It'd be best if ye weren't there when we do our parleying. It might make the others nervous." It sounded pretty lame to Riley, even though it was the truth.

Sharp Hawk nodded. He didn't like it, and more than half suspected that he and his companions were being deliberately shut out, but he knew it was the way it had to be.

Riley fell into step behind the soldiers, without them knowing it. He had been out of the mountains a long time, but he could still call on the skills he had used as a mountain man when necessary. One of those skills was walking silently. In the dark, the soldiers never knew he was there.

Keyes was rather surprised when, just after he had sat on a rock near Gudde's fire, Riley silently plunked himself down cross-legged on the ground a few feet away.

"Is there anyvon else you need here?" Gudde asked.

"A man named Halsey," Keyes said. "Carter Halsey."

Gudde nodded solemnly. "Anyvon else?"

"One of your people a short, small feller with a scar on his face?" Riley interjected.

"Yah. Bob Sprague."

"Git him over here, too."

Gudde talked to his son for a moment, and then everyone sat back to wait. Before long, Halsey and the man named Sprague arrived and sat. Neither seemed mystified or concerned. They looked rather convivial.

"Now, vhat can ve answer questions from you?" Gudde asked. His look had suddenly gone from subservient to smug. He even grinned at Keyes, certain now that he was facing a kindred spirit. Gudde had known from the outset why these soldiers were here, and he now knew that Keyes, at least, would not be one to stir up too much trouble over the deaths of a few Indians.

"I understand you had a little Indian trouble, Mister Gudde," Keyes said unctuously. It was obvious to everyone where he stood on the issue.

"Yah, yah. Ve had much troubles vith them red-skins. They attack von of our huntink parties for no reason. *Herr* Halsey and the men vith him veren't doink nothink wrong. Just huntink vhen those devils attack them."

"You're a lyin' sack of snake shit, boy," Riley growled from the shadows beyond the firelight.

"Vhat? Vhat?" Gudde said angrily. "Vhy do you say dot?"

"Because it's a fact, ye fat, lyin' shit pile."

"How dare you call Mister Gudde a liar," Halsey said tightly.

"I thought your kind was fond of the truth," Riley said easily. "I expect I was wrong on that."

"What do you mean, 'your kind'?" Halsey sputtered, enraged.

"Ye know goddamn well what I mean, unless you're even dumber than I think ye are."

"That'll be enough of such talk, Riley," Keyes snapped. He was losing control of the situation, and he was not about to let it get away from him if he could at all help it.

"Then answer me this, Mister Gudde," Riley said calmly. "Why would Indians attack your hunters? Out here it had to be either Shoshonis or Utes. The Shoshonis've generally been friendly with whites, and the Utes're generally peaceable critters.''

''There's no vay to tell vhat goes on in the minds of those savages,'' Gudde responded.

''Savages, eh? That's int'resting comin' from someone like ye.''

''What's that mean, Pete?'' Lieutenant Browning asked quietly. He generally kept quiet around his superior officer, but he had to know the answer to this one.

''If I remember right, the Saints believe the Indians—all of 'em—are the lost tribes of Israel. So they feel some sort of kinship with 'em. They believe the Indians got lost in more than place, they also lost their souls or some such, so they aim to bring 'em back into the fold, so to speak.'' Riley spit into the fire. ''I got that about right, shit pile?''

''Yah,'' Gudde answered bitterly. ''More or less, though I vouldn't expect somevon like you to understand the intricacies of such a thing.''

''Then why're ye callin' 'em savages?''

''Some of the Lamanites are more reluctant to recognize their true beink und remember vhere they came from,'' Gudde said unapologetically.

''This wouldn't have anything to do with the Shoshonis turnin' away your efforts at missionizin' 'em a couple years back, would it?'' It was hard for Riley to keep the sneer out of his voice, but he thought he succeeded.

''No, it vouldn't,'' Gudde answered testily. ''But, *mein herr,* ve vill prevail in the end. Of dot I can assure you.''

''Ye been out in the sun too long, hoss,'' Riley said, not humorously.

''Jesus, Riley,'' Keyes said, ''that's enough.'' He was worried that Riley might get angry and attack him, but he was still trying to regain control of things. After a moment, he looked at Gudde and said, ''Can you tell me the whole story, Mister Gudde?''

"Vell, since I vasn't there mine self, it vould be better maybe if *Herr* Halsey vas to tell it."

"Fine," Keyes said. "Mister Halsey?"

"Ain't much to tell," the lanky Mormon said easily. He looked almost comical sitting on a low rock, his knees up around ear height. Realizing how foolish he looked, he stretched out, but his feet were almost in the fire. He finally crossed his legs. It was uncomfortable, but at least he didn't look so silly. Or so he told himself.

"Me and four others was out huntin', hopin' to add some meat to everyone's pot, when suddenly up out of nowhere rose maybe a dozen painted Lamanites. We tried talkin' to 'em, tryin' to get 'em to listen to our reason and the words of the Prophet, but it was to no avail. They demanded presents of us, and as we had none to give, they got troublesome. We finally gave them some tobacco. They left, and we thought we were rid of 'em."

Halsey decided his position was too uncomfortable, so he folded his legs under him, one to each side of the rock on which he was sitting. More at ease, he continued.

"Suddenly those devils came rushin' toward us, shootin' arrows. As we were armed for huntin'—and trouble—we returned fire, killing two, maybe three of those benighted souls." He sighed. "If only they had listened to us, had opened their eyes, none would have been killed."

Keyes was about to agree when Riley's voice rumbled out of the shadows again. "You're tryin' to tell me that ye faced a war party of a dozen Shoshonis, and ain't a one of ye come back with so much as a scratch?" he asked, disbelief strong in his voice.

"You don't think that possible?" Halsey countered haughtily.

"Goddamn right I don't."

Halsey smiled smugly. "Faith in the Lord, Mister Riley," he said arrogantly. "With strong enough faith, all things are possible. With the good Lord's help, we were protected from anything the Lamanites could throw at us.''

"If yer God's so almighty powerful, boy, why didn't he make those Shoshonis see the light so's no one had to go under?''

"It's not for me to question God's will," Halsey said evenly. "But if I was presumptuous enough to try guessin' at what he was doin', I'd have to say that he was attemptin' to teach those recalcitrant Lamanites a good lesson.''

Riley shook his head. Faith was a wondrous thing, he thought. It made anything possible in one's mind, no matter how little sense it might make to the rest of the world.

"Are you satisfied now, Riley?" Keyes asked sarcastically.

"Can't say as I am," Riley responded, voice flat. "But I reckon ye are.''

"I am," Keyes said firmly.

"Besides," Riley added sarcastically, "I can set here all day and argue with them pious bastards, but never git a word of truth out of 'em.''

"Dammit, boy, I'm plumb sick and tired of you callin' me a liar," Halsey sputtered, eyes snapping with anger and righteous indignation.

"Then tell the goddamn truth once in a while," Riley said easily. He rose in a smooth, fluid motion as Halsey stood and took a step toward him. "And jist remember, boy, that I stomped yer ass once with no trouble. I can do it again. So come on at me, if ye're in need of another whuppin'.''

Halsey took two steps toward the blacksmith, then stopped. "You ain't worth the effort," he said tightly.

"Faint-hearted toad," Riley snorted.

"That's enough, Riley," Keyes snapped. He wondered how it was that he kept losing control of the situation and then had to struggle so much to get even a bit of his authority back. He was unable to see that he had never had control.

Riley smiled just a bit. One of his pleasures was baiting Keyes, even knowing how easy it was to annoy the lieutenant. "Enough of what?" he asked innocently.

"You know damn well what I'm talking about, Riley," Keyes snapped. He was dangerously close to crossing the line, risking the former mountain man's wrath, but he was irritated enough not to care about it overly much. Besides, Lieutenant Browning was there. The fellow officer, and the soldiers, would protect him if Riley tried anything, he figured.

"I do?" Riley was still playing the innocent. "I ain't done nothin' but invite shit pile over there to exercise his face against my fist for a spell."

"I haff a goot mind to . . . ." Gudde started.

"Ye ain't got no goddamn mind at all, good or otherwise," Riley said with a smirk. "And I'll take on ye *and* your toad-humpin' friend at the same time."

"Goddammit, Riley," Keyes almost shrieked, "I said that was enough!"

Riley smiled serenely in the officer's direction. "Ye say somethin', Lieutenant?" he asked blandly. "I thought I saw your lips movin' there for a moment."

Keyes was livid. He turned and looked at Browning. "Lieutenant," he ordered in a tight voice, "the next time Mister Riley opens his mouth, shoot him. Or have one of the men do it."

"I get shot asswipe," Riley said easily, "and you'll have five angry Shoshonis come down hard on ye."

"We can take care of them." Keyes began to think he had the upper hand again, and his arrogance started to return.

"Even ye ain't so goddamn stupid as to think you'd git away with that. There'd be angry Shoshonis buzzin' all over ye, ye did that."

"They'd never dare to attack an army post—and it'd take them a while to find out what happened." Keyes was still smug.

Riley shook his head, knowing that he would never get through to Keyes. The man was too thick, too full of himself to see what was right in front of him. Riley thought to continue irritating Keyes, knowing that Browning would not shoot him. He wasn't so sure about the soldiers, though. At least two of the five men had little liking for him, and might be dumb enough to kill him, given the opportunity. He decided he would just shut up for a while and see what happened. He spit into the fire and sat again, grinning at Keyes.

"Please be seated again, gentlemen," Keyes said after a few moments, looking from Gudde to Halsey. When they did, he also retook his place and said, "Go on with your report, please, Mister Halsey."

"Like I said before, Lieutenant," Halsey responded, "there's not really much to it. I pretty much told you what happened."

"What did you do after the fight with the Shoshonis?" Keyes asked.

"We rode hell for leather back to the wagons," Halsey said with a shrug. "We didn't know that there might be more of those evil-spirited Lamanites about. When we got to the wagons, we forted up and sat for a while, waiting to see if maybe them savages was to come after us with some of their friends."

"Did they?"

"Nope. Since it was afternoon, we decided we'd make an early stop for the day, so we just stayed where we was and put out extra guards. Just in case."

Keyes nodded in understanding; Riley fought back a derisive snort.

"In the mornin', me and a few others scouted around some. We didn't see no sign of Indians, so we went back to the wagons and gave the go-ahead. We pulled out soon after. Ain't seen hide nor hair of Indians since— till those seemingly repentant ones you brought with you, Lieutenant." He smiled, as if sharing some secret with Keyes.

Riley bit back a retort. He knew it would do no good. He wasn't sure how he knew Halsey was lying, but he did. He supposed it was because there were just too many things unexplained. For one, there was the version of the attack given to him by Sharp Hawk and the other Shoshonis. For another, even if he believed his brother-in-law would lie to him, he knew the Shoshonis too well. They would not unnecessarily attack a white hunting party. And if they were attacked, they would certainly retaliate. Those things did not add up.

Riley was certain there was more to it, too, but he could not figure out what. It would come to him eventually, he was also sure of that. He worried, however, that it might not come to him early enough to do something to help the Shoshonis. Or to make Halsey, Gudde and the others pay.

One other thing the blacksmith knew—he would get absolutely no help from Keyes and the rest of the soldiers. Browning might be willing to throw in with him, but that seemed unlikely. The young officer was too indoctrinated in the military way to go against a superior officer. If Riley could come up with some proof that the members of the Mormon hunting party were lying, that might—but only might—gain him some support. Trouble was, there seemed to be no way he would be able to find proof. Surely none of the Mormons would talk to him, a Gentile, even if they knew anything.

Getting some of these people to talk, though, seemed his only hope, and he determined to at least make an attempt to approach some of them. A feeling of gloom settled over him as he squatted on strong legs.

Keyes, Halsey and Gudde had gotten off the topic of the attack and were just talking of inconsequential things, so Riley slipped away from the fire, heading toward the wagons. He moved as silently as the shadows through which he prowled. He stopped frequently, listening to a few words of a conversation here or there to see if they held any information he might want. He heard nothing of importance.

{ 5 }

Riley knew that someone was shadowing him in the darkness as he wove through the wagons, outside the circles of firelight. It did not worry him; it wasn't the first time he had been stalked. Now that he knew he was being followed, he could pick his spot and time to confront whoever it was.

It soon became apparent to his trained ears that it was more than one person. He let it go on a few more minutes before he slid behind one of the scattered trees just past the last of the wagons and stopped.

To the three men stalking the blacksmith, Riley seemed to have disappeared. A dark, moving figure against the darkness one moment; nothing but darkness the next. They stopped and muttered among themselves for a few moments before deciding to press on. There were few places for Riley to have gone, so they figured they should be able to find him in minutes.

They were a little startled when Riley found them instead just a moment later. He suddenly stepped out from behind the tree, a Colt pistol in one big hand. "Ye fellers've been on my ass for a spell now. Ye want somethin' from me, best git it out in the open so's we can deal with it. I don't like folks skulkin' 'round in the darkness, trailin' me." He paused, but not long enough for any of the others to say anything. "Now, ye shit piles want to cause trouble, git it started."

"We don't mean you no harm, Mister . . . Riley, was it?" one of the three men said.

"Yep."

"We come after you to talk to you."

"Why in hell didn't ye just come up and say what ye had to say?"

"We can't be seen by the others, Mister Riley," the same man said.

Riley nodded, though the others could not see it in the darkness. "What's your name, feller?" he asked.

"Hyram Jenkins. These here are Willard Payson and Orson Haynes."

"Well, Mister Jenkins, what do ye and the others have to say to me?"

Jenkins looked around, as if trying to see if anyone was watching. Trouble was, it was too dark to see more than a few feet. Jenkins took hold of one of Riley's brawny biceps and tugged, indicating he wanted the blacksmith to kneel.

Riley shrugged and squatted. The three Saints followed suit.

"We're scared, Mister Riley. If we're found out talkin' to you with what we got to say, we'd likely be killed."

"Why?" Riley asked, a little surprised.

"The Saints have religious laws calling for blood atonement in many instances. Like talkin' against your own kind to Gentiles—anyone who ain't a Saint. And apostasy will also get a man ritualistically killed, and Brothers Payson, Haynes and me're right on the verge of that, too."

"What in hell's aposty, or whatever the hell it was ye said?"

"Turnin' your back on your faith, Mister Riley," Payson said. "Decidin' that maybe this ain't the path you're supposed to be followin'."

"And is that the way ye boys're feelin'?"

"Let's just say we're doubtin' the choice we made not so long ago," Jenkins responded. "If the others see us talkin' to you, they might figure we're apostates, and our lives wouldn't be worth spit.''

"I see," Riley said truthfully. "Well, boys, since ye come this far, are ye willin' to see it through?''

Three solid, though quiet affirmatives answered him.

"Best get to it, then," Riley encouraged. "The longer you're out here, the greater the chances of someone findin' out about ye.''

"Those hunters weren't attacked by no Indians, Mister Riley," Jenkins said.

"Ye sure?''

"Yes, I'm sure. Brother Halsey and the others weren't shy about talkin' about it." Though he was thinking of leaving the Mormon Church as soon as he got to Salt Lake City, Jenkins still found himself compelled for some reason to use the honorific for Halsey.

"They jist sat and talked about it?" Riley said. He was not really surprised. In a close-knit group like this one was supposed to be, there normally would be no reason for leaders such as Gudde and Halsey to worry about people speaking to outsiders.

"Sure. We were also instructed by the elders not to say anything should anyone like you or the army come along. They didn't expect that to happen, of course, but they wanted to take precautions anyway.''

"What happened?" Riley asked evenly, though his anger was beginning to rise.

"They said they raided an Indian camp a few miles away. Claimed to have killed half a dozen or so of those devils.''

"They kilt three," Riley said tightly, the stranglehold on his anger weakening slightly. "One of 'em a babe in arms.''

"Damn," Haynes muttered.

"Yeah," Riley responded flatly. "I asked this of Halsey before but never got a satisfyin' answer from him. Maybe ye fellers can help. I thought ye Mormons were supposed to be aimin' to convert the Indians to yer ways." It was evident from his tone what he thought about Mormon ways.

"That's true," Payson said tentatively.

"Then what'n hell're some of ye doin' attackin' a peaceful band of Shoshonis?"

"Well, Mister Halsey," Jenkins said slowly, "We're still new to this religion . . ."

"And soon to be out of it," Haynes muttered.

Jenkins agreed, then continued. "So we don't know all the ins and outs of church thinkin', of course. But we have learned some." He paused, then asked, "You know why the Indians have such dark skin, Mister Riley?"

"Figured that was the way the Good Lord made 'em," Riley lied. He knew the Mormon reasoning on this—or at least what it used to be. He wanted to see if anything had changed.

"Not according to the Prophet. You see, the Saints believe the Indians are the lost tribes of Israel who have lost their history and godly ways, revertin' to savagery. Because of that, they wear the mark of Cain on them, so to speak—their dark skin, settin' them apart from . . . good men."

"So?" Riley asked, annoyed. Nothing had changed.

"One of the Saints' main missions is to bring the heathens back into the fold. But that don't mean we'll turn the other cheek when confronted by belligerent Lamanites."

"Those Shoshonis weren't belligerent."

"True, but other tribes have been all along on our journey, includin', one has to assume, Shoshonis at one point or another."

"Damn poor reason for attackin' a band of Indians settin' there mindin' their own business," Riley growled.

"I agree. Which is why we're here now talkin' to you," Jenkins said matter-of-factly. "There's no church reason for the brethren to have done that. None that we can see. And we don't believe the Prophet and Revelator would condone such actions."

"And ye don't like Halsey?" Riley suggested.

"That's true, too," Jenkins said.

"How'd you know that?" Payson asked.

"Jist did," Riley said flatly.

"We think Brother Halsey and a few of the others are assumin' powers beyond their station," Jenkins said. "They act as if they're actin' on orders of the Prophet himself."

"Ye don't believe that?"

"No, sir."

"Why? Brigham Young ain't beyond doin' some purty devious things if he takes a mind to."

"The Saints have been sorely set upon in many places, Mister Riley," Jenkins offered. "Sometimes extraordinary measures have been called for to protect the lives of the Saints and the sanctity of the church. Sure, Brother Young has ordered some things that, accordin' to your lights might've been wrong, but they were all revelations straight from God. The Saints want to convert the Indians, not kill them, though kill them we will, if need be. I doubt that Brother Young would order—or even condone—an attack on a band of peaceful Indians."

"Sounds like ye don't have near as many doubts about your church as ye might've thought, Mister Jenkins," Riley said softly.

"There're many things to admire about this religion, Mister Riley. I would not mock it so easily, if I were you."

The blacksmith shrugged. "So ye think all this was purely Halsey's doin'?" he asked.

Jenkins nodded. "Yep. His and Gudde's."

"Any idea why?" Riley asked.

"Nope," Payson responded. "They might be tryin' to cause trouble, but how or why makes no sense."

Riley nodded. "Who else was with Halsey?" he asked.

"Bob Sprague, Dan Hyde, and Billy Kimball."

"Anything else ye fellers want to tell me?" Riley asked after a short pause.

"Nope," Jenkins answered for himself and the others.

"I'm obliged for what you've done here, boys," Riley said. "Especially since you've put yourselves in danger. Ye fellers best git goin', though, before the others find ye out."

The three Saints moved swiftly away. Riley continued squatting where he was. He wondered if they had really put themselves in danger. They didn't seem too frightened, and Jenkins certainly had seemed defensive when the church's teachings had been challenged.

There was, Riley knew, a good chance that the Mormons were setting him up. It was entirely possible that they were in on the plot—if there was a plot—and that they had been ordered to "confess" to him the way they had. But to what avail? Riley wondered. Would they hope he would go to the Shoshonis and lead a raid on the wagons, thus bringing the wrath of the Mormons and the army down on him and his Indian friends? Did they think he might go to the army with the story and cause such a stink that Major Canby would toss him from the fort, thus lessening his influence with the Shoshonis?

It could be any of those things, he figured. But none of them made sense. As much as he disliked the Mormons, he was not about to jeopardize the Shoshonis to retaliate for something like this. And what good would it do the Saints for him to get thrown off the post? His loss wouldn't mean all that much.

Riley pushed to his feet and stretched. Though he was only thirty-eight, he could feel the years creeping up on him. Years of hard work and hard living. Trying to shrug off the gloom, he headed back toward his camp with Sharp Hawk and the other Shoshonis, and told the warriors what he had learned.

"What're ye gonna do about it?" Sharp Hawk asked. He had learned most of his English from Riley, so his speech sounded a lot like the former mountain man's.

"Ain't sure yet," Riley said, swilling down half a cup of coffee in one gulp. "I don't expect Keyes is gonna be interested, but I'll probably tell him about it anyway. If he ain't interested, I'll wait till we get back to the fort and tell Canby.''

"We're gonna git fucked again, One-Eye," Sharp Hawk said matter-of-factly.

"Wouldn't surprise me," Riley answered flatly.

{ 6 }

Next morning Riley strode up to Keyes's fire, squatted and poured himself a cup of army coffee. It served to annoy Keyes, which was part of Riley's intent. He disliked the officer immensely and often went out of his way to irritate him. Besides, he was in a sour mood, certain of the reaction he would get from the officer, so he saw no reason to be nice to him.

"What the hell do you want here, Riley?" Keyes asked in a sharp voice. He had awoke this morning feeling good. Now the day was ruined and he hadn't even had his breakfast yet.

"Gittin' coffee," Riley retorted, irritating the officer even more. He held up the tin mug and smiled insolently.

"You have coffee at your own fire. Or can't you stand the swill those damn savages brew up?"

"Jist 'cause ye ain't got the stomach for real coffee, shit pile, is no reason to spit on my friends."

Keyes was the only son of a rich plantation owner outside Montgomery, and as such, was used to having his orders obeyed without question or delay. One-Eye Pete Riley confounded him. The former mountain man was the antithesis of everything Keyes stood for—he was slovenly, crude, vicious; he was too close to the savages, defiant of authority and arrogant in a brutish kind of way. All of it added up to an intense dislike of the black-smith on Keyes's part.

"To hell with you, Riley," Keyes spat. "And those god-damn savages of yours. Now, what the hell do you want here?"

"Want to talk to ye."

"What about?"

"About why we're here."

"I ain't interested in anything y'all have to say about this subject, boy," Keyes drawled.

"It puts these doin's in a new light," Riley said evenly. He did not let the snub affect him outwardly.

Keyes sighed, as if burdened by too much responsibility and annoyance. Life, he felt, would be so much simpler if he did not have to deal with civilians. "I doubt it will, boy," he said, seemingly weary, "but go on an' blather, if you have such a great need to."

Riley took a few moments to make sure his temper was in check. Then he said coldly, "Ye know, boy, one of these days you're gonna open that flappin' hole in your face and say somethin' I really take exception to." His stare at Keyes was even chillier than his voice had been.

Keyes had enough sense to know better than to retort when he looked into that flat, brown orb.

Riley let the officer squirm a few more seconds, then sipped some coffee, breaking the spell. Finally he said, "I talked to some of the Mormons last night whilst ye were bein' bamboozled by Gudde and Halsey."

"I was not being bamboozled," Keyes insisted. "I was havin' a serious conversation with two men of intelligence and some breeding."

"Those two got all the breedin' of my Aunt Esther's lame mule, and not nearly the intelligence," Riley snorted.

"Cut the crap, Riley," Keyes snapped. "You got something to say, jus' say it and then get out of my sight."

"The men I talked to told me there was no attack on the huntin' party. The huntin' party attacked the village, jist like the Shoshonis said."

"You're the one was bamboozled, you dumb son of a bitch," Keyes crowed. "You'll believe anything anyone tells you—as long as it fits in with your thinking. If thinking is within your limited capacities."

"That might well be true sometimes," Riley said coldly. "But if it is, I sure as hell ain't the only one doin' such." He looked pointedly at Keyes.

"Believe whatever the hell you want, Riley," Keyes snapped. "But I'm telling you, y'all've been made the fool of by those emigrants."

"I don't believe so, shit pile."

"Doesn't matter anyway," Keyes said. "I have a reasonable explanation for the events, and I'm satisfied with that. We'll be leaving for the fort in half an hour. Y'all best be ready or you can make your own way back —alone."

"We'll be ready," Riley growled. He had expected such a pronouncement from Keyes. He knew how much the officer hated Indians, and he knew that Keyes needed only a flimsy reason to be satisfied.

Riley stood and flung the dregs of his coffee from the cup. As planned, they splattered on the ground and across Keyes's boots. Dropping the tin mug in the fire, he spun and walked off, leaving Keyes steaming in his wake.

At his own fire, Riley quickly explained to the Shoshonis. Since the warriors expected it, they were not too angry. They were concerned, however. Even though Riley had told them he would go to Canby again, they held out little hope that the soldier chief would do anything for them. Riley figured the same.

The six men ate swiftly, downing seared, half-raw antelope meat and black coffee. They were ready well before the soldiers were, and Riley more than half suspected that Keyes was stalling just to irritate him after having told him they would be pulling out in half an hour. Riley considered leaving, but decided that he would wait for Keyes, wanting to keep an eye on the soldiers.

Finally Keyes gave the order to move, and they rode slowly away, heading east. The train had pulled out nearly an hour ago, the creaking wheels screeching in protest at the activity.

Riley fumed as he rode. The Shoshonis, who planned to ride along part of the way before heading toward their village, were angry, and rightfully so, as far as Riley was concerned. He did what he could to soothe their hurt feelings, but there was really little he could do for them. After a while, with the Shoshonis as calm as they were going to be, Riley rode off to the side by himself. He wanted nothing to do with the soldiers, and he was ashamed to ride with the Shoshonis right now. Ashamed because with each step he grew more certain that there would be absolutely nothing he could do to help them in this matter. And he was equally certain that Canby would be unwilling to do much. That shamed and disgusted him, and he did not want to be traveling amid the warriors with the constant reminder of it.

An hour or so out on the trail, a gunshot rang out. Everyone pulled to a stop, looking around in consternation. Then one of the Shoshonis—Empty Horn—toppled from his horse and lay in the dirt.

"What the hell?" Riley mumbled. He had been dozing in the saddle, and it took him a moment to realize what was going on. Then he saw Empty Horn, and the smoke still drifting lazily from Private Chuck Latimer's Springfield rifle. "Son of a bitch," he muttered, quirting his horse. He stopped between Keyes's men, who were unlimbering their guns, and the Shoshonis, who were nocking their bows.

"Hold on, Sharp Hawk!" Riley bellowed.

"Why should we?" the warrior retorted. His face was twisted with rage, and he had trouble controlling his horse, which seemed as eager as its rider to attack.

"Because it's suicide, ye goddamn fool." Riley wheeled his horse to face the soldiers, unconcerned at turning his back on the enraged Shoshonis. "Have your boys put their weapons away, shit pile,'' Riley bellowed at Keyes.

"Like hell I will."

Riley drew his big .44-caliber Colt revolver and thumbed back the hammer. "Now," Riley said quietly, "or I'll shoot your dumb ass right out of the saddle."

"Not till those damn savages ride off," Keyes said adamantly.

"Ye take care of your men. I'll worry about the Shoshonis."

"Like hell. Lieutenant Browning, disarm Mister Riley. Men, prepare to fire!"

"Pete, no!" Browning screeched as he saw—or more likely sensed, he didn't care which at the moment—Riley's finger beginning to squeeze his Colt's trigger. He saw Riley ease off, and he turned to face Keyes. "Lieutenant," he said urgently, "I recommend we pull back a bit and let Mister Riley deal with the Indians."

"Mind your place, Lieutenant," Keyes barked. "I won't run from the enemy."

"It's not running," Browning insisted.

"It's close enough for me to reject the idea." Keyes smiled smugly. "We can take these savages, Lieutenant. Don't you fear about that."

"Sure we can," Browning said soothingly. "But at what cost? We're sure to lose at least a few men."

"And you'll go first, I'll see to it," Riley hissed at Keyes.

Keyes glared at Riley, then at Browning. Finally he snapped, "Put your weapons up, men."

Reluctantly the soldiers did so. Then Riley turned his horse again to face Sharp Hawk and the Shoshonis. "Tell your boys to put their weapons away, Sharp Hawk," he said harshly.

"No. Goddamn soldiers gotta die."

"Buffalo shit. There's been more'n enough bloodshed today."

"They killed Empty Horn," Sharp Hawk said in Shoshoni. "They must pay for that."

"Only one of them killed Empty Horn," Riley said. He was sweating, not only from the heat of the day, but from the responsibility he felt to keep this from turning into a bloodbath. "Not all of them need to pay for the actions of one."

"They must," Sharp Hawk insisted.

"No," Riley growled. "If ye had killed one of the blue coats, and others came and killed some other band of the People in retaliation, ye'd be wild with rage. And that'd be right. If ye attack all these blue coats here for the actions of the one, you'll be as bad as they are."

"But the one must be punished."

"He'll be punished."

"When? Where?"

"First we have to find out what went on."

"There's nothing to learn," Sharp Hawk pressed. "The blue coat shot Empty Horn."

"I need to talk with the blue coats about it. Ye and your men stay here and don't cause any trouble."

Sharp Hawk and the others were not happy about it, but they had calmed down some and were willing to wait a little.

"What the hell was that jabberin' all about, Riley?" Keyes asked when Riley turned toward the soldiers again.

"Keepin' ye and your goddamn soldier boys from gittin' kilt," Riley said flatly. He looked at Private Latimer. "What'n hell'd ye go and shoot Empty Horn for, shit pile?" he asked.

"That goddamn red son of a bitch threatened me," Latimer claimed. "Then he began pulling out his war club, so I shot the dumb bastard in self-defense."

"Ye did, huh?" Riley countered harshly.

"Just said so, didn't I?" Latimer looked mighty pleased with himself.

"And how was it that he was so threatenin' and ye were twenty feet away?"

Latimer shrugged, unconcerned.

"That how it happened, Sharp Hawk?" Riley asked over his shoulder.

"No," the Shoshoni responded angrily. "The white-eye bastard jist shot Empty Horn for no goddamn reason."

"What about it, Latimer?" Riley demanded.

"That's enough, Riley," Keyes said. "Private Latimer told you what happened. If those goddamn bucks don't want to hear the truth, then tell them to come at us. If they're not going to do that, the hell with them, we need to get a move on. So shit or get off the pot."

"Git," Riley said angrily. "We'll see what Major Canby has to say about all this when we git back to Bridger."

Keyes laughed and led his men off. Browning waited a moment, watching Riley, worried. Then he, too, turned and rode off.

The Shoshonis were still agitated as they gathered around Riley. Since most of the warriors spoke at least some English, they knew what had transpired, and they were enraged that nothing was to be done about the killing of their companion.

"Dammit, One-Eye," Sharp Hawk snarled, "this ain't right."

"I know it ain't. But there ain't much we can do about it. Not now."

"Like hell. We're gonna attack the goddamn blue coats soon's we can."

"That'd be the dumbest thing ye could do, Sharp Hawk."

"We supposed to jist take this shit and smile about it?"

"Nope. But if ye go about indiscriminately attackin' soldiers, you're only gonna bring more grief on the People."

Sharp Hawk knew that to be true. "We got to do something," he said, his voice betraying the helplessness he felt within him.

"Look, Sharp Hawk," Riley said soothingly, "ye take Empty Horn back on to the village and see to his burial and all. I'll see that Latimer is punished back at the fort."

Displeased, but knowing that waiting would be best, the Shoshonis accepted Riley's compromise. The blacksmith's word had always been good. With a nod to Riley, they turned away and headed back to their village.

Riley watched for a few seconds, then trotted after the soldiers. It didn't take long to catch up to them. When he did, Keyes grinned insolently. "I appreciate you keeping those devils from attacking," he said dryly.

"Only way I could do it was to give 'em my word I'd see that Private Shit Pile is punished back at the fort."

"Good for you," Keyes said with a laugh. "I'd tell them anything, too, just to keep them from annoying me."

"I give 'em my word," Riley said, glaring at the officer.

Keyes shrugged. "That doesn't mean much."

"I suppose it doesn't—to ye," Riley snapped. He jerked his horse away and rode by himself.

Riley's anger was bubbling when he stomped into Major Edward Canby's office in the morning. He had planned to talk to Canby as soon as they had pulled into the fort last night, but the fort commander had been indisposed, or so the soldier on duty outside Canby's quarters had announced. Stewing, Riley had stalked off.

He was in no better a humor now, and he barely growled a good morning to Canby as he pulled up a chair, swung it around and sat on it with his forearms on the top of the backrest. Browning was just to his left, Keyes several feet to his right.

"All right, Lieutenant," Canby said, looking at Keyes, "now that we're all here, let's have your report."

Keyes did it in three sentences.

"You concur, Lieutenant Browning?"

The junior officer shrugged. He felt extremely uncomfortable, since he did not agree with Keyes's report, but he did not feel it was his place to speak out against his superior officer.

"Oh, come now, Lieutenant," Canby said. "Either you concur or you don't. Now, which is it?"

"Get off the boy's ass, Major," Riley snapped. "Keyes's report is a nose-high pile of buffler shit, and Dwight knows it, but he ain't about to say anything against the man who holds his career in his hand."

Canby's face darkened some, and he stroked his long

chin whiskers. Then he nodded. "Suppose you tell me your version, One-Eye," Canby coaxed.

Riley did. It took a fair amount longer to tell his version than Keyes had taken with his. He reported both about the attack on the Shoshoni village—and what he had learned from Hyram Jenkins, Willard Payson and Orson Haynes—and his thoughts about Empty Horn's death. He ended by asking that Latimer be court-martialed.

When the blacksmith finished, Canby sat in his chair for a while, stroking his beard and mustache with his right hand. His eyes were half closed. After several minutes, he leaned forward, his chair letting out a squawk of protest.

"You say you're satisfied with the version of events Latimer, Halsey and Gudde gave you, Lieutenant?" the commander asked, looking at Keyes.

"Yes, sir, I am," Keyes said firmly. "Just about everything Riley has told you here is a bare-faced lie."

Browning was still too nervous about his position to offer any comment.

Canby sighed. He was sure no good would come of all this. He looked at Riley. "As for the attack on the village —or on the hunting party—I'm afraid I'm going to have to accept Lieutenant Keyes's word on it," he said quietly. "For the same reasons I gave you before."

"But, Major . . ."

"Look, One-Eye, I don't know who to believe in this. Both sides have plausible stories. How the hell am I supposed to sort them out? I can't," he answered his own question. "All I know is that there'll be a hell of a lot more trouble with the Mormons if we make a fuss over this than there will be with the Shoshonis if we don't. And," he added firmly, "the Indians just might take it into their heads to go and attack that wagon train anyway, in retaliation. If they do, I'll have to chase after them, but I promise you that if I'm forced into that, they won't be chased very hard."

Riley nodded. He hadn't expected to win this fight,

and so wasn't too disappointed. "What about the other?" he asked tightly.

"I'm afraid I'm also going to have to deny your request for Latimer's court-martial."

"Jesus goddamn Christ, Major," Riley bellowed, "that was plain out and out goddamn murder."

"It might've been," Canby said evenly, "but we don't have that many men here. I need all the men I have. I can't go hanging a trooper just for killing an Indian." He winced at the assault of heated, blue verbiage from Riley.

When Riley paused for breath, Canby jumped into the breach. "I know Empty Horn was your friend, One-Eye," he said calmly. "But I just can't afford to do something like that. You'll have to go and try to make things right with the Shoshonis. It'll be a damn near impossible job, but if there's anyone can do it, you're that man."

"I'm as like to lose my goddamn hair, ye stupid bastard," Riley shot back.

"It's a risk you'll have to take."

"Sharp Hawk and the others with us was pretty hot over these doin's, Major," Riley said, trying to calm down and speak reasonably. "They ain't gonna be easy to soothe. Especially since I give 'em my word I'd see to it that Latimer was punished here." He paused, thinking, then added, "Now, I ain't askin' ye to hang the bugger, though that'd be preferable. But if ye was to court-martial him and give him some kind of punishment—somethin' the Shoshonis can see—they might accept that."

"No," Canby said. He had made up his mind, and he could be as stubborn as any Missouri mule when he took the notion. "There's also a difference of opinion as to what actually happened out there. You didn't see it, so once again you're relying solely on the word of the Indians. I know how you feel about them, One-Eye. I really do. I also know how you feel about Mormons, and about soldiers who cross you."

"The Shoshonis might consider attackin' the fort."

"If they do, there'll be plenty of dead Shoshonis around."

"They might also consider attackin' farms, ferries, wagon trains and army patrols," Riley pressed. "As well as any other white man they come across."

"I don't think so," Canby said confidently. "They're no fools—as you yourself have told me often enough. And between you and Black Iron and Washakie, you should be able to keep the hot young men under control."

"I sure as hell hope so," Riley said.

Although he was still enraged, Riley was already thinking of the work he had ahead of him, for if he did not succeed, the area from Fort Laramie to Salt Lake City could become a sea of blood, death and despair. And despite his dislike of Mormons, he worried about the Shoshonis. Such a widespread war could devastate the roving bands of Shoshonis, as well as the Utes and others.

"So do I, One-Eye," Canby answered with quiet sincerity. He knew the risk he was taking. But he also knew what could happen if he caused trouble with the Mormons, or if he began punishing soldiers on the word of Indians. There would be no end of trouble then, and the result would be much the same. Besides, he was bound by his oath as an officer in the United States Army, and by the many—often ridiculous—regulations thought up back in the nation's capital. The generals seemed to have nothing better to do, he sometimes thought, than to come up with ever more idiotic rules. He wasn't sure, but he felt certain that there was one of them that said he couldn't punish a U.S. soldier for killing an Indian.

Seeing Keyes's smug smile, Riley rose and turned. In his rage, he almost tore Canby's office door off its hinges when he left the room.

As the door slammed shut, Canby turned to Keyes and fixed him with furious eyes. "You goddamn fool," he roared. "How could you be so goddamn stupid as to let that idiot Latimer kill that Indian right out there in front of everyone?"

"I told you, Major," Keyes said, taken aback by Canby's fury, "the Indian threatened him."

"That's a ridiculous statement and a man as bright as you should know it won't fool anyone. Dammit, Irwin, I cannot let your hateful attitude toward red men threaten the safety of this fort or of Utah Territory."

"Oh, come now, Major," Keyes said, regaining his composure, "you're overreacting to all this."

Canby's eyes bulged with anger. Even his beard seemed to have become prickly. "How dare you say such a thing, Lieutenant?" he hissed. "Sooner or later, these Indians will get tired of being killed and the army turning away from helping them." Then more calmly, "When that happens . . ."

"If that happens," Keyes said quietly.

"*When* that happens," Canby repeated, "you will see a bloodbath, Lieutenant. And you and I and every other soldier in the territory will be swept up by it."

"I look forward to the day, sir," Keyes said confidently.

"Then God help you, Mister Keyes. And God help all of us."

All the way to his shop, Riley fought back his rage. He quickly fired up his forge and began working on the rim of a wagon wheel. The twisting and pounding on hot metal helped his anger ebb. When that happened, he was able to think more clearly.

It was then that he tried to put the events of the past day or so in perspective. He began to suspect that perhaps there was some kind of plot going on, but he had no idea what it could be. He was somewhat certain that the Mormons' attack on the Shoshonis and Latimer's killing of Empty Horn were not related.

He could, if he allowed himself, conjure up a conspiracy by the Mormons to retake the fort, and thereby reestablish their settlements in this pleasant land. But even he had to admit to himself that such a thing was pretty far-fetched. Still, it seemed almost certain that Halsey and Gudde, along with some others, had attacked the Shoshonis on purpose. It was quite likely that the idea behind it was to foment trouble. By killing a couple of Shoshonis, the conspirators, as Riley was beginning to think of them, might figure that the Indians would rise up and attack other wagon trains. That, in turn, would bring the army down on the Shoshonis, possibly removing them from their lands. Then the Mormons could move in and begin new settlements. If the army did not take the bait, the Mormons could raise their own forces—the terrifying, ferocious bands of Avenging Angels—to rid the countryside of the Indians.

It made some sense, but after sleeping on it, Riley began to think that perhaps he was letting his mind run away with him.

Seeing how troubled he was, Spirit Grass questioned him about it.

He smiled wanly at his wife, then explained it to her.

"Ye must tell the major," Spirit Grass said after Riley was done.

"He'll think I'm a fool."

"Maybe," Spirit Grass said with a wife's assurance in her husband. "Maybe not. But the People could react that way, even if there isn't a plot. If that happens, the People'll be hurt bad. Ye gotta tell him."

Riley looked up at his wife's dusky face and he patted the hand she had on his shoulder. She was a fine woman, he thought for the thousandth time. She was showing signs of her age, though she was not yet thirty. Still, she had weathered the years better than most of her female kinsfolk had. Her short frame had filled out in womanly fashion in the thirteen or fourteen years they had been together. He liked that, and it made him love her all the more. She was a kind and giving woman. He knew she felt out of place here at the fort and he tried to compensate for that with frequent trips to her village. It was too bad, though, that she was not more accepted at the fort. She had come a long way toward living like a white woman. But even the common soldiers' wives wanted little to do with her.

"Maybe you're right," he said, standing. He took her shoulders in his big hands and pulled her to him. "That a new dress?" he asked.

"Yes," Spirit Grass replied in her whispery voice. "I made it with the cloth ye got from Judge Carter's store."

"Ye look shinin' in it, woman," Riley said honestly. The pale-yellow calico dress set off her deep, rich skin nicely, and hugged her form in a way he appreciated. He kissed her. "Well, if I'm gonna go talk to Major Canby, I best be on my way."

Shortly afterward, he was in the commander's office, sitting in a high-backed chair, puffing on one of Canby's cigars and waiting for Keyes and Browning. He hadn't liked the idea of bringing in the two other officers again, but Canby had insisted.

"You say this has something to do with our recent troubles," Canby said quietly. "If that's the case, they need to be here."

When all four were seated, Riley, feeling like a fool, outlined his suspicions.

Keyes snorted in derision; Browning, as usual, kept silent, though he seemed to be considering it.

Canby didn't want to hear it. "Aren't you carrying your dislike for the Saints too far? Isn't that what's hatched this conspiracy in your mind?"

"No, sir, I don't think that. I told ye it was just a suspicion, and that maybe it didn't make any sense." Riley was embarrassed and uncomfortable.

"Just how long have you been against the Mormons anyway, One-Eye?" Canby asked.

"Since before they run off Bridger back in '53."

"What happened back in those days?" Browning suddenly asked.

"Yes, tell us, One-Eye," Canby said. "I haven't been out here that long, and I've always been curious about the fort's history. I know a little of the old days here, from tales and rumors. But I've never heard much of it firsthand.''

''Well I sure as hell ain't interested,'' Keyes said, rising from his chair.

''Sit down, Lieutenant,'' Canby ordered. ''Who knows, even an arrogant snot like you might learn something.''

''I'll need some tongue oil,'' Riley hinted.

''Of course,'' Canby said. He pulled a bottle and four glasses out of his desk. Drinks were poured all around.

''I'll have to go back a bit further than '53, though,'' he said. ''To the days when I first come out here to these Rocky Mountains.''

PART 2

Sixteen-year-old Pete Riley sat on his horse atop a small bluff and looked out over the sprawling rendezvous on the flats where Horse Creek died, bleeding its life away into the Seeds-Kee-Dee Agie. Despite his young age, Riley was already a burly fellow. He was dressed in worn wool trousers held up by plain black suspenders, a homespun shirt, leather boots, and a floppy felt hat.

He had a hard time believing what he saw out there. For a boy straight from the farm in Virginia, it was some sight, even at this distance. He had run away from home, sick of farming, and looking for adventure. In Missouri, he had hired on as a laborer for Sir William Drummond Stewart, a Scottish nobleman who was making yet another trip to the far west for the annual mountain man rendezvous. Stewart had done this several times before, and had made a few fast friends among the traders and trappers. Along the trail, he would regale his employees with stories of the wildness at rendezvous.

Riley had not believed much of what he had heard during those nights around the campfires, but now, despite the distance, he could see that there was a heap of truth in what Stewart had said. He couldn't wait to get down there, draw his pay and take part in some of the festivities.

There was a lot of work for a common laborer like

him, though, before he could join the frivolity. That rankled him a bit, but not too much. Stewart had been more than fair to him. Riley finally finished all he had to do, and then waited impatiently in line with the other laborers to get some money in his hands. He wandered off, his coins tucked safely in a pouch hanging under his shirt.

He soon found that some of the Indian girls were unconcerned that he was a laborer. As long as he had some money or foofaraw to give them, they were willing to let him have his way with them. He decided this was a good deal, and partook of their giving natures more than once. He also found that whiskey was a great way to loosen tongues and get the men talking about their adventures in the mountains.

He felt out of place, though, among the mountain men, traders and Indians. He was not one of them, and they all knew it. Not that any of them treated him poorly or said anything about it to him. He just knew he was an outsider here.

All this was expensive, and he soon ran out of money. He was lucky in that Stewart could always find some task for him to do for a few coins.

As rendezvous progressed, Riley began to consider trying to hire on with one of the trapping or trading parties. He knew he was expected to make the trip back to Missouri with Stewart, but he felt sure the Scotsman would let him out of his contract. Though he had met some of the trappers and traders at the rendezvous, he didn't know anyone well enough to just up and ask for a job. Not when he had no experience, no gear, nothing but the clothes on his back and what little things Stewart had supplied and might allow him to keep.

He knew the rendezvous wouldn't last much longer, and he would have to make a decision. It perplexed him. He was sitting with his back against a tree stump, drinking a jug of whiskey he had bought with the last of his money, when the decision was made.

There was a roar of voices, which wasn't unusual at

the rendezvous, and he almost ignored it. But something made him lurch to his feet and stagger off to see what the rumpus was about.

What he saw almost made him chuck his whiskey jug away and swear off spiritous liquors forever. Clanking across the rendezvous grounds was a man in a suit of metal. He had never seen the likes of it, not even in the few picture books he had come across. "I'll be goddamned," he muttered at the spectacle.

Thinking about it a little later, he decided that any man who would parade around in such a costume was the kind of man he wanted to work for.

It didn't take long to find out that the man was named Jim Bridger, one of the most respected men in all the mountains. The old mountain man seemed to have been around forever, if even half the tales about him were to be believed. Stewart had told a good many of the tales himself. The Scottish nobleman considered Bridger his best friend among the mountain men.

Hitching up his courage, Riley wandered around the rendezvous the next day looking for Bridger. When he spotted the big, bull-necked mountain man, Riley simply walked up and said, "I'd like to hire on to ye, Mister Bridger."

Bridger was far bigger close up than he had appeared from a short distance away. And he did not look entirely pleased at having been interrupted in mid-discourse among several friends. Besides, he seemed decidedly drunk. Riley suddenly thought he might've made a mistake.

"That so, sonny?" Bridger inquired, fixing Riley with a baleful glare. He didn't sound drunk.

"Yessir." Riley wasn't entirely sure his voice had actually come out.

"Doin' what, hoss?"

"Whatever it'll take for ye to hire me on."

"That covers a heap of territory," Bridger said, as the other men laughed.

"So do I," Riley said with a shy grin.

"Goddamn, I think ye might do, boy," Bridger said with a deep laugh. "Ye willin' to be a camp helper, boy?"

"Yessir," Riley said without hesitation.

"Ye got any supplies or possibles?"

"Not a damn thing," Riley said, almost ashamed.

"Such doin's ain't uncommon," Bridger allowed. "Ye free to join up with my party? Not contracted out to anyone else?"

"Well, Mister Bridger, I'm consigned to Mister Stewart, but I . . ."

"The Scotsman?"

"Yessir." Riley began to worry, thinking that perhaps there was bad blood between Bridger and Stewart; that perhaps Stewart had overestimated his friendship with the mountain man.

"That ol' hoss shines with this chil'," Bridger whooped. "Damn if he don't. Give me a goddamn set of armor, he did. Said the knights of olden times wore such things. He may be givin' me a line of buffler shit, but that metal suit sure shines."

"I was thinkin' Sir Stewart would let me out of my contract," Riley finally managed to finish.

"Ye really set on stayin' in the mountains, boy?" Bridger asked, squinting at Riley.

"I am."

"I figure you're right about Ol' Sir Bill lettin' ye out of your contract, hoss," Bridger said with a nod. "He gives ye a hard time about it, ye come see me. I'll straighten it out for ye."

"Supplies and gear?"

"I'll see you're set up." He grinned and then added, "Now go away, hoss. I got doin's goin' on here."

Riley got in three fair years before the beaver trade was pretty well dead. But he learned a lot in those three years. For most of the first half of his first year in the mountains he was strictly a camp helper, but Bridger had seen something in the young man and during the long winter had started teaching him to be a trapper and a trader. By the spring hunting season, Riley had moved out of the ranks of camp helpers into the position of company trapper.

The next two seasons were pretty poor, and the drab, sparsely attended rendezvous seemed to be the clincher for the vast majority of the beaver men. Bridger, though, was not about to give up yet. Drunk and angry, he had raged around the poor rendezvous camp cursing the fates and the fickleness of men in the States as well as in Europe. "If them sons of bitches hadn't gone over to usin' silk for their goddamn hats, beaver'd still shine."

"Buffler shit," an old-timer named Grosvenor said. "Hell, we all knew this was comin'."

"Like hell," Bridger insisted.

"Besides, Jim, there ain't no goddamn beaver left in the mountains anyway."

"This ol' chil' can find beaver, goddammit," Bridger roared. "And I'll show ye all, too. There any of ye boys aim to ride with this ol' hoss?"

Riley and several others agreed. Most had nothing better to do with their lives anyway. Two days later they pulled out.

Riley and Bridger stuck it out for another year, but by then it had become evident even to Bridger that the beaver trade had gone under for good. Bridger, Riley and the several other men who had hung on sat around a meager fire.

"Damn, boys, when even this ol' hoss can't make beaver shine, there just ain't no beaver left," Bridger said sadly.

"What're ye gonna do, Jim?" Riley asked. The past four years had been all he had hoped for and more. He had traded with some Indians and fought others; he had taken part in rendezvous; trapped his share of beaver; run buffalo on horseback; bedded Indian women; tangled with drunken revelers and with an angry griz. He felt a deep sense of loss now that it was all gone, and he seemed to have little future.

"I ain't certain," Bridger said. "I'll have to see what some of the ol' boys're doin'. How about ye all?"

"There's money to be made with buffler robes and wolf pelts," Grosvenor said. "Reckon that'd suit this ol' hoss." He cackled with glee. "Especially seein's how I don't know nothin' else."

Others felt the same, figuring to trap wolf or otter or hunt buffalo, or maybe work out of Bent's Fort or Fort Laramie, or even at Fort Union on the Upper Missouri.

Riley didn't know what to do. He was not nearly as expert in trapping and hunting as the others, and he did not have the connections they did. He had hoped that Bridger had more of a plan, and that he would be able to stay with him, but it was apparent now that the footloose Bridger wasn't quite ready for settling down.

When they broke camp, Bridger and Riley headed east. A few days later, they met up with Henry Fraeb, a former partner of Bridger's. That night, Bridger and Fraeb talked quietly for several hours. Riley was not really invited into the conversation, and sat off to the side until he got tired and turned in. All he overheard was that the two men were talking about building a trading post somewhere.

The next morning, over a sparse breakfast of stringy antelope and weak coffee, Bridger said to Riley, "Me'n Ol' Fraeb here have gone partners, and we're fixin' to build us a tradin' post up near the Seeds-Kee-Dee."

"Oh," Riley said sadly. He figured he was on his own now, and his prospects were not all that good.

"We was wonderin' if ye might like to hire on to us."

"To do what?" Riley asked, brightening. He really didn't care; he'd do just about anything to stay out in the mountains, living this life of freedom. He just wanted to know so he could fix it in his mind.

"Huntin', I reckon. Though I might teach ye a little blacksmithin'. Ye know I was apprenticed for such way back in my youth, don't ye, boy?" When Riley nodded,

Bridger continued. "We'll need a blacksmith there, and I sure as hell ain't gonna do it."

"Suits me." Riley kept his face expressionless, despite the roaring of excitement inside. It would not do to act too eager.

They turned north, heading for Fort Laramie, where the partners hoped to find some laborers for the actual construction of the post, though they did not yet really know where they were going to build it.

Two weeks later, a dozen men had been hired on, and the party moved toward the Green River—called the Seeds-Kee-Dee Agie by the Shoshoni. They crossed the river on a ferry run by one of their old friends from their beaver trapping days, and turned downriver. A few miles on, they stopped. From a bluff overlooking the Green, Bridger pointed. "There's whar we'll build 'er," he announced.

Workers were sent south into the Uinta Mountains the next morning to begin cutting logs for the fort. Bridger headed back to Fort Laramie to get more workers. Work on the post began a little more than a week after the group had arrived, though Bridger had not yet returned.

Bridger brought twenty men back with him, along with a couple of wagons of supplies and tools. Then work began in earnest.

With nearly three dozen men at the site, plus whatever old friends of Bridger and Fraeb showed up for a day or two, plenty of meat was needed to keep them all fed. That kept Fraeb and Riley busy, as they had been designated the hunters. Bridger, when he was around, bossed the laborers, though he did wander out to do a little hunting now and again.

When a party of twenty-five or thirty mountain men showed up, they decided that they'd go out and make meat, enough to feed them all, plus the workers. Riley and Fraeb decided that they would go along.

They headed southeast, secure in the knowledge that

most Indians would not bother such a large group of mountain men.

But the war party of Sioux, Cheyenne and Arapaho—nearly seventy strong—didn't think much of the mountain men's arrogance. They struck out of nowhere as the mountain men were just breaking camp the morning after they had left the fort. The men were scattered among the trees and thick brush along a creek when the warriors hit.

Half a dozen whites went down right off, two of them dead, the others wounded to one degree or another. However, this was a seasoned group of men, long used to the tricks of hostile Indians, and just as brave and resourceful as they. Two volleys from well-made rifles, in the hands of men who knew how to use them, gave the warriors something to think about as several of them fell.

When the warriors withdrew, the mountain men used the brief respite to regroup. There was not much they could do, other than just try to continue withstanding the Indian charges, and take out as many enemies as they could.

Riley held his position in some brush, trying not to be too scared. He had been in battle before, but this was something a little different, considering the number of Indians they faced. The warriors' tactics also were unnerving, what with them popping up individually from behind a rock or bush or tree. He was certain one of them would do so right next to him and carve his scalp off before he even knew the man was there.

Watching the other men in his party was giving him some courage, though. Despite the sweltering August heat and the tension of the spasmodic battle, they seemed calm and in control. Riley tried to emulate them.

Things dragged on for more than an hour, with little happening. But then Riley sensed something. He didn't know what it was; he just became certain that something was imminent.

Several minutes later the Indians charged, rushing through the brush, seeking to overwhelm the mountain men through sheer numbers.

Riley fired his rifle, knocking a warrior down. Then, dropping his rifle, he pulled out one of his two single-shot pistols. He fired one, but before he could fire the other, a warrior jumped on him, knife in hand.

More out of desperation than planning, Riley managed to stab the Indian in the ear with the patch knife he had snatched out of its sheath on the strap of his shooting bag. The warrior howled and fell back, clutching the injured ear.

Riley leaped up and slid the small knife away. He grabbed the handle of his big belt knife from the sheath on his right side, the thumb of his fist outward. He drew it and swept it backhanded across the warrior's throat in one swift motion.

He heard Fraeb's thick, guttural curses and swung his head that way. Three Sioux surrounded the tough German, who was defending himself with a knife in one hand and a tomahawk in the other. Then one warrior slipped in and shoved his knife to the hilt into Fraeb's lower back.

Fraeb turned like an enraged grizzly and hacked the man down, but that left his back exposed to the other two warriors. Slowed as he was by the wound, he could not swing back again fast enough.

Riley began running, seeing one of the warriors swing his war club at Fraeb's head. He missed, but the stone ball broke Fraeb's shoulder. One-handed, the old mountain man slashed wildly, but hit nothing.

Just as the other warrior cracked Fraeb's skull with his tomahawk, Riley smashed into the one with the war club, who had fallen onto his back. It was but a few seconds before he had gutted the Sioux. He pushed himself up and turned.

The pain in his left eye was more staggering than anything he had ever experienced before. It was as if someone had driven a freezing steel knife blade into the soft tissue. He reacted by instinct, head butting the warrior, who fell. Riley fell atop him.

He didn't remember much after that. Not until later.

Riley awoke inside a tent in the camp where Bridger's and Fraeb's trading post was being built. His left eye hurt like hell, and he generally felt poor all around. It was frightening, wondering if he had lost sight in the eye. It was covered by a patch, so he had hope that he might recover, though rationally he knew that was plumb foolish; the patch more than likely meant the eye was useless. Still, he was too much of an optimist to let reality intrude.

Dim recollections of what had happened during the fight filtered into his consciousness. With all his pain, he had turned savage, feral, hacking unconsciously at the Sioux with his knife. Vaguely he could see in his mind chunks of flesh flying off the warrior's body, seeming to sail in slow motion.

He could remember, too, feeling something warm and sticky seeping out of his left eye. Then the pain had overridden even the savage fury he felt, and there came a blessed blackness.

Bridger and several other mountain men entered the tent where Riley had awakened. "How's doin's, hoss?" Bridger asked.

"I felt a mite better at times," Riley said, mostly truthfully.

"That's good," Bridger said distractedly as he squatted next to Riley. "I hate to bring ye the bad news, boy, but it's best gotten out in the open right off."

"What's that?" Riley asked, licking his lips.

"Ye ain't ary gonna use that eye no more, hoss. I don't know how that ol' cuss managed not to stuff his blade clean through your eye and out the back of your head, but he did. In the doin', though, he cut that eyeball to hell and back."

Riley nodded. He had known it deep in his heart since it had happened. It was something he would have to live with. Others had gotten along with worse injuries; he could do the same. As long as infection didn't set in and kill him, he figured he'd be all right. "And Frapp?" he asked, using the common pronunciation of Fraeb.

"Gone under," Bridger said flatly. He and Fraeb had been friends a long time, and had been partners several times over the years. He felt the German's loss heavily. "The boys tell me ye tried to help him."

"Didn't do a very good job, did I?" Riley said sourly.

"Ye did as good as anybody could've, hoss," another of the men said. The others agreed.

Riley shrugged. He did not consider himself a hero, and he did not want the others having any such notions either. "What's gonna happen now?" he asked.

"Well, I ain't of a mood fer buildin' this goddamn fort no more," Bridger said. "I think I'll jist mosey on a little higher in the mountains for a spell, see if I cain't raise beaver somewhere. The rest of the boys are headin' in different directions. Several of 'em's goin' back to the Settlements. I suggest ye go with 'em, boy. Ye can recover there for a spell."

"I'd as soon go with ye, Jim."

"No," Bridger said harshly. His usual cantankerousness was worsened by the death of his friend.

Riley nodded again, suddenly feeling unwanted and out of place.

"We'd be glad to have ya along, One-Eye," a trapper named Ed Perkins said, giving Riley the nickname that would stick to him from here on.

"Ye sure?"

"Certain. Ain't that right, boys?"

There was no dissent that Riley could hear.

"Hell, any man can make chunked stew meat out of some damned ol' Injin as easy as you did is welcome to travel wit' us boys any time," Perkins said with a laugh.

The others—including Bridger—chuckled in agreement.

"Goddamn, boy, you shoulda seen yourself dere, sendin' parts a dat Innian sailin' all which ways." Perkins was laughing hard now. "All da while, dat Sioux was screechin' and hollerin' and clobberin' you wit' anything he could find, but you . . . you . . . wasn't payin' him no mind. Just kept on flingin' baits a his carcass hither and yon and . . ." He finally had to stop, he was laughing so hard.

"You're a putrid pile of shit, Perkins, ye know that?" Riley said in disgust. He did not like the idea of what he had done to that warrior. Not one bit. His own savagery frightened him.

Perkins was still laughing, and he slapped his left palm into the crook of his right elbow and jerked the right forearm upward.

"Jesus Christ, will ye boys git him the hell out of here?" Riley said, but he was grinning. He couldn't help himself. Perkins was a purely jovial man. "I'll be ready to pull out when ye all are."

In Independence, Missouri, Riley tried his hand at a number of things, but he had little luck or success with any of them. Finally he remembered something Bridger had said—about teaching him some of the blacksmith's trade. He thought that might be a useful craft, whether he stayed here in the States or went back to the mountains one day.

He started asking around, and finally managed to sign on as a blacksmith's apprentice. He did well, but not well enough—or so his master, a man named Charles Flannigan, kept telling him. Besides, he was so poorly paid that he knew he would never be able to save enough to start his own shop. Not with the way he spent money, most of it on whiskey, whores and gambling.

The only thing he seemed to be good at was getting in trouble. He spent more than one night in the city jail for public drunkenness, brawling and assorted other offenses. Finally he was encouraged to depart Independence, so he moved up the Missouri River to Saint Joseph and found a job with a blacksmith there. A few wagon trains were heading west toward Oregon every year, and the wagons needed work before pulling out. That was enough to keep him occupied, if not overly busy. He was all right there for a year or so, but then, as he had in Independence, he started finding trouble too often again.

In 1844, three years after he had left the mountains, Old Broken Hand Fitzpatrick strolled into the blacksmith shop. "Hey, hoss," the big Irishman said, "how's doin's?"

Riley grinned, but then shrugged. "I've seen better times."

"Ye lookin' to get out of here?" Fitzpatrick asked.

"It'd shine with me. Why, ye got somethin' in mind?"

"I'm leadin' a big ol' wagon train to Oregon. Ye want to join on?"

"Doin' what?"

"Looks like ye know the blacksmithin' business. We can always use such a hand. Ye can help out with the huntin', too, if that'd suit ye."

Riley didn't have to think about it. "When do we leave?"

"Three days. See me sometime before that and I'll set ye up with your possibles."

Riley nodded, then asked, "Ye heard anything about Ol' Jim?"

"Bridger? Sure. Him and Louis Vasquez built a trading post last year up on Black's Fork of the Seeds-Kee-Dee."

"This wagon train goin' by there?" Riley asked, a burst of anger sweeping through him.

"Yep. Why?"

"No reason," Riley said. He was not about to voice his sudden anger at Bridger having partnered with Vasquez instead of him. After all that he and Bridger had been through—especially Fraeb's battle—he would've thought Bridger would have looked him up to see about going into business together.

"Ye sure?" Fitzpatrick asked skeptically.

"Yep. I'll be by tomorrow to see about my possibles."

The trip was even longer and more boring than Riley had thought it would be. After so much traveling with the mountain men and their Indian women, he was used to a far swifter pace than could be hoped for with this oxen-driven plodding.

Blacksmithing work kept him fairly busy, and he rode out to hunt whenever he could. One of the reasons he was so eager to leave St. Joseph was that he didn't like the crowds. He had come to enjoy the relative solitude of traveling and working with a small group of men in the mountains. He saw the wagon train as little more than a moving city, one filled with all the same problems as a stationary one, and none of the benefits. Hunting gave him a chance to be away from the wagons and the bickering that went on among the people in them. Being with two or three men, even if they were emigrants, was a lot better than being with the entire group.

Despite the work, the journey was long and dull enough to give him a heap of time to think. Because of that, he gradually began to look at Bridger's new partnership a bit differently. He found he could not stay angry at Bridger, not after all the old mountain man had done for him. Without Bridger, Riley would've never been able to stay in the mountains when Stewart had left. Whatever Riley had—and it was not much, if one only counted worldly possessions—was because of Bridger. But he figured he had plenty—memories of

cold mountain streams; of frigid beaver ponds; of the
lush, almost sensual feeling of a prime, finely cured beaver plew; of the intimacies of Indian women, who had
taught him so much about being a man; of the blood-
curdling fear of facing off an Indian war party. All that,
and more.

Truth be told, Riley finally admitted to himself,
Bridger had been smart in choosing a man like Vasquez
to be his partner. Bridger had little business sense, but it
was more than Riley possessed. Riley knew that if he and
Bridger had partnered up, their enterprise would have
been doomed from the start.

Still, Riley wondered how Bridger could have chosen
Louis Vasquez to be his partner. Riley considered Vasquez somewhat pompous. Even though the Spaniard
had gone west with Bridger and a heap of the old boys
more than two decades ago, he retained an aristocratic
bearing—one gotten through the simple feat of having
been born—that grated on Riley.

Despite his deep thoughts on the journey, Riley never
realized that he had somehow managed to transform
his anger at Bridger into resentment of Vasquez.

Riley did make up his mind on something, though,
through all the self-examination: He had no real desire
to go to Oregon, or even California. As the wagon train
slowly approached the Green River, he made his decision. Over their fire that night, he asked, "Would ye
mind much if I was to see if Ol' Jim'd hire me on at his
tradin' post, Mister Fitzpatrick?"

"*Mister* Fitzpatrick now, hoss?" the former mountain
man said with a big laugh. "If Jim'll hire ye on, I'll let ye
out of your deal with me."

"I'm obliged, Tom," Riley said seriously. Some
doubts lingered, mostly about how he would get along
with Vasquez. That could be a tricky situation. He
wouldn't know, of course, until he and Vasquez came
face to face. He would deal with it then.

Two days later, they had crossed the Seeds-Kee-Dee
and arrived at the fort on an 'island' between the two

branches of Black's Fork. It was not much to look at—a simple structure, about one hundred feet wide by perhaps one hundred twenty long, made of small logs, with cabins making up most of two walls on either side of the small courtyard. A large corral was at one side. Shoshoni and Ute lodges were scattered around the outside of the fort, and Indians and former mountain men wandered in and out through the wide gates in the front wall.

Bridger was surprised to see Riley, but he seemed pleased about his arrival. The old mountaineer was glad to give his friend a job, especially when he found out that Riley had indeed become a blacksmith. "Hell, boy," he said in his normally rough voice, "we need an experienced hand for such work more'n ever. And I know ye to be a man I can trust. I been doin' the blacksmithin' here this season, since the idjit we hired on last year turned out to be a connivin' son of a bitch." He laughed a little, not unusual for him despite his curmudgeonliness. Riley had gotten used to such ways from Bridger. "There was a damn good reason I left Saint Louis as young as I did, boy. I tell ye, I ain't fond of blacksmithin'."

A day later, a rather revived Pete Riley—eye-patch in place as it had been for almost four years now—waved farewell to Tom Fitzpatrick and the wagon train. Then he went to work.

He kept his distance from Vasquez, believing that saying the wrong thing would hurt his position. And he did feel that he had a good situation here. He was paid well, and he could sleep in his shop for free. The shop was large enough for him, and it was, in essence, his own. That was something he never thought he would see.

Only one thing bothered him—his want of a woman. He was twenty-four now, and thought it time to take a wife. Every time he saw Bridger's Flathead woman go strolling by, the yearning inside him would start all over again.

Since the wagon trains were coming in force now, he was kept mighty busy, which helped him avoid Vasquez *and* keep his mind off the fact that he had no woman. Besides, he liked to work. He never had been the kind to sit around doing nothing. Working gave him a feeling of accomplishment.

{ 10 }

Riley heard a commotion, and he went to investigate. Seeing that it was only a small group of Shoshonis, he was about to return to his work when something stopped him. His one good eye fixed on a young Shoshoni woman. Riley had had his share of Indian women, both in the beaver trapping days and since coming to Bridger's fort a few months ago, but he had never seen one as fetching as this one.

She was maybe fifteen, Riley figured, short and slender. Her eyes were set deep in a rather flat and circular face, below a smooth, high forehead and above a somewhat large nose. Her skin was rich, dark and smooth; her lips thin and straight. The braids of her long, silky black hair were wrapped in rabbit fur and rested on her collarbone. Her beaded, double-yoked elkskin dress could not disguise her curvaceous figure, though it revealed nothing.

Riley had never been so awestruck by a woman, and he stood in the doorway of his small shop, filled with desire. Finally, though, she was swept away amid other women and lost to his gaze. Dumbly, he turned and went back to work, doing it more by instinct now than by thought and reason.

As the morning wore on, Riley began to think that he had merely had a vision, that the young woman was either a product of his imagination, or that he had seen her as something far more than she was. That settled him, and he even managed to chuckle at his foolishness. "Damn, hoss, ye best go git yourself a woman. And soon," he muttered to himself.

Near noon, he cut off a hunk of buffalo meat the hunters had brought in an hour ago, and jammed a metal spit through it. He arranged it over his forge to roast, while he finished the link of chain he was fixing. The fort was built to serve emigrants on the California and Oregon Trails, and the wagon trains would be arriving soon. Because of that, Riley was busy at this time of year, making up chains, horseshoes, wheel rims, wheels, nails, hinges, basic cooking and eating utensils, trivets, cooking tripods, Dutch ovens and other items the emigrants would need. They might not be just what the travelers wanted or needed, as far as size went, but he could adjust these a lot easier than he could make them from scratch.

Finished, he grabbed his spit of meat and a large tin mug of coffee and went outside. He sat on a small bench made of poorly hewn logs and set his cup on a tree stump next to it. Leaving the meat on the spit, he simply tore off chunks of it with his teeth.

While he was eating, he saw the young woman again. She and several other women were headed for the trading room. "Goddamn," he mumbled, "it weren't no vision." He was just as struck with her this time as he had been earlier.

Just then Bridger happened by. "Hey, Jim," Riley called excitedly. When Bridger stopped and looked at him in question, Riley asked, "Who's that gal there?" He pointed.

"The purty one with the sunburst design on her dress?"

"Yep."

"Ye don't recognize her, ol' hoss?" Bridger said with a laugh. "That there's Spirit Grass, youngest daughter of ol' Black Iron."

"No. Spirit Grass is jist a chil'."

"Like hell she is, boy. When's the last time ye seen her?"

"Back in '38 or '39, I reckon."

"No wonder ye don't recognize her no more."

"She married?"

"Widowed. She was married to a hoss named Bull Hide, but he was kilt by the Arapaho nearabout a year ago. Jist afore ye come back out here, I'm thinkin'." He paused and squinted at Riley in mock surprise. "Ye ain't got designs on that gal, do ye, hoss?" he said in jest.

But Riley was deadly serious in answering. "I ain't ever seen one like her, Jim. She plumb outshines any other woman I ever set eye on."

"Damn, boy, ye got it bad," Bridger said, surprised for real this time. "It'll take a heap of specie to pry her away from ol' Black Iron. I figure that ol' hoss is holdin' out for a heap and has many warriors in the biddin'."

Riley nodded sadly. "I expected as such."

"And ye ain't got a damn thing to offer for her, do ye, boy?"

"Nope." Riley paused, then swallowed all his pride. "I was wonderin', Jim, if ye could maybe . . . well, maybe advance me a few ponies and some trade goods that I could offer Black Iron for her."

"I ain't in the business of helpin' folks get wives, boy," Bridger said, not all that seriously.

Riley couldn't see Bridger's attempt at humor, though. "Sorry I asked. I didn't mean to put ye out none. I jist wasn't thinkin' is all."

"Goddamn, you're a sour-faced ol' fart, ain't ye? I was just pullin' your leg some, hoss. Sure I'll let ye have such things as ye need to trap that gal. Hell, I'll even go to talk to Black Iron with ye."

Riley didn't know how to thank Bridger, and knew that an effusive show of gratitude wouldn't be wanted or accepted. So he simply muttered, "Thanks, ol' hoss."

There wasn't really anything to the ceremony, but the small band of visiting Shoshonis thought Riley's marriage to Spirit Grass a fine excuse for a celebration. With the enthusiastic help of the resident mountain men—and ample whiskey supplied by Bridger—there was feasting, dancing and singing.

Riley watched his intake of whiskey and food, not wanting to be too drunk or too bloated with buffalo meat to be able to perform with his new bride. He and Spirit Grass sat together for a while during the celebration, talking, getting to know each other a little. Since Spirit Grass spoke almost no English, they conversed in Shoshoni. Riley wasn't completely fluent in it, but he knew it well enough for them to make each other known. He silently vowed right off that he would perfect his ability with the Shoshoni language, and begin teaching Spirit Grass English as soon as possible.

While the festivities were in full flower, they slipped out of the small fort, and headed for the lodge that Black Iron had supplied for them. The tipi was set up in a comfortable spot alongside Black's Fork, amid willows, cottonwoods and brush. It was less than fifty yards from the fort gate, but to the newlyweds, it seemed far removed.

Both Riley and Spirit Grass were a little nervous as they entered the lodge, mainly because they were new to each other. It seemed silent inside the tipi after the din of the celebration, even though the drums and shouting could still be heard.

Riley took the woman in his arms and kissed her gently, though with longing. A rush of desire pulsed through him as he tasted her sweet mouth, and felt her supple young body moving strongly against his.

When they broke apart, Spirit Grass raised a hand and stroked one of her husband's cheeks. She was glad that he had shaved for her. She did not like the look of a white man's beard or mustache; such things were simply too strange. Most white men knew facial hair bothered Indian women, and Riley's having shaved showed that he cared about her feelings.

He thought at first that she was reaching to touch his

eye patch. He was still sensitive about it, even after four years. That was especially true right now, seeing as how he was here with his new bride. "Does this bother ye?" he asked in Shoshoni, touching the patch himself. Even though he knew by now that that was not where she was heading with her hand, he had to ask. "It doesn't make ye think I'm not a whole man or something?"

Spirit Grass smiled up at Riley, marveling again at his size. He was so tall and wide compared with most of the men of her tribe. His muscles felt like iron, too, she was learning already. She had wondered what had happened to his left eye that required it to be covered with the leather patch all the time. But it didn't matter to her. She was discovering that she quite liked this large, powerful white man. "It's all right," she responded in her own language. "It shows you're a brave man. A mighty warrior."

Spirit Grass moved back a step, still smiling, turned and took his hand. She tugged him toward the neat bed of blankets and buffalo robes. She untied the thongs at her shoulders and let her dress slither down her to the floor. Bending, she quickly shucked her moccasins and leggings, then slid under a thick, six-point blanket. Lacing her hands behind her, she grinned and said, "Well?"

Riley had been mesmerized by the sight of Spirit Grass disrobing. Her word finally shook him out of his trance. He nodded and hastily began tossing off his clothes. In moments he was lying beside her, up on one elbow. He peeled back the blanket so he could drink in the sight of her strong young body. Each breast was large, firm and capped by a dark point surrounded by a darker circle. Her belly was slightly rounded, her hips wide and gently curved. Spirit Grass's skin was soft under Riley's rough hands as he began stroking her from neck to pelvis.

Spirit Grass enjoyed the touch of her new husband. His hands were experienced and gentle, knowledgeable yet questing. His lips were exciting as they began following the flow of her chin, neck, breasts and lower body.

She reached out for him then, running her blunt, cracked fingernails through the mat of hair on his chest. How odd, she thought, that he would have hair there, yet a smooth, hairless stomach before his pubic hair began. She didn't mind, though. She found this difference between Riley and Shoshoni men exciting and interesting. She quit thinking about such things soon enough, as pleasure rippled and then pounded through her. She shuddered and groaned as the feelings grew, exploded, ebbed and rose again.

Riley eventually rolled atop Spirit Grass, with her willing help and considerable cooperation. Then he was inside her, thrusting with his powerful body, both of them crying out with the intensity of it. They burst in a sudden convulsion of extreme pleasure, clinging to each other as they bucked and writhed wildly.

"Ye don't mind being married to a white man?" Riley asked in Shoshoni when they were done—for the third time that night. The drums had finally stopped and the celebration was over. It was quiet now, except for the normal night sounds: the yelp of a coyote, the croaking of frogs in the stream, the buzz of insects. They were comforting sounds, ones both were used to.

"It's strange," Spirit Grass answered in Shoshoni. She smiled and touched his face. "But not bad strange. Good strange."

"I'm not sure how I should take that," Riley said with a small laugh.

Spirit Grass laughed a little, too, then grew serious. "You should take it as it was meant—I like it, I think, but it'll take getting used to."

"I suppose it will," Riley agreed.

Spirit Grass's small, pink tongue edged out of her mouth and licked at her dry lips. "And how do you feel about this?" she finally asked nervously.

"When I saw ye the first time, when ye and your family got here to the fort, I just knew I had to have ye, woman.'' Riley felt embarrassed saying such things, especially since he was having a hard time forming the words in Shoshoni. His knowledge of that language was inadequate for the task, he thought.

Spirit Grass looked at him in surprise. "How can that be?'' she asked.

He shrugged. "I don't know. All I know is that it's true.'' He paused again, unsure of himself. "And I'm glad ye were available. I don't know what I might've done if ye were still married.''

"I'm happy we didn't have to worry about that," Spirit Grass said firmly. "Are you hungry?''

"Man's big as me's hungry all the time," he said in English. When he saw Spirit Grass's blank look, he repeated—more or less—in Shoshoni.

The woman smiled and rose, stretching the lithe, strong muscles in her legs, back and arms.

Riley enjoyed watching the display, and he kept his eyes glued to her nude form as she headed toward the fire. She moved like a mountain cat, he thought, all suppleness and sleek strength. Her dark skin seemed to ripple with every movement, and her hair, now loose, flowed in an ebony cascade over her shoulders and back. The sight of her almost took his breath away.

Spirit Grass brought Riley a bowl of antelope stew and a tin mug of coffee, then got the same for herself. The two sat on their bed of robes and blankets, facing each other, slowly eating.

Riley was surprised at how comfortable he was with Spirit Grass already. It was as if they had been together for years, rather than hours.

Spirit Grass felt the same way, and it was reflected in her eyes.

With a mischievous grin, Riley loaded up his horn spoon with stew and moved it toward Spirit Grass's mouth. She was momentarily shocked, but recovered quickly. She smiled and accepted the offering. A moment later, she returned the favor. Laughing, they continued to feed each other.

And when they were done, they reached out for each other and rolled onto the robes again.

R iley walked uncomfortably into Louis Vasquez's small office in one of the log buildings at Fort Bridger. He felt like a small boy called by his father, certain that he was about to be taken behind the woodshed but having no idea why. Despite the fort owner's resolve to overcome the rift with Riley, a wide chasm still separated the two men.

"Take a seat, *Señor* Riley," Vasquez said. He had only a trace of an accent.

Riley sat, wondering what this was all about. He was fairly sure that with winter coming on, Vasquez was going to tell him his services were no longer needed. That didn't worry Riley; he could always find other work after spending the winter in Black Iron's village. It did annoy him, though. He thought he deserved better, after the long and faithful service he had given to Bridger.

"What're your plans for the winter, Pedro?" Vasquez asked.

Riley shrugged. "I was fixin' to stay right here—with your approval. And Jim's, of course," he added pointedly. He didn't really mind losing his job, but he'd be damned if he'd let Vasquez do it without Bridger's having some say in the matter.

"That's good to hear," Vasquez said, confusing Riley all the more. "I can't bear the thought of spending another winter in this place. Not at all." The Spaniard was in charge of the trading post, mostly because Bridger was as footloose as ever, and was away from the fort as often as not.

"What's this got to do with me?" Riley asked. "Ye figurin' on shuttin' the fort down for the winter?"

"Hell, no," Vasquez said in some surprise. "What makes you think that?"

Riley shrugged again. "Jist a hunch I had."

"No. I wanted to know if your plans for the winter included thoughts of leaving here. Since they don't, I wanted to ask if you'd stay and look after the post."

"What about ye?" Riley managed to ask despite his surprise. He never would have thought Vasquez would ask him to run the fort, even over the winter when there were few, if any, visitors.

"I will be enjoying the pleasures of Saint Louis," Vasquez said with a big smile. He could envision the women there, and the fine foods and wines, the company of refined men and women. Such a life was far more to his liking than spending another winter hunkered down hundreds of miles from anything. "So I'd like you to be in charge here until I get back, or until Jim does."

"Ye sure?" Riley asked. He was still a little bewildered. He had come in here expecting to be told to leave the fort, and instead was being put in charge of it.

"*Sí,*" Vasquez answered without hesitation. "You've worked with Jim a long time, and for me not so long, but long enough. You're the only *hombre* I can trust. Hell, you're about the only *hombre* who won't steal us blind if both Jim and I're gone. So, what do you say?"

"I reckon I could do such for ye," Riley said tentatively.

"You don' sound so sure, *amigo.*"

"Well," Riley responded after only a moment's hesitation, "I'm jist surprised by the offer is all, considerin' how . . . less than friendly I've been toward ye."

Vasquez shrugged. It bothered him some that Riley didn't like him, but that was Riley's business, he told himself. He had his own concerns in running the fort and much of the business as Bridger's partner. That had to be foremost. "You're a good worker and I can trust you."

"Folks don't usually trust those that don't like 'em."

"We're different men, with different ways, Pedro. Because of that, we don't get along so good. That doesn't mean we can't work together without trying to kill each other. That's enough some times."

"I reckon it is," Riley agreed, a little surprised. Maybe he had been wrong to resent and dislike Vasquez so much, he thought. That was a question he could look at later.

"Then it's settled?" Vasquez asked.

"Reckon so," Riley offered. But his brain was catching up to what had just gone on, and he began really thinking again. "But I expect I'll need a bit more specie for my added responsibilities." He had the sudden thought that this might help him decide if Vasquez wasn't perhaps trying to play some kind of trick on him. Then he realized that it didn't matter—he still wanted more money, even if the responsibility really wasn't all that great.

"Of course," Vasquez said without hesitation. He had no objection to paying Riley more, but he had not been planning to offer higher wages. He wanted to see if Riley asked for them, fairly certain that he would. "You make a dollar a day?"

"Ye know damn well what I make, ye bug-eatin' son of a bitch," Riley growled, but not very harshly.

"*Sí,* I do," Vasquez admitted. "Well, I will raise your wages to a dollar fifty a day, How's that?"

"Three dollars. In Mexican gold pieces," Riley countered.

"Don't abuse my generosity, *señor,*" a tight-lipped Vasquez said.

"Then don't abuse my good nature and my loyalty to Ol' Jim with such a piddly offer," Riley responded a little hotly.

"You're a hard bargainer, *Pedro.* . . ."

"Buffler dicks," Riley shot back. "I ain't no such thing and ye know it. I'm jist some ol' hoss tryin' to keep hisself from gittin' took advantage of by a goddamn thievin' half-breed Spaniard."

Vasquez sneered. "So, you'd rather be taken advantage of by an irascible reprobate of an American?" He was basically a good man, but he could be as hard as any man who roamed these mountains, and he could be pushed only so far.

"Best watch your words when it comes to Ol' Jim Bridger, ye bean-fartin' snake dick," Riley growled. "Jim Bridger's the best friend this chil's ary had, and I ain't about to let no son of a bitch—even his partner—disparage his character." Riley began to reconsider his recent reconsideration of his feelings toward Vasquez.

"I'm not disparaging my partner's character," Vasquez protested with a smile. "He is irascible. And a reprobate. No more so than you and even me. You can't disparage a man's character when you speak the truth, señor."

"Hell, you're not only a goddamn bean-eater, you're an annoyin' son of a bitch, too," Riley said in reluctant agreement.

"Sí," Vasquez said with a nod and a laugh. "And you have not disparaged this hombre's character in saying that." He stopped laughing seconds later, and said, "Two dollars a day is the best I can do, Pedro. In Mexican gold."

Riley nodded. "I accept, Señor Vasquez," he said, holding out his hand.

They shook, and Vasquez poured them each a drink. They downed them in one swift gulp each, before Riley rose and left.

Riley hurried to his lodge, bursting with the news. It was still almost inconceivable to him that he had been entrusted with such responsibility when he had only been at the fort for three, almost four months. He had to force himself to speak slowly and calmly when he told Spirit Grass about it. When she understood the importance of it—or at least its importance to her husband—she was as happy as he. To celebrate, they spent an hour in the robes.

Jim Bridger rode back into the fort just before winter really laid its ungentle hand over the landscape. Riley heard the noise, and came out of his shop and stood watching. He grinned when Bridger stopped and dismounted. They shook hands and exchanged greetings, then Bridger asked, "Where's Louis got to?"

"He's in Saint Louis," Riley said. He began to wonder a little. When he had thought Vasquez was going to fire him two months ago, he hadn't wanted it to happen without Bridger's say-so, thinking that Bridger was sure to reject Vasquez's effort. Standing here, though, he wasn't at all sure that Bridger wouldn't just up and fire him now.

"What the hell's he doin' in Saint Louis?" Bridger growled. He was a cantankerous fellow most of the time, and most of the men he dealt with knew it. His friends also accepted it.

"What the hell do ye think he's doin' there?" Riley growled right back. Just because he accepted Bridger's quarrelsome ways didn't mean he couldn't or wouldn't hold his own.

Bridger grinned. "Prob'ly dunkin' his puny little pecker in any woman fool enough to let him," he said. Then he stopped, looking puzzled. "Then who's in charge here?" he demanded.

"I am," Riley said defiantly. "At least I was."

"What the hell's that mean?"

"Louie put me in charge until one of ye two come back. Now you're here, looks like I'm out of a job."

"Buffler balls," Bridger snorted. "Ye had any trouble?"

"Nope."

"Then ye must be doin' a good job, ol' son. I don't see no reason to give it up."

"What about ye? What're ye gonna do?"

"Hell, maybe head back east myself. Give ol' Louis some grief. That lazy bastard give ye more specie for bein' in charge of things?" Bridger might be irascible, but he believed that if a man did a job, he should be paid for it.

"Yep."

Bridger nodded. "Probably not enough, but if ye think it's fair . . . ?"

"Hell, a man can always use more money," Riley said with a laugh.

Bridger nodded, then asked, "I don't suppose there's any of the other ol' boys about?"

"Jist me and Jack Robinson. Ye jist missed Broken Hand. He was here a few days ago, but rode out. Said he was hopin' to make the Settlements before winter come on."

Bridger thought that over. "I might try'n catch that son of a bitch," he offered.

"Then ye best be quick about it. He was aimin' to move fast." Riley paused. "Might be, though, that he's stopped by Fort Laramie for a bit. He does that, ye might run him down somewhere near there."

Bridger nodded. "I'll cogitate on it. There any meat on in here someplace?"

"I got a bit over the forge, but it ain't enough to satisfy a man. Why'n't ye go on over to my lodge. Spirit Grass'll fill your meatbag for ye."

"Obliged, One-Eye. Ye mind takin' a look at my horse here?" It was not really a question. "I think the shoe on the right foreleg's comin' loose."

"That's what I'm here for," Riley said. "I'll unsaddle him and tend him for ye, too, while I'm at it."

Bridger nodded and walked off.

Bridger stayed the rest of that day and all the next, but the following morning he rode out, leaving the fort in peace and solitude once again. Riley decided that he liked it that way, even if it did mean he was in charge of almost nothing.

* * *

Bridger and Vasquez returned to the fort together, though winter had not fully left yet. As soon as they were settled in, they called Riley into their joint office on a gray, wintry day that threatened yet more snow. Vasquez had the chair behind the table. Bridger stood leaning against the wall a few feet to Vasquez's left, and behind him a bit.

"Looks like a goddamn funeral in here," Riley said as he turned the seat so the back was facing the desk. He plopped down in the chair and rested his forearms across the back. He was mostly right. The only light inside came from one small window and from two lanterns that threw a ghastly orangish glow around the room. Bridger blended into the shadows.

"It ain't near so much fun as that," Bridger growled. Then he laughed, a deep, rumbling sound.

Vasquez was smiling. When Bridger's laughter faded, Vasquez said, "Jim and I just wanted to see how things went over the winter, Pedro."

"It was duller'n dog shit. A few of the ol' boys come along and wintered up here, but otherwise it was real quiet."

"That's a relief," Vasquez said, though it was what he had expected. The previous two winters had been the same.

Riley nodded. When he saw that the partners had nothing else to say, he asked, "Any news from back in the Settlements?"

"Hell, big news, boy," Bridger said with a grin. "Big news. Ol' Broken Hand's been named Injin agent."

"The hell ye say," Riley shot back. "What Indians?"

"As far as I can tell, every goddamn Injin 'tween the Mississippi and the High Sierra. At least that's the way he's talkin'. He might be by here one of these days. He's tryin' to parley with all the tribes he can, hopin' to set up peace parleys amongst 'em."

"Hell, he might's well try to find gold up in the Sierra as try'n git the Shoshonis to set down with the Crows or such. I think he's pissin' into the wind on this one."

Bridger laughed. "Damn if I didn't tell him the same. Son of a bitch won't listen, though. Poor bastard thinks he can win over all them Injins with his Irish charm, and ye should know better'n most folks how useful that is."

"Shit, it wasn't for us Irishmen, you'd of been suckin' dirt years ago and your scalp'd be hangin' from some shit pile's lodgepole."

"There ain't ary gonna be a day I'll need the help of no goddamn Irishman," Bridger groused. But there was a twinkle of humor in his eyes. "There ain't a one of ye that's worth the sweat off a buffler's balls." He laughed.

Riley had a quick flash of anger at several remembrances, but he calmed down almost immediately. He knew Bridger wasn't being serious. A moment later he could hold out no longer. He also started laughing, joining in with his two companions.

When the onslaught of wagons started arriving, Riley began to believe they would never stop. There seemed to be no end of blacksmithing work for him.

Sometimes, though, things worked out even when they weren't planned. Riley walked into his shop one July day and found a young man working at his forge. "Hey, shit pile, jist what the hell do ye think you're doin' here?" Riley demanded. Tired and irritated, he was about ready to hammer this young fellow into the ground.

The youth held up the pair of tongs he gripped in one hand. Clenched in the tongs was a metal U used for yoking oxen. "This ox bow broke. I'm fixin' it for me mother. Without it, we'd nae be able to go much farther."

"Ye from Ireland, boy?" Riley asked, some of his anger dissipating.

"I am. Three years off the boat from County Cork."

"A fine place, lad," Riley said. It was only a small lie. He had been born in Virginia, though his parents had come to America only a year before. He had heard them talking enough about the old country. He knew nothing specific about County Cork, but he figured it was pretty much like County Clavan, where his parents were from.

"That 'tis, sir." He went back to working on the ox bow.

"Why'd ye leave it?"

"Potato famine. Wasn't a damn thing to eat for none of us."

Riley nodded. "What's your name, son?"

"Patrick McGinnis. Most folks call me Paddy. And who're ye?"

"Pete Riley. Most folks call me One-Eye, though I cain't figure out why," Riley said dryly. He was rewarded with the spark of a smile by the young man. "Ye with that wagon train came along day before yesterday?"

McGinnis nodded, and then began hammering the piece of metal, working it around the anvil's horn.

"Ye know, boy," Riley said, growing agitated again, "I don't like folks who jist up and wander into my shop and start usin' my gear."

"I won't be but a minute more." McGinnis said, hardly paying Riley any attention.

The big blacksmith watched for a few seconds, then decided that McGinnis wasn't trying to snub him; he was simply trying to get his small job finished and get out without irritating him any more than necessary.

"There, done," McGinnis said, straightening up and sticking the ox bow into a bucket of water, where it hissed angrily. He set down his hammer and looked at Riley. "Thankee, sir, for lettin' me use your tools. And I apologize for havin' done so without askin' permission."

"That's all right, son," Riley said, thinking. Suddenly he asked, "Is that all ye can do at the forge?"

"Oh, no, sir. I'm a fair hand at all blacksmithin'." As he had all along, he spoke with directness, but with no arrogance or disrespect.

"Ye got brothers and sisters along?"

"Aye." McGinnis seemed puzzled. "But why would ye ask me that?"

Riley grinned a little. "We got two wagon trains settin' around the fort now, one jist left, and I hear there'll be another here in a day or two. And that's jist the beginnin', really. All of which means I'm up to my ass in work here, and wouldn't mind havin' a capable assistant. Ye interested?"

"I'd have to think on it some, Mister Riley."

"I understand. Ye go talk it over with your folks. But don't take too long about it. If ye ain't up for the job, I've got to find someone else who is."

"Yes, sir," McGinnis said. "And thankee for the offer, Mister Riley."

Riley watched as the young man ran off. It created something of a wistful feeling in him. He could remember when he was that young and carefree. Then he laughed. Those days were not all that long ago—less than a decade, though it seemed as if several lifetimes had passed. He turned and went back into the shop.

McGinnis returned first thing the next morning. One look at the youth's face gave Riley the answer. "Your ma said no, did she, boy?" he asked.

"Me mother didn't say much at all," McGinnis said angrily. "It was me stepfather who put his foot down."

"Needs your help, does he?"

"Damn right he does," the youth groused. "Since he doesn't do a goddamn thing himself. Makes me and me sisters and brother do it all. Lazy bastard just sits on his skinny ass all the day, givin' orders and drinkin' whate'er whiskey he can find."

"Would ye like me to have a word with him, Paddy?"

McGinnis's eyes brightened. "Ye think ye could?" he asked eagerly, the hope of youth filling him. "I'd sure like to work for ye here."

"Let's do it straight off."

A few minutes later the two rode out, McGinnis on a borrowed horse, and minutes after that they stopped at McGinnis's wagon. "What's your steppa's name?" Riley asked as the two dismounted.

"Eamon O'Neill."

"Mornin', ma'am," Riley said as he walked up to Mc-Ginnis's mother, who was crouched at the fire, cooking. She had once been a fairly good-looking woman, Riley saw when she looked up at him. But seven children, a hard life, and a new husband who treated her poorly had aged and worn her.

"This is Mister Riley, Ma," McGinnis said. "He's the one I was tellin' ye about."

"Mornin'," Mrs. O'Neill said gruffly.

"Would ye mind your boy stayin' over here at the fort to work for me—if we can talk Mister O'Neill into it?" Riley asked.

The woman smiled wearily but with true sentiment. "I'd be proud to have me boy doin' such an important thing, Mister Riley," she said.

"Good. Where is your husband, ma'am?"

"Down by the crick." She pointed.

Riley nodded and headed that way, with McGinnis trying to match his strides. McGinnis was tall for his age —fifteen—with long, strong legs, but he had a little trouble keeping up. All his siblings followed at a little distance.

"That's him," McGinnis whispered when they saw a man leaning against a tree, looking out over the stream. He was smoking but otherwise doing nothing but staring.

"Mister O'Neill?" Riley said.

The man turned. He wore a scowl on his reddish face, as if he had been born with it there. "What do ye want?" he growled. "Did that little bastard bring ye here?"

"My name's Pete Riley, and I've come here to plead Paddy's case for . . ."

"Ye look like the type who does a lot of pleadin'," O'Neill said. "Ye can plead all ye want, lad, but ye won't be takin' me property away from me."

Riley had heard a lot of insulting things about people before; had even dished some out. But he had never heard a white man refer to his white stepson as property. He was enraged. "Reckon pleadin' wouldn't do no good with ye, shit pile,'' he said in a low voice. Out of the corner of his eye, Riley could see gloom descend once more on McGinnis's face, ''seein's how ye got no more sense than a rock. So let me address ye in a way you'll understand.'' He hammered O'Neill in the forehead with a mighty fist.

O'Neill's eyes were even dimmer than normal. They turned upward and he weaved, but he stayed on his feet.

''Now that I got your attention, shit pile,'' Riley said, ''maybe you'll understand what I'm sayin' to ye.''

''Fuck ye,'' O'Neill growled as he launched himself at the blacksmith.

Riley jerked his left shoulder forward as O'Neill charged, and the Irishman slammed into it and stopped cold. Riley calmly pounded O'Neill three times: once in the stomach, doubling him over; once in the face, half straightening him up again; and finally a powerful blow to the back of the neck that dropped O'Neill like a stone.

Riley knelt and grabbed O'Neill's hair, pulling the man's head up a little. He was conscious, but groggy and in pain. ''Paddy's comin' to work with me at the fort, shit pile,'' he growled. ''He has his ma's approval for it. Ye best be treatin' her with respect and start doin' your share of the work. Ye fuck up, and I'll hear about it, shit pile. I got friends from Saint Louis to Oregon and Californy. I'll hear about ye.''

Leaving O'Neill where he lay, Riley strode back to the wagon, McGinnis walking proudly by his side. ''Mister O'Neill has no objection to Paddy takin' employment at the fort, ma'am,'' Riley said. ''He might need some tendin', though, since it took a mite of convincin'. I wouldn't worry about hurryin' out there, though.''

Kathleen McGinnis O'Neill smiled through tears, and took one of Riley's hands. ''Thank ye, sir. Thank ye.''

''None needed, ma'am,'' Riley said uncomfortably. He was happy to leave.

12

It was with considerable joy that he saw his old friend Ed Perkins pull in, guiding a wagon train.

"Hey, ol' hoss, how's doin's?" Riley said with a grin as Perkins stopped at the blacksmith's shop.

Perkins grinned as he dismounted, "Shinin', ya toad-humpin' skunk. And you?" He was a short, rotund man, with a cheery, lightly pocked but still cherubic face under a trimmed beard and mustache, and an overall demeanor of joviality. His tiny, round, wire-rimmed glasses glinted in the sun.

The two embraced briefly, and McGinnis, watching, thought it was a comical sight—both men equally burly, but one a fair amount taller than the other.

"Dis ol' chil' still shines, ya snake-humpin' son of a bitch. And ye?"

"Nary been better. How many wagons ye got with ye this time?"

"A hundred and twenty, by God, and I swear, each and every one a dem damn wagons has at least one asswipe along for da ride," Perkins said with a laugh. His voice was raspy, as it always had been.

"Hell, we jist got rid of a whole wagon train of idjits. Such folks sure can be tryin' on a man."

"Dat dey can. Ol' Jim around?"

Riley shook his head. "Hell, ye know that ol' cuss. He cain't set in one place more'n a few minutes. Louie's around, though. I'm surprised he ain't come out to see what the commotion's all about. He's over yonder." Riley pointed.

"Obliged, One-Eye. Ya got a jug a to share with this parched ol' feller once I've taken care of business?"

" 'Course I do. Brewed it up right in the shop here all by my lonesome. It's some powerful medicine, boy, I'll tell ye that."

Perkins laughed. "Sounds just like what dis ol' chil' needs. Be back before long."

Within an hour Perkins strode into Riley's shop, shouting, "Where da hell's 'at awardenty ya promised, ya flea-bitten sack of shit ya?"

"Ye got the balls for such potent medicine, boy?" Riley shouted back.

"It'll be a hundred goddamn degrees here in January before dis ol' chil'd back off from a swig a home-brewed lightnin'. Now shut your trap and pass 'at jug over here. I'll show ya how a real man can drink."

"As if some fat-bellied fool of a Scotsman could compare with this chil'," Riley scoffed.

"Hell, boy, ya keep on da way you're goin' and you'll be every bit as fat as 'is shinin' Scotsman." He laughed. Perkins was a Scot only in that his parents had come from Scotland long before he was born. He grabbed the buffalo loin roasting on a spit over Riley's forge.

"Who's da young snake humper over dere?" Perkins asked, pointing the meat at McGinnis.

"That there's Paddy McGinnis, a new friend. He's a snotty little bastard, but he works hard, so I put up with him. Paddy, this here's an ol' friend, Ed Perkins. He's a strange little shit pile, but we used to keep him 'round 'cause he was amusin'."

The two shook hands.

"I'm pleased to meet a fella who comes so highly recommended by me feeble-minded friend over there," McGinnis said with a chortle.

"Same here. And I'm glad to see dis big walkin' wad a

buffler snot ain't changed none a his ways since I saw him last.''

"I ain't known him but a couple months, but he's been this way since the day I was unfortunate enough to meet up with him.''

"Well, if ye two're done singin' my praises,'' Riley said, having gotten a bottle of his home brew, "there's some awardenty jist cryin' out to be drunk.''

"I'll sit this one out, One-Eye,'' McGinnis said. "There's a plenty of work to be done yet. And I don't want to get 'tween ye and your old friend.''

"Wise chil','' Perkins said as Riley nodded.

With Perkins carrying the meat, and Riley the whiskey, the two walked outside. The heat was formidable, though afternoon was drawing to a close. They walked to a shady spot along the creek not far from Riley's lodge and sat, cross-legged. Perkins jammed one end of the spit into the ground, so the meat was handy to both men.

Riley handed Perkins the jug. "Hospitality says I should give ye first swaller, Ed, but if ye don't take it soon, my good manners're gonna disappear in a sprightly hurry.''

"Damn, you're an eager one, ain't ye?'' Perkins laughed. He pulled off his slouch hat and tossed it aside, then ran a thick-fingered hand through his shock of dark brown hair. Perkins finally took a long, long pull from the earthen container, then swiped the residue off his mouth with the back of his shattered hand, a legacy of a rifle that had burst when he fired it once, years ago. He handed the jug to Riley, pulled his sheath knife and sliced off some meat. He ate slowly.

Riley took a drink, too, then set the jug down between him and Perkins. "Where'd ye park them emigrants, Ed?'' he asked.

"About a half-mile northwest. It's where Louis told me to set 'em.''

"Louie seems to be mighty distracted about somethin' these days,'' Riley said quietly. He and Vasquez still didn't get along very well. Vasquez had even given up trying to win Riley over, though he was generally still polite enough. They tolerated each other, and respected the other's accomplishments, but that was about it. Riley didn't really like talking ill of his boss, but he knew the words would go no further.

"I got da same impression," Perkins agreed. "You got any idea what's brought it on?"

"Not really." Riley took some meat and chewed slowly. "Mayhap he's jist pent up over how busy we've been."

"What 'at ol' boy needs is to get his carcass back to da Settlements for a good spree."

Riley laughed a little. "Hell, that'd shine with this son of a bitch, too."

They continued drinking and chewing at the meat, occasionally taking time to puff a pipe or a cigarillo. They talked of the old days, mostly. Like rendezvous of '37—the last great one. They laughed at the remembrance of Bridger with his suit of armor. And they recalled the painter—Alfred Jacob Miller—who had been brought along by Sir William Drummond Stewart to paint the scenes of the rendezvous and the west for Stewart, who was about to head back to Scotland to take his titles. The Scottish adventurer did not think he would ever be able to get back to the American West, and wanted a vivid record of his times there.

Stewart had come back, in '41 and even put on a rendezvous for the mountain men. Riley, Bridger and Perkins had heard that the Scotsman had returned, and hurried to see him. But it wasn't like it had been in the old days. There were few of the true mountain men left in the mountains; most had drifted off to other places and other jobs. The rendezvous that year was a sad, pitiful affair, and broke up soon. Stewart went back to Scotland. Only a few weeks later, Bridger and the few others still trapping realized just how foolish they were being.

"Them were the days," Riley said half-drunkenly at some point after dark.

"Yeah, 'at dey were," Perkins said, waxing somewhat philosophic with a heap of whiskey roiling through his system. "But dem days're gone for all times. All times. Damn."

Riley woke to the sound of screeching, as if all the devils in hell had come to pay him an unwelcome visit. He sat up groggily, trying to remember where he was and why he was there, as well as to discover just what maniacal demon was making such un-humanlike sounds nearby.

Slowly the howling began forming into words. Moments later, Riley realized he could understand some of them. That was a little frightening, though he wasn't sure why.

The answer came to him in a flash. The words were in Shoshoni. He groaned as his body protested the offenses he had committed against it last night. Then the words became more intelligible.

"Get up, ye lazy dog," Spirit Grass screeched at her husband for perhaps the tenth time. "Get up before the coyotes and crows come to feast on your stinking flesh. Rise, ye pitiful worm. It's a new day, and ye have things to do, though ye are less than a man. Come, greet the new day."

Spirit Grass knew exactly how piercing her voice was, since she was using that pitch and tone on purpose. She wanted Riley to know just how displeased she was with him. She knew the agony he was suffering, too, and she took some delight in exacerbating the pain. When Riley had not come to her bed last night, she had even considered leaving him, of taking her things and going back to her people. There would be plenty of warriors there who would be glad to have her, and not treat her as poorly as Riley had. Then she realized such a thing was foolish. They hadn't been married very long—not quite a year—and Riley had never caused her any trouble or heartache. He was, all in all, a good husband. But she had to let him know right now, with no uncertainty, that she would not put up with him getting drunk and leaving her alone in the robes.

"Jesus goddamn Christ," Perkins moaned, rolling onto his back, "shut 'at screechin' critter up before I take a tomahawk to it. Whatever it is." He threw an arm over his eyes to blot out the sun that poured through the leafy canopy.

Riley cracked his eye open and was startled by the searing pain of the sunlight. He clapped the lid shut, but the eye had been open long enough to see Spirit Grass still standing over him screaming epithets at him in Shoshoni. After a few moments, Riley decided to try it again. It worked a little better this time, though his eye was so bloodshot that it was difficult to see anything clearly. He did note, however, that a small group had gathered and was growing. All the fort workers were there, as well as some of the emigrants from Perkins's wagon train.

Riley managed to get to his feet and glare threateningly at Spirit Grass. "Shut up, woman!" he roared, hoping not to show the fresh burst of pain that splattered across his head like bird shit. He had to grit his teeth trying to keep his brain from exploding out his eye sockets.

His words had no effect on Spirit Grass, and now there were assorted chuckles from the still-growing audience to his abasement. He advanced, raising a big hand threateningly. That did not faze Spirit Grass either, and he wondered what to do now. He was not the type to lodgepole his woman, even with some reason.

Perkins took the opportunity to escape. Noticing that everyone's eyes were on Riley and Spirit Grass, the Scotsman rolled onto hands and knees and pushed himself to his feet. He was unsteady, but vertical. He slipped into the trees, feeling like he would be violently sick at any moment, but at least he was now out of the public's view. All he wanted now was a spot where no one would find him so that he could sleep off the worst hangover he could remember in some years.

Still standing there with his hand in the air, Riley felt like a complete idiot. Spirit Grass was still screaming at him, calling him all kinds of unflattering names. He was just glad it was in Shoshoni, since no one else here would understand her. He knew he had to do something, but his brain, still besotted with home-made whiskey, wasn't working very well. Still, an idea dimly dribbled up out of the sodden morass of his mind. He suddenly bent and scooped Spirit Grass up. Throwing her over his shoulder, he bulled his way forward, Spirit Grass yelling the whole while, until he was in the sanctity of their lodge.

Riley unceremoniously dumped Spirit Grass in their robes. That shut her up, if only momentarily.

With injured pride and a system gorged with anger, the woman scrambled up, ready to begin her tirade anew. Before she could get started, though, Riley warned in English—he didn't think his head could stand the effort of translating—"Don't start again, woman. I cain't take it. I ain't been this sickly since I had a bout of the shits some years ago. Jesus."

"Ye shouldn't got drunk," she said in English. Her tone was normal, though touched with anger. Her English had improved considerably since they had married, but it still wasn't all that good.

"I know." Riley stood there weaving, trying to keep upright.

"I missed ye in the robes," Spirit Grass said petulantly. It was the first night they had not spent together since they had wed. She knew there would be times that would happen, but she would not accept Riley's drunkenness as a reason for it.

"I know." Riley gritted his teeth again, trying to keep his gorge from erupting up and out.

"I don't want ye drinkin' no damn whiskey," Spirit Grass insisted.

"I cain't promise ye that, Spirit Grass," Riley said quietly. "But I promise ye I won't git stinkin' drunk again. That suit ye?"

Spirit Grass thought about it a moment, and then nodded. Men were men, and had to have their freedom to do foolish things. "You'll keep ye word?"

Riley nodded, which he found was a stupid thing to do. "Ye still mad at me?" he asked when he thought he had his head and stomach under control again.

"Yep," Spirit Grass answered honestly. "But not bad as before."

"Why'd ye go and . . ." Riley could not complete the question. He turned and bolted out of the lodge, tearing the flap loose and almost knocking the whole tipi down. He raced into the bushes and vomited, long and poisonously.

Some minutes later, about the time he thought it safe to head back to the lodge, he realized that he had a case of the runs. He ripped down his trousers and squatted.

Finally he seemed to be dry inside, and the maelstrom that had raged inside him subsided at least somewhat. He slunk down to the stream and thrust his head into the water. He gulped deeply, hoping the cool water would extinguish the fires that still burned in his guts. It didn't, but he felt minutely better after having been rehydrated some.

At last he headed back to the lodge, a miserable creature indeed. He had been gone almost half an hour. He crawled onto the robes, blankly took some potion Spirit Grass had concocted for him, and fell into a deep slumber.

He felt almost human again when he woke. He pushed himself up until he was sitting. "How long I been out, Spirit Grass?" he asked quietly.

The Shoshoni smiled at him. "Half-day. Mayhap more. Hungry?"

"Some. But not fer anything heavy. It'd only end up on the ground outside," he said sourly.

"I'm not fool," Spirit Grass said. "I know things."

"Sorry," Riley said. "I ain't thinkin' too well yet."

Spirit Grass brought her husband a wooden bowl filled with steaming antelope stew. He dug into it right away, using a horn spoon to scoop the hot broth and bits of meat into his mouth. Spirit Grass went back to the fire and filled a tin mug with coffee and brought that to Riley, too.

After his third bowl of stew, Riley relaxed. He lit his pipe and sipped his fourth cup of coffee. "Why'd ye wake me like that, Spirit Grass?" he asked. "Damn."

Spirit Grass shrugged. "I needed to do it," she said in Shoshoni. "I had to let ye know I wouldn't put up with such things. If I didn't do something like that this time, then next time, you'd think you could get away with it."

"Think you're pretty tough, don't ye, woman?" Riley joked.

Spirit Grass smiled. "Yep," she said without shame. "Ye best remember it, too," she added.

"Yes, ma'am."

Riley slept soundly that night, but in the morning he began to dread going out where people could see him. He was certain that everyone from Fort Laramie to Taos would be waiting to make fun of him. He finally shoved out into the already rising heat and strolled to the fort and into his shop. Several emigrants were waiting for him, having things they needed made or repaired. None said anything to him, and he quickly became immersed in his work.

Perkins wandered in around midmorning. He looked better than he had the last time Riley had seen him, but not really all that well.

"Ye all right, hoss?" Riley asked, concerned. Riley took the long piece of iron he was working and thrust an end into the fire to heat. He moved away from the forge a few steps, wiping his forehead with a ragged piece of cloth.

Perkins nodded. "Right as rain." He grinned ruefully. "Actually I still feel like shit. Them doin's da other night has shown dis ol' chil' 'at he's a mite long inna tooth for such goddamn nonsense."

"I ain't nearly as old as ye are, ol' man, but I've been havin' some of the same thoughts."

"As well ya should, hoss," Perkins said, laughing, "after 'at takin' down 'at woman give ye. She your wife?"

Riley nodded. "Spirit Grass. She's the daughter of Black Iron, a Shoshoni war chief."

"I've heard a him," Perkins said with a nod. "He's got quite a name for himself."

Riley nodded proudly. "When're ye pullin' out?" he finally asked.

"Couple more days, I reckon. Soon's 'ese goddamn pilgrims get what dey got to done. Damn, I am pure sick a leadin' 'ese goddamn fools out this way."

"Find yourself somethin' else to do, Ed."

Perkins laughed a little sadly. " 'At ain't so easy for a man like me, One-Eye. You had a trade you could turn to. But me, I don't know anything but trappin' beaver and 'is land out here."

"There's plenty of jobs for ye, Ed, if ye jist look for 'em. Talk to some of the ol' boys when ye git back to the States. Bill Sublette or Bob Campbell ought to be able to help ye some."

"I'll keep 'at to mind, hoss," Perkins said thoughtfully. "Well, I best get out to da camp and see how dem pilgrims're gettin' on. I'll stop by afore we pull out."

Riley nodded and went back to work. Not long after, Vasquez arrived. "Quite a show you and your woman put on yesterday, *amigo*," he said haughtily, his voice only slightly accented.

"Glad ye enjoyed it," Riley responded with barely concealed annoyance.

"You know, Pedro"—he refused to use Riley's nickname—"we can't have such displays, especially when an emigrant train is here."

"Since when did ye become a priest?" Riley countered. He slammed his hammer on the anvil with a loud clang.

"What's that mean?" Vasquez asked angrily.

"It means, goddammit, that I've seen ye dead drunk more'n once."

"That was some time ago."

Riley shrugged. "Don't matter none. My business is my business, Louie. Keep your nose out of it."

"It becomes my business when it affects the running of this trading station," Vasquez said with a touch of arrogance.

"My gittin' drunk don't mean shit to the runnin' of this place. Even my wife raisin' bloody hell out in the open about it don't make no difference to the fort. Where else're these emigrants gonna go? Besides, even if there was someplace else for 'em to go, I don't think such doin's'd scare 'em off."

"I just want to make certain that this place . . ."

"Ye ain't foolin' nobody. What ye want to make sure of is that ye control everyone and everything in and around this fort. Jist 'cause you're head fly of this shit hole don't mean ye can go givin' me and the others a hard time over such unimportant nonsense."

Vasquez laughed. "Don' get your *cojones* all in a knot, Pedro," he said.

"Goddammit, Louie," Riley said with a shake of his head, "ye can be a most annoyin' critter sometimes."

"I suppose I can," Vasquez readily agreed. He paused, then sighed. "Despite our differences, I don' hold you in low regard, and so yesterday's exhibition was a little shocking."

Riley shrugged. He was not about to apologize.

Vasquez turned and began walking away, then stopped and spun back. "By the way, *hombre,* they really was some doin's. That wife of yours shines, *amigo.* You better treat her right."

Riley grinned a little. "I aim to, Louie."

It was some time before the business at the trading post slowed down, but it finally did, and the men could really relax for the first time since the wagons had started coming in the spring. With some free time, Vasquez strolled into Riley's shop.

Wondering what the boss wanted, Riley set down his eight-pound cross-peen hammer and the cutting hardie and wiped his sweating head with a rag. "Let's go outside, Louie, if ye want to talk. It's hot enough in here to make jerky out of a man." Without waiting for Vasquez's consent, Riley stomped out the back door into the corral. He poked around in his pockets until he found pipe, tobacco and matches.

Vasquez had followed, annoyed at not having been consulted. But he said nothing, since it was abominably hot in the shop. He followed Riley outside, oblivious to the pungency of horse and cattle dung and urine.

"So, what brings ye to such wonderful surroundin's, Louis?" Riley asked. He got his pipe going.

Vasquez looked at Riley in irritation, tired of the blacksmith's insolence. He sighed. "Pedro, we need to talk about your assistant."

"Paddy? What the hell's wrong with Paddy?"

"Well, I never said anything before because we were too damned busy, but I don' like the idea that you hired him without checking with me. Or Jim, for that matter."

Riley looked at his boss with disbelief. "Ye mean ye expected me to bother such a busy man as ye—or, worse, try'n find Ol' Jim—jist to hire an assistant when he was busier'n a one-legged hound crawlin' with fleas? I didn't hire Paddy, I would've been eyeball deep in work."

Vasquez knew that Riley was right—had known all along. He just wanted to let Riley know who was boss. Besides, he was making a point that would be important in just a short while. "True enough," he said evenly. "But what you didn't think of when you hired him, is that you put a man on the company payroll without checking with me or Jim. Did I say anything about that, though? No. I just paid him, without question. You could've at least mentioned it to me sometime. Perhaps even actually introduced us."

"I guess that would've been the right thing," Riley conceded. But he shrugged. He figured he had been too busy to worry about such niceties. "Ye know, ye could've stopped by and introduced yourself, too."

"I suppose that's true. But do you think I'm any less busy than you?" This was getting further afield than he had wanted to go. He should have expected it, he thought, considering Riley's usual obstinacy.

"Reckon not." Riley, who had been looking out across the filthy corral, looked at Vasquez. "That all ye brought me in here for, Louie?" he asked. "To piss and moan 'cause I didn't introduce ye to Paddy?"

"Well, no, not really, Pedro. I just wanted to mention that."

"So what else is eatin' at ye?" Riley settled back against the wall, puffing on his pipe.

"We've got to let your friend go, Pedro."

"Ye lost your reason?" a shocked Riley responded tightly, looking sharply at Vasquez.

"No."

"Then why?" Riley asked. "He done somethin' to rile your feathers? Or are ye jist half froze to give me some comeuppance for not introducin' ye?" The latter was too ridiculous to even consider, he was fairly certain, but one could never tell.

"Neither. I've seen nothing wrong with him. Or you, either—except for your bullheadedness. It's a business decision, Pedro. That's all. With winter coming on, we have too little work for two blacksmiths. I'm also going to get rid of some of the other workers."

"So I expect ye want me to fire him?" Riley asked harshly.

Vasquez nodded firmly.

"Why?"

"You hired him—without checking with me, I remind you—so you can fire him."

Riley thought that over for a few moments, then said slowly, "I cain't do that, shit pile."

"Why not?" Vasquez asked, surprise added to his irritation.

"Because I don't work for ye no more." Riley began peeling off his heavy blacksmith's apron.

"Don't ye dare do that, One-Eye," McGinnis said, stepping out of the shop and stopping between Riley and Vasquez. He looked at Vasquez. "I take it ye're Mister Vasquez, one of the owners of the fort?" he asked.

"*Sí.*"

"Pleased to make yer acquaintance, Mister Vasquez," McGinnis said with a short, dignified nod.

"A bit late for such a thing, no?"

"Better late than ne'er, me mother always said," McGinnis answered with a shrug. He turned again to look at Riley. "Ye can't quit here, One-Eye," he repeated, voice firm. "Not when it's me Mister Vasquez has the trouble with."

Riley grinned. "Don't ye worry about it, boy," he said. "Louis and me ain't ever seen eye to eye on anything. He'll probably be jist as glad to see me ride out of here. Ain't that right, Louie?" He didn't expect a response from Vasquez, so he didn't wait for one. "Of course, Paddy, that means he ain't gonna have no blacksmith 'round, and not a heap of tools fer such work neither, since all of 'em—includin' that portable forge in there—are mine and I'll be takin' 'em." He had managed to buy all the equipment from Bridger at an excellent price.

"Calm down, One-Eye," McGinnis said soothingly. "As one of the owners, Mister Vasquez has the right to take on or let go anyone he sees fit to. And, while ye two might've never gotten along, ye've worked for him a long time, and he's appreciated that work."

"Right on all counts, young man," Vasquez said stiffly.

"Thankee. Now, One-Eye, ye don't have a thing else to do, and ye can use the money ye make here, what with a babe on the way and all. And ye like what ye do here, and ye're a friend of Mister Bridger, as ye've told me often enough."

"Those're facts, boy," Riley grudgingly allowed.

"Well, then, me head and me heart tell me there should be no partin' of the ways here 'tween ye two. Me heart and me head tell me ye should put aside your diff'rences for the good of the company—and for each other."

"I ain't so sure that's a good idee, boy," Riley said. "I cain't see me'n Louie ever gittin' along."

"*Sí*,"Vasquez agreed. "Pedro is an insufferable *hijo de puta*, and I can't see any way he can become acceptable."

"Now, now, ye two," McGinnis said, chiding the men as if they were wayward children. He thought for a moment, then said, "How about this, then. One-Eye, ye continue to work here, doing yer blacksmithin', but ye do so independently. Ye charge the emigrants whate'er ye want. Ye can pay Mister Vasquez rent fer the shop space. And ye, Mister Vasquez, ye leave One-Eye in peace. He'll no longer be yer employee, so ye can't order him about, and ye'd have no reason to deal with One-Eye, except perhaps when he comes to pay ye rental for the shop."

"And what about ye, boy?" Riley asked.

"I'll take me leave of the fort. Try to find a way to get to Oregon."

Vasquez had been thinking it over. Now he nodded. "Such a deal is acceptable," he said.

"Good," McGinnis said, smiling. "How about ye, One-Eye?"

"Nope." He was secretly pleased at having shocked the other two. "As long as ye ain't workin' here, Paddy boy, I ain't neither."

"Then get out of . . ." Vasquez started.

"A moment, Mister Vasquez," McGinnis interrupted. "I think I've come up with a solution." He smiled softly. "If ye're workin' here independently, One-Eye, ye could hire men, if ye feel strongly enough about it. Then neither of us'd be in Mister Vasquez's employ." He smiled again, this time almost sadly. "Of course, ye'll have to pay me wages instead of the company's doin' so, which might mean ye won't want me around no more."

Riley was thinking it over. The whole thing made sense to him. He would be out from under Vasquez's yoke, yet still be here at the fort, amid the Shoshonis, and still somewhat connected with Bridger business-wise. He nodded. "That'll suit—long as shit pile over there don't fleece me on the rent."

"I don't think Mister Vasquez'll do that, One-Eye," McGinnis said, voice stronger as he had gained confidence. "Since if that was to happen, ye and me could move a half-mile down the trail and start up our own little place. If we did that, the emigrants might not be able to get supplies there, but on the other hand, they'd not be able to get blacksmithin' services here."

"You're a conniving little bastard, boy, you know that," Vasquez said rhetorically, but he was smiling a little. "It's no wonder you have taken up with that cunning son of a bitch."

"I'm not connivin', Mister Vasquez," McGinnis said with boyish charm. "I just happened to find it in me to head off problems sometimes. That's all. Now, are ye willin', Mister Vasquez?"

"I suppose I am," Vasquez said a bit reluctantly. He was troubled, though, and cursed himself silently for having started this in the first place. He could never understand why he did such things with Riley. He never did it with anyone else. There was just something about Riley that drove him toward such disturbances. "But there's still the matter of the rent on the shop."

McGinnis nodded. "How much're ye askin'?"

"Fifty dollars for the rest of the summer."

Riley snorted in derision. "There ain't no rest of the summer, shit pile."

"All right, then, thirty, dammit," Vasquez snapped. "That'll hold it over the winter for you."

"Ten."

"That's preposterous. You'll make far more than that from the emigrants next year."

"And you'll save a pretty penny not havin' to pay me or Paddy."

The two old adversaries haggled for a little before settling on a price of seventeen dollars and fifty cents for the fall and winter. It included two meals a day and rough quarters for McGinnis through the winter, and it was to be paid right away. Riley went into the shop and found the old iron box in which he kept most of his money. He counted it out carefully, and went back outside, where he handed the hard cash to Vasquez.

The two men shook hands on their new agreement, and Vasquez swiftly walked away. When he was gone, McGinnis looked at Riley and grinned.

"Ye done all right, boy," Riley said, smiling back. "I don't think Louie was right when he said ye was a connivin' critter, but ye sure are a shrewd feller."

McGinnis nodded, accepting the compliment. Then he grinned again and said, "Well, while I have ye in such a good humor, I think it's time we talk about me pay, since I'll be workin' for ye."

"Damn," Riley laughed, "I thought ye was mayhap gonna forget all about that."

"Hardly."

"Well, how's about I pay ye what you've been gittin' here?"

"I . . . Well, One-Eye, I sort of had another plan in mind."

"Don't go shy on me now, boy," Riley said. "Ye got an idee, let it out and we'll see which way the wind takes it."

"I was hopin' ye might make me yer partner. And before ye answer, let me say this. I don't mean a full partner, but I thought that maybe ye'd not mind much if I was to share in the money made, say twenty-five percent?"

Riley thought that over for a few moments, and he saw no problem with it. Paddy McGinnis had shown himself to be a willing and hard worker. He was also better at some of the things required of a blacksmith than Riley himself was. They complemented each other nicely in the work that they could do, and they worked well together.

"That don't suit this ol' hoss," Riley said, suppressing a grin. He could see the disappointment writ large on McGinnis's young face. "Since that'd mean you'd have to take twenty-five percent of the risks, too, and that ain't right. So I'll tell ye what, boy, I'll pay ye twenty-five percent of whatever we make, but I'll take on the cash risks."

"I can't ask ye to do that, One-Eye," McGinnis protested.

"Ye didn't ask, ye little fart. I jist tol' ye that's how it's gonna be. Take it or don't, but make up your mind."

"I'll take it," McGinnis said with a beaming grin.

A few weeks later, Riley rode out of the fort, planning to spend the winter in Black Iron's village. Spirit Grass was pretty close to having her first child, and both wanted her to be back in the safety and relative comfort of the village. That way, Spirit Grass could have the help of friends and relatives during the birth. Shoshoni males had nothing to do with birthing, leaving it to the females to handle. Riley thought it a fine idea and subscribed to it himself.

Throughout the journey, he was as nervous as a cat afraid that Spirit Grass would go into labor along the way. The possibility struck sheer terror in Riley's heart, though he had known Indian women, ready to give birth, who had simply pulled to the side of the trail and handled it alone. He wasn't nearly so sure that Spirit Grass could do such a thing, though he didn't know why. She was one of the hardiest women he had ever seen.

The only adventure on the trip was sitting out an early snowstorm that stalled the couple for more than a day. It was a harbinger of what was to come. Two weeks after they reached the village—about the end of October— Spirit Grass gave birth to a son. She and Riley called him Flat Nose, for the prominent feature of his small, wrinkled, dark face.

After Flat Nose was born, Riley headed out with several Shoshoni warriors to hunt. By the time winter really hit, the mountain man and the Shoshonis figured they had an ample supply of meat. Riley settled back to relax, which was something he rarely had an opportunity to do.

The winter, while uneventful, was one of the harshest Riley had ever faced. The wind screeched and roared, and snow fell several feet deep. Drifts piled up wherever there was something to give it a framework, though arctic winds scoured the open spots bare. The People were kept inside their lodges for days on end at times, which didn't bother Riley that much. He, Spirit Grass and infant Flat Nose were warm and cozy in their tight buffalohide lodge. The meat lasted, though it was getting a little sparse as winter dragged on and on, seemingly without end. But finally things eased up.

By then, Riley had had his fill of relaxing. He was a man used to working, and there was little he could do all winter, considering its harshness. So at the first signs of spring, he made plans to leave. First, for the fun of it, he accompanied Black Iron's band on their annual spring buffalo hunt. It was hugely successful, and the people celebrated for several days. Finally, though, Riley and his family headed south toward the trading post.

When they arrived at the fort, Riley had his wife put their lodge up along the easternmost branch of Black's Fork, maybe fifty feet beyond the "back" fort wall. It was near enough to the fort so they could get there in a hurry, if there was an emergency, but far enough away to not be too fouled by the noise and stench coming from inside the trading post's picket walls.

The wagon trains began arriving a few weeks later, and with them came Mormons for the first time. The first arrival this year was a seventy-two-wagon train with one hundred forty-three Mormons.

Riley had never even heard of such people before, and thought at first that they were just like all the other emigrants struggling to get to California or Oregon. But they were different, he was quick to learn. He found that the Saints, as they preferred to call themselves, were reserved, aloof, virtually unwilling to speak with those not of their group. Riley wondered why.

So did McGinnis, who asked Riley about them.

"I don't know nothin' about them folks, boy," Riley responded. "Never heard of 'em before, but they sure seem a queersome people."

"That ain't much of an answer, One-Eye," McGinnis said.

Riley laughed. "It's the best I can do, boy," he said. "Ye want to know about 'em, go ask 'em."

"Hell, One-Eye, ye're more curious about 'em than I am. Ye go talk to 'em."

Riley had never been one for doing nothing when something was on his mind, so he did just that. He headed toward their camp, which was a couple hundred yards away. The Mormon wagon train was the first of the season, so there was plenty of good grass close to the fort.

It didn't take long for Riley to learn who the leader of these people was, or to find his large, commodious wagon.

Brigham Young did not impress Riley much, though he laid it to the fact that the Mormon leader had Rocky Mountain spotted fever and was confined to his bed. He wouldn't even see Riley, until Riley persisted. The boyish-faced Young allowed the blacksmith into his wagon then, just long enough to tell him that he was too ill to deal with questions and that he would have to talk with someone else. "Unless," Young ended, "you're here to convert to our path. The only path that is the true way into God's favor."

"I don't think that'd shine with this ol' hoss," Riley grumbled, wondering who the several women in the wagon were. He figured one was a wife, but Young was not old enough to have daughters that age. Riley finally decided they were the wives of other Mormon men who had come to help their leader.

"Then speak with Brother Rockwell," Young said in dismissal.

Riley shrugged, left, and went looking for Orrin Porter Rockwell. He found a medium-tall man with a strong build and flat, deadly eyes. He seemed short of temper and fervent in his love of his faith and his religious leader. "I'm Rockwell," he growled, surliness the major tone in his voice. "What do you want with me?"

"Mister Young sent me to ye."

"You been troublin' Brother Young?" Rockwell asked roughly.

"Jist long enough to be told to find ye." Riley's hackles began to rise. Despite Rockwell's look of deadly competence, Riley held no fear of the Mormon, and he was damn sure not going to be intimidated by him.

"What fer?"

"To ask about your people."

"Why? You don't look like no goddamn convert to me."

"Even if I had been considerin' such a damnfool move, I'd certainly disabuse myself of the notion now, boy," Riley said, his tone taking a decidedly cooler timbre.

Rockwell almost smiled. He figured he had found out that Riley was not a seeker, and so he could treat him like he would any other Gentile. "So, why'd Brother Young send you to see me?"

"I was interested in knowin' more about ye people. He was too sick to talk, so he sent me to ye." Riley was still battling his rising temper.

"Why?"

"Why do I want to know more about your people?" When Rockwell nodded, Riley shrugged. "I ain't sure, really. I never met Mormons before. Y'all seem different from the other emigrants who come along this way."

"I don't think our ways are any of your goddamn business, pal," Rockwell snapped.

Riley had had just about enough of this obnoxious, insufferable man, but he decided he would try one more time. "Ye so afeared of me that ye won't even talk to me some?" he demanded.

Rockwell laughed, a harsh, hollow sound. "I ain't afraid of no man God ever put on this earth, boy," Rockwell growled. "None."

"Then why're ye—and the rest of your people—so close-mouthed?" Riley asked, trying to keep his voice reasoned and calm. "Y'all, as a people, seem to be mighty afeared of something."

Rockwell felt rage burst through him, and he came mighty close to pulling a pistol on Riley, but he managed to catch himself in time. His eyes piercingly searched Riley's face. Rockwell quickly decided that Riley was not a troublemaker in the sense that most other Gentiles had been for the Saints. He tried to calm down some. "You just want to know about us because you're interested?" he queried.

Riley nodded.

For some reason, Rockwell believed him. "You got a place where we can set a spell, and maybe pull a cork?"

Riley led Rockwell to his shop, where he pulled up an earthen jug from a small bucket of cool water. They sat in a far rear corner, where the sun couldn't reach them and the heat was at least bearable. Riley rested back against a large box in which he stored fuel for his forge; Rockwell leaned against the log wall.

There was silence for some minutes, as the two men passed the jug back and forth. Each lit a pipe. Finally Rockwell spoke, voice low, still rough and irritated, but calm. "The Saints've been put upon by Gentiles wherever . . ."

"Gentiles?" Riley prodded.

"Those not of the faith." When Riley nodded, Rockwell continued. "The Gentiles've always set on us, no matter where we've gone—Ohio, later Missouri, then Illinois." The latter was said with a foulness that bespoke a deep-seated rage. "That's where they killed the Prophet, those sons of bitches. They . . ."

"Prophet?"

"Joseph Smith, the founder of our church, which is properly called the Church of Jesus Christ of Latter-day Saints. He was killed in jail there, which is why the new Prophet—Brother Young—is leading the Saints into the wilderness. This way, we hope to get away from the goddamn Gentiles who continually persecute us." He was looking angrily at Riley again.

"Why have ye been so put upon?" Riley asked, curious. "Do ye have such strange ways that Gentiles can't take to ye or somethin'?"

"Some of our ways're strange to Gentiles," Rockwell admitted. "Especially the Principle." He paused for a swallow of whiskey. "There's two parts to it, basically. The first is that when Saints marry, it's not just for our lifetimes, but for eternity. Married men and women are reunited in the hereafter."

"Makes sense, I reckon," Riley said through a fog of pipe smoke.

"The other part's the one that Gentiles most take exception to. You see, male Saints're allowed to take more than one wife," Rockwell said defiantly.

The blacksmith was nonplussed by the statement. "Most of the Indians I know of allow the same," he said, thinking it was a sensible way to live sometimes. "It doesn't happen too often, but any warrior who can afford it and needs extra wifely help around the lodge can take as many wives as he can support." Riley paused a moment, then continued. "It does strike me as odd, though, that white women would take to such a notion. It doesn't seem to be in their natures to welcome such an arrangement."

Rockwell was surprised at Riley's acceptance of the Principle. Most Gentile men were as outraged by it as their women were. "When the word comes straight from God—given directly to the Prophet—those of the faith do not question it," Rockwell said, a little defensively.

"I suppose that's true enough," Riley said with a nod, again surprising Rockwell with his equanimity about it all. "I can see how most Gentiles might frown on it, though." Riley paused to refill his pipe and light it. "But ye said that was a small part of why the Morm—er, Saints—were set on so much. What causes folks to rise up against ye?"

"The words of God're sometimes hard to live up to, but we Saints try our damnedest to do so. Even if that means settin' ourselves agin the Gentiles. Not that we look for trouble with Gentiles, you understand. It just works out that way sometimes. Right from the start, though, the Saints were looked on poorly by others, so we tended to stick to ourselves."

"So would anyone else," Riley interjected.

"We set up what we had hoped would be our Zion—our kingdom of God—in Ohio some years ago. With our own hands, we built the city, set up shops and farms and businesses. The Gentiles didn't mind at first, but as a close-knit people, we began buyin' at Saints' shops and takin' our business to other Saints, bypassin' the Gentiles. They quickly turned on us then, jealous of our prosperity. The Saints're hardworkin' people, Mister Riley, and frugal when the need is there. We can also be open to our own who might be havin' difficulties. Wherever we've gone, we've quickly become prosperous and self-reliant. That's brought resentment from the Gentiles around us."

His pipe had gone out, and he knocked the ashes free and shoved the pipe into a pocket. "Outsiders also seem to resent our ability to live in peace and harmony amongst ourselves, our ability to do for ourselves, without the help or compliance of Gentiles."

"I can see where that'd breed poor feelin's," Riley said. "There's far too many people who're jealous of the gains of others, even when those gains're made as the result of hard work and sacrifice."

"You don't seem to be among them," Rockwell noted.

Riley shrugged. "It ain't that I don't like prosperity, but I've always had a free hand. Comes from my days as a beaver trapper. Most of us ol' boys're that way—we git some specie in our pockets, and it jist burns a hole there, so we spend it on foofaraw for our women and presents for their families, and on whiskey and gamblin' and damn near anythin' else we take a shine to."

"Sounds reckless. Many's the man who's ended his life destitute for havin' spent so freely in his younger days."

"I suppose that's true," Riley acknowledged. "But I'm hopin' the Great Spirit'll watch out for me when it comes my time to cross the divide."

"You're close to Indians, then?" Rockwell asked.

"The Shoshonis mostly. But I've dealt with others, includin' the goddamn Sioux." He unconsciously touched the patch over his left eye. "Got a Shoshoni wife and a youngster." He paused. "Ye know, Mister

Rockwell," he finally continued, "the Saints seem mighty like Indians in some ways. Indians generally pull together to help their own durin' hard times. There's hardly any of what we'd call crimes in an Indian village. Little robbery or murder or such. And at those rare times when someone does do somethin' against one of his own, it usually can be worked out with no more blood bein' shed."

"A communal spirit is very important to the Saints," Rockwell agreed. "The land in a Mormon town is divvied up by the church's leaders. Each Saint family gets a plot of farmland just outside town, and a house lot in town. We tithe faithfully, and that allows the church to run its institutions, buy more land, and care for its needy, among other things."

"Except for jealousy and resentment over your good fortune . . ."

"Our prosperity and gains haven't been good fortune, Mister Riley," Rockwell interjected. "They're the result of hard work. As a people, in many other ways, our fortune hasn't been particularly good."

Riley nodded. "I didn't mean to indicate your people haven't had more than their share of hard times," Riley said calmly. "I was jist aimin' to make the point that ye ain't told me anything that'd cause a reasonable man to persecute a people so harshly as the Saints've been, other than their resentment and jealousy. Most of what you've said here today makes a whole lot of sense."

Rockwell's eyes widened a little. "Then perhaps you'd consider becomin' one of the Saints."

"No, sir. Such ain't my style. While it works for ye, I don't think it'd do much for me. Ye ain't exactly said, but I git the feelin' your people're mighty constrained by the church." It was a question.

"We don't consider them constraints," Rockwell said thoughtfully. "Such rules that we live by—and, yes, there are many of them and sometimes they are harsh— are passed down from God himself, through the Prophet. So, we're glad to live within those rules. They

ain't like the onerous constraints under which the pa-
pists must live."

Riley was almost amused at Rockwell's vehemence,
and his comment about followers of Catholicism, but he
was still not swayed. "Mayhap, Mister Rockwell," he said
quietly, "I ain't the kind to willingly live under such
rules, no matter that they might've come from the Almighty himself. This chil's got too much of an indepen-
dent and adventuresome spirit."

"It's your loss, Mister Riley," Rockwell said, almost
sadly. "Your loss indeed."

Despite his talk with Rockwell, Riley found little lessening in the standoffishness of the Mormons. He tried a
few times to strike up conversations with the Saints, but
they would have none of it. They were unfailingly polite,
but unfailingly uninterested. Finally, Rockwell showed
up in Riley's shop. He was far less friendly than last time.

"Unless you've changed your mind about convertin',
Riley, stay away from the Saints," Rockwell growled.

Riley did not take to being lectured to, nor challenged. "What business is it of yours?" he countered,
voice even but showing an edge of anger.

"Anything that has to do with safety and peace of the
Saints *is* my business, boy," Rockwell said. "I am one of
Brother Young's inner circle, and he has entrusted me
with keeping a close watch over him and all the other
Saints."

"Think a heap of yourself, don't ye, shit pile," Riley
said rather than asked.

"Yep." There was no doubt in the man's hard voice.
He stood, feet slightly spread, thumbs hooked into his
belt, where his hands would be near the two Colt Paterson revolvers he had stuck there.

"It'd be interestin' to see if ye can live up to your high
opinion of yourself," Riley said quietly.

"Any time you're of a mind to find out, come look me
up. Till that day, though, keep away from the Saints."

"I'll give it due consideration," Riley said dryly.

Rockwell shrugged. He didn't care much one way or the other. "It also goes for the Saints who follow. And there'll be many."

"Seein' how joyful ye people are," Riley countered, "havin' no dealin's with ye won't put me out none. But I think," Riley continued, giving it one more chance, "that it'd do your people a heap better if they was a little more open to outsiders. I know what ye told me of your troubles, but ain't every outsider is like them folks. I was jist tryin' to be friendly, strike up a conversation here and there. Ain't no harm in that, is there?"

"All them others started out bein' friendly, too, before they turned against us."

"Goddamn, boy, ye think everyone's against ye and your people?" Riley asked.

"Until I learn better, I believe the worst," Rockwell said evenly. "There's less trouble that way."

Riley shook his head. It was sad to see people so. As a gregarious man, he liked meeting people—all kinds of people—and conversing with them. He had learned a great deal that way. But these people appeared to be so bitter, so turned against anyone not of their faith, that they couldn't see the hand of friendship extended to them. If what Rockwell had told him was true, the Mormons might have good reason to be suspicious of all Gentiles, but that still went against Riley's grain.

Riley sighed. There was nothing he could do about it, so he would ignore the Saints as best as he could. This group should be leaving in the next day or so anyway. And he vowed silently to leave other Mormons alone when their wagon trains rolled into the fort. There would be plenty of other wagon trains without Saints.

"I'll keep away from your people," he finally said.

Rockwell nodded once, turned and walked away.

"One thing, though," Riley said coldly. When Rockwell had stopped and turned to face him, Riley continued. "Ye tell your people to stay away from my wife."

"She been bothered?" Rockwell asked, showing a little surprise.

"Some folks've come 'round pesterin' her. I don't know if they aim to steal her away from me or convert her to your ways, but it don't really matter. The next one comes 'round'll find out what it's like to have his hair parted by a tomahawk in the hands of a man who knows how to use one."

"It's unlikely a Saint'd bother your wife," Rockwell said. He was puzzled.

"There's many a folk who don't think much of botherin' Indians."

"That's right, you said your wife is an Injun," Rockwell said. "That might explain it then, Mister Riley." Rockwell saw no reason not to be polite now. "The Injuns of the Americas're among the lost tribes of Israel. These Lamanites have lost the true ways, and have fallen into wickedness, savagery and degradation. God gave 'em their dark skin as a punishment for their rejection of His enlightenment."

"What's it got to do with your people pesterin' my woman?"

"One of the tasks God has given the Saints is to bring the Lamanites back to the true path toward God's wisdom and light. To do so, we must convert 'em, return 'em to the fold, so to speak."

"Well Spirit Grass don't need—nor want—no convertin'. And I figure ye ain't gonna find any Indian 'tween the States and the far side of the Sierra Nevada gonna want any convertin' to your ways."

"We'll see about that, Riley," Rockwell said, the glint of fanaticism in his eyes.

"See all ye want, shit pile, but if any more people come 'round my lodge, you're gonna be a few Saints short."

"That could be troublesome."

Riley shrugged. "Trouble don't bother me."

Rockwell nodded curtly and left.

All in all, Riley was relieved when Young's wagon train pulled out, though Rockwell had kept his word. Riley never saw another Saint near his lodge. Nor did he try to converse with any of them, other than what was necessary in the course of doing what work they required of him.

15

A rider came pounding into the fort. "Injins!" he shouted. "Injins attackin' our camp!" He pulled to a halt in front of Riley's shop.

The blacksmith grabbed the man's bridle and kept the horse from dancing away. "What's happened, boy?" he asked.

"I told ya. Injins're attackin' our camp."

"What goddamn camp?" Riley roared. "We got five caravans out there."

"Cap'n Breyer's."

Riley nodded. That fixed the spot for him. "Go tend to your horse, boy. Then git somethin' to eat and drink. We'll take care of the rest. Go on." He turned and began hollering orders: "Paddy, saddle us a couple of horses. Lloyd, pass out powder and ball for all who need it. Weapons, too." He spotted an old mountain man— there were usually a number of them around the fort at this time of year. "Purdy!" he shouted at the man. "Grab your horse and git out there. See what's goin' on. Tell 'em to hang on, we'll be there in minutes."

"Where, One-Eye?" Mordechai Purdy asked, jumping into the saddle.

"North. First big bend of Ham's Fork."

Purdy slapped his horse's rump with his rifle barrel and thundered off.

Other men were lining up at the trading room, drawing arms and supplies as needed. Riley nodded in satisfaction. Vasquez was out of the fort, making a quick trip to Fort Laramie, so Riley was in charge.

Within ten minutes of word of the attack, a dozen mounted men—led by Riley—were galloping out of the fort. They stopped at Riley's lodge.

Spirit Grass had known something was going on, and she was standing outside the tipi, her husband's rifle in hand. She was beginning to show her second pregnancy a little. "Go on into the fort, woman," Riley said calmly, taking his rifle. "There's been an attack on one of the camps, and I ain't sure who's responsible. Lloyd's there, and he knows to lock the doors as soon as ye git there." He reached down, touched her cheek once and then dashed off, his men right behind him.

They met Purdy just before getting to the camp. "Blackfeet," the old mountaineer said sourly. Like all mountain men, he hated the Blackfeet.

"They still there?" Riley asked, wondering. It seemed unusual that Blackfeet would be causing trouble these days.

"Nope. They were headin' almost due south."

"Shit," Riley snapped. "There's another camp down on Muddy Creek. There ain't no way in hell those Blackfeet'll miss that camp. Let's ride." As they pounded along, Riley pulled up alongside Purdy. "How many of 'em was there?" he shouted.

"Twelve, maybe fifteen," Purdy shouted back. "But I cain't be sure. Christ, those damnfool emigrants tried to tell me there was a couple hundred of 'em. I did jist a bit of trackin' and seen sign of a dozen or so."

They could hear the battle when they were a quarter of a mile from the camp, and they urged a little more speed out of their overworked horses. Finally, they slowed. All the men save for McGinnis were experienced in such fracases, and they needed no telling to know what to do. They began to spread out into a ragged battle line, since there were no trees along the creek, which was fairly dry.

"Ye mind if I stick close to ye, One-Eye?" McGinnis asked as he rode alongside his partner. "I've never done anything like this before."

Riley nodded. "Jist don't git in my way, boy. These here are serious doin's." He moved on slowly.

The whole line of men had stopped, and each man was looking at Riley. Being in charge of the fort, he was also the leader of this expedition, and to him fell the order to charge. It had been a few years since he had done something like this, and Riley could feel a little rush of excitement building inside him. He raised his old Hawken rifle and bellowed. There were no words, just sounds.

The others joined in the cacophony, and charged forward. The horses, having gotten a few moments' rest, seemed to have caught the excitement and urgency of the moment. They raced forward as if freshly saddled.

The camp was a little less than a hundred yards long, with wagons lined up on both sides of a sluggishly running stream of water several inches deep and about two feet wide. Most of the forty-two wagons were close to the creek, since there was brush there, which provided a little shade and fuel for fires.

Riley could see Blackfeet darting in and out of the wagons, firing arrows mostly, though a few warriors had guns. Most of the emigrants cowered in, under and around wagons. Some of the men were firing back, but they seemed to be having little effect.

Riley blasted a Blackfoot out of the saddle with three shots from one of his two Colt Paterson revolvers. He kept charging, jumped his horse over a wagon tongue and splattered across the creek. As he was turning his horse, an arrow thudded into the animal's neck. The horse squealed and fell.

The blacksmith managed to roll before his leg was trapped. On his knees, he waddled over to the horse, which was struggling to get back up. He swiftly fired a ball into the horse's head, putting the animal out of its misery. He moved back a few feet while the beast shivered in its death throes.

He put his rifle down and began reloading the Colt. He was almost done when a bullet punched into his shoulder on the left side, just above the collarbone. The impact knocked him onto his back. He grabbed his rifle and crawled to his horse to use the carcass for protection.

He took a swift look around. The Blackfeet had realized right off that this new force was a lot more dangerous than the few men firing from the camp, and so were directing their attention toward the rescue party. Three warriors were racing toward him, but were still a bit off yet. He glanced behind, wondering where McGinnis was.

The young blacksmith had been right behind Riley when he saw his mentor's mount go down. He wanted to stop his own horse and go back and help his friend, but the animal appeared to have other ideas, and in moments he found himself twenty yards from the wagons with possible protection from the brush near the creek. He was out in the open with two Indians bearing down on him.

He was fascinated with the charging warriors. Their horses were painted with various symbols he did not understand, and the animals had feathers and other decorations tied to their manes, tails and hackamores. The warriors themselves were frightening. One had the top half of his face painted black. The rest of his face and his chest were painted a bright yellow. The other had two triangles of rich blue paint on his face, surrounding his eyes, the points reaching to his jawbone on each side of the chin. A stripe of the same color paint started on the bridge of the man's nose and went straight down across the nose and both lips, ending on the underside of the chin. Stripes of red paint radiated upward across his chest from a spot just above his navel.

Each warrior had a shield on his left arm and carried a bow in the other hand.

An arrow thudding into his rifle stock finally woke McGinnis up. "Jesus, Mary and Joseph," he breathed, as real fright crawled into his belly and snuggled up there. He tried to pull the arrow free, but couldn't, and finally snapped it off as near to the rifle stock as he could. He cocked the rifle, aimed and fired. He hit nothing. He blamed it on the arrow in his rifle, but it was too late to worry about that now. He tossed the rifle aside and scrambled for the pistol in his belt.

Almost laughing the two warriors decided not to waste any more arrows on this foolish man. They raced in on him and each swatted him as hard as they could with their bows, counting coup. They whooped as they rode by, and turned, making another dash at him.

Hurting from the assault, McGinnis had finally managed to free his pistol. He jerked the hammer back and was ready to fire when he got hit with a bow again. He dropped the revolver. Then the other warrior hit him, and he fell out of the saddle. He felt mortified at his uselessness, and saddened to know that he was about to die. He got up with an effort and saw that the warriors were coming for him again. He spun and ran toward the wagons and the creek.

The Blackfeet rushed at him, and smote him down as they roared past, laughing now. They both stopped then and dismounted. Each slung his bow across his back. On foot they moved toward McGinnis, pulling knives as they did. They laughed and joked about what they were about to do to this pitiful creature.

McGinnis fought like a demon as the Blackfeet crouched over him. He might not be much with a pistol or rifle, but he knew how to kick and bite and scratch and claw. The fear seemed to leave him as he struggled. Suddenly there was a gunshot and one of the warriors fell on him. The other Indian was almost magically lifted away. He looked up, blinking in surprise to see old Mordechai Purdy slitting the Blackfoot's throat.

Purdy dropped the body and wiped his knife on his filthy buckskin pants. He grinned, showing rotting teeth. "I ain't nary in all my whole days seed sich a way of fightin' red devils as ye showed, boy," he said, laughing. The sound was deep and rich, where most people expected a high-pitched cackle.

McGinnis shoved the other Indian's body off him. "Well," he said lamely, "I was figurin' to lull them into thinkin' they had me beat. Then I was going to snatch out me knife and carve 'em new assholes."

Purdy laughed some more and held out his hand. He pulled the young man up.

Suddenly McGinnis got worried again. "One-Eye!" he said urgently. "We've got to help him. And fast. I saw his horse go down. I don't know whether One-Eye was hurt or not."

"Ol' One-Eye's jist fine, boy. Took him a bullet in the shoulder, but it ain't likely to slow him down much."

"And the Blackfeet?"

"Them that ain't gone off to the Happy Huntin' Ground at our invite has tucked tail and run, boy. Jist like I knew they would. Them Blackfeet ain't got no more balls'n a buffler cow. Goddamn savages're lower'n snake dicks."

Despite his renewed fear and concern, McGinnis couldn't help but laugh at Purdy's descriptions. And at his appearance. Purdy was as tall as Riley, but nowhere near as powerfully built. His clothing was well beyond frayed and filthy. His whole outfit looked as if he had been wearing it since he joined the fur trade more than twenty years ago, and had never once cleaned it. He had a scraggly beard, a creased face and bloodshot eyes. Right now, though, McGinnis didn't care what the old reprobate looked like.

"Let's go see how One-Eye's doing, then," McGinnis suggested.

Riley lay behind the carcass of his horse, watching the three Blackfeet coming for him. He felt a lot more rage than he did pain from the wound. He wasn't about to let these warriors get away with putting a bullet in him. He slid his rifle across the carcass and took out one Blackfoot right away. He dropped the rifle, not having enough time to reload, and pulled out both small Colts.

Two arrows suddenly appeared in the dead horse just to Riley's left. "Jesus Christ," he muttered, jerking his head around to see another warrior coming at him from that side. He rolled onto his back, so the horse's carcass would protect him from the original two warriors. This way he could fire at the other one, which he did. He emptied one of the .36-caliber revolvers without hitting the Blackfoot that he could tell. It took three more shots from the other revolver before the Indian went down.

Sweating now, knowing that the other two Blackfeet must be within inches of him, he rolled over and popped up over the carcass, pistol ready, though he only had two shots left in it. He breathed a sigh of relief when he saw the two warriors surrounded by six of his own men, who made quick work of them. He stood looking around. Across the creek he could see a cloud of dust, and he figured that whatever Blackfeet had survived were racing for home.

Peeling his shirt off, he finally looked at his wounded shoulder. There was no exit wound, which meant the ball was still in there. "Damn," he muttered, knowing that it would have to come out. It was not something he looked forward to.

Purdy and McGinnis rode up, the former trailing a Blackfoot pony. "Looks like trouble come grab your ass, One-Eye," Purdy said with a laugh. Danger, bloodshed, even death seemed to have no effect on him.

Riley laughed, too. He was relieved that the battle was over, and he could afford some humor. "That a Blackfoot pony I see behind ye, fart face?" Riley queried.

"Damn if it ain't," Purdy said, looking back as if surprised to see the animal. "Critter must've been lured by my kind heart and strikin' handsomeness."

"Shit," Riley laughed. "It's more like he was drawn to

your stench, ye scabrous ol' bastard. Probably reminded that pony of a corral somewhere. A corral that nary had its years of horseshit took away."

Purdy took no offense. He simply laughed some more and agreed, then handed over the horse.

Riley jumped on the pony, which snorted and stomped a few times, not favoring Riley's weight on him. "Settle down, horse," Riley muttered low. "I ain't above bustin' your goddamn noggin, ye don't." The pony became calmer, as if understanding, and Riley headed the small procession toward the camp.

The other men met them there. Three—including Riley—had been injured, none seriously, and none killed. When they toted it up, the rescue party figured they had killed eight Blackfeet.

"How could you let this happen, Riley?" the wagon master, Jon Coates, bellowed, stomping forward.

Riley slid off his horse. He was beginning to feel some real pain from the wound, though not more than he could tolerate. It didn't help his mood any. "I ain't your goddamn nursemaid, Coates," he growled. "Ye were told to keep a guard out for Indians, or any other trouble."

"Don't matter none," Coates insisted. "We're supposed to be under the fort's protection."

"Ye got attacked, we protected ye," Riley said with an angry shrug. "Ye don't like it, Mister Coates, ye can go suck the ass out of a buffler."

Coates sputtered, and several women gasped in disgust at the vulgarism. Riley didn't much care. "Ye got anything else to say, boy?" the blacksmith asked.

"Yes, by God," Coates snapped. "Yes, I do. I'll pass word about this, about your lack of protection for travelers. Once word gets around, travelers won't stop here any more, and you'll lose all your business."

"Your word don't mean shit to anyone who counts," Riley said sharply. "And I don't think you'll be travelin' this trail again."

"Our guide will, and he'll tell others of what happened here."

"Like hell I will, sonny," the guide, Bob Cameron, chimed in. "I don't owe you no goddamn allegiance, sonny. But I do owe some to Ol' Jim Bridger. Any words git said about someone's nature wantin', it'll be tales about you. And if you want me to stay on as your guide, you'll button your hole."

"Ye lose anyone?" Riley asked, after nodding thanks in Cameron's direction.

"None dead," Coates said angrily. "Several were wounded, though."

"Be thankful then," Riley spat harshly. "Them Blackfeet attacked another wagon train over on Ham's Fork jist before they come on ye folks. Half a dozen people there lost their lives to the Blackfeet. Ye and yours got off easy."

Without waiting for further comment or complaint from Coates, Riley leaped onto the Indian pony and led his men back toward the fort. As he rode the three-quarters of a mile, he hoped that this was not a harbinger of the way the rest of the summer was going to go.

⟪ 16 ⟫

It took everyone at the fort a couple of days to realize there would be no more wagon trains that year, so they began to relax. The summer had been as busy as the only bull elk during rutting season, and the sudden peace was highly welcomed.

"Goddamn if there weren't more Mormons this year than I ary want to see again," Riley said as he and McGinnis sat outside the shop. They had managed to trade some work for a few bottles of Irish stout, and were sipping the lukewarm brew.

"They're sure some strange folk," McGinnis agreed. "Odd as a cat wearin' buckskins."

Riley belched loudly. "I still cain't understand people like that, ones who spit on the hand of friendship when it's offered."

"They're just jackasses, One-Eye."

"I'd think so, too, but one of 'em told me some of their history. It weren't pretty."

"And ye believed him?"

"Not whole hog. Not at first. But since then, I've asked some of the other boys about it. Ones that've been back to the States enough to know what's gone on there. Damn if they didn't verify jist about everything that one Mormon told me." He shook his head, still wanting to disbelieve. "It'd be easy to take a dislikin' to 'em, but knowin' such things about 'em makes it some harder.''

"I guess what ye see is deceivin' at times," McGinnis agreed.

The two were in good spirits. They had made far more money than they would have had they still been on the company payroll. Riley hadn't gotten around to figuring out exactly how much, but it was a favorable sum, of that he was sure.

They drank a little and watched as Vasquez approached them. He had returned a week after the fight with the Blackfeet—just about a month ago now—and had immediately irked Riley, who was still recovering from the wound suffered in the fight.

The blacksmith had just come out of the shop for a breath of fresh air when Vasquez had ridden in. "Have any trouble, Pedro?" Vasquez asked, stopping.

"Had some Blackfeet pay a visit on a couple of camps."

"Blackfeet?" Vasquez asked, surprised. "Those cursed devils were pretty well wiped out ten years ago or so with the smallpox, and good riddance. You certain they weren't Sioux or Cheyenne?"

Riley looked up at Vasquez, who was still on his horse. Then he jabbed his hammer in the Spaniard's direction. "Now, I know I ain't been in the mountains as long as ye and Ol' Jim and some of the others, but I been out here long goddamn enough and been in enough fracases with Indians to know the difference 'tween the Blackfoot and the Sioux or Cheyenne, goddammit, and ye sure as hell ought to know it, too."

"Calm down, damn you," Vasquez snapped. "I was just checking."

"Jist checkin', my ass," Riley retorted. "Ye was makin' light of me again, and I'll tell ye, Louie, I ain't of a mind to listen to it."

"You're too sensitive, Pedro," Vasquez said evenly. "You take too much to heart. I just had to make sure."

"Fuck ye," Riley growled. "Ye say somethin' like that

again, and your partner'll have to come pick your stinkin' remains out of the horseshit.''

''I was kicking the ass of young bucks like you long before you came along,'' Vasquez said tightly. He wasn't that old, but he was considerably older than the twenty-six-year-old blacksmith.

''Anytime ye want to prove yourself, boy, jist come on at me.''

Riley spun and walked back inside, leaving Vasquez sitting there by himself. He was still angry when he spotted Vasquez coming toward him again. ''Wonder what the hell he wants this time,'' Riley muttered.

Vasquez stopped in front of the blacksmiths and said pleasantly, ''A word with you, Pedro, if you don't mind. And with you, McGinnis.''

''Have at it,'' Riley said evenly. He was determined not to let Vasquez rile him, not on such a fine day.

''I wondered if you two would mind watching over the fort again for a spell.''

''How long?'' Riley asked.

''Couple of months maybe. I'll be back sometime in the fall.'' He seemed mighty nervous.

''Make it early fall,'' Riley said after a swig of ale. ''Spirit Grass'll be close to droppin' our second, and I want to git her to Black Iron's village before she does.''

''I'll be back early enough,'' Vasquez promised.

''I don't mind,'' Riley said. ''How about ye, Paddy?''

''Doesn't put me out any.''

Vasquez left, and Riley and McGinnis spent the rest of the afternoon doing little of anything besides drinking the thick beer and gabbing. Just before dark, they closed up the shop and headed to Riley's lodge. McGinnis had been staying there since the spring. He had felt a little awkward about it at first, thinking he was intruding where he did not belong, but he had gotten used to it over the past couple of months. There wasn't much he could do about it yet, though he had a plan.

Riley felt it wise that he and his friend had not had too much ale. He could've easily sat there drinking it until he was roaring drunk again. And *that,* he knew, would have Spirit Grass out for his scalp.

As it was, she frowned at him when he came in the lodge, showing her disapproval when she smelled the ale on his breath.

"Dammit, Spirit Grass, stop givin' me that wicked look," Riley said in irritation. "I ain't drunk. Me and Paddy jist had us a few bottles of ale is all."

"Ye ain't drunk?" she asked suspiciously.

"I jist tol' ye, didn't I."

"I don't want ye gittin' drunk," Spirit Grass insisted.

"I know. And I ain't, so quit your fussin'."

Spirit Grass hesitated only a few seconds. Then she grinned.

Vasquez returned to the fort by late September. When he arrived, he was accompanied by a woman—a white woman he introduced as his new wife—and two small children.

"My family, Pedro," Vasquez said after he had helped the woman and children down from the wagon. "My wife, Narcissa, and her children, Hiram and Susanah."

Riley doffed his battered old hat. "Pleasure to meet ye, ma'am," he said politely. "Ye and your young'ns." He knelt and shook young Hiram's hand seriously. He was surprised to the point of shock, but he thought he covered it well.

"And you, sir," Narcissa said when Riley had stood again. It was apparent from her soft drawl that she was from Kentucky.

From what Riley could see, Narcissa was a plain-looking woman, strong and used to hard living, in her mid-twenties or so, and just beginning to show a bit of dowdiness. She appeared to be a jolly sort, though right now she was overwhelmed by everything, and Riley guessed that Vasquez had exaggerated the fort's amenities.

"I'll need to speak to you, Pedro, soon as I get Narcissa and the children settled."

"I ain't goin' anywhere," Riley said with a shrug. He wondered what this was all about, but brushed it from his mind as he went back to the shop. He figured he would find out within minutes.

His timing was off by a little—it was nearly a half-hour later before Vasquez returned.

Riley and McGinnis were sitting outside. They had no pressing work, and were taking advantage of a fine Indian summer day. "That was some surprise ye sprung on us, Louie," Riley said.

"I thought it would be," he said a little shyly. He seemed almost embarrassed that he now had a wife.

"Well it was." There was a little silence, before Riley asked, "What'd ye want to talk to me about, Louie?"

Vasquez hesitated a moment, then cleared his throat. He could see no reason for feeling so discomfited. "With having brought my family to the fort, we need more rooms here," he said stiffly.

"And?" Riley queried.

"Well, Pedro, I'd be obliged if you could handle the construction of extra rooms."

"How much're ye payin'?"

"I figure we can work something out, Pedro."

Riley looked at McGinnis. "Ye game fer this, boy?"

"It'll suit," McGinnis answered with a little smile. He had picked up quite a bit of Riley's jargon.

Riley nodded at Vasquez. "Looks like ye got some laborers, Louie," he said. "Jist one question—why us?"

Vasquez shrugged and looked uncomfortable again. "Not many others around now that things've slowed down. Besides, I trust you two to do it right."

Riley nodded again. "Makes sense," he said dryly. "Well, it's set then. But it's too nice a day here to ruin it over hagglin' and other business. Come on over here in the mornin' and we'll parley."

"Just one other thing—I want you to start right away. I know your woman's near her time, but I figure there's a few weeks left of decent weather where we—you—

could get a start. Then you could leave for Black
Iron's.''

Riley thought it over for a moment, then nodded.
''I'm still in—if we can reach an agreement on a price.''

''I figure that's likely.''

The parley with Vasquez didn't go as poorly as Riley had
expected it would, and he credited McGinnis with making it so. The young Irishman seemed to have a knack
for finding common ground between adversaries, of
having just the right phrase to cool down rising tensions. He also seemed to have a streak of iron in him
that would make him as obstinate as either Riley or
Vasquez when he wanted to show it.

The deal was set, with all three parties more or less
pleased. Riley and McGinnis spent the rest of the day
trying to find some help for the project. It was difficult,
considering that most of the fort laborers had packed
up their Indian wives and headed off to winter in the
villages; the single men headed toward Fort Laramie or
to the Settlements.

After a few days' search, four men were found and
convinced to winter at the fort. The pay of a dollar a day
through the winter, even when they would not be working on the building project, went a long way toward
making up their minds.

Work started the next morning and progressed fairly
well. First they had to ride off a little way with a large
wagon. Finding a good stand of cottonwoods was not
difficult, and they began chopping lumber. It took several days before they figured they had enough. Then
the actual construction began.

Things went well, although one problem arose early
on. One of the workers, a laborer named Wood Caldwell, had gotten hold of a bottle of whiskey during a
noon meal break. He was staggering when he returned
to work.

''Hey, Wood,'' Riley called, trying to keep the annoyance out of his voice, "ye in all right enough shape to continue?"

"Sure I am," Caldwell said. His words were slurred, his eyes blurry.

"Like hell," Riley snapped. "Git your ass out of here and come back tomorrow when ye ain't so full of fire water."

"I'm fine," the laborer insisted.

"Ye can hardly stand up, shit pile."

"You sayin' you never got drunk?" Caldwell snapped. "If y'are, you're a damn liar."

"I've poured a heap of awardenty down my throat in my time," Riley growled. "But never when there was work to be done—work I was bein' paid well to do. Now git the hell out of here. Ye ever come back like this again, shit pile, you'll regret it." He grabbed Caldwell's shoulder and shoved him, in case he hadn't gotten the point.

Caldwell lurched off, muttering in drunken impotence. He was back the next morning, slightly hungover but apparently willing to work. Riley was pleased to see it.

The men were working hard and fast, and things settled into a routine. Winter was fast approaching, and while they knew they could not finish before then, they wanted as much done as possible. That would leave them less to do in the spring. But Riley was eager to be on his way to Black Iron's village. Judging by her size, Spirit Grass was near her term.

Because of that, he drove the men fairly hard. In return, he made sure they were well-fed, paying out of his own pocket to have one of the hunters give him some of the choicest cuts of buffalo and antelope he caught. Riley also made sure the men had some whiskey—but not very much and always after the day's work was done.

The men appreciated such gestures, and their pay, and so were willing to work hard. But Caldwell, after being taken down by Riley in front of the others, was reluctant to keep up the pace, angering his comrades.

They were working harder than he, yet were paid the same. Quietly, out of the hearing of Riley and McGinnis, the three other laborers began taking him to task for it.

Riley was unaware of it, thinking everything was fine. Walls to make separate rooms were going up in the two long cabins that had been there since the fort was built. The first order of business was trying to get Vasquez and his family a home rather than just having them in the large cabins with all the stored goods, visitors, trading activity and more. Pleased with the way everything was going, Vasquez left Riley and McGinnis alone, which suited the blacksmiths just fine.

Though he had been a blacksmith now for four, nearly five years, Riley had lost none of the instincts and reflexes that had kept him alive during his several years trapping with Bridger. Working in what would become the quarters for the Vasquez family, Riley suddenly dove to the side. He had moved automatically, not really knowing why, just sensing that danger was there. He hit hard on his side and rolled a few times. Somewhere in the back of his mind he was grateful he did not carry his revolvers in his belt while he was working; they would've hurt like hell.

Riley came to his feet quickly, moving like a big cat. He spotted Caldwell yanking a hatchet out of the wood wall near where the blacksmith had been working.

"Think you'll make light of me, will ya, goddammit?" Caldwell mumbled. "Turn the others against me? I'll teach ya, goddammit. By God, I will!"

"Ye gone mad, shit pile?" Riley countered.

"Mad, hell. You turned my friends agin me, you son of a bitch, and now you're gonna pay for it."

"Now jist hol' on a minute here," Riley said, hoping to gain some time to think of something—other than just charging Caldwell and killing him.

"Scared, ain't ya, goddamn dog humper?" Caldwell said with a sneer. He advanced, brandishing the weapon, which had a sharp blade at one end of the head and a flat section for use as a hammer on the other.

"Scared of ye?" Riley said, laughing a little. Even if he were, he wouldn't admit it.

Caldwell charged, swinging the hatchet. Riley ducked, then rose and turned as the blade chunked into the wall. As the laborer tried to free the weapon, Riley slammed a big fist down on Caldwell's arm between elbow and shoulder.

Caldwell groaned and sagged as his humerus broke. But he pushed himself back up and yanked the hatchet free with his left hand. His right arm hung disjointedly at his side.

"Don't be a goddamn fool," Riley barked.

Caldwell said nothing. He just advanced, the weapon swinging in his left hand.

Riley backed toward the door, keeping a watchful eye on the laborer. When he felt the door jamb right behind him, he sighed in relief. He would be outside in a second, and then he would have room to deal with this wild man who had turned on him. He was still trying to get set to step outside, going backward, when Caldwell jumped at him.

At the same instant, McGinnis stuck his head in the door. "There ye are . . ."

Riley swept his powerful left arm out, hitting McGinnis across the bridge of the nose, knocking him outside. He sucked in a breath as Caldwell's hatchet bit into his forearm, ripping out a dollar-size chunk of flesh. "Ye craptious little toad fucker," he growled. Heedless of the blood dribbling onto the floor, he grabbed Caldwell's throat with his blood-covered left hand. With his right, he grabbed his foe's hatchet arm so that Caldwell could not bring the weapon into play again.

Riley squeezed Caldwell's wrist until the laborer dropped the hatchet. Then, keeping a tight grasp on Caldwell's throat, Riley slammed the man's head against the log wall, and again. Then he calmly clamped off the laborer's windpipe, crushing the trachea.

Caldwell struggled feebly for a few seconds before the life was squashed out of him. Riley turned and shoved the lifeless body out through the doorway. McGinnis caught it, realized who it was and dropped it in the dust.

"Ye all right, Paddy?" Riley asked.

McGinnis nodded, though his face was red from where Riley had hit him.

"Good. Run on out to the lodge and git Spirit Grass. Tell her to bring her bag of herb cures and such." When McGinnis had run off, Riley turned to the three other laborers. "Ye boys best go bury shit pile. I don't care where ye do it, jist git it done. Then ye can take the rest of the afternoon off for yourselves."

The three had not been pleased with being assigned the burial duty, but they brightened when they learned of their bonus. All three grabbed Caldwell's body and carted him off.

Riley sat on a wood bench and filled and lit his pipe. The arm was beginning to hurt. Sticking the pipe stem between his teeth, he pulled off his bandanna, rolled it some and then tied it as tightly as he could around his wound. Then he leaned back against the wall and waited for Spirit Grass, absently puffing his pipe.

Minutes later, McGinnis and Spirit Grass galloped into the fort enclosure on the same horse. Spirit Grass slid off the animal, buckskin bag in hand, as soon as the Irishman stopped. She knelt in front of her husband and peeled away the bandanna.

"It ain't so bad," he said quietly.

Spirit Grass looked up at him, stuck out her tongue and then lowered her eyes back to the wound. "What'd ye go'n do this fer?" she demanded, paying attention to the wound as she cleaned some of the blood away.

"Tryin' to save ol' Paddy's goddamn neck, worthless as it is. Damnfool Irishman jist cain't keep himself out of trouble."

"Go to hell, One-Eye," McGinnis said with a grin.

"Both shut up," Spirit Grass ordered. She had stanched the blood and was preparing a poultice. She slapped that on, then used some almost-clean cloth to tie it down.

Riley looked at McGinnis. "Best take that horse back to the corral and tend him."

When McGinnis was gone, Spirit Grass reached up and ran a hand across Riley's stubbled cheek. "Ye all right?" she asked, showing her concern for the first time.

"I'll be fine, woman," Riley said with a soft smile. "Long's I got ye lookin' after me."

"Let's go home," she said, pushing herself up. As they began walking toward the gate, Spirit Grass said shyly in Shoshoni, "I wish we had our lodge to ourselves again."

"I know," Riley replied in kind. "We will some day, but it'll be after the winter. We can't just throw Paddy out."

"No, I wouldn't want that."

"Maybe he'll find a wife with one of the caravans next season."

Spirit Grass nodded and pushed a wisp of hair off her forehead.

{ 17 }

With more than a taste of winter in the mountain air, Riley decided it was time to put the work on the fort to rest and head to Black Iron's village. He told that to Vasquez in no uncertain terms, so that Vasquez would not even think of arguing.

The fort owner nodded. "That's right, Spirit Grass is near her time, isn't she?"

"Yep."

"You'll be coming back?" Vasquez asked, a little concerned.

"Yep. And I'll want the shop for the next emigrant season."

"More parleying?" Vasquez asked wryly.

"Not if I can help it," Riley said. "I'll give ye fifty dollars for the whole season."

Vasquez didn't have the heart for dickering. He just nodded and said, "Deal."

Riley handed Vasquez the money, all in gold coins.

"Can you afford this right now, Pedro?" Vasquez asked, surprised. "I can wait till the first wagons come."

"I'll be fine, Louie. I'll need ye to arrange to git some things from back in the States, though. Supplies for the shop."

"Write down what you need and . . ." Vasquez stumbled to a halt. "That's right, you can't write, can you?"

Riley thought he detected a note of derision in the

words, and it angered him. He could read and write well enough. He just had not made the fact public—in part because he hadn't wanted to insult Bridger, who did not possess those skills. He just shrugged.

"I can write some," McGinnis said. "I'll do our list, *Louie.*"

Vasquez's eyes widened. "A disrespectful tone isn't good in one so young," he said, chastising the Irishman.

"That may be true, mate, but disrespect comin' from an aristocratic ass like ye ain't neither. There's no wrong in not bein' able to read or write. Hell, I hear Mister Bridger can't. There's no call for ye to make light of One-Eye for it."

"I didn't . . ."

"Ye sure as hell did, mate." McGinnis smiled a little. "But there's no reason to ruin the day with such bickerin'."

"As you wish," Vasquez said. His pomposity had grown considerably in the past few seconds. He stuck his money in an inside pocket of his frock coat, turned and left.

"Ye didn't need to stick up fer me like that, boy," Riley said quietly as he and McGinnis walked off.

McGinnis stopped, grabbed Riley's cloth sleeve and jerked him around to face him, no easy task, considering Riley's size. "Now ye listen to me, One-Eye," McGinnis said hotly, "ye've been more of a father than I e'er had. Ye pulled me from a life of drudgery and who knows what and give me a chance to make somethin' of meself. Ye've made me a partner with ye in your business, and ye saved me neck from that crazy Wood Caldwell. Ye and Spirit Grass've given me a place to live that's filled with warmth, good food and carin' folks. I ain't done a damn thing to help ye or her. It's about time I stood up and was counted."

"Goddamn, boy," Riley said with a grin, "you've sure gotten windy in your old age."

"I suppose I have," McGinnis grudgingly admitted. "But it's all true just the same."

"Well, then, thankee, boy," Riley said honestly. He was actually quite proud. He wasn't sure when he had taken the youth on that he was doing the right thing. Now he knew he had. McGinnis was turning into a fine young man, and Riley felt a gush of pride in knowing he had had at least something to do with the youth's maturing.

"No thanks needed, One-Eye. Not among friends."

"And that's what we are, boy. Shinin' *amigos.*"

A rush of warmth and pride flooded through McGinnis, and he grinned. "I'm glad to hear ye say that, One-Eye," he finally said, "seein' as I've a favor to ask of ye."

"Ask away, boy. But let's walk while ye do."

"I'd like to go with ye when ye take Spirit Grass to her father's village."

"What fer?" Riley asked out of curiosity.

McGinnis shrugged. "I'd just like to see an Indian village." He suddenly laughed a little. "I'd like to see a *peaceful* Indian village. One where I wouldn't be unwelcome. I've seen some of the Shoshonis and the Utes who come to the fort to trade, but I've ne'er seen them too close up, or had a chance to see the way they live and such."

Riley laughed. "You're one eager beaver, ain't ye."

"Well, another reason is that I don't look with favor on the idee of spending another winter cramped up here."

"I don't see why ye cain't come along. But," he warned, "we'll have to see what Spirit Grass says about it. She has some objection to ye comin' along, you're gonna stay put right here."

"Yessir," the youth said seriously. "After all the good things Spirit Grass's done for me, I'd not want to put her out in any way."

"Glad to hear it, boy." They were back in the shop by now, and Riley said, "There's jist one more thing, boy."

"Oh?" McGinnis asked, surprised.

"This here's a secret, boy, so don't ye go flappin' your

lips about it none. I can read and write jist fine. But only a few folks know about it.''

''Ye devilish son of a bitch,'' McGinnis said with a laugh. ''I won't tell no one. Does Mister Bridger know?''

''Yep. But I nary told Louie. Shit pile thinks he's somethin' special 'cause he likes to read books. I do, too, but I ain't usually got the time for it. Hell, I'm in the midst of readin' somethin' called *Tales of the Grotesque and Arabesque* by some feller named Edgar Allan Poe.''

''Sounds interestin','' McGinnis said, eyes wide. ''Ye mind lettin' me have a read at it when ye're done?''

''Be glad to, but it might be a spell.''

Spirit Grass had no objections to McGinnis coming along.

In the two days before the three rode out, McGinnis had neatly written out the list of supplies he and Riley needed and gave it to Vasquez. They had also made sure their shop and all the tools were secured.

Finally they were ready. Both men helped Spirit Grass lower the lodge and fashion a travois out of it to carry their personal possessions. McGinnis saddled horses for the three of them while Riley loaded a mule with food supplies and some trade goods, most of which he would give to Black Iron's band of Shoshonis as presents. Flat Nose, who was just over a year old, rode in a cradleboard hanging from Spirit Grass's saddle horn.

That afternoon, they crossed the Green River via one of the ferries, making the passage without having to pay. All of the ferries were operated by former mountain men, and Riley knew just about all of them.

They turned upriver, following it. They didn't make much progress, since Riley kept stopping to greet the men operating other ferries. It was a necessary ritual to greet everyone he knew, have a drink or a bite of meat, lingering a half-hour or more.

They made camp along the river that evening, about five miles beyond the last ferry. Though the nights were already quite cold, Riley decided the lodge wasn't needed. The three were supplied with thick six-point blankets and a few buffalo robes. Over Spirit Grass's protestations, Riley made her sit and rest while he and McGinnis did the necessary camp work.

Finally Spirit Grass could sit no longer. She pushed herself awkwardly to her feet, waddled over to Riley and grabbed the iron frying pan from his hand. "I ain't eatin' your cookin'," she said firmly.

"But . . ."

"Go," Spirit Grass ordered, pointing a withering finger toward a rock where she wanted her husband to sit.

Riley meekly did as he was told. As he sat, he glanced askance at McGinnis. "One word out of ye, boy," he muttered low, "and you'll be worm food right off."

"I haven't said anything," McGinnis responded, still trying to stifle a chuckle.

"Best not." But Riley was having trouble not laughing himself.

Two days later, after having turned more northeasterly, Spirit Grass suddenly called out. Riley jerked his horse around, eyes wide with worry. "What is it, woman?" he called.

"The baby," she gasped. "It's comin' . . ."

"Goddamn son of a bitch," Riley muttered. Aloud, he asked in Shoshoni, "What do you want me to do?"

"Just stop. Wait." Spirit Grass was having trouble getting off her pony, so Riley jumped off his own horse and hurried to help her. "This ain't your doin's," she said sternly.

"Helping my woman down off her horse ain't my business?"

"I'll be all right," Spirit Grass said after weathering another contraction. "Watch Flat Nose. Care for horses. I'll be done soon." With her feet firmly on the ground, Spirit Grass waddled away, looking for some kind of cover. There wasn't much of anything out on these sere plains except sage. *That'll have to do,* she thought. She squatted down behind a large sage, after trying to make sure there were no snakes around the bush. She wished she had a pole or something to grip as she tried to push the baby out. But she didn't and she knew she would have to do without.

Some yards away, Riley paced, worried. He muttered curses against Vasquez, blaming his trouble on the fort owner for having kept him working so long.

McGinnis left him alone for a little as he loosened the saddles so the horses could have a breather. He hobbled all the animals, leaned the cradleboard against a sage bush, and then rolled a corn husk cigarillo. With that going, he found a bottle of Riley's homemade whiskey among the packs and brought it to Riley. "Here, have a swallow of this, me friend," he said.

The big blacksmith took the bottle and drank deeply. He handed the bottle back. "Thanks," he mumbled, and then went back to pacing.

McGinnis shook his head. He had trouble understanding why Riley was so nervous, since he had been through this before. He figured it was due to the fact that the birth was going to be out here in the open, with no women to help. Men weren't supposed to have any part in all this.

A sudden scream from Spirit Grass brought Riley to a halt. He stood there, heart pounding, more frightened than he had been since the first time he had ever faced Indians in battle. He had no more idea of what to do now than he had then, and so he was frozen. But another scream from Spirit Grass galvanized him into action. He ran for his wife, not knowing what he would do when he got there.

Riley found Spirit Grass on her back, dress pulled high up over her still bulging belly. Her face was contorted with pain and covered with sweat, though the temperature was only in the upper thirties, and a light snow had begun falling. She emitted animal-like grunts and moans. The baby's head was out of the birth canal, but the child seemed stuck.

"Cord," Spirit Grass gasped in Shoshoni. "Cut cord." She groaned.

"What?" Riley asked stupidly. He wasn't sure he had understood what she said, or what she was talking about if he had.

"Look, One-Eye," McGinnis said urgently. He had been only moments behind Riley in rushing here, delaying just long enough to grab Flat Nose. He set the cradleboard down against the bush and pointed. "Look, somethin's wrapped around the babe's neck."

"Shit," Riley said when he saw the umbilical cord tightening on the infant's neck as Spirit Grass pressed to give birth. "Cut the cord around the baby's neck?" he asked in Shoshoni. His mouth was dry.

"Yes," Spirit Grass grunted. Then she screamed again as pain ripped through her insides.

Riley drew his big knife and knelt on his shins alongside Spirit Grass's left thigh. The baby's face was turned toward him, and he could see the perfect nose, broad lips and thatch of dark hair, slicked down by placental material. Gulping in fear, he reached out to grab hold of the umbilical cord.

"Jesus goddamn Christ," he breathed, almost in tears. He could see the life draining from his child right before his eyes, and he could not help. For the first time in his life he cursed his great size—his thick, sausage-like fingers could not pry free the cord, which was tightening ever more as each second passed.

"Get yer big mitts out of the way, me friend," McGinnis said with urgency. He was outwardly calm, but inside he was terrified.

"What?" Riley was almost paralyzed with worry.

"Get out of me way, ye big goddamn fool," McGinnis snapped, shoving Riley's hands. As Riley sat blankly back, the youth drew his own knife. Beginning to sweat, McGinnis stuck the knife blade between his teeth. Pushing gently on the baby's throat and chest flesh, making an indentation, he managed to wriggle a long, thin pinkie under the umbilical at one point.

"Cut it boy, cut it," Riley hissed. He had recovered his senses somewhat.

"In due time," McGinnis said, his voice muffled by the knife blade. He pulled upward on the cord a little, knowing he was hurting the child but also knowing it had to be done. He got a fraction of an inch worth of clearance, grabbed the knife from his teeth and with a frighteningly fast move, sliced through the cord. He dropped the knife and swiftly unwrapped the cord from the baby's neck.

Spirit Grass suddenly grunted again and pushed hard. Several more times, and the baby—a son, it was plain to see—was out, lying in Riley's big, bloody, now-capable hands.

Riley's relief was short-lived, however. "He ain't breathin'," he said, his fear and worry renewed.

McGinnis reached across and forced the infant's mouth open. He scooped out some muck and flung it aside. "I ain't sure it'll do any good, but I've seen times when me mother had such troubles they turned the babe upside down and whacked his bottom."

"Ye gone mad, boy?" Riley asked in disbelief.

"Do it," Spirit Grass groaned. "Quickly."

Riley lost all doubt. Grasping the tiny boy's ankles in his left hand, he reared back to swat him.

"Not too hard now, ye big ox," McGinnis cautioned.

Riley tapped the baby.

"Harder than that, me friend," McGinnis said in annoyance.

Riley spanked the child's buttocks somewhat harder. Nothing happened.

"Again," Spirit Grass said in a raspy voice, trying to sit up.

Riley did so, and a moment later there was a feeble squawk from the child. Riley smiled, his relief more potent than anything he had ever experienced. He grinned widely when his son began crying softly.

"Give me," Spirit Grass said weakly, holding out her arms. She had sunk back down when her infant had come alive. Riley gently handed her the child. "A son," she said proudly.

Riley nodded, his face split by a huge grin.

Spirit Grass grimaced again, turning Riley's relief to fear, but a moment later she smiled. "It's the way of these things," she said quietly in Shoshoni. "Go now. There is more to be done, but it is not for men to do."

"Ye sure?" Riley asked, also in Shoshoni.

She nodded.

"What'd she say?" McGinnis asked as Riley started to rise.

"The rest is her work, boy," Riley said gruffly. "Let's go."

The two sheathed their knives and wiped their bloody hands on their clothes. Riley picked up Flat Nose, and he and McGinnis headed toward their horses. Riley leaned his son against the bush again and picked up the whiskey bottle McGinnis had dropped when the two men had run to help Spirit Grass. "Goddamn, if I don't need this now, boy," he said, pulling the cork and pouring a good dose down his throat.

"Well don't hog it all, One-Eye," McGinnis said, grabbing the bottle.

It didn't take them long to finish the whiskey, and Riley pitched the bottle away. Neither was drunk, but they were a lot calmer than they had been. "We best git a camp made up, boy," Riley said. "We'll be stayin' here tonight."

They were almost done when Spirit Grass came shuffling gingerly back toward them. She was drawn and weak, and looked exhausted, but she smiled.

"Ye all right, woman?" Riley asked.

She nodded. Holding out her child, now wrapped in a small blanket she had had with her for just this occasion. "And our son—Arrives With Trouble—is doin' good, too." She paused. "His name is all right?"

"It's a fine name, Spirit Grass," Riley said with a proud smile. "Well, ye jist sit fer a spell. Me and Paddy'll finish up here and then make us some grub."

"That's my work," Spirit Grass said.

"On usual days, maybe. But this ain't normal. Now ye do as I say."

Four days later, the small group rode into Black Iron's village, where Spirit Grass was greeted by the women with great exclamations of joy. She was the center of attention for some days, and she enjoyed every moment of it.

Riley was ribaldly regaled by the warriors, and once word got out of his and McGinnis's role in the birth, the two were favored with almost as much respectful attention as Spirit Grass was.

18

Knowing he had the work on the fort to complete, as well as preparing for the emigrants, Riley led his small group home as early in the spring as he could.

McGinnis brought a woman back with him. Doing so, Riley had learned, had been his partner's primary reason for wanting to go to Black Iron's village. He had asked Riley some leading questions on the ride out—so many that Riley caught on right away and McGinnis finally admitted it. Riley offered to help, but the young Irishman would have none of it, so Riley let him be.

Riley didn't know how his young friend did it, but only several days into their stay at the village, McGinnis had himself a wife—Praises the Sky, daughter of Black Dog. Praises the Sky was a pretty girl of only thirteen summers, but she proudly wore the full bloom of womanhood in her softly curved, rounded figure. She had a streak of wildness in her, but McGinnis was capable of handling that. Or at least *he* thought so. Riley didn't, and told him so often and with great humor at McGinnis's discomfiture.

Vasquez showed up within minutes of Riley's lodge going up near the fort. Spirit Grass was not even prepared to serve coffee or welcoming food, and that upset her no end.

"Now see what ye done, dammit," Riley snapped at Vasquez. "Spirit Grass's gonna have the goddamn sulks most of the day now 'cause ye come up here botherin' us already. Jesus, couldn't ye have waited an hour before comin' over here to pester me? Damn.''

Vasquez ignored the question. "It's about goddamn time you got back.''

Riley shook his head, annoyed. He walked away, filling his pipe. After a moment, Vasquez followed. Riley found a clear spot along the creek and squatted there. Once his pipe was going, he looked at the Spaniard and said, "You're lucky I come back early.''

"Early?" Vasquez exploded. He muttered a little Spanish, then said in English, "You should've been back a week ago. More.''

"What the hell's got your nuts in an uproar, Louie?'' Riley asked, an edge of annoyance evident.

"We need to get those damn rooms finished before the emigrants start arriving.''

"So?" Riley asked, purposely insolent.

McGinnis wandered up and took a seat. Vasquez looked at him in irritation for a second, during which time the Irishman's eyes never flinched. Vasquez looked back at Riley. "Dammit, you hard-headed Irishman,'' he snapped, "you know goddamn well what that means. You . . .'' He stopped, realizing he was playing into Riley's hands. He drew in a long breath and then spit it out. "When do you plan to get back to it?'' he demanded, though his voice was mostly calm.

"Soon.''

"You know, Riley,'' Vasquez said in resignation, "talking to you isn't like talking to another human being. It's more like talking to a mule—a big, strong mule, granted, but a mule, an ugly, dumb-as-a-rock goddamn mule.''

Riley laughed heartily.

"What's so goddamn funny?''

"It's always a pleasure when I can git your asshole all bound up like this,'' Riley said, still laughing.

"You're an exasperating man, Pedro. Damn exasperating.'' Vasquez stood up. ''I expect you to be working on those rooms tomorrow. First thing.''

''Day after,'' Riley said evenly.

Vasquez's eyebrows rose, then settled back to normal. He nodded and left. As Vasquez walked away, Riley looked over at McGinnis and winked.

Just southwest of the fort, along the eastern branch of Black's Fork, Spirit Grass and Praises the Sky erected their tipis next to each other, with enough room between them for privacy. Coming from the same band, the two women knew each other, though not well, because of the difference in their ages. Still, they felt almost like sisters, with their common bonds and background.

No sooner had Spirit Grass and Praises the Sky set up their lodges than others began springing up, too. The other lodges were set off a bit from theirs, in deference to Riley's position within the fort, as well as his reputation. Within two days, there was a small village of nine lodges. All belonged to men who worked at the fort, and their Shoshoni, Ute or Piute wives.

The rooms were done, and Riley and McGinnis paid, long before the first wagon trains appeared. The six rooms made life more comfortable for Vasquez and his family, but didn't do a thing for the looks of the trading post.

The fort was still a small log stockade with living and working quarters along the north and south sides, facing each other across a small dirt square. Now, the single, long log building on each side was divided into three cabins—or rooms—each. The west wall had a long, small open stable that was also used for the storage of firewood and hay. Riley's blacksmith shop was the first room to the right when one entered the gate on the east side of the fort. A door opened at the back, into the corral, which was also enclosed by a log stockade. Riley's working quarters and part of the room next door formed a portion of the corral wall. The gate to the corral—large enough to admit wagons—was on the south side, at a right angle to the main gate of the fort.

It was obvious to anyone who stopped there that the place had seen better days. After more than a decade of use, the fort was shabby and worn, though it was sturdy enough. The co-owners didn't really care, though. They had set it up to serve the emigrants, not to emulate a fancy Saint Louis hotel.

Once the work of dividing the buildings was done, there was still no respite for the men. There was plenty of work to be done, and they went right to it. Most of the fort employees living in the little village were hunters and trappers, and had to ride out to their work. Riley and McGinnis were kept busy laying in a sufficient supply of fuel for the forge, and making sure their tools were in proper working order after lying around for the winter. They worked feverishly, though they figured it would be some time yet before the emigrants began arriving. Most of the wagon trains would have just left the States, or be waiting for the jump off.

That didn't mean no one came to the trading post, though. Trappers who had spent the winter up in the mountains came in, looking for supplies, a few weeks of whiskey—and, hopefully, some time with a woman. Indians also began showing up at the fort to trade. Most of those were Shoshonis, but there were a smattering of Flatheads and Bannocks who didn't want to trade at Fort Hall for one reason or another, and some Piutes. Soon after, Utes began arriving from the other side of the Uinta Mountains to the south.

Less than a month after Riley had returned from Black Iron's village, Jim Bridger pulled into the fort. Riley, who had heard some commotion, looked out of his shop. When he spotted Bridger, he walked outside.

Bridger dismounted at the corner of the building catty-corner to Riley, and stood there a moment, stretching. Vasquez came out of the next building. "*Hola*, Jim," he said in greeting. The two shook hands.

"Looks like ya done a good job here, Louis," Bridger said, waving a hand around the fort.

"Riley and McGinnis did it," Vasquez said. "Narcissa, the kids and I have taken this corner apartment. If you're of a mind to get married one of these days, the one up at the end of this side's for you. The middle one here's the one I've been using for an office."

Bridger nodded acceptance. "What's on the other side?" he asked, turning. He waved when he spotted Riley heading toward him.

"That's Riley's, of course," Vasquez said. "Middle one's the trade room. The other's for whatever we need it for, at least for the time being."

Bridger nodded and turned again. He pointed. "Ye say that'n's mine?" he asked.

"*Sí.*"

"It's funny ye should mention marriage."

"Oh?" Vasquez said, surprised.

"I aim to bring my own wife out here now that the cabins're built."

"Ye what?" Riley asked as he strode up alongside Bridger.

"Hell, boy, your ears got stoppered up over the winter or somethin'?" Bridger said with a grin. "I said I'm aimin' to bring my wife here."

"*Como?* But who . . . ?" Vasquez sputtered. "Where . . . ? When did this . . . ?"

"Ye finally talked some drunk, dumb-ass Bannock chief into givin' over his daughter to ye, didn't ye?" Riley said with a laugh.

"Like hell. This here's a white woman." He sounded neither angry nor defensive, though he knew he was likely to take some teasing.

"A white woman?" Riley said, fighting off a grin. "She must be deranged. Lost all her faculties if she's willin' to take up with the likes of ye, boy." He burst out laughing.

"Worse than that," Vasquez added, joining in the

laughter, "she must be blind as a bat and have no sense of smell."

"Eat skunk shit, the both of ya," Bridger said with a wide grin.

"Well, dammit, who is she? Where'd ye meet her?" Riley asked.

"Met her back in the Settlements when I was there a couple years ago arrangin' for supplies. I . . ."

"Hell, we've been mighty inhospitable," Vasquez said. "Making you stand out here in the sun and all. Come on, *amigo,* and let's go inside and set a spell."

"Ye do have somethin' to cut the dry, don't ya?" Bridger asked.

"You'd even doubt such a thing?" Vasquez responded, faking hurt.

"Hell, not ye, boy, him." Bridger jerked a thumb over his shoulder in Riley's direction. "I was some suspicious that goddamn Irishman'd drank up ever' drop in the post here."

Riley snorted in disgust, but grinned.

"I always make sure I keep some hidden from the Irish when they're around," Vasquez said innocently. He found this a perfect opportunity to get back at Riley —and McGinnis—a little for the times he had fallen into their traps and tricks.

Riley couldn't think of any response to that, other than to get angry, which he was not about to do when his boss and longtime friend had such news. He neither said nor did anything other than to follow Bridger and Vasquez into the latter's living quarters. In minutes they were seated, had some antelope soup set before them and were filling tin mugs with whiskey.

"To your almost new bride, *amigo,*" Vasquez said in a toast. The three drank, then Vasquez said, "Now, just when the hell did you marry her?"

"Back there. Not too long after I met her. She was in Choteau's store. Him and I were hagglin' over our supplies, so I told him to take care of her first. She thanked me, and we got to talkin' some. She seemed powerful interested in me once she found out I know everything there is to know about these western lands.''

There was no arrogance in the latter, just his own acknowledgment of fact. His friends would not argue the point. Anyone who had been out here more than a few weeks knew that Old Jim Bridger had seen more of the western lands than any man alive. Hell, he had been the one to discover the Great Salt Lake so many years ago. He had trapped and traded from Santa Fe to Canada, from the Settlements to Fort Vancouver.

"I was taken by her, damn if I wasn't. So I started squirin' her around Independence. Just before winter, we was wed. I planned to bring her out here last summer, but she was with chil', and this place wasn't suitable yet.''

"What?'' Riley exploded, spitting a mouthful of whiskey across the table, almost hitting Vasquez.

"Ye heard me, ya shit-brained idiot.'' He grinned hugely. "Ye two ain't the only ones got a full load of man juice in his nuts.''

"Well, goddamn, ye lecherous ol' bastard,'' Riley whooped. "Boy or girl?''

"A son, of course,'' Bridger said. "I named him Jim.'' He laughed.

Another toast was made, this one to James Bridger Junior.

"Well, when're she and your boy getting here?'' Vasquez asked.

"Soon. I left her and her folks at Fort Laramie. Her folks're headin' on beyond here. They're gonna wait for their caravan there.''

"Well, what's her name, dammit?'' Riley demanded.

"Sarah Lockwood.''

"So why'd you come on ahead instead of waiting there with her?'' Vasquez asked.

"Wanted to make sure the cabins were finished,'' Bridger responded, draining the mug of whiskey and pouring another. "And, soon's she gits here, I aim to have us one hell of a welcomin' fandango."

Vasquez nodded. "Well, then, there's a heap of work to be done before that. How long you expect it'll be before she gets here?"

"A month, tops. Her party was plannin' on gittin' an early start."

Vasquez nodded. "We'll get to work and shape this place up. But we're going to need supplies. Where're our wagons?"

"Couple days back. When I left Laramie, I pushed on ahead. They'll be along directly."

"Good," Vasquez said. He raised his glass again. "Another toast," he said.

Bridger did not raise his mug. He just sat for a few moments, then said quietly, "Before ye go and git all excited, boys, there's something else I figure I ought to tell ye."

"After them little surprises, what else can ye say that'll shock us?" Riley asked. But suddenly seeing the solemn look on Bridger's face, he and Vasquez grew quiet with interest and some concern.

"Sarah's a Mormon," Bridger said flatly.

Vasquez slowly lowered his mug, face screwed up in wonder and surprise. Riley was too stunned to say anything. He just sat, eyes wide. He couldn't have been more surprised if Bridger had up and told them he was planning to give up the mountains and go east to some place like Indiana and run a haberdashery.

"Ain't ye boys got nothin' to say to that?" Bridger asked, looking from one to the other.

"I think you're a damn fool, Jim," Riley allowed, finding his tongue again. "A *Mormon?* Goddamn. That can cause a heap of trouble."

"I ain't askin' ye to like her, One-Eye," Bridger said with a scowl. "I'm jist tellin' ye the way it is."

"It don't have anything to do with likin' somebody, Jim. Ye know me better'n that. I wouldn't give a good goddamn if ye was to hanker to wed yourself to a goddamn buffler cow. But this here's gonna be nothin' but trouble.''

"Damn, boy, stop thinkin' of yourself for once.''

"Shit on ye, Jim. I'm concerned about all the ol' boys around here. How do ye knew that shit pile Young doesn't covet this land? The Salt Lake Valley sure as hell don't have no promise. Was I him, I'd sure take a look at workin' my way in here. And if he does, all of us're gonna git hurt.''

"None of that's likely, One-Eye,'' Bridger said calmly.

"It ain't? Christ, thousands of Mormons come through here last year headin' that way. I'll wager there'll be even more this season. That valley can't support that many people—ye cain't no more grow crops out by that goddamn salt lake than you can grow 'em on the top of the Wasatch Mountains in the winter time. Young's gonna have to find somewhere to put 'em.''

"And ye think that place'll be here, do ya?''

"It's the best place around.''

"I figure you're jist tryin' to find things to worry about, One-Eye. The Saints ain't so bad once ye git to know 'em.''

"I tried that, Jim. Ye know I did.''

Bridger shrugged. "Maybe that first group that passed by here was jist too worried about findin' a place where they'd be left alone to be too neighborly to strangers. 'Specially after what all they'd been through, and so recently. Might be that now they're settled, they'll be more hospitable.''

Riley grinned ruefully. "I reckon you're right, Jim. Mayhap it was that I met the wrong ones first.'' He paused, then asked, "Ye aimin' to convert?''

"To Mormonism?'' Bridger said with a laugh. "Can ye see this ol' chil' as one of them pious bastards, bein' ordered about all the time by some idjit thinks he's God's own handpicked servant? Ain't goddamn likely.''

Riley laughed, since it was rather a ludicrous thought, but he was still a little worried down deep. He could see no good coming of this marriage. Not for anyone. But he raised his glass and said, "Then I wish ye the best of luck, my friend."

Bridger and Vasquez joined in the toast, then got down to talking business.

19

When the emigrants began coming, there was a torrent of them, and a good many were Mormons. One of the first wagon trains to arrive brought Sarah Lockwood Bridger. She was quiet, reserved, a fair, almost fragile-looking woman with a pale prettiness about her. Riley could not imagine a more unlikely mate for a wild, tough, crotchety man like Jim Bridger.

Riley said nothing, though. In the several weeks since Bridger had broken the news, Riley had had plenty of time to think about things, and he had concluded that he might have been too quick to judge. This lot of Saints seemed a little more pleasant than the many who had passed through the fort last year.

A rider had gone out from Sarah's wagon train when it was only a few miles from the fort, so that last-minute preparations could be made. The emigrants would not be able to stay at the fort more than a few days, and they wanted the celebration to take place without delay.

Sarah was cordially welcomed to the fort and shown to her new apartment.

Riley felt an edge of uneasiness build in him when he realized that Brigham Young was leading this wagon train. The blacksmith remembered his reception the year before when he had tried to talk with Young. Of course, Young had been mighty sick then, and Riley knew it was not fair to judge him that way.

Riley also noticed that Porter Rockwell was along, sticking close to Young at all times. Riley wanted to go talk to the hard-eyed man, but he was not sure how he would be received, so he figured he would wait until a better opportunity presented itself.

The day after Sarah's arrival, a throng of Saints and mountain men crowded into the fort's small confines to hear Elder Elizear Flake bless the 16-month-old union of the mountain curmudgeon and his sweet bride. Sarah wore her wedding dress for the event, and she was radiant in these dull surroundings.

Bridger had paid a Shoshoni woman well to make him a fine pair of buckskins. They were soft elkskin, both shirt and pants heavily fringed. A bullhide belt held in place the old mountain man's two pistols, big butcher knife, tomahawk and his small sack of possibles. He had new moccasins of buffalo hide, decorated with beads. A silk top hat was perched on his head.

Then the party began. Several one-time mountain men joined some Mormons in a corner of the square. Among them they had three fiddles, a guitar, four squeeze boxes and several harmonicas. The impromptu band wasted no time in beginning a sprightly tune.

Rough-hewn men who had made their living for years in beaver streams throughout the mountains lined up to dance with the few single Mormon girls. The men's buckskins, fur hats and wild abandon clashed with the Mormon girls' simple calico dresses, their light feet and their gentle deportment.

Someone broke off the top of a barrel of whiskey and began dispensing the fiery liquid with a large ladle. Tables of all kinds of food were set up along the front wall of the fort, near Bridger's apartment. Mormon women gladly dished out the victuals with a free hand.

Riley felt strangely detached from all the goings-on, though he didn't really know why. He knew it had something to do with the possibility of trouble because Bridger had married a Mormon, but beyond that he wasn't so certain. He filled a large tin cup with whiskey and sipped at it as he walked around. He stopped occasionally to chat with old friends from the mountain days, many of whom he didn't get to see much any more.

McGinnis, on the other hand, was so worried about Praises the Sky's wildness, afraid that she would take up with someone else, that he wouldn't leave her side, even though she was standing in a corner with the other Indian women, detached from the frolicking going on.

Riley finally decided he would give the Mormons another chance, and he approached three men standing to one side, drinking and watching the dancers swinging around the small square. "Mind if I join ye, boys?" he asked.

"Not at all," one man said. He was short, round and balding. His face was nicked in several places from where he had shaved. "My name's Edson Gurdy."

"One-Eye Riley."

"John Donaldson," the second said.

"Millard Halsey," the third added.

"You're the blacksmith here, aren't you?" Gurdy asked.

"One of 'em. Me and my partner, Paddy McGinnis, handle most of the work."

"Been here long?" Donaldson asked. "At the fort, I mean."

"Few years. I knew Jim back in the old days. I'd been back in Missouri, not enjoyin' it a lick, when I come back out here with a wagon train of emigrants. When we got this far, I told Jim I was lookin' for work. He needed a blacksmith. So here I am."

"You do fine work, Mister Riley," Gurdy said. "I sent my boy over to you yesterday with a couple of pieces I needed repaired. Your workmanship was such that I couldn't tell where the original problem had been."

"Thankee. It always does a man good to hear his work's appreciated."

Riley was momentarily distracted when he heard a mountain man and a Saint behind him discussing the ferrying business. The mountain men had run ferries across the Green River since before the fort was built, and were making out well in doing so. The Mormon asked about that, and the mountain man replied, "Hell, the boys runnin' those ferries down there brought in maybe ten thousand dollars last year. We expect we'll do a heap better this year."

Idiot, Riley thought, listening to the mountaineer. It was plumb foolish to reveal to anyone how lucrative the ferries were. "What's that ye said?" Riley questioned, bringing his mind back to Gurdy, who had just said something to him.

"Have you ever thought of convertin' to the Mormon church, Mister Riley?" Gurdy asked evenly.

"Convertin' from what?" Riley countered, a smile tugging his lips. "From a blacksmith?"

"The church appreciates men with humor, Mister Riley," Gurdy said with a chuckle. "It also appreciates fine craftsmen. We have need of blacksmiths in Zion, sir, and . . ."

"Where?"

"Salt Lake City," Gurdy corrected himself. "As I was sayin', the church has need of blacksmiths, and one of your caliber could do well for himself."

"I'm doin' jist fine where I'm at," Riley said flatly.

"But sir, you . . ."

"Leave him be, Edson," Halsey said. "He can't be so good a blacksmith that you should grovel before him to get him to see the light. He looks disreputable and untrustworthy, if you ask me. And he appears to be a troublemaker."

"The church needs men with such talents at times," Gurdy chided.

"Damn right it does," Rockwell said, walking up. "Is Mister Riley botherin' you, brothers?"

It was almost startling to see the light of fear that overcame all three men as soon as Rockwell had announced his presence, Riley thought. "Botherin' 'em, hell," he growled. "They were tryin' to convert me. Damn, but ye folks're sure big on that."

Rockwell shrugged. "We're blessed with knowin' we're followin' the Lord's true path. So we feel compelled to spread the glorious news to everyone."

"Ain't everybody wants to hear that news," Riley said evenly.

"As we have learned. However, you can't fault the elders for tryin'."

"I don't. I do fault 'em, however, for not knowin' when to back off. And for not knowin' when a man ain't interested right from the git go."

"Some folks take more learnin' than others, Riley." He looked at Gurdy. "Why don't you boys go have somethin' to eat."

He tone was soft, the words unthreatening in themselves, but the effect was instant in the three other Saints. They almost cringed as they slunk away. Riley suspected that Porter Rockwell had that effect on a lot of men.

"So, how's the blacksmithin' business, Riley?" Rockwell asked.

"I'm gittin' by. How's things goin' out by the Salt Lake?"

Rockwell almost grinned. "Quite well," he said in a vigorous voice, showing a strong spark of interest. "All the Saints who arrived last year have homes, and there's already a few businesses goin'. We made it through the winter on what we brought, but now we must plant. That should be well under way by the time we get there."

"Ye really think ye can make somethin' out there in that wasteland?" Riley asked. He thought they were lunatics for even trying.

Rockwell nodded. "The Lord didn't direct us to the Salt Lake Valley for no reason, Mister Riley. We were led there for a purpose. Mark my words, one day—and not very far off—you'll see the Salt Lake Valley a veritable Garden of Eden."

"Y'all're crazier'n bedbugs," Riley said with a shake

of the head. "But it ain't my place to tell anybody not to try anything they set their hearts on."

"A wise attitude for one so unenlightened," Rockwell said. Riley was not certain whether he was being sarcastic. "I suggest you stay away from the Saints, Mister Riley, unless you have an affection for bein' pressed to convert."

"Ye don't think you're gonna convert Ol' Jim, do ye? Ye got about as much chance of that as ye do of changin' me to your ways. Mayhap less."

"Mister Bridger has taken the first step. He'll eventually come to see the light. We'll see to that," Rockwell said confidently.

"Buffler turds," Riley snorted. "I'll tell ye, though: If ye git Ol' Jim to convert whole hog, ye can have me, too."

"I'll hold you to them words, Mister Riley. Good day." Rockwell touched the brim of his hat, spun and strutted off. Mormons stepped out of his way, looking as frightened as Gurdy, Donaldson and Halsey had.

Riley sipped some whiskey, grimaced and poured the rest onto the ground. He had been drinking rotgut for so long that fine whiskey just didn't taste right to him any more. He also suspected that his vow to Spirit Grass kept him from wanting to drink too much. Tying the cup to his belt with a small buckskin thong, he headed for the tables of food.

Riley dropped his plate of buffalo and onions—it was his fourth, so he wasn't too disappointed—and ran toward the band, shoving past people who had stopped dancing and were looking that way. He got to the scene of the fight he had seen starting just as Porter Rockwell was about to plunge a butcher knife into a mountain man.

Riley grabbed Rockwell's knife arm, pulled him up a little, and kicked him in the stomach.

Rockwell dropped the knife and fell to one side, but

he was on his feet in an instant. He looked like an enraged bull, and he was ready to charge.

"Calm yourself, Brother Rockwell," Brigham Young said in his deep, booming voice. It was enough to make just about anyone pause.

Rockwell breathed deeply and then straightened, but he kept his eyes on the blacksmith. "One day you and I're gonna tangle for real, Riley," he snarled.

"Anytime, anyplace, shit pile," Riley responded easily. Rockwell might scare these Mormons, but Riley was not worried about him. Cautious, yes—it was obvious that Rockwell was a tough man—but not worried.

"What's this all about, Brother Rockwell?" Young asked, walking up.

"That son of a bi . . ." He realized there were women around, and so he changed his tune a bit. "That scurrilous coward," he went on, pointing to the mountain man he had been about to kill, "dragged one of our young women into a room and debased her."

The mountain main—Elmo Rutledge—had risen and was rubbing his head. Rockwell had clouted him good with something hard. "I didn't do no such thing," he protested. "I was dancin' with her and suggested we retire to a secluded place and have us a little fun." Now that he was on his feet and the other mountain men were massed behind him, he was feeling more cocky. "She was a willin' and eager participant in the delights we was havin'. Until that ox come rumblin' in and clobbered me while my attention was on more pleasurable pursuits."

"That's not true," a fetching fifteen-year-old said. She was disheveled and crying. "He forced me . . . and then he tried to . . . then he did . . ." An older woman began comforting her.

Riley got the impression the girl was lying, at least somewhat. He suspected she had gone willingly with Rutledge, and then, when found out, had begun yelling rape. But he couldn't be sure. Rutledge was not the most pleasant of men and had a reputation for pressing himself on women far more than he should.

"Well, sir?" Young asked, looking at Riley.

Riley shrugged. "This ain't a decision for me to make. That'll be made by Mister Bridger or Mister Vasquez. I'm jist here to keep Rockwell from killin' one of us."

Bridger and Vasquez were standing right behind Rutledge, and they both stepped forward. Vasquez spoke. "Rutledge'll be punished for what he did here, Mister Young. You have my word on that."

"You ain't gonna listen to him, are you, Brother Brigham?" Rockwell asked incredulously.

Young did not answer for some seconds, then he nodded. "I think Mister Vasquez is a man we can trust," he said. "And a man we can work with." His eyes bored into Vasquez's, and the two men seemed to reach some sort of silent understanding.

Finally Vasquez turned his head. "Pedro, please escort Elmo out of the fort and send him on his way. We'll deal with him when the festivities are over." As Riley shoved Rutledge toward the gate, Vasquez said to Young, "I hope this disgraceful incident hasn't spoilt the celebrations entirely."

"The Saints've persevered through far more terrible things, Mister Vasquez. I think we can continue our revels. But I assume," he added pointedly, "that there'll be no more trouble."

"One of our boys causes any kind of ruction, I'll set your Mister Rockwell *and* our own Mister Riley on the miscreant," Bridger said harshly.

Outside the fort, Riley turned Rutledge toward the corral. "Jist what the hell did ye think ye were doin' with that girl, Rutledge?" Riley asked.

"Goddamn, boy, ye got to this age and still ain't figured out what to do with a woman?" Rutledge jibed. He figured Riley would set him on his horse and send him home. He'd come back in a few days, when the Saints were gone, and everything would have blown over.

"Ye ain't very funny, shit pile."

Rutledge stopped and turned to face Riley. "Hell, One-Eye," he said. "That little harlot was askin' for it. Ye could see that plain as day."

"So she went with ye willingly?" Riley asked, trying to stay calm.

"Well, hell, she had to put on an act in case anyone was lookin'. But once in that room, goddamn if she wasn't plumb shinin'. Buckin' and kickin' and all." Rutledge laughed.

"Ye sure she wasn't fightin' to git away?"

"Well, hell, she might've been a wee bit resistant at first, but she was comin' around, sure as shit she was. Then that big, ugly son of a bitch had to interfere. Goddamn, if he'd only waited another minute, I'd of had my fill of that pristine little gal. Christ, I'm still hard from it, and my nuts're achin'." He laughed again.

"You're a disgustin' piece of shit, Rutledge."

"Ye turnin' into one of them pious turds or somethin'?" Rutledge asked, his laughter gone now. "Jesus, One-Eye, ain't you ever had to use a little more persuadin' some times than others to get a woman in the robes?"

"Depends on the kind of persuadin', I suppose."

"A friendly little tap or somethin'."

"Tell me straight, shit pile," Riley growled. "Did ye force that gal into the room?"

Rutledge shrugged. "Nope. She went on her own. Then she got a little reluctant. So I used some charm on her. You know, a couple of cuffs on the side of the head. What of it?"

Riley kicked Rutledge in the crotch.

Rutledge fell, his breath hissing in and out as he grabbed his injured testicles. "What . . . the . . . hell . . . was . . . that . . . all . . . about?" he gasped.

"I got a particular dislike for muskrat-humpin' shit piles like ye who got to use force to git a woman. And I cain't see no reason why I should let ye continue a life of such deviltry."

"What're ye gonna do?" Rutledge asked, half sneeringly, half in fright.

Riley grabbed the man's hair and hauled him to his feet, then shoved him toward the corral. When Rutledge balked, Riley said harshly, "Walk, shit pile, or I'll drag ye."

Rutledge shuffled ahead, pain racking his groin.

Riley opened the wide corral gate and shoved Rutledge through. Rutledge stopped and looked at him. "Hold up, One-Eye," he said, "you've had your fun. Jesus, ye busted my nuts. I git the idear. I won't go tryin' to screw any of them Mormon gals again. Now let me get on out of here and git home so's I can pray that my nuts'll work again."

Riley pulled his knife—one that he had made himself —and stepped toward Rutledge, who was still in too much pain to run. The blacksmith slashed Rutledge's abdomen from side to side, deep enough for his guts to start spilling out. Then he shoved the mountain man, who staggered back a few steps and fell into a large mound of horse manure.

Rutledge clutched his innards and looked with shocked eyes at Riley. The blacksmith calmly pulled out a bandanna and wiped the blood off the knife. He turned and walked out of the corral.

"Adios," he said, "shit pile."

Riley strolled back into the fort and wandered around until he spotted Rockwell. He walked up to the broad-shouldered Saint, who looked at him warily. "Ye needn't worry about Rutledge lustin' after none of your women again."

It took only an eye blink before Rockwell caught on. "You should've let me finish him off in the first place," he said angrily.

"Don't ye believe in justice?" Riley asked.

"Of course, but . . ."

"That gal didn't look all that virginal, and she could've been puttin' on them tears to make it look like she was innocent. Ain't no reason for ye to jist go and kill a man before ye git the facts."

Rockwell nodded. He hated to agree with Riley, but the blacksmith was right.

As Riley headed toward the whiskey barrel, McGinnis strode up alongside him. "Ye left Praises the Sky?" Riley asked in mock surprise.

McGinnis grinned. "I tell ye, One-Eye, there's times when I almost wish some fool'd come along and take that willful woman off me hands." Then he grew serious. "Ye done the right thing, One-Eye," he said quietly.

"Right what thing?"

"I wanted to see what ye were going to do with Rutledge," the young Irishman said without shame, "so I followed ye. I heard the chat ye two had. When ye started again toward the corral, I went into the shop and poked my head out the back door. I saw what ye did, and I think ye done right."

Riley nodded. "Thankee, fellow mick."

McGinnis grinned. "I best be gettin' back to Praises the Sky, though. There's no tellin' what that woman'll do if I ain't around."

Relations with the Mormons did not improve, not even after what Riley had done. Still, the blacksmith found he disliked the Saints just a little bit less. They were not the only ones who could cause trouble for others, as Rutledge had amply shown. And Riley had heard no protests about the marriage of Sarah Lockwood and Jim Bridger. He had thought that Brigham Young especially would have had something to say about that, but he had kept quiet, at least in public.

Riley tried to put all the potential troubles he could see out of his mind. He had more success at some times than at others. Work helped, and soon after the celebration, more and more wagon trains began arriving. He was astounded at the number of Mormons. There were more than last year, and there had been plenty of them then. He wondered where they would all go. He knew the Salt Lake Valley, and he was certain there wasn't room for all of them.

Not that he cared much. All these emigrants, Mormon or not, were good for business. He had no objection to that. He'd do business—honest business—with anyone.

Quite a few Saints were heading east, too, not because they were beaten and slinking home, as Riley had first suspected, but to help even more Mormon emigrants prepare for the journey to Salt Lake City. These people, and non-Mormons who had passed through the Salt Lake Valley, brought tales of a growing, vibrant city on the slash of land between the high ridge of stark mountains on the east and the huge body of salt water on the west. The land, these travelers said, was becoming fertile through the Saints' hard work, and crops grew in what had been a desolate hunk of land that even the Indians had not wanted much to do with.

Riley was amazed, and when the flood of wagon trains dwindled to a trickle as summer wore down, he felt he had to go see for himself. Leaving the women at the fort under the watchful eyes of Bridger and a few of the other men, Riley and McGinnis made the trip to Salt Lake City in only three days. Along the way they passed two mail carriers and one stagecoach filled with passengers.

Much to Riley's dismay, he and McGinnis found that the tales were true. They could see the Salt Lake Valley blooming with life almost as soon as they had ridden through Emigration Canyon. Between that and the knowledge that the Mormons had contracted to carry the mail between Salt Lake City and the States as well as to run a stage line along the same route, Riley was somewhat worried. Also troublesome was the fact that the Saints were opening their own trading stores in and around the city, plus other shops that could serve emigrants as well as, if not better than, the fort could.

Safe and secure in their numbers, and in their distance from the mainstream, the Saints had seemed a lot more friendly toward outsiders while the two blacksmiths were there. Riley was glad Porter Rockwell hadn't been around, though. He certainly would have crowed about having been right in his predictions for the valley. That would have galled Riley to no end.

So it was with some concern that Riley headed back to the fort.

McGinnis knew something was bothering Riley, but he didn't know what. Riley had, uncharacteristically, been rather close-mouthed since the two men had arrived in Salt Lake City, and he showed little signs of opening up any when they left there. On the second day out, McGinnis, a talkative young man, had had enough of the silence. Seeing as how he was a hardheaded Irishman like his big friend, he made a point of saying something about it.

Riley just grunted, then mumbled, "I got things on my mind, boy."

"Like hell, One-Eye," McGinnis scoffed. "Some kind of bug's gone and crawled up your ass pipe and ye ain't gonna be right till ye shit it on out again."

"Ye certainly got a way with words, boy," Riley said in annoyance. He shut up again, but cursed himself silently. There was no reason for him to take out his concerns on his young friend. The guilt nearly opened him up, but he had a bit yet. All he did say was, "It's time for us to be settlin' in for the night, boy."

They rode on a little way, the high Wasatch Mountain air already chilly. Riley found them a meadow along a bubbling stream. It had been used plenty, but it was still a good spot. There was sufficient wood, water and grass.

While McGinnis began the camp chores—unloading their pack mule, unsaddling his horse, caring for the two animals, gathering fuel and building a fire—Riley went off hunting. Since the area abounded with game, he was back quickly, a small deer carcass over his saddle.

McGinnis was still busy, so Riley unsaddled and tended his horse, then skinned and butchered the deer. Finally meat was cooking and coffee heating.

McGinnis chafed as the two men ate silently. He wanted to talk, wanted to know what was bothering Riley, but he was reluctant to ask again after having been rebuffed. Not that he was really afraid that Riley would do something; it was just that he could see no reason for angering his friend for no good reason. He ate and said nothing.

When he was done, Riley pulled out his pipe and got it going. "I'm worried about them Mormons, boy," he said softly, with no preliminaries.

"Ye can't be that much against 'em, can ye?" McGinnis asked, a little surprised. "They're just folks is all. Sure, they have some different ways about 'em. Well, strange to us. But so do the Shoshonis. Ye don't have no trouble with their ways.''

Riley thought that over, and pondered his answer. McGinnis was right, of course, and he knew it. It wasn't even as if he hated the Saints really. He didn't like them much, mainly because to him they seemed so unfriendly, even hostile. While he figured they had some good reason for such, it didn't seem to him that they should turn down friendship when it was offered. He wasn't fond of their predilection for proselytizing, either, but that was more of an annoyance than a reason to dislike those people.

Something about it all went deeper, and that was why Riley was so sullen. "I can't put my finger on it, Paddy," he finally said, slowly, still cogitating as he spoke, "but I know them Mormon's gonna be trouble for all of us out by the Seeds-Kee-Dee.''

"How? They keep to themselves, not wantin' to mix with the likes of us.''

"I don't know, boy. I jist know it's true. I've noticed that they're a mite more fond of money than most folks in general,'' he continued after a bit.

"No harm in that,'' McGinnis said with a grin. "I'm kind of fond of money meself.''

"So'm I, boy. So'm I.'' Riley sighed. "I dunno, but with the stage contract and the mail contract, they seem to be makin' a push for . . . what, I ain't sure. But I wager ye that as soon as a couple thousand more Mormons git to Salt Lake City, Brigham Young's gonna be looking to make the area a territory so he can keep control over it.''

"Ye're a wee bit touched, One-Eye,'' McGinnis said. "Ye've gone and let yer dislike of those folks overcome yer sense and ye've conjured up a mirage.''

"Mayhap, boy, mayhap. What really bothers me, though, is the number of stores and workshops they've got goin' there already.''

"They're a hardworkin' people, One-Eye. No wrong in that.''

"No, no there sure ain't. But think on this, boy. With all them places open and bein' only a bit more'n a hundred miles from the fort, do ye think Mormon emigrants're gonna stop at our place for their services? When the same things're available from their own kind only four, mayhap five days on? And when that's where they're goin' anyway?"

McGinnis's eyes widened. "I ne'er thought of that," he said quietly. "But now that ye speak of it, it does make a heap of sense. That could hurt us somethin' awful."

"Damn right it could. And once that happens, how long do ye think it'll be before they start turnin' their eyes to the ferries on the Seeds-Kee-Dee?"

"That's gettin' kind of far removed from Salt Lake City, ain't it?" McGinnis said, but Riley's comments had gotten him to pondering already, and he was no longer sure.

"I overheard one of the ferrymen tellin' some Mormon at Bridger's fandango how much money those boys pulled in last year. That Mormon was powerful interested, I can tell ye. They don't like payin' the old mountain boys for the ferryin', 'specially with so many of 'em emigratin', and if they was to git control of the ferries, they could fleece the Gentiles, as they like to call us, whilst givin' their feller Mormons a good deal."

McGinnis could think of no response to that, so he kept quiet. He did begin to worry some, though. The concern stayed with him for a while, but he was too young and too happy-go-lucky to allow it to rule his life, and it soon faded.

Riley mentioned his concerns to Bridger and Vasquez when he returned to the fort. Neither was impressed, or worried.

"Hell, One-Eye," Bridger said, "we been here more'n ten goddamn years. We've faced hard winters, raids by the goddamn Sioux and Blackfoot, drought, starvin' times and every other kind of poor doin's you can think of, and we ain't been run out yet. I don't expect no herd of sermon-spoutin' folks is gonna do us in.''

"You worry too much, Pedro," Vasquez said in condescension. "It's why you'll never have a good head for business. You see dangers and threats where there are none."

"I'll remember ye said that, Louie, when . . ." He stopped, knowing his words would have no effect on Vasquez. He turned his attention to Bridger. "You've known me a long time, Jim. And ye know I don't make such things up. I can't prove none of this, of course, and I don't really figure you're gonna take my word as gospel. I jist wanted to let ye know my thoughts on the matter, so's ye can be on guard."

"I ain't been caught unawares on anything yet, hoss," Bridger said with a grin. It wasn't entirely the truth, but it was more true than not. "I'll keep my nose in the wind."

Riley nodded and left. He was beginning to think that maybe he was overreacting, and he didn't want to press the point. Nor did it seem as if the Saints were going to do anything imminently, even if they were planning something. It was not his concern, he decided. Besides, he and McGinnis still had plenty to do in getting a head start on the following year's emigrant season. And as winter nosed into the high country not long after, the two blacksmiths said their farewells, packed up their families and moved on toward Black Iron's village, where they would spend the winter.

Praises the Sky was pregnant, though she was not showing much yet. That had served to tame her wild streak a little bit, which was a relief to her husband. She seemed to be settling down, becoming more accustomed to married life and what was expected of a wife.

Sometime in the midst of the winter—which rivaled the one two years before in accursedness—Praises the Sky gave birth. She and McGinnis called their new daughter Winter Sings.

⇥{ 21 }⇤

It took only a day or so for the small group to get reacclimated to life outside the fort. There was still plenty of snow on the ground, especially along Cache Creek and Yellow Creek, but that didn't bother anyone. Neither did the still-frigid nights.

As soon as their lodges were up and their camps set, Riley and McGinnis set about opening their shop and preparing for the emigrants to come. First they stopped by Vasquez's office—since he managed the trading post, it was considered his office, not Bridger's.

The Spaniard was not very happy to see the two; without them around, the fort was a much more peaceful place. "You're back," he said disinterestedly.

"I'm overwhelmed by your joy," Riley said sarcastically.

"You want something here—besides a jolly greeting? If that's all you want, you better leave now, because you're not about to get it."

"Your warmth is touchin'," Riley said dryly. "There any mail or such for me or Paddy?"

"There's something for your associate. None for you."

"Well?" McGinnis asked. "Where's me mail, ye festerin' pile of dog meat?" He had been at the fort long enough to be tired of Vasquez's pomposity.

"It's around somewhere. I'll have to dig it up. But I'm busy right now. I'll get to it when I have time."

"Ye'll do it now, friend," McGinnis said harshly. "Or I'll kick your ass around the tradin' post."

"If you insist," Vasquez said wearily. He was not afraid of McGinnis, but he did not want to cause unnecessary trouble either. As he stood and began looking through piles of papers, books and other paraphernalia, he wondered just what it was about Riley and McGinnis that drove him to distraction. He was generally an outgoing, ebullient man, friendly with any and all. But One-Eye Riley had grated on his nerves from the first time they met. Their relationship had only grown worse over the years. It angered and frustrated Vasquez that he could be so without reason when he dealt with Riley.

Now he felt the same way about McGinnis. He wondered if it was just McGinnis's friendship with Riley that made him dislike the young man; that perhaps McGinnis had become somehow tainted by the relationship. It couldn't be that both men were Irish—he had many a friend who was, like Tom Fitzpatrick, and he had no trouble with them.

He sighed, thinking that he would never figure it out. And maybe, he conceded, that would be for the best. He found the two letters, turned and gave them to McGinnis. "They came in from Oregon a few months ago. Not long after you left for Black Iron's," he said, trying to be cordial.

"Thankee, Louie," McGinnis said with an ingratiating tone.

"You two need anything else?" Vasquez asked tightly.

"There any news?" Riley asked, ignoring Vasquez's irritation.

"None that'd concern the likes of you, Riley."

Riley shrugged, masking his own irritation. "You'd probably fuck up the tellin' of it anyhow," he said. He turned and walked out, McGinnis beside him. The two stopped, and Riley took off his hat, allowing the biting wind to riffle his long, wavy hair. "There's somethin' goin' on here, boy," Riley said. "I jist know there is. And Vasquez ain't tellin' us jist to git our goats."

"Somebody'll know," McGinnis said. "One of the other workers."

Riley nodded. "Let's go see if ol' Jack Robinson's around.

It didn't take long to find the one-time mountain man. He was about Bridger's age or so, and a strong-looking man. His hair was as long as Riley's, but it was graying rapidly. His beard was white.

"Ho, Jack, how's doin's?" Riley asked as he and McGinnis knelt on the ground outside Robinson's lodge.

"Middlin'. How's about ye two boys?"

"I been better," Riley allowed. He grinned. "But I been a heap worse, too."

"Fine, Jack," McGinnis said quietly.

"What brings ye two to my lodge?" Robinson was making lead rifle balls, and his hands never ceased their work even while he was talking. He kept a pipe clenched in his teeth.

"We jist got back from Black Iron's village. I sense there's some news about, but Vasquez won't say anything. Ye know how it is 'tween him and me."

Robinson nodded. "Ye boys ought to bury the hatchet," he said. "It'd make life around here a hell of a lot more peaceful."

"Talk to him."

"Shoot," Robinson said with a grin. "Well, fust thing I'll say is that them Mormon folks has declared theyselves a state—and it includes the Green River Valley here."

"The whole valley?" Riley asked in surprise.

"Yep. All the way to the Seeds-Kee-Dee itself. They call it Deseret—Land of the Honeybees."

"I told ye those shit piles coveted this valley, Paddy," Riley said almost self-righteously. "Damn."

"I wouldn't worry none too much about it, One-Eye," Robinson said. "Jist 'cause they say it's so don't make it so. I don't figure the Americans're gonna take too kindly to sich an idear. Not when them Mormons don't plan on joinin' the Union anytime soon, or so I hear it." He paused a moment. " 'Course, it won't bode well fer none of us boys if they press the point."

"What's Ol' Jim got to say about all this?" Riley asked.

"Cain't rightly say. Ain't seed him much."

"Ain't he stayin' with that wife and kid of his?"

"Kids. She calved about two months ago. But he weren't around for it. Ain't nobody come out and say it, but ever'body figgers she was a naggin' ol' witch. Been pesterin' him somethin' awful to join that accursed church of hers. Goddamn fool should have knowed sich a union weren't gonna work."

"So what happened?" McGinnis asked impatiently.

"Hell, he packed up, left that cursed female and the fust boy here and rode on off somewhere. Ain't nobody knows where. Ye know that ol' hoss. He showed up again mayhap a week ago. Stayed a day—no, two—some of it in his place in the post. Waugh! There was screechin' comin' from that lodge, I can tell ye boys that." Robinson gave out a hoarse laugh around the pipe. "Goddamn, ye would've thunk a passel of Sioux and Shoshoni was in there havin' a right wild go at each other."

Riley couldn't help but laugh. Bridger was such a hardheaded man, so taciturn, contentious and wild that the thought of him having a set-to with the pale, frail Sarah Lockwood Bridger was ludicrous. And the way Robinson told it, it sounded as if his wife had gotten the better of the old mountaineer.

"Then what?" Riley asked, still smiling.

"Well, after all that fussin' and feudin' for two days, next thing we all know, Ol' Jim was ridin' out again, but this time he had that woman and both boys—the new one was a male chil', too—with him. He nary said where they was goin' but from some of them shoutin' matches, and the fact he went near due west, we figger he's gone to take that woman back to her people."

"Damn," Riley breathed. "but them doin's would've

been somethin' to have been around for.'' He paused, grinning again. "I'd plumb like to be there in Salt Lake City when he unloads his wife. I'd wager there's gonna be a heap of pissed Mormons out there.''

"I reckon," Robinson said. He wasn't concerned, since angry Mormons in Salt Lake City had no bearing on his life, he figured.

"Any other news for us, hoss?" Riley asked. "Not that I can recall.''

Riley nodded, and he and McGinnis rose. As they turned to leave, Riley said, "Why don't ye go on in your lodge and read them letters of yours in quiet, Paddy. I'll be over to the shop.''

As Riley walked toward the fort, he wondered why there were only five lodges, including his and McGinnis's. He spotted Lloyd Black, who traded livestock for Bridger and Vasquez. As he fell into step alongside Black, he asked about the dearth of tipis.

"Ain't ye heard?" Black countered. His voice sounded like frozen bones cracking in the cold. "Vasquez went and fired six of the boys. Hired three Mormons to replace 'em.''

"Three to replace six?" Riley asked in surprise.

"You know how them Saints like to work. They ain't shirkers like some of those boys we had on last year.''

"You sound like ye admire 'em.''

"Who? The Saints?" Black shrugged. "Can't say as I admire their beliefs much, but they're a hardworkin', honorable people in all.''

Riley thought Black was touched, but he kept his mouth shut. He was beginning to think that he might be the only one to have a problem with the Mormons. He figured he might have to take another look at his feelings toward them. "Where're they gonna stay?"

"That empty cabin down at the other end of where your shop is.''

"Well," Riley said, stopping in front of his workshop, "I hope Louie knows what he's doin'." He sure doubted it, though. He shoved the door open, not really looking forward to cleaning up and getting ready for a new season of emigrants after a long, hard winter, but wanting to be by himself for a while.

Bridger finally rode in about a week later, with a very pregnant Ute in tow. "Goddamn, Jim, ye didn't waste no time, did ye?" Riley joshed when he spotted his long-time friend.

Bridger scowled but then grinned. "I had to do *somethin'* over the winter," he noted.

"Ye leave Sarah with her people?"

"Hell, yes," Bridger said with a look of distaste. "Damn but I couldn't take that woman's sermonizin' no more. I think her mam and pap put her up to most of it. Lord a'mighty, but I ain't ary seen a people for tryin' to convert folks like them pontificatin' people."

"Ye expect ye leavin' Sarah off there is gonna cause any trouble, Mister Bridger?" McGinnis asked.

"Knowin' ol' skunk-humpin' Brigham Young like I do, I figure he'll use this to his advantage somehow. He ain't ary took to me, ya know."

"Nor any of us ol' mountain boys," Riley tagged on. When Bridger had nodded agreement, Riley looked him in the eye. "Ye think there might be another reason for Sarah tryin' so hard to bring ye into her church?" he asked.

"Like what?" Bridger asked, puzzled.

"Like mayhap if ye was a member of their tribe, they might find it easier to expand their holdin's into the Green River Valley here?"

Bridger's eyebrows arched, but he said nothing for a bit. He dismounted and handed the reins of his horse to the woman. "Take the animals back into the corral and tend 'em good," he said to her. He watched her ride back out the gate, but he was thinking all the while.

Finally Bridger turned back to face Riley. "Your mam raised herself one goddamn suspicious critter for a son," he said. "I ain't ary thought of that, but I'd wager my last piece of Mexican gold that it's true. Now I know at least one reason me and goddamn Young nary got along. He saw me as somethin' in his way, I suspect. Well that baby-faced ol' bastard's got him a hard row to hoe if he thinks he's gonna get this here valley from me. I'll fight that cunnin' dog ever' step of the way and that's a fact.

"Well," he said with a sigh, "I best go git Mary settled in. She's gonna . . ."

"Mary?" Riley asked.

"Well, I ain't gonna call her by her real name, since I cain't even pronounce it, and the translation's dumber'n hell. So she's Mary to me." He squinted in mock fierceness. "And to everybody else, hoss."

"Suits me," Riley said with a grin.

"And me," McGinnis added.

The men at the fort were not prepared for the deluge of travelers, even though they had gotten the news in the spring that gold had been discovered the year before at Sutter's Mill in California. They figured they might see an increase in emigrants, but nothing like the mad rush that came. The gold-hungry travelers arrived on foot, in carts, in wagons, with wagon trains, on horseback, riding mules. And each one seemed to have some need to fill at the Bridger and Vasquez trading post, which was on the easiest trail to California.

There seemed to be as many Mormon emigrants as the year before, too, and between the Mormons, the gold hunters and the regular emigrants, Riley's fears of the Saints draining away the fort's business seemed to fade. Besides, he and McGinnis were too busy to think of such things.

One of those arriving with a Mormon wagon train was a hard-eyed man who reminded Riley of Porter Rockwell, which left Riley instantly disliking the Saint. "Ye know who that critter is, Jim?" he asked Bridger, pointing.

"Name's Bill Hickman. He's one of Young's closest men. A guard for him or something."

"I thought Rockwell was Young's guard."

"Reckon they both are, hoss," Bridger said. "The way I hear it, there ain't no love lost 'tween the two of 'em.

But that don't mean they're to be trifled with where the church is concerned, boy. Both of 'em're zealots, jist like the rest of them Mormons. And while neither of them scare me none, I'd hate to have either one of 'em on my ass. I'd stay away from him was I ye."

"I got no thoughts of bein' friendly to him or any other Mormon," Riley said.

"Somethin' else maybe ye ought to know, One-Eye," Bridger said thoughtfully. "The Saints've got themselves a group called the Danites. They're actin' sort of as a Mormon police force. There's also talk that they might be used as a Mormon army."

"That doesn't sound good," Riley said dryly.

"Nope, hoss, it sure don't. It does lend credence to your concerns that the Mormons're eyein' this here valley."

"Damn." Riley felt no sense of pride or smugness because his worries seemed to be coming true. It was too serious a situation, and could very easily turn deadly if such a thing came to pass.

"Well, I wouldn't worry too much about it, One-Eye," Bridger said. "I think it's gonna take a while for Young to pull anything, if he even plans to."

"Don't seem like he's gonna wait forever, Jim. Lest ye forget, he's claimed this whole area for that damn state he decided to create for himself."

"Oh, yeah, I meant to tell ye about that," Bridger said. "We been so goddamn busy 'round here that I plumb forgot. Word is, he's askin' to have Deseret made a state of the Union."

"Ye think the federal gov'mint in Washington is gonna allow that?" Riley asked.

"Doubt it. I ain't privy to nothin' that goes on back in that goddamn place, but from what I been hearin', Young ain't got a prayer of Deseret becomin' a state. Not so long as they keep the Principle."

"I expect you're right." Riley paused. "Still, we best keep a close watch on them Mormons."

"I aim to. I got eyes and ears all over this country,

boy, ye know that. If they're plannin' somethin' I'll hear about it.''

The gold seekers kept coming and coming, until Riley and everyone else thought there would never be an end to it.

Vasquez, who had fired many of the fort workers in order to hire on a few Saints, had to reverse himself and find more workers in a hurry. He didn't like the idea, because it cost him more, but he got over that quickly enough when he saw how much extra money was being brought in.

Bridger twice rode to Fort Laramie to scrounge up more supplies for his own trading post, and Vasquez made a trip to Salt Lake City to buy supplies from the Mormons. That upset the Spaniard, too, since Young made sure his people charged the Gentiles as high a price as they could get.

In addition to the overwhelming influx of emigrants, there was a small but steady flow of people heading east. Most of them were Saints, but not all. The Saints heading east rarely stopped at Bridger's fort, since they had come only from Salt Lake City, but those returning from California—many of them already realizing that there was more money to be made selling goods to miners than in prospecting—were going for supplies to open stores back in the gold fields.

It was a hectic, crazy time, especially as summer wore on. The grass within a mile of the fort soon began to disappear, meaning wagon trains had to camp farther and farther from the trading post to find good grass and water. That brought arguments as wagon masters jockeyed for the best positions. And with this many people, fistfights and other altercations were inevitable. Most were minor and ended with a couple of men with bloody or broken noses and some bruises. A few turned deadly, however, before wagon captains or the fort's owners could intercede. In such cases, the bodies were generally buried in the fort's fast-growing cemetery, a trial was convened and justice dispensed. In those cases, the murderer frequently found his final resting place next to his victim, usually to the chagrin of both families.

Even worse were the increasingly frequent Indian raids. The Sioux, Cheyenne and Arapaho all seemed to be on the prod more this year than they had been in a while. Riley, Bridger and Vasquez figured it was because of the huge increase in emigrants crossing their land. Whatever the reason, it was troublesome. The men at the fort warned wagon captains as soon as they arrived that they should be vigilant because of the Indian trouble. Most took the advice to heart. A few did not, and their people suffered for it.

When they learned of an attack on a wagon camp, Bridger or Vasquez would hastily form a party and race out there, trying to run the Indians off and perhaps gain a little revenge in the process. They were usually too late to be of any good.

Friendly Indians—Shoshonis and Utes mostly—still came to the shabby fort to trade. That often caused consternation among the emigrants. When the Indians were approaching the fort and came across camps, the settlers would fly into an uproar and be ready to attack. Most did not, though on occasion some men in the camps took potshots at the Indians. Generally, though, they had sense enough and had heard enough about Indian raids that they did not want to precipitate an attack on themselves, so they stood ready, but did little.

By the time Independence Day loomed, the men at the fort were exhausted and in need of a fandango. For the holiday, Bridger and Vasquez ordered that the trade room and the shops be closed, and the fort gates opened to all who wanted to come. A large American flag—its thirty stars gleaming brightly in the hot sun—beckoned several hundred people. There was not nearly enough room for them all in the courtyard, so they spilled outside the fort enclosure, up and down Black's Fork and into the fort workers' lodge village.

Since their shop was closed, Riley and McGinnis stayed in the village. There was too much of a crowd for their tastes. They also wanted to prevent the possibility of some fool trying to bother their women and children, or walking right into the lodges. There were far too many whites who saw an Indian tipi and figured it was open to anyone who was nosy.

The two blacksmiths sat outside Riley's lodge just watching the world go round. Their women had rolled up the bottoms of the tipis to let the breeze in, and they sat inside working. The children played in and around all the lodges, heedless of the white people who milled about watching, some with interest and curiosity, others with hate and disgust in their eyes.

Gunfire popped from the fort and most of the camps with some regularity during the sweltering day, and an occasional cannon shot echoed off the mountains. Many of the old mountain men who were in the vicinity had heard of the festivities and had shown up. Quite a few came by to talk to Riley. Others started up card games and horse races and shooting contests and wrestling matches with the emigrants. Money was won and lost. Most of the sporting was good-natured, though a few problems cropped up, as was usual when such gatherings were held.

"Goddamn, if this ain't like rendezvous," Riley said at one point. He had a wistful look in his eyes.

"Those must've been some times," McGinnis said.

"Well, the one in '37 sure as hell was, and the ol' boys like Jim and Ol' Tom Fitzpatrick tell me there were others before it was even better. The couple after '37 were pretty poor, though they still had some good times."

"Sounds like ye miss 'em, One-Eye."

Riley grinned with a touch of sadness. "Well, now, boy, I do. Yep. I purely do." He sighed. "But them days is gone forever."

"Well, at least ye had some of those days, One-Eye," McGinnis said. He was trying to cheer his friend up, but he felt somewhat sad himself at having missed such adventures.

"That's a fact. Ain't no one can take that from me." He shut up and watched as Lloyd Black ran toward him. "Wonder what's up with ol' Lloyd," he muttered.

Black stopped, puffing, in front of Riley and McGinnis and knelt. He took a moment to catch his breath. "Jim needs ya down to his cabin. Pronto. And bring your woman."

"Trouble?" Riley asked, beginning to worry a little.

Black nodded. "His woman's time has come, and somethin' ain't right. He figures your woman can help."

Riley shoved up. "Spirit Grass," he called urgently. "Grab your herb bag. Hurry."

Spirit Grass did not question the order. She just jumped up and went for the buckskin sack of herbs and roots she used in healing.

While she did that, Riley looked at McGinnis, who was on his feet, too. "Stay here, my friend," Riley said. "I'll need ye to watch over my lodge and young'ns whilst I'm gone."

McGinnis wanted to go with Riley, but he nodded. "Ye or Jim need anything, ye come get me," he said.

"I will." Neither thought there would be any call for it.

Riley and Spirit Grass sped off, surprising many of the people who were hanging around the area. At the fort, Riley used his size and ferocity to create a path through the throng for himself and his wife. One man got indignant when Riley shoved him, and pushed back. Riley stopped short and smashed the man's face with a fist. The only reason he didn't fall was because of the crush of the crowd around him.

Riley plunged on, and finally made it to Bridger's door. Seven hard-jawed mountain men had created some space in front of the cabin and were making sure no one who wasn't wanted invaded that area. Bridger nodded at Riley, who said quietly to Spirit Grass, "Go on in, woman and see what ye can do."

When she had closed the door behind her, Riley turned to Bridger. "How bad ye think it is, ol' friend?"

"Hell if I know," Bridger responded somewhat testily. "These here are women's doin's, and a man don't git involved in 'em."

"Unless there ain't no other choice," Riley muttered.

"What's that?" Bridger asked, looking askance at Riley.

"Ye never heard the story of how Arrives With Trouble was borned?"

"Nope."

Riley told him, hoping it would keep Bridger's mind off what was going on inside the cabin. He was not sure it worked, but Bridger did seem to settle down a bit.

It was more than an hour by the pocketwatch Riley wore on a chain around his neck before they heard a newborn squawking inside. Bridger looked relieved, and Riley smiled. The blacksmith was about to say something congratulatory, but for some reason he held himself in check.

Minutes later, Spirit Grass walked out of the cabin, clutching a blanket-wrapped child in her arms. She held the baby out for Bridger to see. "A daughter," she said.

Bridger only glanced at the baby, then looked at Spirit Grass. "How's Mary?" he asked softly.

Spirit Grass shook her head and looked down, not wanting to say the words.

"I'm sorry, hoss," Riley said, putting a hand gently on Bridger's big, hard shoulder.

The others who were protecting Bridger's privacy added their quiet condolences.

"I'm gonna go in and see Mary one last time, One-Eye," Bridger said. "I'd be obliged if ye was to wait here. Spirit Grass, too."

Riley nodded.

Bridger was gone only a few minutes. He didn't look

too upset when he came out, but Riley wasn't sure. Bridger could be mighty taciturn when he wanted to be.

"Ye all right, Jim?" Riley asked.

Bridger nodded. "I've had better times, for certain, but I've had some worse. Me and Mary didn't know each other too long. She was a good woman, all in all, and I'll miss her. But I cain't grieve too hard for her, since we was together so little a time." He tried to smile a little but couldn't quite pull it off. "I got the chil' to worry about now, though, and that's why I wanted ye and Spirit Grass to stay around. Your boy's still sucklin', ain't he?"

Riley nodded.

"I'll care for the chil', Mister Jim," Spirit Grass said without prompting.

"I was hopin' we could reach such an agreement, Spirit Grass," Bridger said. "But are ya sure? I don't want to put ye and your man out none."

"I got me plenty of milk," Spirit Grass said, bouncing a little. "Both full most of the time. Another one on a teat won't matter. Don't ye worry."

"That's all right with ye, One-Eye?" Bridger asked.

"Long as Spirit Grass don't mind, it's fine with me."

"It won't be too long, I hope, Spirit Grass," Bridger said quietly. "I aim to find me another woman soon's I can git away for a spell."

"I ain't worried none. I'll keep her as long as needed." She paused. "What're ye gonna call her?"

"Virginia," Bridger said without hesitation.

"Anything else we can do, ol' hoss?" Riley asked.

"Nah. You've done enough fer me already. That and takin' care of little Virginia."

"All right. Ye need anything, though, ye come see me." He smiled a little then at Spirit Grass. "Ye make sure ye got hold of that chil' good and tight, woman," he said. Then he led the way through the mob of people, nearly all of them unaware of the tragedy that moments ago had been played out in their midst.

{ 23 }

The activity at the fort continued without letup, never really giving Bridger a chance to get away. Spirit Grass didn't mind. She enjoyed having a girl baby around; had always wanted one of her own.

Riley didn't mind too much, either, though once in a while, having an extra suckling child around was annoying. There were times when he got irritated by being woken not once but two or three times; or when he was in an amorous mood and was put off because Spirit Grass had to tend one or another of the children. But all in all he had no problem with it.

Finally, though, the flood of emigrants began to slow some, and the men at the fort began to think that the end was near. Emigrants were still arriving, and there was still some traffic moving eastward, but at least they didn't have to work at a constant breakneck pace. Indeed, they even had time to stop work now and then and enjoy a bit of fresh air.

Riley was doing so one afternoon, leaning against the outside wall of the shop, puffing on a pipe, when a small group of warriors rode into the fort. That, in and of itself, was nothing unusual, but seeing the two Shoshonis named Old Elk and Wakara among them was. The two war chiefs normally didn't venture this far east, preferring to stay on the other side of the Wasatches. He wondered what they were doing here.

Riley watched as Bridger and Vasquez came out to greet them. After a few minutes, the fort's co-owners and the six warriors went over to the open-front stables at the rear of the fort. It was relatively cool there, out of the sun, and since there were no animals there right now, it made a good place to parley.

Riley wandered up and stopped, leaning against one of the rickety posts holding up the thin log roof. Since he spoke Shoshoni better than anyone at the fort except Bridger himself, he had no trouble understanding.

Old Elk did most of the talking, but the warriors and the other war chief were in full agreement with him. What he spoke about was war.

"We won't attack around here," Old Elk finally said. "You and your friends have nothing to fear from us, but you should keep away from the settlements of the . . ." He was suddenly at a loss for words.

"The Mormons?" Riley helped.

Old Elk nodded. "They're the ones. The white-eyes who don't just pass through our land, but stay and scratch at the ground, and hunt our buffalo and elk and antelope. Who bring ever more people to live in our lands."

"The Mormons're branchin' out, Jim?" Riley asked quietly.

Bridger nodded. "They been pushin' north up past Bear Lake and south as far as Spanish Fork. They cain't go west because of that salt desert out there. And they cain't come east because of us."

"Why'd ye come here, Old Elk?" Riley asked in Shoshoni. "Not just to tell us you're planning to make war on the Mormons three, four days west of here."

"No," Old Elk said with a shake of his head. "We came to trade for guns with Blanket Chief." He pointed to Bridger.

"Ye have guns," Bridger noted, pointing to the few pistols and rifles the warriors sported.

"My men need more. And powder, ball and other supplies."

"What've ye got to trade?" Bridger asked. "I'm not just going to give you those things."

"We have ponies to trade. Twelve fine ponies."

"They belong to whites?" Bridger asked.

"Does it matter?" Old Elk countered.

"Not to me," Bridger said with a shrug. "I was just wondering." He paused. "Where are these ponies?"

"Cache Creek. Not far."

Bridger nodded. "Have one of your men go get those horses, Old Elk. When they get back here, take them straight into the corral."

Old Elk spoke to one of his men, who rose, hopped on his pony and galloped out of the fort.

"One-Eye, go and tell Lloyd what's gone on. Tell him to look those damn ponies over good, then let me know what they're worth."

Riley nodded and went through the shop toward the corral.

"What's goin' on out there, One-Eye?" McGinnis asked.

Riley stopped and explained.

"That's good," McGinnis said. "Ain't' it?"

"I reckon so. As long as they keep the ruction-makin' out west of here." He went outside, spoke to Lloyd Black, and then headed back to where Bridger was still sitting, talking with Old Elk and the other Shoshonis.

Within twenty minutes, they heard a rumble of horses' hooves and watched as several Shoshonis drove horses into the corral. It was another thirty minutes before Black and the Shoshonis strolled up. The Indians sat, comfortably cross-legged. Black squatted next to Bridger and spoke quietly to him.

Bridger nodded. "One-Eye, go git Louis fer me."

Riley went and did so, then headed back to the shop. He didn't figure there'd be much of interest in watching Bridger and Old Elk haggle over how much the horses were worth, and then the dispensing of the goods. He did come out of the shop when he heard the Indians leaving, and watched as they trotted away.

As soon as the Shoshonis left, Bridger sent someone for Riley. When the blacksmith entered the fort office, Bridger and Vasquez were there.

"I got a job fer ye, One-Eye. But there's somethin' else got to be done first. Louis, I want ye to take a letter down fer me." He waited impatiently as Vasquez got out some paper, made sure the nib on his pen was sharp and swiftly mixed up some fresh ink in a pewter well. Then Bridger began dictating.

Finally Vasquez blotted the paper, sealed the letter and handed it to Bridger, who in turn gave it to Riley.

"I want ye to ride to Salt Lake City and give this to Young," Bridger said. "Nobody else."

Riley grinned. "Be happy to," Riley said. Knowing what was in the letter made this task something of a pleasure.

He rode out first thing the next morning, leaving Spirit Grass and the children in McGinnis's care. He was dressed for the trail in old, serviceable buckskin pants, bullhide moccasins, a calico shirt and a floppy, battered felt hat. He carried his two Colt Paterson revolvers in his belt as well as his ever-present knife. His old Hawken percussion rifle was in a loop on the front of his saddle, just behind the horn.

Riding alone, and without wanting to waste time, he made the trip in three days, pulling into the city just before dark. It took him a while before he found out where Young's office was, not even certain that he would find the Mormon leader there at this time. He figured that was the place to start.

He entered a stone building and spotted Rockwell standing in front of an office door. He assumed it was Young's. He walked there, under Rockwell's watchful eyes.

"What do you want here, Riley?" Rockwell growled, his imposing bulk blocking the door.

"Got a letter for your big chief."

"From who?" Rockwell countered, ignoring the jibe.

"That ain't none of your goddamn business," Riley said evenly.

"It is if it concerns Brother Young," Rockwell said flatly.

Riley thought to argue about it, but decided there was no point to it. He had wanted to bring this letter to see Young's reaction. The only way he was going to do that was to get into the office, and that meant playing Rockwell's game. At least to a point. "It's from Bridger."

"Hand it over. I'll see that Brother Young gets it."

"In a pig's eye, shit pile. Ol' Jim asked me to be certain it got into Young's hands, not yours."

Rockwell glowered, then said, "My hands are Brother Young's hands."

"Regardless, shit pile, I ain't givin' this letter to no one but Young himself."

Rockwell thought it over for a few moments, then said in a tight voice, "Stay here or I'll kill you."

"Ooh, I'm scared now," Riley said sarcastically. Then his face hardened. "Don't try that buffler shit with me. I know you're a hard man. Well, so am I, and there's no reason fer us two to stand here growlin' at each other—unless ye want to have a real set-to."

Rockwell nodded once, turned and entered the office. Waiting outside, Riley could hear their voices, though he could not understand what was said. Some seconds later, Rockwell came out and told him to go inside. He did and handed Young the letter. "I'll wait a bit," he said, "in case you're of a mind to answer."

Young scowled but then sat at an old desk and opened the letter. "You know what it says?" he asked when he had finished reading it.

"Mostly."

"This is distressing," Young said. He stood and paced. "I had hoped Mister Bridger and his cohorts would control the Indians."

"No Indians I know of are controlled by whites," Riley said.

"Is there nothing your Mister Bridger can do to head off this war led by Old Elk and Walker?"

"His name's Wakara. And, no, there's nothin' we can do. Besides, Mister Bridger don't think they'll attack over in the Green River Valley."

"Oh?" Young asked, eyes wide. "Is Mister Bridger able to control the Indians in this vicinity, but not elsewhere?" he asked suspiciously.

"Nope. It's jist that Wakara and Old Elk make their homes closer to the city here than to the Black's Fork area. The reason Jim sent this letter—and made sure it got into your hands—was to give you warnin' of somethin' we heard that's likely to affect ye." Riley tried to keep the smugness out of his voice.

"How was it that you heard of this impending war?" Young asked suspiciously.

"The Shoshonis come to the fort all the time to trade. A couple of 'em we know did so a few days ago. They'd been visitin' with some of the bands allied with Wakara. They told us that talk in the villages there was of makin' war on ye and the rest of the Saints," Riley lied smoothly. "As soon as we heard, Ol' Jim got this letter up and sent me here with it." He couldn't believe Young was swallowing the lies with such ease.

"Seems a strange thing for Mister Bridger to do," Young noted. "Or for you. We've all had some problems in getting along."

Riley shrugged. "I cain't say as I'm fond of the Saints, considerin' that all my efforts at friendliness were so rudely spurned by ye. I don't know that Jim has a problem with ye, though. He ain't spoke of it. He said he thought it'd be the neighborly thing to warn ye so ye can prepare. I'm jist a messenger. Jim asked me to deliver that letter, and bring back any reply you might want to make. Since I'm in his employ, I do what he says."

"Commendable," Young said, glaring at Riley. "But I thought he was illiterate." Young made it into a question. "So Sarah had led us to believe."

"He is. His partner, Mister Vasquez, wrote as Jim dictated."

"I see," Young said. "Well, maybe they won't be able to find supplies," he said hopefully. Riley tried to suppress a grin. "None of the Saints'll supply them," Young added with absolute certainty. "Mister Bridger wouldn't do such a thing, now, would he?"

"Not that I know of," Riley lied without missing a beat.

Young nodded distractedly. He paced a little more and then said, "I don't see that a response to this is warranted. Just tell Mister Bridger that I appreciate his concern and his warnin'. It'll be taken into account, and our people'll be ready when—if—the Indians attack." He paused, then added, "Oh, and you might tell him that Sarah is doing well, and that both his sons're fine. She has remarried, and James and John now have a father—one who will take care of them." The last was said rather disdainfully.

"I'll tell him. Ye mind if I stay the night in the city?"

"No. Not at all. There are several fine places to stay. Enjoy yourself."

"Son of a bitch never batted an eye when he read the letter and I gave him a pack of lies," Riley said. "Believed everything I tol' him."

Bridger nodded. "It's a good thing, I suppose."

"You suppose?"

"I jist don't trust that ol' bastard no more—if I ever did. He's a slick critter, that one. I wouldn't put it past him to stand there as straight-faced as you was and let you believe he believed."

"I reckon he could've," Riley said thoughtfully. "Well, even if he did, he's got some things to think about for a spell. Especially if Old Elk and Wakara—Young called him Walker, if ye can believe that—actually raid a few Mormon settlements."

"I expect they will. And before long. Whether they continue to do so after the winter, who knows." Bridger sat there, chewing on a sliver of wood. "Ye think Spirit Grass'd mind keepin' little Virginia a bit longer?" he finally asked.

Riley laughed a little. "As it is now, you're gonna have your hands full tryin' to git that chil' back, ol' hoss. Spirit Grass's becomin' right attached to her."

"That gonna be a problem?" Bridger asked, almost horrified.

"Nah," Riley said, "not really. Spirit Grass'll miss her, but she won't try'n keep someone's chil'. I don't expect she'll mind havin' that babe around for a bit longer. Why? Ye aimin' to fetch yourself a new wife?"

"Eventually," Bridger said with a sigh. "But I got to make a run to the States. We need some supplies soon, if I can git any back here, and I got to make arrangements for next year. That'll take a spell. Then I hope to find me a woman—with luck before winter sets in."

"We'll make do." He chewed his lip. "That mean ye want me and Spirit Grass to stay here for the winter?"

"You plannin' to go to Black Iron's?"

"I was. But I can stick things out here, if that's your desire."

Bridger thought that over for a while. "Ye mind makin' it a short stay? Let's say, till around Christmas?"

"Reckon that'll be all right. Ye expect to be back by then?"

Bridger nodded.

Bridger didn't get back until just days after the new year had turned, and when he did, he had himself a fetching Shoshoni woman along. "This here's Elizabeth," he announced before shepherding the woman into his cabin.

The next day, he came to Riley's lodge with Elizabeth. After the formalities, he said, seemingly uncomfortably, "I come to git my little Virginia back, One-Eye."

Riley nodded. Out of the corner of his only eye he could see a sudden painful look come over Spirit Grass's face.

"And I am obliged for ye to have looked after her all

this time. To show my thanks, I've brung you a few things. For ye and Spirit Grass.'' He set four big revolvers on a blanket in front of Riley. "These here're new, ol' hoss," he said. "Some feller down in Texas come up with the idear and took it to Mister Colt. They're called Colt Walkers. They're .44-caliber and ought to have a heap more punch than them small Colt Patersons of yours.''

Riley picked one up and hefted it. "Heavy," he commented. He checked the weapon over, breaking it down and putting it back together. "These shine, ol' friend,'' he said solemnly. "Damn if they don't. But why four?''

"Ye know how hard these revolvers are to reload, especially whilst you're ridin' hard. This way ye got two for in your belt, and two for saddle holsters. It'll be a week afore ye have to reload.''

Riley grinned. "I'll be a heap big warrior now,'' he crowed, laughing.

While Riley was looking at the guns, Spirit Grass had handed the baby to Elizabeth and then sat next to her husband. She was very sad at having to give up the girl, but she was pregnant again, and she hoped that maybe she would have her own daughter this time. She also was filled with anticipation, since she was certain that Bridger had brought her gifts, too.

Bridger knew she knew and he cracked a smile at her. "And for ye, Spirit Grass, fer bein' such a help durin' my tryin' times, I've brung ye these things.'' He set out a tortoise shell comb, a bottle of perfume, several bracelets of good silver and a fancy-back mirror.

Spirit Grass squealed with delight and she touched each item, then tested it. She splashed on far too much perfume, but she didn't care. This medicine water was a gift almost beyond comprehension.

While Spirit Grass was enjoying herself, Bridger and Elizabeth stood. Bridger winked at Riley, and he and his new wife left the lodge.

R iley knew when he heard the war whoops that he was too late, but he dropped his hammer and grabbed his pistols anyway. He raced out the back door of the shop into the corral just in time to see a young Sioux warrior pushing the last of several horses out the gate. "Shit pile," he shouted as he snapped off a shot. He didn't hit anything but one of the stockade logs.

He turned and ran for the few horses that were left. McGinnis paced him. Their black leather aprons flapped, almost spooking the horses, who were already nervous enough. "What were they?" McGinnis shouted as they ran. "Blackfeet again?"

"Sioux," Riley said, wheezing a little.

Each man managed to grab a horse and jump on, bareback. As they raced across the corral, Riley saw the body of Jesus Escobar. The fourteen-year-old stock tender had three arrows in his back. A second later, Riley and McGinnis charged out the gate, hot on the heels of the Sioux.

Three men, including Jack Robinson and Lloyd Black galloped out of the fort gate at about the same time, and the five men almost collided. They all managed to get straightened out, the horses slipping some on the slick mud created by snow that had been trampled into the ground. Then the men were back on the trail.

Snow still covered the ground for the most part,

though in some places it was spotty. The streams and creeks rushed fast and were bitter cold, the spray chilling the men as they galloped through them. They raced along, jumping an occasional log, dodging trees and boulders, hoping the horses didn't fall on the slippery snow.

Riley lay low on his horse, guiding it by knee and with a grip on the animal's mane. He still had the two Walkers in his hands. The wind stung his face, but he tried to ignore it, keeping his eye on the warriors and stolen horses ahead. He had spotted four Sioux, and he estimated the young warriors had gotten fifteen, maybe eighteen horses.

The Indians yipped and whooped as they rode, almost as if challenging their pursuers. The white men rode silently, seeing no reason to waste energy just to make noise.

The five whites closed the gap fast, and within half a mile of the fort, they were a few dozen feet from their quarry. Riley was on the left, trying to get to the front of the horse-stealing party and turn the ponies; McGinnis was a few feet behind him. Robinson and a young Mormon named Ezra Smith were on the far side from Riley. Black was bringing up the rear.

One warrior twisted on his pony's back and let fly three arrows in the span of an eye blink. One thudded into Riley's side. He sucked in a breath, but tried to ignore the pain, and the arrow itself. There was nothing he could do about it now anyway.

Another arrow tore a chunk of skin and muscle out of McGinnis's left arm just below the crook of the elbow. He watched with some fascination as his arm suddenly spurted a bloody opening.

Riley closed in on the warrior who had shot him. He was focused on that warrior for the moment. Nothing else mattered or had meaning to him. He shoved one of the Walkers inside his apron, where it lay tight across his big chest. It would be safe there, he figured. If not, well, he still had another. Riley half hung off the right side of his horse, reached out, grabbed the back of the warrior's shirt and yanked him from his mount.

The Sioux bounced and rolled, and was almost trampled by McGinnis's pony. The young blacksmith jerked his horse to a halt and jumped off. He ran back to the warrior, but the Indian could put up little fight after his brutal landing. McGinnis had dispatched him in a minute. Then he got sick, realizing that he had just killed a man close up, tearing his innards out as if he were simply gutting a deer. He did not like the feeling.

Ahead, Riley pulled up close to another Sioux. He simply blasted this one with two shots from one of his new Walkers. At a distance of less than eight feet, it was a messy business.

Having taken care of the two Sioux nearest to him, Riley was just about at the head of the herd of stolen horses. He got a little more speed out of his own mount and managed to pull ahead of the lead horses. Shouting himself hoarse, firing one of his Walkers, and just through force of will, it seemed, he began turning the ponies.

Riley saw Robinson, Smith and Black, but he saw no other Sioux. He figured they had fled, or else his friends had taken care of them. It didn't matter now.

As he got the horses turned and starting to head back toward the fort, he saw Smith's horse slip on the snow. The animal managed to right itself, but not before Smith had fallen off. He disappeared under the feet of the stolen horse herd.

"Goddamn son of a bitch!" Riley howled. There was no way in heaven or earth he could turn the herd fast enough to save Smith's life. Smith might be a Mormon, but he was still a boy, and a pretty decent one at that.

Robinson saw it, too, and shook his head at the inability to do anything.

Black joined Riley and Robinson in trying to get the horses stopped now, but it took a little while. When they finally did, Riley tried to get the arrow out of his side, but it was stuck good and solid in one of his ribs. He cursed and snapped the shaft off, fairly close to the wound. Then he galloped back to where Smith was.

He stopped, dismounted and, with some trepidation, approached the body. He expected to see a mangled mass of blood, flesh and shattered bones, but what he found was a living, though unconscious, young man with only one mark on him—a large, discolored bruise just in front of his left temple.

"I'll be good and goddamned," he muttered as he knelt at the boy's side.

Robinson walked up. "He don't look none too bad, does he?" he said, a note of wonder in his voice.

"This boy's got some powerful medicine," Riley said. "He got kicked in the head once. Might've scrambled his brains somethin' awful, but he's alive. I expect that counts for something."

"If I wasn't standin' here lookin' at it, I'd never have believed it," Robinson said, still baffled.

Riley shoved his other Walker into his apron and lifted Smith gently. The youth groaned, and his head lolled. "Ye seen Paddy?" he asked Robinson as he stood.

Robinson pointed. "It appears killin' don't sit with that chil'," he said casually.

"It ain't ever easy the first time. Go git him and then let's git home."

"Scared?" Robinson joked.

"Well, them young bucks might have a heap of big brothers lurkin' about, and I don't figure we're in the best of shape for dealin' with 'em."

"A tellin' point, *amigo.*" Robinson mounted his horse and trotted over to McGinnis.

Riley walked slowly toward the horses, carrying Smith. He let Black hold the youth while he jumped on a horse, and then he took Smith back. Moments later Robinson and McGinnis rode up. "Ye look like hell, boy," Riley said gleefully at McGinnis.

"Kiss my ass," McGinnis mumbled.

"Ye help him raise that buck's hair, Jack?" Riley asked, enjoying himself a little.

"I were gonna," Robinson responded, getting into the spirit, "but he kept pukin' so much I was afeared I were gonna see his stomach come up out of him. And sich ain't a sight this chil' wants to see."

"I hope ye both get large festerin' boils all over your dicks and ye die slow, painful deaths."

"I think he'll live, Jack, don't ye?" Riley said.

"Could be. But I think we best wait a while before we go wagerin' on it."

They took their time riding back to the fort. Men and animals had taken enough of a beating for one day. Riley sent Black on ahead to tell the others at the fort what had happened.

Riley let the others corral the horses while he rode into the fort. There was a reception committee waiting for them. Vasquez directed two men to take Smith from Riley and bring him into his cabin.

"Looks like ye had a little trouble, One-Eye," Bridger said, pointing to the arrow shaft.

Riley nodded and dismounted. "It ain't so bad really, 'cept it's stuck in the rib bone."

"I ary tell ye the story of the time I had that arrowhead taken out of my back at rendezvous back in . . ."

"Only two, three hundred times," Riley said with a chuckle.

The others returned from the corral. "Ye all right, Jack?" Bridger asked.

Robinson nodded. "Nary a scratch."

"I'd be obliged if ye was to ride to Salt Lake City and tell Ezra's folks what's happened. Guide 'em back here if they want to come see him."

Robinson nodded again. "I'll jist grab me a bite, let my horse rest some and be on my way."

"I'll have Lloyd cut ye a horse out of the cavvy. Yours is about played out. Ye go on and eat. Everything'll be ready when you're done."

When Robinson had strolled off, Bridger looked at Riley and then McGinnis. "Looks like we best see about gittin' ye boys fixed up. I expect we'll have to cut that arrowhead out of ye, One-Eye." He seemed almost happy at the prospect.

"I'd as soon let one of them quacks from back in the States come at me with his goddamn leeches and calomel as I would let ye git near my hide with a knife," Riley growled.

"Ungrateful son of a bitch," Bridger muttered. He looked at McGinnis. "I suppose ye don't want my doctorin' services neither?" he questioned.

"Who's gonna work on ye, One-Eye?" McGinnis asked.

"Spirit Grass."

"Reckon she'll do for me, too," McGinnis said. "I'm obliged for the offer, though, Mister Bridger." He was feeling quite a bit better, in some ways. The memory of killing the Sioux warrior seemed far away now. He was in pain from his arm, but all in all he didn't feel too bad.

"We best git goin', boy," Riley said, a grin tugging at his lips, "before Ol' Jim here ties us down and starts drainin' our blood and fillin' us with calomel."

"I'll be butt-humped by a goddamn buffler bull afore I'd use such tactics on friends, goddammit, and ye know that." Bridger grinned. "Go on, git."

Spirit Grass and Praises the Sky were waiting for them. All went into Riley's lodge. "Ye want to go first, Paddy?" Riley asked. "Or would ye rather see how a real man handles such doin's?"

"I'm in no hurry," McGinnis answered firmly.

Riley let Spirit Grass cut his shirt off, and he removed the watch from around his neck. Taking the bottle of whiskey his wife handed him, he slugged back several deep mouthfuls. He sat, leaning his back against his saddle and clasping his hands behind his head.

"Ain't ye worried?" McGinnis asked.

"About what?"

"About it hurting."

"Well, hell, of course it's gonna hurt, boy. What the

hell do ye expect? Ye deal with it the best ye can. Spirit Grass ain't gonna do nothin' bad to me. I trust her."

Spirit Grass shoved a stick between his teeth, ready to go to work. She had the blade of a large butcher knife in the fire, heating; a small, sharp patch knife, a large, sturdy needle, some sinew, a poultice and some bandaging lay within reach. "Ready?" she asked.

Riley nodded, closed his eyes and bit down on the sturdy stick.

Spirit Grass picked up the patch knife and quickly, easily sliced open the skin and muscle around the arrow shaft. She ignored Riley's tenseness and the hissing from behind the stick. Opening a large enough hole to give her some working room, she stuck a finger in and probed gently. "It ain't stuck in bone," she said in English. "It's stuck between two ribs."

Riley just nodded, indicating he wanted her to do what she had to and get this over with.

But Spirit Grass was already working the broad iron arrowhead, carefully trying to turn it and tug it through the ribs. In less than two minutes, she had the bloody thing out and had tossed it aside. She grabbed the hot blade from the fire, said, "Heat comin'," to warn Riley, and slapped it on the gaping wound. Flesh sizzled, and some putrid smoke curled up from Riley's side, but then the knife was gone.

Spirit Grass swiftly, surely stitched up the ends of the wound, laid the poultice on and bandaged her husband. She smiled at him in reassurance, and handed him the bottle of whiskey.

Riley spit the stick out and drank deeply. Then he sighed, thankful that the ordeal was over.

"Your turn," Spirit Grass said to McGinnis.

"Like hell," McGinnis protested. "I ain't havin' ye come at me with that hot knife and such. I . . ."

"I'm gonna be mighty put out if ye force me to git up and wrassle your stupid ass down," Riley said. He was deadly serious. "Now show your woman what you're made of, boy." He held out the bottle.

Without another word, McGinnis drank, then lay down, wounded arm stretched out toward Spirit Grass. Praises the Sky stuck the same stick Riley had used between McGinnis's teeth. Spirit Grass quickly stitched up most of the wound and seared it with the hot knife to stanch the flow of blood. In minutes, he, too, had a poultice on and his arm was bandaged. He sat up and grinned at Riley. "Hey, One-Eye, that wasn't nearly so bad as I feared."

Then he passed out.

Riley and McGinnis took a few days to recover, and then went back to work. Almost a week after the Sioux attack, Robinson rode into the fort with Smith's mother and father plus several other Mormon men. Smith had been up and about since late in the day after the attack. He was grateful to see his parents and asked to be taken home.

"That's why we come here, son," his father said. "We've brought some of the brethren with us to make the journey. We'll leave straight off."

One of those traveling with the Smith family was William Hickman, who gave Bridger a letter of some kind. Being polite, Bridger did not open it until the Mormon party had left. Then he went back into his office to have Vasquez read it to him.

Moments later Bridger came roaring out of the office, bellowing for every man in the fort to assemble, with their arms.

Riley and McGinnis ran out of their shop. Seeing Vasquez trying to stop Bridger from going anywhere, Riley and his partner moved there in a hurry. There was no way Vasquez could hold back an enraged Bridger, considering the difference in their sizes. Riley, however, was another story. He went chest to chest with Bridger and wrapped his arms around the old mountain man.

"I don't know what this is about, Jim, but ye best settle down now. Ye don't, I'll have to flatten ye. Now git hold of yourself."

It took a few more seconds, but Bridger finally came to his senses and relaxed.

"Now," Riley said, letting him go, but watching him warily, "what's this all about?"

"This," Vasquez said, holding out a paper.

"The letter from Hickman?" Riley asked.

"*Sí*. The Mormon Legislature has granted ferry rights on the Seeds-Kee-Dee to Mormons."

"What about all the old mountain boys who've been runnin' them ferries for years?"

"You think those Mormon devils care any about our old friends? Hah!" Vasquez grinned without humor. "Jim wanted to go after Hickman. I tried to convince him that would do no good, since he's only the messenger."

"He's right, Jim," Riley said.

"Well, I'll be damned if I'll set here on my ass while that goddamn pious peckerwood tries takin' over everything we've worked for here."

"I know that," Riley said soothingly. "Look, he ain't gonna be able to do much yet. Hell, winter ain't even full over yet. First thing we got to do is get word to the boys who run the ferries. Then we'll worry about how to head this off. But we cain't do that whilst you're actin' crazy."

Bridger breathed deeply, letting the air out slowly. Then he nodded.

{ 25 }

It was the largest gathering of mountain men since the rendezvous of 1837, Riley figured. Even old friends who had no real interests in the Green River Valley showed up, some coming from as far as Fort Laramie and Taos. Those men felt that any assault on old friends' independence or livelihood affected them all, and as soon as they had heard the news, they had headed to Bridger's fort.

More than a hundred one-time beaver trappers crowded into the rickety fort's small, muddy square, buzzing angrily. Bridger finally climbed up on a wagon that had been set in front of the open stables deep inside the fort. He fired a pistol—loaded with powder and a wad, but no ball—into the air.

The men finally quieted, waiting for Bridger to speak. Some leaned on rifles or against the cabins. Many pulled out pipes or rolled corn-husk cigarettes.

"Well, boys," Bridger drawled, still angry despite the fact that almost a month had passed since getting the edict from Young, "Looks like ol' Brigham's gone and shown his true colors. That craptious bastard ain't gonna be satisfied till he owns everything from the Salt Lake to the plains—unless we decide to stop him. And I'll tell ye, boys, this ol' chil's not about to let Young and his cursed flock take over this valley. Leastways not without a fight."

Howls of anger arose from the crowd of men.

"I take it ye boys're in agreement," Bridger said to more whoops and growls. "Now all we got to do is decide what to do about it."

"Kill 'em all!" someone shouted, a sentiment echoed by a majority of the men.

Riley swiftly jumped on the wagon beside Bridger. "Hold on, boys!" he shouted, "Hold on!" He glanced at Bridger, who was looking at him in surprise and annoyance. Riley would not back down, though. He turned toward the now-quiet crowd. "Ye boys cain't do that," he said evenly, his big, hard voice carrying easily over the throng.

"Why not?" someone shouted. "Ye gone fainthearted?"

"I'll ignore that," Riley said harshly, "as the rantin's of a man who's gone touched in the head." He paused. "Think about what you're proposin', boys," he continued. "Ye mean to head for Salt Lake City and start killin' Mormons? Or maybe attack some of their settlements? Or their wagon trains?"

"Suits this chil'," more than one man yelled from the crowd.

"Suits me, too," Bridger growled low at Riley.

The blacksmith ignored him. "Since when did any of ye boys turn to the massacrin' of innocent women and children?" Riley demanded. " 'Cause that's what you'll be doin' if ye take to attackin' Mormons."

That got the men buzzing in consternation, and Riley let the hubbub run its course. While waiting, Bridger grabbed his shoulder and jerked him around. "Goddamn ye, boy," Bridger snarled, "ye got a lot more goddamn brains than I ary figured."

Riley shrugged, a little embarrassed by the gruff praise.

"I should've listened to ye a long time ago, ol' hoss. When ye suspected Young had his sights on this valley and all them other things. Goddamn, I wish I nary helped them people in the first place." He paused. "Ye know, hoss, I think mayhap ye was right, too, about Young and his Saints turnin' against me 'cause of Sarah. Like ye said, he might've thunk that if that ol' nag had converted me to their cursed ways, he might've had some claim to this here land.''

Riley didn't know what to say to that. He wasn't the kind of man who would say, "I told you so," especially to a friend. He was somewhat happy that he had been shown to have been right, and that Bridger had acknowledged it, no small act in and of itself.

Riley faced the crowd again, which had almost settled down. Before he could say anything, though, Bridger shouted, "Ye boys best listen to ol' One-Eye here. I'm more'n half froze to raise hair on them goddamn Mormons, but One-Eye spoke true. I still aim to do somethin' about Young's people, but I ain't sure jist what, now.''

Silence fell, as everyone stood around trying to think of a solution. Into the stillness, Riley suddenly said, "Indians.''

"What about 'em?" someone yelled.

"Well, Wakara and Old Elk kept them Mormons hoppin' for a spell last year when they were ridin' against their settlements.''

"Yeah, but them boys can't keep it up for any length of time," someone shouted, sparking some sniggers of derision as well as of humor.

"That's a fact," Riley said. "Both ways.'' He paused, then said, "All of us boys got friends among the tribes. Let's stir 'em up. Ain't a one of us who cain't stretch a tale a mite. I reckon we can all tell the Shoshonis and the Utes that the Mormons are makin' covetous glances at their land—which, when ye come down to it, is the truth. We can jist embellish it a bit to make sure we git them stirred up good and proper against Young's cursed tribe. Hell, if the Shoshonis and Utes can keep up their raidin' fer the summer, that ought to put an end to Young's goddamn plans for a spell.''

More whoops erupted from the crowd of mountain

men. The idea seemed fine to them. All of them had friends among the Shoshonis and the Utes, as well as other tribes, and they had no love for the Mormon people. Not when Young's government was trying to take away the lucrative ferrying business many of the mountain men had turned to when the fur trade died.

"Anyone don't agree with this?" Bridger called out.

Only two men raised their hands. "That don't shine here," one said. "Sendin' Injins out to kill Mormons is as bad as doin' it ourselves. I'll have no part of it."

"I'm with Horace," the other man said.

Bridger nodded, accepting their reasoning. There was no need for him to warn the two to keep their mouths shut. "Then it's settled. Spread out as soon as ye can, boys, and spread your tales. They don't believe ye, tell 'em to come on in here and we'll parley over it. Ye can also tell all the tribes that they can trade here for powder, ball and other such possibles they'll need."

He paused, looking out over the lake of solemn faces. Then he said, "I expect we can hold off one more day in such doin's. Let's celebrate our upcomin' venture."

Minutes later, a barrel of whiskey was rolled out and opened. Soon some of the men were pairing off, one of each pair wearing a yellow handkerchief to signify that for the purpose of this one dance, he had the woman's role. It was, for the men, like the old days, when they would be at rendezvous and there was a serious dearth of women to dance with——there were plenty of Indian women there, of course, but the men felt they were near useless for dancing.

Riley headed for his lodge, not feeling like joining the festivities. He was troubled in some ways. Seeing that his concerns were coming true did not please him. It was bound to bring only death and hurt and trouble for everyone involved. Still, he felt, the Saints could not be allowed to get away with this plan. If they did, he and many other men like him would lose about everything they had. Men like Bridger and Vasquez could weather such a storm financially, having the connections to move on and do something else. Men like Riley had no such opportunity.

Just over a month later, a large group of Shoshonis arrived at the fort. At first, Riley thought they were there only to trade, since many women and children were along, and such a thing was not unusual. But he rode out right away to talk with Black Iron, and found out that the warriors were there to parley about the war the whites were trying to stir up.

Black Iron led a fair-sized contingent of Shoshoni warriors into the fort the next morning. Riley, Bridger and Vasquez were waiting in the center of the dusty courtyard, sitting at a small fire. Black Iron sat across the fire from the three white men. Sharp Hawk took the place to Black Iron's right, and Black Dog sat to his war leader's left. The rest of the warriors sat in a circle around the small core of men. The white workers had climbed to the tops of the cabins and were watching intently.

"Welcome, my friends," Bridger said in Shoshoni. "It's good to see our brothers within our walls."

"It's been some time since we were here," Black Iron said. It wasn't true, really, though it was a fact that the Shoshonis hadn't been here for such a formal occasion in some time.

"What brings my brothers here?" Bridger asked.

"Many of our white friends—those who came in the old days to trap and trade for beaver—have encouraged us to make war on the white men in the Salt Lake Valley. Those with the strange medicine ways."

"The Mormons?"

Black Iron nodded solemnly. "We have some reason for going to war against them, we all know. Those people have come to our land to stay, and more of them are coming every day. But we want to know why you and your people are so eager to have us do this." The war chief looked expectantly at Bridger, waiting for an answer.

"Smart-mouth goddamn Injin," Bridger muttered so low only Riley could hear him. Bridger sat in silence for some time. When he spoke, it was in Shoshoni, the words slow, thoughtful and edged with dignity, as befitted a man the Indians called Casapy—the Blanket Chief. "My words mean little in such matters. I can't sit here and *tell* your men to go to war, my friend. Nor can the others who live in peace and comfort in the land of the Shoshonis. But I can say that if ye were to make war on the Mormons—at your own insistence—it'll help your people and mine."

"How is that?" Black Iron asked.

"The chief of the Mormons has decided he should rule all the lands from the Salt Lake to the Seeds-Kee-Dee. He has formed a council to make laws . . ."

"What are these 'laws'?" Black Iron asked.

"Shit," Bridger mumbled under his breath, "I was afeared he was gonna ask that." Once again he sat, trying to think of how to phrase this.

Riley saved him. "These laws're a little like your medicine, in some ways," he said in Shoshoni. "When ye make your medicine, you're given certain rules that, if not followed, will lessen or even break your medicine. These laws go further than that. They're rules for the way the Mormons will conduct their lives. Since there's less trust among some peoples than among the Shoshoni, these laws are written on paper for all to see. They won't follow them if they're not on paper."

"That's right, Black Iron," Bridger added. "And this council that makes these laws expects everyone who is in 'their' land to live by them. And whether ye know it or not, he means to include ye in those laws."

A baffled look crossed Black Iron's face. "We do not live in their lands," he said, still puzzled. "We aren't of his people."

"That's not the way the Mormon chief thinks, Black Iron," Riley said. "He's claimed all this land and expects everybody in it to live by his laws."

"You, too?"

Riley nodded. "And worse, he's trying to take over the ferries on the Seeds-Kee-Dee. Take them right out from under the men who've been running them all these years."

"Bad shit," Black Iron said in English.

"Damn right," Riley agreed. Then in Shoshoni he added, "But the worst of all things is that, if the Mormon chief gets his way, his people will take over the fort owned by Casapy and his partner. Then the People will have no one to trade with but the Mormons."

Now Black Iron sat silently, thinking all this over. He and the bands he held some sway over had not had much trouble with the Mormons, though there had been some encounters. Still, it was plain that the Mormons were not going to go away, and even more plain that they were going to expand, reaching ever outward for more land—and the Shoshonis were the ones mostly in their path. Behind him, he could hear his warriors conferring among themselves.

Several warriors rose, one by one, and spoke their minds. All spoke of war.

When everyone who wanted to had spoken, Black Iron asked, "If we go to war against these people, will you and your men join us, Casapy?"

"We can't do that, Black Iron," Bridger said tightly. "The Mormon chief has many men at his disposal, and he'll send them against us here at the fort, if we take the war trail."

"He'll fight us, too," Black Iron said simply.

"He won't send his people out lookin' for your villages, Black Iron," Bridger said.

"Why not?"

"They're afraid of the People." Bridger didn't know if that was true or not, but he knew that Black Iron, as a proud, successful warrior, was arrogant enough to believe it.

Black Iron finally nodded solemnly. "We will make war," he said.

Bridger nodded. "It is good." After pausing, he

added, "If you're certain ye want to do this ye must take up the cause soon. If not, they will be as many as the pebbles in the creeks and streams that feed the Seeds-Kee-Dee Valley. Then ye will have no chance of winning."

"And now?" Black Iron asked.

"Ye have little chance now," Bridger said seriously.

"What do you say, One-Eye?" Black Iron asked.

"I think Casapy is right," Riley said quietly. "I'd hate to see any of my friends killed in useless war. But," he added sadly, "many white men won't leave ye be, as we here have done."

Black Iron nodded once more. He was not eager for war, but he and his people had reason for it, and they could see what the future held. Before long, he thought, there would be white men all over the lands the Shoshonis roamed. "Our friends said you'd supply us with guns and other things we'll need to make war on those white-eyes?"

"Those words are true," Bridger said. "But only in trade, though we'll be very generous with the People. You know I speak true."

Black Iron nodded. Bridger and Vasquez weren't the most honest traders the Shoshonis had ever met, but they were far from the worst. And Bridger had never been known to lie to the People, not in any major way. He figured he would get a good enough deal here.

Sitting next to Bridger, Riley was a little surprised. "Ye sure ye want to make 'em trade for guns and other plunder they'll need?" he asked in a whisper.

"Certain. We jist gave 'em the possibles, the Shoshonis mayhap would see it as a gift, and then they might think twice before goin' to war on those damn Mormons. But if they have to pay for that truck, even if it is small, they'd look on it differently. Like it had some better value."

Riley nodded. Then he grinned. "If Young ever hears you're armin' the Shoshonis to go to war against him, he'll shit his britches."

Bridger laughed. ''I do expect he'd be more'n half froze to raise my hair,'' he agreed.

They all smoked a pipe to solemnize the Shoshonis' decision, did some trading, and then the Indians rode off.

Riley went back to his shop, but while there, he began to wonder if they had done the right thing. He had not realized the Shoshonis' depth of anger at the emigrants in general and the Mormons in particular. Now that it was clear to him, he was filled with uncertainty. On one hand, he could understand the Indians' desire to try to drive the Mormons out of their lands, since the Saints had shown such a strong determination not only to settle this country but to wrest even more of it from the Shoshonis and Utes and Piutes. That would be enough to make most men want to go to war.

On the other hand, he was afraid for the Shoshonis. They could not win a fight against the white man—even just the Mormons—over the long run, and everyone but them knew it. He would hate to see any of his friends— Black Iron, and his brother-in-law, Sharp Hawk, and Black Dog, Running Bull, Empty Horn and Crow Lance —die in such a futile cause.

He almost wished he could join them in the war, since he had as much to lose as many of the Shoshonis, but that, he knew, would be foolish. To do so would send the Mormons—and probably the federal government, too—against the fort and the Shoshonis. Everyone would lose.

26

A rider thundered into the fort, his shouts stopping work and drawing everyone outside.

Not knowing what the hell was going on, Riley and McGinnis dropped their blacksmithing tools and ran toward the fort office, where the man—whom Riley quickly recognized as Fred Wetherall—had stopped.

Bridger and Vasquez had already come out of the office and were standing there, looking at Wetherall in puzzlement.

"There's Mormon posse headin' this way," Wetherall said, panting from his hard ride. "Though damn if it don't look more like a small army than a posse." Wetherall was an excitable man, often given to exaggerating danger or trouble.

"What'n hell fer?" Bridger asked, unconcerned yet. He well knew Wetherall's foibles, and wasn't very willing to just accept what the man had to say.

"Comin' to arrest ye, boy." Despite his bad news, Wetherall almost crowed. He was mighty proud to be the bearer of such important news, especially if it was going to save Bridger's hide. He'd be an important man, then, he figured. Those pert young squaws wouldn't laugh at his enlarged head or his scrawny body or his nearly toothless mouth then, no sir.

"What'n hell do they want to arrest this peaceable ol' chil' fer?" Bridger asked.

"From what I heared, ol' Brigham Young's got his nuts in a knot 'cause ye been sellin' guns and plunder to the Shoshonis to make war on his people."

"Wonder where he got such a damnfool notion," Bridger said dryly.

"Be damned if I know," Wetherall said with a small, tight grin. "But if that ain't enough fer ya, they got other reasons—like not payin' taxes to the territorial gummint like you're supposed to."

"Ye tellin' me those jackasses're serious about all this shit?" Bridger asked. He was surprised at being surprised. He should've known something like this was coming ever since Young had claimed this land and more for the state of Deseret in '49. Sometime the next year, the American government had formed Utah Territory from Deseret. It, like the Mormon state, included this area. Bridger had thought that might rein in the Mormons some, until he heard the other news: The president had appointed Young as the governor of the new territory. That had truly soured Bridger's humor, and for a while he was more curmudgeonly than usual.

Things had not gone too poorly, though. Soon after, the Mormons had negotiated an agreement with one band of Shoshonis to allow them to found a settlement in the Green River Valley. The rest of the Shoshoni bands, however, kept up their small but annoying war against what Mormon settlements there were, preventing the Mormons from ever starting their new colony.

Things had stayed relatively quiet during the past three years. There were still raids by the Sioux or Cheyenne or Arapaho on the fort or the camps; caravans of wagons still came and went, as did the mail and the stage service. The mountain men running the ferries across the Seeds-Kee-Dee had fought off a couple of Mormon attempts at competing.

The one big difference the men did note, however, was the lessening of business at the fort. Salt Lake City had siphoned off a fair amount of the fort's trade, even with the Indians. It was more convenient for Piutes and western Shoshonis and western Utes to go there or to one of the Mormon settlements to trade than it was to come this far east. There were even some Indians who thought the Mormons gave them a better deal than their old friend Bridger did. Few Saints stopped at the fort any more, at least not for trading. Their wagon trains gave the fort a wide berth, skirting the area to the north or south.

Bridger had heard, of course, that Governor Brigham Young had started his own police force, which ranged over the entire Utah Territory chasing down miscreants whether Mormon, Gentile or Indian.

Because of all that, Bridger knew Young would come against the fort again sooner or later, and he should not have been surprised when Wetherall brought the news moments ago. Still, he found that he wasn't quite prepared for this.

"Damn sure they're serious about this," Wetherall said. "I expect Young figures you've been a thorn in his pious ass long enough, and he's determined to git rid of ya once and for all."

"It ain't gonna be as easy as he might think," Bridger muttered. Aloud, he asked, "How far off are they?"

"Not more'n a couple hours, Jim. Maybe a little less."

"Damn." The old mountain man, still strong, determined and active at forty-nine, stood there thinking.

To Riley, though, there was no need for thought. "Ye got to git your ass out of here, ol' hoss," he said firmly.

"I ain't runnin' from those skunk-humpers."

"To hell with such nonsense, Jim. We got, what, half a dozen men here right now." He looked up at Wetherall, who still sat on his horse. He was guzzling from a canteen someone had handed to him. "How many of them shit piles're comin', Fred?"

"I counted maybe a hundred and fifty," Wetherall said, taking a break from the canteen. "And they ain't lookin' friendly neither. Prob'ly gonna butcher ever'body here."

Riley shook his head at the nervous man's probable

overstatement. "We cain't hold off even a quarter of that many men, Jim. Ye know that. So git your orn'ry ol' ass out of here. I don't imagine they're gonna bother the rest of us much. If they do, at least you'll be free to raise up some of the boys and take revenge for all us poor souls."

Bridger nodded. "Lloyd," he said to Black, "saddle my horse. Louis, I want ye and One-Eye there to make sure those two ol' boxes of gold don't git took by them Mormons. I was plannin' to send it east anyway with Charlie Quinlan, who's supposed to come through here on his stage in two days. He didn't want to take it without it bein' counted, so soon's ye can do that and divide it up into smaller parcels and hide it till Charlie gits here."

Both men nodded solemnly.

"Fred, I'm grateful fer ye comin' to warn me. Take what food and plunder ye need from the fort when ya leave." He spun on a moccasined heel and headed toward his quarters, leaving the rest of the men standing there pondering their future.

Riley was not nearly as sure as he had sounded that Young's men would not bother the people at the fort. He knew Bridger was the prime target, but he also knew he was pretty high up on Young's hate list. That could mean trouble for him. He sighed, deciding he would worry about that later. There were other things to be done first.

Bridger came out a few minutes later, carrying a sack, just after Lloyd Black had returned with a saddled horse. He hung the bag of food over his saddle horn. "One-Eye," he said, "I need to gab with ya. Alone."

Surprised and wondering, Riley said, "Sure," and followed Bridger back to his quarters.

Inside, Bridger turned to him and said, "I'm gonna go stay up near the head of Willow Creek Fork . . ."

"Where me'n ol' Fraeb . . ." Riley unconsciously touched the buckskin patch over his left eye.

"That's the place, hoss. It's a good spot to cache, and

mayhap its medicine has changed some over these twelve years."

Riley nodded, and smiled a little ruefully. "It don't bother me none, Jim. Not really. 'Course, I ain't been back there either, but that's all right, too, I suppose. Why're ye tellin' me this?"

"Only other one who knows where I'll be is my woman."

Riley felt his chest swell with pride, if he was the only man at the fort Bridger was going to tell this to.

"She'll be bringin' me some victuals and such ever' other day or so. But I want ye to know where I'll be in case somethin' happens to Elizabeth. Or in case ya need to git hold of me right quick."

"Why tell me and not Louie?" Riley asked, still stunned about it.

"He'll have a heap of other shit to do that'll occupy his mind. Plus, if worse comes to worst, and they start gettin' rough tryin' to extract information about me, I figure you'll stand it better'n he will. Not that he ain't got a heap of sand in him, don't git me wrong, boy. It's jist that you're a lot younger, and ye got a wild streak in ya that won't give in to nobody."

Riley wasn't sure if his voice would work right now even if he knew what to say. So he just nodded.

"There's those boxes of gold, there, One-eye," Bridger said, pointing. "Now I reckon I best drag my ass out of here."

When Bridger had ridden hard out of the fort, Riley turned to Vasquez. "Ye want to see to the gold before the Mormons git here? Or would ye rather wait here to be ready for 'em when they arrive?"

Vasquez seemed distracted and he suddenly asked, "What'd Jim need to talk to you about?"

"Nothin' of importance. He jist wanted me to take care of Virginia if things got rough," Riley lied smoothly.

"Why didn't he ask me?" Vasquez seemed quite angry.

"Said ye had too much to think about, what with bein' in charge of the fort and havin' to deal with the Mormons when they git here. It's a big responsibility, this fort."

Vasquez grudgingly accepted that. "Why don' you see to the gold," he said. He didn't feel the need to warn Riley not to slip a coin or two into his possibles sack. The two might not get along, but Vasquez could trust the blacksmith around his money. "But be quick about it," he added.

Riley turned and hurried to his lodge. "Come, Spirit Grass," he said urgently, "There's work to do. Leave the children with Praises the Sky."

Spirit Grass jumped up and took the children to McGinnis's lodge. Then she and Riley rushed back to Bridger's cabin. There he explained in Shoshoni what was to be done—the women would stack the gold coins in neat piles of five, and he would take the count.

They heard the Mormons arrive, but Riley figured it would take a little while for them to come into the cabin. He was wrong. Minutes later, McGinnis popped his head in the door. "A couple of them Saints is comin'," he said urgently, then ducked out.

"Shit," Riley muttered. The money was spread out over a blanket along one wall. There was no time to gather it up and hide it.

But calm as you please, Elizabeth, who was wearing a white woman's calico dress, rose and then squatted down on the blanket, her full skirt covering the cash. Spirit Grass smiled and sat in front of her and the two held hands.

"I'll be damned," Riley breathed, grinning just a bit. The smile left his face as a familiar-looking man shoved through the door, followed by three others. "Where's Bridger?" the first one asked.

"How the hell should I know?" Riley spat. "He's often gone from the post."

"Then what're you doin' in his quarters?" the man demanded.

"Lookin' in on his wife and young'ns. Not that it's any of your affair, shit pile."

"I'm Bill Hickman," the man said. "An officer of the territorial Legislature. I ain't gonna listen to such venom from the likes of you, boy. Now, since Bridger ain't here, my men and I're hungry. Have the squaws fix us some food."

"Go hump a muskrat, ye pusillanimous pile of shit," Riley said easily.

Hickman's deadly eyes widened in anger. "We're here at the order of the duly constituted governor of this goddamn territory," he said harshly, "and you'll do what the hell I say, goddamn your hide."

"I wouldn't do anything ye had to say, even if ye sent over all your whorish wives to ask me nice." He was prepared for the attack when Hickman lunged at him. He sidestepped the attempt, spun, grabbed the back of Hickman's shirt and launched him toward the wall.

Hickman hit the logs with a loud crack and went down without a sound.

Riley turned and faced the three other Mormons—one a tall, overweight young man who could barely raise a mustache; another of medium height and stockily built, with a decidedly hard look about him; the third about the same size as the second, but rather older. "Any of ye other shit piles want to start tossin' 'round some orders?" Riley asked.

"Make us some food," the young one commanded. He was sure that Riley had caught Hickman by surprise, and the same would not happen to him.

Riley laughed.

The young man reddened. "Why you insolent . . ."

"Ye jist gonna stand there and call me names? I always knew all ye goddamn Mormons was lily-livered dogs."

When the young man jumped at Riley, the other two Mormons were right behind him, figuring to overwhelm the big blacksmith with numbers.

Riley grabbed the big one in a bear hug and smashed the man's face with his forehead. The Mormon groaned and wobbled. Riley let him go just as the hard-eyed Saint grabbed his left arm and jerked him around.

Riley allowed himself to be pulled, but kept going, figuring the third Mormon was about to hit him in the back of the head. He had been right, and the man stumbled after hitting only air. Riley yanked his left arm free, and with the right punched the hard-eyed man in the face three times.

When that Mormon stumbled back against the wall, Riley turned. The third Saint had gotten a pistol out, and fired as Riley jumped at him. Riley felt a burning punch in the left shoulder, just under the collarbone. He slammed his other shoulder into the man's chest, and grabbed his gun hand. The blacksmith drove him backward until the Mormon smashed up against the wall. Jerking him forward, Riley pounded him against the wall twice more, each time a little harder.

The Mormon dropped his pistol and fell in a heap.

As he turned, Riley saw the tall young man just getting up. Riley kicked him just under the chin, then in the side.

The hard-eyed Saint slammed into Riley, and they fell, rolling and clutching at each other. Finally the Mormon broke free and rose to one knee, trying to get his revolver out. Riley managed to sweep an arm out and knock the man's legs out from under him. Scrambling to his feet, he grabbed the Saint and threw him through the door.

With a shrug, Riley went back, grabbed each of the three other Mormons and tossed them out into the courtyard, too, Hickman being the last. Riley thought they made a nice little pile out there in the dust.

''What's the meaning of this?'' a tall, pleasant-looking man with a neatly waxed mustache asked as he strode over.

''Who're ye?'' Riley countered.

''Sheriff Jim Ferguson. I'm in charge of this posse, under the direction of General Lewis Robison. What's your name, boy?''

"Pete Riley. Most folks call me One-Eye."

"Seems I've heard that name bandied about Salt Lake City of a time," Ferguson said dryly.

"All good, I presume," Riley added in like tones.

"Hardly." Ferguson almost grinned. "Now, sir, would you mind tellin' me just what this is all about?" He indicated the pile of groaning men.

Riley shrugged. "Those four shit piles come bustin' into Mister Bridger's quarters and, seein' that Mister Bridger wasn't there, began orderin' his wife—and mine—to start makin' 'em food."

"And I presume you took exception to that?"

"I did. Then Hickman attacked me. When I laid him out, the three others come at me."

Ferguson looked impressed. Bill Hickman was one of the toughest men he knew, almost as tough as Porter Rockwell. "My apologies for their behavior, Mister Riley." He paused, then asked, "Well, since Mister Bridger is not in his quarters, would you know where he happens to be? We do have an official warrant for his arrest."

"I have no idea where he is, Sheriff." Riley even managed to say it with a blank face.

Ferguson nodded. "What's your place here?"

"I'm the blacksmith."

"Well, again, my apologies." Ferguson turned and walked away.

Riley watched for a moment, then said over his shoulder, in Shoshoni, "Finish your task. Put all the gold in small sacks, and let Spirit Grass hide it under her clothes. If you can't take it all at once, Spirit Grass, take what you can, and let Elizabeth keep the rest, hiding it the same way. We can get it later."

{ 27 }

Riley tried to keep to himself over the next several days. With more than a hundred Mormon posse men in and around the fort, he could easily be in danger. Helping was the fact that Ferguson had sent Hickman out at the head of a troop to take over the mountain men's ferries down on the Seeds-Kee-Dee. That kept him away from Riley for a while, at least.

Spirit Grass had had to make three trips with bags hidden under her clothes to get all the gold to their lodge. She managed it all in that first day, moving easily through the Mormon posse members. That night, Riley and Spirit Grass shoved the small fire out of the way, dug a hole there, buried the gold, and then rebuilt the fire over it. They would have to go through the entire thing again in a couple of days when Charlie Quinlan brought his stage around, but this way Riley was as certain as he could be that the gold would not be found.

For the most part, the Mormons left the people at the fort alone—except for Vasquez. The posse had orders to destroy all the fort's liquor supplies, and confiscate all powder, lead and other items the Legislature had deemed illegal for trade to the Indians. Vasquez was stuck with the unenviable job of having to help the posse men as they went through the fort looking for contraband. The Mormons probed every nook and cranny, or so it seemed, including Riley and McGinnis's shop, which set the two blacksmiths' teeth on edge.

Things got a little tense when the posse men found Riley's small still in a dark corner. It was still perking merrily along when a young man stumbled on it. "Captain Cummings," he called, "come here, sir, and look at this."

A spare, somber-looking man marched over. He took one look at the still and commanded, "Destroy it."

Riley slammed his hammer on the anvil with a clang that echoed through the room and brought all movement to a stop. "Any of ye shit piles touches my still is gonna git his head pounded flat. That there's my personal still, and its product ain't for use in tradin' to the Indians nor no one else. There ain't no call for ye to go destroyin' a man's personal property."

Cummings turned and walked toward Riley, as if thinking. Unbeknownst to the Mormon, McGinnis had slipped up behind him, three-pound hammer in hand. "I suppose we can leave it," he finally said, as if he had just made some momentous decision. "But I must tell you, sir, that whiskey is the devil's own water. Evil it is, sir. Pure evil."

"Don't preach to me," Riley growled. The Mormon posse had been at the fort only two days and already it seemed like an eternity. "Go preach to your own people about it."

"They don't need it," Cummings said huffily.

"In a pig's ass they don't. Them boys're supposed to be pourin' that whiskey out, but it seems there's a passel of 'em pourin' more down their gullets than they're pourin' on the ground."

"That's a bare-faced lie, you ignorant ape," Cummings said in high dudgeon.

"If ye and your boys're done stickin' your noses up my ass, pull 'em out and go elsewhere before there's some violence committed against ye."

"I have a good mind to . . ."

"Ye don't have any goddamn mind at all. Now git lost before I lose my temper."

Sniffing in indignation, Cummings and his small troop left stiffly.

McGinnis grinned a little. "Guess we showed them, didn't we, One-Eye?"

"Reckon so, boy." Riley didn't feel much like grinning, though.

It wasn't long before Ferguson showed up, alone. "I'll tell you this jist one time, Mister Riley," he said. He still looked pleasant, but his words were as hard as the iron Riley worked with. "You will treat my men with respect or I'll have you in chains. Is that clear?"

"Ye ain't got enough men to get me in chains," Riley bragged.

"Oh, I think we do, sir. And if, by some chance, we don't, we'll just shoot you down."

"I'll take as many Mormons with me as I can," Riley warned.

"The Saints've been through more terrors than you'll ever conceive, Mister Riley," Ferguson said evenly. "We have no fear of death. We live life to the fullest, gettin' all the enjoyment we can from life's bounty. But it is no hardship for a Saint to go to meet his Maker. Indeed, any of us would greet that day with a cry of welcome on our lips. Thus, we are afraid of no man, of no hardship, of no burden the good Lord could put before us. You might kill one or two of the brethren, maybe even several of us, but you'd die, too, as sure as I stand here now."

Riley could see the truth of Ferguson's words in his clear, unwavering eyes. The blacksmith also realized that he would have to get Bridger's gold out that afternoon so it could be taken east. He couldn't do that if he was dead or chained up. He nodded. "Jist as long as your boys leave me alone."

"Acceptable, Mister Riley. I had no trouble accepting the other day's little imbroglio, nor would I have trouble if you had to defend yourself again. But what you did to Captain Cummings was wrong. I forgive it of you since these are strange and heated times. But it won't happen again without serious consequences to you."

Riley nodded again. He found he could accept Ferguson, even as he accepted Rockwell. He didn't agree with much of what they believed in, but they were honorable men nonetheless.

About an hour after Ferguson had left, Riley pulled off his apron. "I'm gonna go take care of that business for Jim," he said to McGinnis.

"Ye want some help? It might take some doin's if what ye told me the other day is true."

"It is. But ye can be of most help here, I think. This way we don't have to worry about some of those shit piles sneakin' back in here whilst we're gone and bustin' the place up. The hardest part's going to be gettin' it down here."

"Do it the same way ye got it to yer lodge, One-Eye," McGinnis said.

"It took Spirit Grass three trips. That might be a little suspicious lookin'."

"Damn fool, ye. Have Praises the Sky take a load. And if ye need a third, get Elizabeth. It wouldn't be all that unusual for the three of 'em to be walkin' together to stop and give a greetin' to the husbands of two of 'em."

"What about the young'ns?"

"Hell, have Lloyd's woman tend to 'em."

"I cain't stand that witch," Riley grumbled.

"I can't either, but it ain't gonna be but a few minutes."

Riley nodded. "Ye ain't so dumb as ye look, Paddy," he said with a grin. He left and went to Bridger's quarters, spoke to Elizabeth for a few minutes and then left. At his lodge, he had Spirit Grass tell Praises the Sky of the plan, and had her wait just outside the tipi to keep watch while he retrieved the bags of gold.

When he was done, and everything was back in order, he called Spirit Grass. Elizabeth and Praises the Sky were with her, having left their children with Lloyd

Black's Piute wife, Big Round. Riley kept watch outside
while the three women prepared themselves. Then the
four walked casually toward the fort—and Riley's shop.

McGinnis went to watch at the back door, while Riley
stood in the front one. Just as the women were beginning to unload their bags of gold, Riley saw Ferguson
heading his way. He hissed a whispered warning, then
casually filled and lit his pipe. "Somethin' I can do fer
ye, Sheriff?" he asked.

"My horse's bit broke. I was wonderin' if you could fix
it."

"Don't see why not. Come on in."

"Looks like you're busy," Ferguson said when he got
inside.

"Not really. You've met Elizabeth, Mister Bridger's
wife?" Riley pointed to her.

"Oh, yes."

"This here is Spirit Grass, my wife," Riley said, plac-
ing an arm around Spirit Grass's shoulders. "The other
is Praises the Sky. She's my partner's woman. They jist
come down here to pay us a visit."

"Well, if I'm not in the way . . ."

"Nope." He took the bit and checked it over. One
side had cracked. It didn't take Riley long to weld the
piece back together. He handed it to Ferguson. "Ought
to be better'n new, Sheriff," he said.

"Much obliged, Mister Riley. Good day to you all."

Riley followed him to the door and then stood there.
Finally he called quietly, "All clear."

McGinnis returned to his post at the back door.
Within minutes, the women had divested themselves of
the small sacks of gold and stashed them behind tools
along one wall. Then they left, strolling out of the fort as
if they had not a care in the world.

"That was cuttin' it close," Riley said as he heard the
stage rattling and jangling into the fort. The few passengers got off the stage and went into one of the cabins
that was serving as a dining room. Then Charlie Quin-

lan drove the stage into the corral so the horses could be changed over.

While Black and another man went about taking care of the horses, Riley and McGinnis swiftly put the bags of gold into two burlap sacks and carried them out to the stage. Quinlan stored them under his seat, covered by an old coat, some rope and various other junk. No one would see them, or notice anything untoward if they did.

"Ye watch over that gold good, boy," Riley said gruffly, but he was grinning.

"Hell, I thought I'd go have myself a little spree somewhere on the trail," Quinlan said dryly. "How much is there?"

"Two thousand, six hundred and fifty-six dollars."

Quinlan whistled. "Tidy little sum."

"Ye bet. Jist make certain it gits to Bill Sublette out there."

"No problem."

The next morning, Indian whoops had the men tumbling out of cabins into the blistering heat of another August day, to see what was going on. A band of Shoshonis rode into the fort, led by a ferryman named Elisha Ryan.

"Goddamn you festerin' shits, git out of this here fort!" Ryan bellowed. "Goddamn scurrilous Mormon bastards."

Everyone stood kind of dumbfounded for a bit, as Ryan continued his profane discourse on the ancestry, habits, sexual practices and customs of the Saints. Finally a Captain Robert Burton shouted, "Arrest that man!"

No one moved, since nearly a dozen Shoshoni warriors were sitting there looking like they were about to attack. One of them was Sharp Hawk. Riley edged up to his brother-in-law's pony and asked, "What the hell're ye doin' here, Sharp Hawk?"

Sharp Hawk shrugged. "Runnin' Bull called for a war

party," he responded in English. "I wasn't doin' nothin', so I joined in. I didn't know Ryan'd be leadin' us. Goddamn idiot."

"You're bein' too kind," Riley said in distaste. As far as Riley was concerned, Elisha Ryan was a degenerate, drunken reprobate, without a single redeeming quality.

"I think you're right, One-Eye." Sharp Hawk looked over at Ryan, who was still bellowing a blue streak.

"Well, I'd advise ye to git your ass out of here. Take the others with ye and let Ryan hang himself with his cursed nastiness."

Sharp Hawk looked around again, seeing the angry faces of the Mormon posse members, and beginning to count them. He nodded, then leaned toward his left and whispered rapidly into a fellow warrior's ear. That Shoshoni nodded and spoke softly to another. Within two minutes, all the Shoshonis had gotten the message.

Almost as one, the Indians spun their ponies and raced out of the fort, whooping and shouting.

As soon as the Shoshonis were gone, a group of Mormons surrounded Ryan's horse. "Submit peaceably," Burton commanded, "or you'll be shot down."

"Son of a bitch," Ryan muttered. "Well, what the hell, why not." He slipped off his horse. "Scurrilous bastards."

"I was ye, I'd shoot that shit pile, Sheriff," Riley said to Ferguson, who happened to be standing nearby.

"What, one of your own kind?" Ferguson asked, smiling to take the sting out of it.

"Ye mean an ol' mountain feller? He don't hardly count. I'd as soon be a friend with one of the Saints as I would with that son of a bitch." He, too, grinned.

"That'd be a first, I reckon."

"I suppose it would," Riley agreed with a laugh.

Most of the posse men spent their time scouring the surrounding countryside looking for Bridger. But the old mountain man was too wily for such an amateurish bunch. Elizabeth slipped out of the fort on foot every few days, to bring food to her husband. It was easy for her to do, since she always took a little basket and always returned with some kind of berries. Though she was Bridger's wife, the Saints paid little attention to her.

At the same time, a troop under Hickman went toward the Green River with the purpose of taking over the mountain men-run ferries there. About half the posse returned in a day or so, reporting that they had killed several of the mountain men and were in control of the ferries.

Hickman seemed mighty pleased with himself after killing the ferrymen. Riley bit back his anger, knowing there was nothing he could do now. He wondered who the men were, and if they were among those he called friends. Still, he would grieve for almost any of the former mountain men. He decided he was glad that he had pounded the snot out of Hickman.

After a few weeks, most of the posse headed back to Salt Lake City, leaving a contingent of only twenty men under General Lewis Robison. The general, with Vasquez at his side, toted up the cost of all the goods that had been confiscated, borrowed, used, destroyed or otherwise appropriated by the posse. It came to a tidy sum.

The search for Bridger continued even under the reduced posse, but without any success. Riley kept a straight face about it, but he was pleased inside. He talked with some of the ferrymen who drifted in and out of the fort, making plans to take back the fort and the ferry crossings just after winter hit.

By early October, the Mormons decided they had been in the vicinity long enough. They felt sure that Bridger had fled the area or, if not, that he was finished in this region anyway. So they headed home, leaving the depleted fort in the hands of Vasquez, who looked almost forlorn.

Bridger reappeared the next day, having waited to make sure the posse was really gone. He and Vasquez talked the morning away in their office, their sometimes heated words drifting out over the cold, forsaken court-yard.

Late in the afternoon, Bridger wandered into Riley's shop. "I'm pullin' out come mornin', One-Eye," he said without preliminary. "I'm gonna take Elizabeth and my little Virginia back to the States."

"Then what?"

"Then I aim to see about gittin' paid back for all the plunder them sons of bitches took from me." He paused to regain his calm. "I'd be obliged if ye was to stick things out here, help Louis as much as ye can. I know ye two don't git along real well, but you've made out all right."

With some trepidation, Riley nodded.

"Besides, there's always a chance the posse'll come back lookin' for Louis. If that happens, ol' hoss, the fort's all yours till I can git things straightened out."

Riley didn't like it, but he was willing to accept it.

{ 28 }

Some of the mountain men from down by the ferries, as well as others from outlying areas, began drifting into the fort soon after, until, three weeks after the Mormons had left, about a dozen of them were holed up there. They were angry and bored and even a bit confused by all that had gone on in the past few months, and so they congregated in solidarity.

Riley's old friend Ed Perkins rode in a few days after most of the others.

"Ed!" Riley roared in joy. "By Christ, I thought I'd nary see ye again. How are ye, ol' hoss?"

"Best as ever."

"What brings ye here, Ed?" Riley asked.

"I heard about da troubles ya had here of recent, boy, and I come to see what da hell it was about." His voice was as raspy as ever, but more high-pitched with the addition of a decade or so.

"Ain't much to tell. The goddamn Mormons're movin' in on us. Been headin' toward it for a while, but they've been pressin' hard the past few years. Hell, they come to try'n arrest Ol' Jim, but he outfoxed 'em. They're gone now, though, a couple of weeks ago."

"Dey'll be back, don'tcha think?"

"I figure so."

"So, maybe I brought some good news for ya."

"That'd be a right welcome thing," Riley said dryly.

"Dey are comin', dem Mormon fellers," Perkins said, not looking at all upset at the prospect.

"That's good news? Shit," Riley said disgustedly.

"Well, it's good news 'at ya know it beforehand, heh? Besides, dere's more. About twenty a da boys ain't far from here. Up inna mountains wid a Ute war party. Dey can be here right quick if trouble shows up."

"I expect that is a bit of good news," Riley allowed. "Now, c'mon inside the shop and wet your dry."

"I been wonderin' how long it was gonna be afore ya offered an ol' friend some hospitality."

"Eat a dead skunk, ye fart-filled sack of muskrat innards," Riley said as he led Perkins into the shop.

"I ate dat before, goddammit. And muskrat guts, too." He laughed. "Tasted worse dan da worse thing ya ever ate, but dey kept me alive one time."

"And, that, my friend, is all that counts." Riley stopped.

"Hey, Ed," McGinnis called out. "Welcome back."

"Good to be here. You keepin' 'is fractious critter out a trouble?"

"I keep tryin', but it ain't no use."

Riley brought out a bottle of his home brew.

"Goddamn," Perkins said, grabbing the bottle, "it's a good thing some habits don't change none." He drank deeply, eyes watering as the foul liquid ate its way down into his stomach. "Ain't as good as buffler piss," he said when he had finished the long swallow, "but it'll do for now."

The three spent the afternoon drinking a little, eating and reminiscing. Perkins, unencumbered at the moment by a wife who would crucify him for overindulging, threw caution to the winds and got roaring, stinking drunk. Riley and McGinnis, whose wives would not put up with such behavior, watched their intake of the poisonous whiskey.

The two blacksmiths left Perkins alone in the shop with the bottle and went to their lodges. Perkins was still ambulatory, but barely. He was nowhere to be seen the next morning.

"Probably got himself off in some hidey-hole somewhere sleepin' it off," Riley responded when McGinnis asked. He grinned. "Bet ye a dollar we don't see him today."

"Ye're on," McGinnis said. "He'll come draggin' his ass in here sometime today lookin' for a little hair of the dog."

"No he won't," Riley said with a knowing smile. Perkins had a habit of slinking off into the underbrush like a wounded animal, and not coming out again until the hangover had worked its way out of his system. Riley won the bet.

Perkins did show up the following day, looking none the worse. He made his greetings, then went out and hunted up a card game with some of the other former mountain men. Riley and McGinnis joined them after a while, since there was little to do in the shop.

"There's Mormons comin'," Jack Robinson said, sticking his head inside the door of the cabin being used as a dining room. It was also where the men played cards, which several of them were doing at that moment.

"How many?" Riley asked lazily, looking up from his cards.

"Looks like a couple dozen or more. And they're headin' straight for here, too. No doubt."

Riley nodded and stood. "Reckon we ought to go give them a welcome," he said. "Jack, if ye don't mind, go round up the other boys."

"Courtyard?" Robinson asked. "Couple minutes?"

Riley nodded. "See to your weapons, boys," he said. "Those shit piles might be lookin' for a fight."

"They are, there's gonna be some goddamn dead Mormons here right quick," one of the mountain men said. He had been close friends with two of the three ferrymen killed by the Mormon posse.

There was a growled chorus of assent while the men

checked their pistols. When they were ready, they tramped outside. Robinson and several other men joined them. Vasquez was already there.

"A couple of you boys get up on the roofs," Vasquez ordered. "A few more head into the corral. *Pronto.*" When some did, Vasquez walked out ahead of the men in the courtyard and waited patiently.

Before long a group of Mormons began riding through the gate. "That's far enough," Vasquez said.

Most had not yet gotten into the fort. A man who appeared to be the leader stopped, the men behind him doing the same. He frowned. "I'm Captain John Nebecker," he announced. "My company is here to colonize the area, and by order of the Utah Territorial Legislature, we commandeer this fort as our headquarters. We . . ."

He stopped when the hooting and laughter from the assembled mountain men threatened to drown him out.

"It's about time we had some entertainment around here," Riley said when the laughter died down a little. "It's been a mighty glum time since the last time ye shit piles come through."

"I'm here by the authority of Governor Young himself," Nebecker said, beginning to sound unsure of himself.

"I'm sorry, *Capitan,*" Vasquez said soothingly, "but there's just no room here for you and your men, and we are woefully short on supplies."

"Don't apologize, Louie," Riley snapped. "They ain't worth it."

"There's no need for violence or confrontation here, Pedro," Vasquez said stiffly. "These men are, after all, the representatives of the duly appointed territorial government."

"Dese men're nothin' but goddamn cold-blooded killers," Perkins said harshly. He owed no allegiance to Vasquez.

"This is my fort," Vasquez snapped. "And I'll make the decisions and give the orders."

"You don't have da backin' of da men here, Vasquez," Perkins said. "Especially if ya plan to kiss da ass a dem killers dere. Now step aside and let us handle dis."

"Best do it, Mister Vasquez," Riley said deferentially. "It'll be best for all."

"I'm not about to . . ."

The Saints used the argument between the three men to surge fully into the fort. Riley acted almost instinctively, jumping forward and slamming into Vasquez.

"What the hell . . . ?" Vasquez started, but the sudden spurt of gunfire shut him up. He heard Riley grunt, and he looked up, worried. Riley was up and moving already, without Vasquez getting a chance to thank the burly blacksmith, who jumped up amid the gunfire that had broken out from both sides.

Riley felt the searing fire of a bullet scrape across his back as he knocked the Spaniard to the ground. He hoped it wasn't too bad. The bullets stopped flying almost immediately when it became obvious that, with so many men packed in the close confines of the fort, it was as easy to shoot a companion as it was to shoot an enemy.

Riley, like most of the other mountain men, preferred hand to hand fighting in such a situation anyway. He was a serious threat with fist, feet or knife, as were quite a few of his companions.

To the mountain men's disadvantage, the Mormons were still mounted. The Saints' advantage started to dwindle rapidly though, as the mountain men began to haul them off their horses.

Riley grabbed one man's bridle and jerked as hard as he could. The horse went down, falling to one side. The surprised rider could not leap free, and his leg was caught under the animal. He looked with frightened eyes as Riley loomed over him, but the blacksmith only smashed the Saint in the face, putting him out of the fight.

The bulky blacksmith was still bending over the man when someone plowed into him from behind with enough force to knock even a man as big as Riley down. Instinctively, he jerked an elbow up and connected with his attacker. He didn't know how much damage he did, but he knocked the man off him, shoved up and spun, ready for another assault.

The Saint had his knife out and was already lunging toward Riley, who did not really have time to react. But Perkins had landed on the Mormon's back, driving him to his knees. He pulled his own knife and slit the Saint's throat.

"Obliged," Riley said, and charged back into the midst of the dusty, loud, chaotic melee.

Perkins was right behind him.

The two of them mowed a pretty good swath through the swirling Mormons and mountain men. They were not bloodthirsty, preferring to just toss people out of the way when they could, but more than once they were forced to bring their knives into play.

Almost as quickly as it started, the fracas stopped. Mormons streamed out of the fort as fast as they could get through the gate, some on foot, some still on horseback. A few mountain men chased them, shouting and firing an occasional shot. Others spooked the Mormon horses out. Then the fort gate was slammed shut.

Riley stood looking around. The dust was beginning to settle in the chilly November afternoon. "Any of us kilt?" he asked.

"Al Fancher crossed the divide," someone said. He didn't sound too sorrowful.

"Anybody hurt bad?"

No one said anything, and Riley nodded. "Louie, how're ye doin' . . . ?" Riley suddenly sprinted to where a mountain man named Moore was fixing to raise the hair of the Saint whom Perkins had killed. Riley pounded the man on the back of the head. Moore fell, half rolled and looked at Riley as if he had lost his mind.

"What in the name of sweet Jesus was that all about?" he asked, rubbing the back of his head.

"That ain't no Blackfoot or Sioux there, boy," Riley

said angrily, pointing to the Mormon. "He's a white man, and ye ain't gonna raise no hair on him."

"You come to love them Saints all to a sudden?" Moore questioned, baffled.

"Ye know better'n that. There jist ain't no need for butcherin' a white man is all."

"Go hump a squirrel, One-Eye," Moore growled as he got to his feet. "Ye ain't got the gumption to raise hair no more, fine. But don't you try'n stop me from doin' it."

"I'll stomp ye into the ground," Riley said, still angry.

"Oh, you will, eh?" Moore snarled.

"Goddamn right I will."

"And I'll help him, goddammit," Perkins said, moving up alongside Riley.

"So'll I." McGinnis took his place on Riley's other side. "Not that he'd need any help with the likes of ye."

"Who the hell is this jackass?" Moore asked, pointing at McGinnis.

"Me goddamn partner," Riley said. "Would ye like him to introduce himself to ye?"

"If he's got the stones."

Riley grinned and looked at his friend. "He's all yours, Paddy," he said.

"Do ye mind if I damage him?" McGinnis asked with a smirk.

"He don't look like he can take much damagin'," Perkins threw in, chuckling just a bit.

"Do with him what ye will, Paddy," Riley said.

McGinnis slid his knife away and edged up on Moore. He wasn't nearly as confident as he looked and sounded, but he wasn't too worried either. He gave away twenty or thirty pounds to Moore, but the former mountain man looked like he had gone to seed over the years. McGinnis was still young and strong.

Moore was wily, however, and he sprang into action seemingly out of nowhere, landing a hard right fist to McGinnis's breadbasket. The Irishman had become aware of it at the last moment and managed to tighten his stomach muscles and absorb much of the blow.

Ignoring the little ball of fire that had erupted in his abdomen, McGinnis suddenly grabbed Moore by the ears and jerked his head forward, while snapping his own toward Moore. His forehead connected with the lower portion of the mountain man's face. McGinnis let go of Moore's ears and stepped back.

Moore looked dazed, and he spit out what few rotten teeth he'd had left. He mumbled something, but it wasn't coherent to the others. He spit blood, on the ground, and then at McGinnis's face.

The Irishman ducked reflexively, which allowed Moore to jump on him and begin punching him as hard, as fast and as often as he could.

McGinnis covered up for a bit, then began getting angry as the blows began to tell on him. "Begorrah!" he finally yelled. "Get your goddamn hands off me, ye pustulent Limey bastard." He slammed an elbow into Moore's throat, knocking him back. Then he whirled and grabbed Moore's shirt. He shoved him, and the mountain man went stumbling backward, and again and again.

McGinnis kicked Moore in the stomach, doubling him over, spun him and then shoved him forward as hard as he could. Moore hit the fort wall head first, and fell to the ground, unconscious.

"Goddamn, but that was harder than I thought it was going to be," McGinnis said, panting.

"Never underestimate anybody, my friend," Riley advised him.

Vasquez seemed distracted the rest of the day, so Riley took over the cleanup of the fort. Some of the mountain men were, as usual, cantankerous, and not in a mood to be ordered about. But Riley went about his business, ignoring them, until finally Jack Robinson called for a vote to elect a leader.

"If we're gonna stay here and keep this fort till Ol'

Jim comes back," he told the men, "we'll need some goddamn order."

Riley was elected by a wide margin.

Riley had Spirit Grass tend to his wound—fortunately, the ball had just skipped across his back—that evening. The next morning, he sent Perkins out to find where the Mormons had gotten off to.

"They're a couple miles past where Willow Creek and Smith's Fork join," his old friend said when he returned. "About twelve miles from here, I'd say."

Riley nodded. He asked Robinson and Lloyd Black to take the Saint's body back to his people for burial, under a white flag. He wasn't sure, but he hoped that the gesture would ease some of the enmity between his group and the Mormons.

"Them boys said to tell ye that they appreciate ye sendin' their *compañero* back to 'em." Robinson said. "They was some amazed, I'll tell ye, when they found out that a cantankerous ol' bunch of mountain men'd do somethin' so civilized. Don't know as if it'll do any good, but it sure as hell won't do no harm."

Riley nodded again. He was not so much pleased with himself as he was relieved. He thought that perhaps he had bought a little peace, at least for a time.

❧ 29 ❧

"I'm heading east, Pedro," Vasquez said flatly. He and Riley were sitting in the office on the morning of the second day after the battle with the Mormon colonizers. "I'm worried about Narcissa and the children, and I want to get them out of here. I think Jim had the right idea."

"Ye git along well with the Saints, Louie," Riley said evenly. "Hell, ye damn near opened up that mercantile store over in Salt Lake City before things started to git really sour 'tween us and them."

"I know. I just worry that something will set the whole region ablaze. *Madre mia.* You and Jim've been telling lies about the Saints to the Indians, and lies about the Indians to the Mormons. Brigham Young's still after the ferries, which the old boys aren' going to give up easy. Now the Mormons're trying to colonize the valley. Everybody is on edge, just waiting for things to explode. I don't want Narcissa and the children to be here if that happens."

"Ye got to do what ye feel is best for ye and your family, Louie," Riley said without rancor. He didn't blame the man for it. He might've thought Vasquez cowardly if he had been married to an Indian woman, but a white woman, alone out here with God knew what about to happen; no, he could not find a bad thing to say about Vasquez's decision.

"I also have to think of the company. I don' know exactly where Jim's gotten to, but I've got some ideas on that. While he's gone, I'm supposed to represent the company here, which puts me in something of a bind right now."

"It would that, yep," Riley acknowledged.

Vasquez knew that beating around the bush would not accomplish anything. Looking Riley square in the eye, he said, "I know you still resent me for . . . Well, that was a long time ago, Pedro, and I think some of your feelings were misplaced, shall I say. Be that as it may, we have always worked pretty well together when it came to this post and the company. You've watched over the fort in our absence before, Pedro, and I'm asking you to do it again."

Riley smiled a little lopsidedly. "Gonna give me five dollars a day for it?" he asked.

"Como? What?" Vasquez said, eyes growing wide. Then he laughed. "A good one, Pedro." He paused. "To tell you the truth . . . One-Eye . . . I don' know if we'll be able to pay anyone anything for quite some time."

"I know that, Louis. I don't expect nothin'. Someday ye and Jim git all this settled, well, then, maybe you'll owe me a few dollars. Let me ask this, though—are ye plannin' to come back here anytime soon?"

"No," Vasquez said flatly.

"I'll watch over your fort for ye," Riley said calmly, "under one condition."

"What's that?"

"That ye come back here as soon as ye can with a load of goods. Ye can turn around and head right back east again, but we need supplies bad."

"That's reasonable, I suppose, but I don' know how doable it'll be. Hell, it's November already. By the time I get back to the Settlements, get the family settled, buy supplies, get wagons and all, it'll be Christmas. You know as well as I do how hard the winters are out here."

"You're damn right I do. And that's why I want ye to

git us some supplies. We ain't gonna make it through the whole winter on what we got.''

Vasquez leaned back in his chair. What Riley had asked was perfectly reasonable. It was also smart from a business standpoint. If they could get some supplies in here, they could still deal with whatever emigrants came through. But his family had to come first, and then there would be the awful journey back in the dead of winter. Not that he was afraid of such a journey, but he did not look forward to it, not while his family was still trying to get settled in Missouri. And he would also miss them for Christmas. Then it came to him.

''How about this, Pedro,'' he said, leaning forward to rest his arms on the rickety, handmade table that served as a desk. ''I'm planning to take several of the men with me, for protection. I'll take a couple extra—men we trust. Along about Fort Laramie, I'll send them ahead, with a letter from me as representative of the Bridger-Vasquez Company. They'll be able to buy supplies in Independence drawn on company funds. They can be halfway back here before my family and I reach the States.''

Riley thought that over. He filled his pipe and lit it, then nodded. ''That'll suit. Who do ye want to take?''

''Jack and your friend Perkins?''

''They'll do,'' Riley agreed. ''When're ye leavin'?''

Vasquez sighed. ''Morning. I want to get on the trail before hard weather begins to set in. Hell, we've had snow a couple of times already.''

''Looks like more on the way, too.'' He started to rise.

''Another moment, Pedro, please.'' When a surprised Riley had settled back into the chair, Vasquez said, ''I'm really obliged to you for this, Pedro. It's a great imposition, I realize. But I want you to know I have complete faith and trust in you. Not just to keep the fort out of Mormon hands, if at all possible, but also to represent the Bridger-Vasquez Company here. To make sure that everyone knows that you're representing the company, before I leave tomorrow, I'll give you a letter stating that. You can find someone to read it for you if anyone wants to know what's in it.''

Riley was flabbergasted and didn't know what to say. He just sat, smoking pipe in hand, mouth slightly agape.

''And, as a bonus, you can move your family into my quarters—if you want, of course. You don' have to.''

''I must be havin' a medicine vision or somethin','' Riley said in confusion. ''For this sure cain't be real.''

''Why not?''

''After the troubles I've given ye all these years?''

''I told you a long time ago, Pedro, that I bore no ill will against you, and that you were wrong in resenting me my partnership with Jim. Maybe now you'll believe me.''

''Mayhap I will. I reckon this ol' hoss ain't so ol' he cain't change his ways some.'' He rose and stuck out his hand. ''It's me who's obliged to ye, Louis.''

''Let's just say it's mutual,'' Vasquez said as he stood and shook Riley's hand.

Riley stopped at the door and looked back. He grinned a little. ''By the way, Louis, about that letter—I can read. And write.'' Then he left.

Winter wasn't long in coming, and the men hunkered down inside the fort to wait it out. Riley wasn't too worried. They had enough supplies to get them through a month or so, though if Perkins and Robinson didn't get back in good time, there'd be starvin' times for all.

The arrival of winter had one advantage—it brought peace to the Green River Valley. All the Indians were wintered up somewhere, most of the Mormons stayed in their relatively comfortable Salt Lake City homes, and the Saints were trying to survive in their new colony, called Fort Supply, just like the mountain men were in Bridger's old trading post.

Still, there were things to worry about for Riley. Both Spirit Grass and Praises the Sky were pregnant and nearing their terms. Riley, who had moved his family into Vasquez's quarters, came out one morning, heading toward the shop. He and McGinnis knew of nothing else to do, so they went there every day. This day, however, instead of McGinnis, he found Praises the Sky waiting for him. The young woman looked full of despair.

"What's wrong?" Riley asked in Shoshoni. Praises the Sky spoke English fairly well by now, but when she was this upset, Riley figured, she would communicate better in her native language.

"My husband is sick," Praises the Sky said plaintively.

"What's wrong with him?"

Praises the Sky shrugged. She had never felt so helpless. McGinnis had taken such fine care of her these past seven years, but now that he needed help, she could do nothing for him. "He shakes, as if he is cold, but he burns with fever. He has much pain in his head."

"Damn," Riley muttered. "Sounds like ague or grippe. Mayhap might even be recurrin' fever," he added in English. There were really no words for such things in Praises the Sky's language. Riley wasn't even sure she understood what he had said.

"Is that bad?" Praises the Sky asked nervously.

"Could be. But maybe not." He paused, sighing. He wanted nothing more right now than to just saddle a horse, throw a few supplies on a pack mule and ride out, heading into the real high country up north in Blackfoot land. He could be free there. But he knew it could not be. He had been entrusted with a large responsibility in minding the fort. Plus there was Spirit Grass, and Flat Nose and Arrives With Trouble, and the new child on the way.

"Go on back to him now," Riley told the woman in Shoshoni. "Put a cold cloth on his head to help ease his head pain. I'll bring Spirit Grass up to your lodge soon. Maybe we can do something for him. Go on now. And don't ye worry too much."

Praises the Sky nodded, though she was not convinced that anything could be done. Still, Riley was someone both she and McGinnis looked up to, and if anyone could help it would be he. Well, he and Spirit

Grass, who had been almost like a mother to Praises the Sky, though she was only a few years older. She left, walking sadly through the tingling cold of late November.

Riley spun and hurried back to his cabin. "Paddy's ailin'," he said urgently. "It sounds bad, but I ain't sure. I figure we'll try some of my medicines on him first. They don't work, we can try your herbs and such."

Spirit Grass nodded. "Want me to come with ye?"

"Of course. I always feel better about such things when you're along." There wasn't much in the way of medicines at the fort, but Riley got what few were around and put them in a sack. Then he and Spirit Grass hurried over to the village, and into McGinnis's lodge.

The young Irishman lay on his robes, face bathed in sweat. Praises the Sky was kneeling beside him looking more worried than she had only a few minutes ago, outside the blacksmith shop.

Spirit Grass took Praises the Sky by the shoulders and tugged gently until she rose. Then she led the younger woman over to the fire, talking to her quietly in Shoshoni.

Riley squatted next to his friend. "Damn, boy," he said cheerily, "I never would've took ye for a loafer. Ye should be up and workin'."

"Maybe tomorrow," McGinnis said softly, wincing in pain.

"What's ailin' ye, boy?" Riley asked, trying to keep up the facade of joviality but not succeeding very well.

"Damned if I know, One-Eye," McGinnis groaned. "I'm burnin' up, but shakin' with cold at the same time, my heart's racin' like hell, I'm painin' like a son of a bitch and I feel like I got to puke."

"Shit, ye got a hangover is all, boy," Riley said gruffly. He took the cup of water that Spirit Grass handed him and added some quinine to it. "Here ye go, hoss, have a swaller of this." He lifted McGinnis's head and helped him drink the potion down. Then he eased his friend's head back.

"I feel better already," McGinnis croaked.

"Jist wait till I finish dosin' ye, boy. You'll be up and about before ye know it."

"What other kind of poisons're ye plannin' to make me imbibe?"

"Jist some laudanum, boy. It won't cure ye, but it'll ease the painin' in your head and mayhap let ye sleep some so's your body can mend itself."

"Ye ain't fit t' doctor horses, and we both know it, ye one-eyed blitherin' idiot."

"Ye ain't gonna die on me, ye fractious little shit pile. Not without a fight. Now shut your trap." Riley pulled out a bottle of laudanum, and helped McGinnis take a few swallows. Then he laid him down again. "Ye rest a while, Paddy. I'll be back after a spell to look in on ye."

Riley rose and went to where Spirit Grass and Praises the Sky were sitting together. "I think he'll sleep for a while now, Praises the Sky," he said quietly. "I'll look in on him later."

"You're worried, ain't ye?" Spirit Grass asked as she and Riley walked back to their cabin.

Riley nodded. "It don't look good."

"Ye know what he's got?"

"Looks like recurrin' fever to me. But I cain't be sure. It could be ague, maybe lots of other things, too."

"Which means we cain't be sure of how to fix it, right?"

"Right."

Riley spent a considerable portion of the next three days in McGinnis's lodge, pouring quinine and laudanum into his friend. He did a lot of thinking, too, while he sat there, looking at McGinnis in a new light. He hadn't realized before how good a friend the young Irishman had become, but now he jumped from considering McGinnis as "just" a friend to begin thinking of him as a younger brother. It was something of a revelation for him.

Because of that, he worried more and more about McGinnis. The young man didn't seem to be getting any better. So Riley spent more time at his friend's side, thankful that there was little work that needed doing around the fort.

But the third morning, McGinnis was awake, lucid and apparently over the worst of whatever had plagued him. "Ye take another day to rest up and make sure you're better," Riley told him.

The next day, McGinnis showed up at the shop like he normally did, much to Riley's relief. A week later, he was back in bed, the same symptoms hitting him hard again.

Angry, worried and frustrated, Riley asked Spirit Grass if she had anything in her herb bag that would work.

"I ain't sure," she said. "But I've got a few things I can try, if ye want."

Riley nodded. Once again he spent much of his time at his friend's side, but this time he let Spirit Grass dose McGinnis with whatever concoctions she had. At first it seemed to have little effect, but this time the sickness lasted only two days. After that, McGinnis was up and working again.

Six days after, almost as if it were running on a regular schedule, the fever and head pain returned. More annoyed than ever, Riley decided on a full-scale attack. Both he and Spirit Grass spent a considerable amount of time dosing McGinnis with their respective medicines, hoping that the combination would work.

They worried even after McGinnis had seemed to recover, wondering whether the illness would mysteriously appear again in a week or so. As time passed, McGinnis, Praises the Sky, Riley and Spirit Grass grew more tense. A week went by, then eight days, then ten, and McGinnis remained well. The four breathed a collective sigh of relief, and life soon got back to normal.

Well into December now, Riley found a new worry. Supplies were getting low, and concern grew over whether Robinson and Perkins would arrive in time to do the fort's residents some good.

As Christmas neared, Riley tried to shake off the gloom, and set about planning a small celebration, using up a fair portion of the meager goods. The snow stopped enough to allow a couple of the men to go out hunting, and they brought down two buffalo and an elk, which made the celebration a bit brighter.

On the first day of the new year, Spirit Grass went into labor. Assisted by a pregnant Praises the Sky, Spirit Grass gave birth to a girl—Laughing Swan—with no trouble or complications. It seemed to Riley as if that had been the first thing to go right at the fort since the fracas with the Mormon colonizers.

Two weeks later, Riley ordered that food be rationed, since there was little left. Hunters went out as often as they could, but they frequently had no luck. Winter tightened its grip, with frequent snows, bitter temperatures and often hellacious winds, making life even gloomier at the forlorn trading post.

As time dragged on Riley began trying to figure out whether he should cut back rations even more and make a greater effort at hunting, or try to make it to either Salt Lake City or Fort Laramie.

Just as things were getting to the point of desperation, Bob Cameron trotted into the fort from the midst of another snowstorm. "Wagons'll be here tomorrow," he gasped into the fierce wind. He looked half frozen, and icicles dripped from his beard and mustache. "Day after at the latest."

Riley heaved a sigh of relief as the other men in the fort whooped in joy.

The fragile peace continued in the Green River Valley—now designated Green River County by the territorial Legislature—for two years. Life at the fort went on pretty much the way it had before the attempted Mormon takeover. During the winter the men kept inside as much as the winter demanded; in summer, they serviced emigrant wagon trains and traded with some of the tribes who still preferred dealing with the Bridger-Vasquez Company instead of the Mormons.

Vasquez made sure supply trains made the run from the Settlements with some frequency. He always sent a letter asking how things were going. Riley usually had little to say, since not much out of the ordinary seemed to happen. One of the few things that did was the birth of McGinnis and Praises the Sky's third child in the late spring of '54. Other things—a run-in with Cheyennes, another with the Arapahos, an exchange of angry letters with Fort Supply, the Mormon colony not far from the fort, the death of a man in a fight brought on by boredom—were not worthy of bothering the trading post's owner with, Riley figured.

In one letter, though, Riley asked about Bridger. He learned through Vasquez's reply some months later that Bridger was trying to win reparations from the federal government for what he saw as a takeover of the fort. He was also trying to get the government to either run the Saints out or to at least confine them—and their influence—to the Salt Lake Valley. Apparently he wasn't having much success with either effort.

Riley was conscientious, too, of sending fort profits back to Vasquez whenever he could. His old friends Jack Robinson and Ed Perkins were regularly making the runs between the fort and Independence, which made it easier to do, since both Riley and Vasquez trusted the two couriers.

There had, fortunately, been no more sickness at the fort. Not real sickness. A case of dysentery now and again, a cold, someone's arthritis flaring up, a baby's bout with colic, all things that could be dealt with easily enough.

Illness among the arriving emigrants was a different story. They generally showed up with a fair number of their people suffering dysentery, scurvy, ague, Rocky Mountain spotted fever, even cholera and smallpox. The latter two were the most worrisome, of course, and

Riley made sure those emigrants stayed in their camps and didn't come into the fort itself.

Mountain men and workers came and went as they chose, but there were always enough men around to do what work needed doing. Some opted to head back with the wagons, so they'd have a chance to see civilization again. Some stayed in the Settlements, others returned to the fort with supply trains, sated, even burned out, by their frolicking in the cities.

In winter, Riley provided a haven at the fort for any of the mountain men who needed shelter and food. Nothing was expected of the men who availed themselves of the hospitality, though most made some effort to work off the debt—hunting or doing repairs or odd jobs.

The mountain men had retaken most of the ferries, though the Saints had started up several of their own. The southern Mormon ferry got the most business, since it was right near the colony of Fort Supply. It meant that the fort rarely saw any more Mormon emigrants. That was something of a relief to Riley, who figured that the less he had to do with the Saints the better off he was.

A solemn Jim Bridger rode into the wobbly old post in the company of Robinson and Perkins.

Riley was flabbergasted to see him. "Louie never sent word ye was comin', Jim," he said as the three new arrivals dismounted.

"Wasn't really time, One-Eye," Bridger said, shaking Riley's hand. "I jist made up my mind a little while back. Louis was gonna write, but hell, that wagon train's still a couple weeks behind us."

"Well, I'm glad you're back. I'm relieved to be relieved of my command over the tradin' post here."

"Don't git so eager, hoss. I ain't certain how long I'm gonna be here. Ye jist keep on doin' what ye been doin'. Louis tells me you've been doin' a fine job. 'Course, he's complainin' that not enough money's bein' made."

"I've told him in my letters that we don't see any Mormon emigrant trains any more," Riley said more than a little defensively, "and that's cut into our profits somethin' fierce."

"He knows that. So do I. He was jist joshin' ye."

"Ye need me to show ye anything or make some kind of report or somethin'?" Riley asked, somewhat mollified.

"Nope. Git Lloyd to tend horses. You and your friends can go on and git reacquainted."

Riley didn't see much of Bridger over the next week.

He had a little work to do, but mostly he spent time with McGinnis, Perkins and Robinson, playing cards, drinking, yarning, and hunting.

When they returned from hunting one day, Riley spotted an unknown horse in front of the office. He wondered who it belonged to, but then he shrugged. He and his friends had fresh meat and they aimed to enjoy it—as soon as they dropped some off for the other fort workers.

As they finished doing that, Riley looked up and saw Bridger coming out of his office with William Hickman. The two spoke for a moment, then Hickman mounted his horse and rode out of the fort.

"C'mon, One-Eye," McGinnis said, "get your fat ass movin'."

Riley hadn't realized he wasn't paying attention. He looked up at the other three, all mounted already. "Ye go on to the lodges. I'll be along direct."

"Somethin' up?" Perkins asked.

"I don't reckon so. I jist need to go talk to Jim a bit."

The others nodded and pulled their horses around. As they rode off, Riley walked slowly across the square, battling back the anger that had suddenly found a comfortable spot in his chest. He entered the dim office and saw Bridger sitting back in the chair, feet up on the table. The old trader had a small pipe in his teeth, supported by one hand. His eyes were closed. "Who's that?" he asked, not opening his eyes.

"One-Eye." He took a seat and filled and lit his own pipe. Once it was going, he asked bluntly, "What was Hickman doin' here?"

Bridger's eyes opened, and he glared at Riley. "None of your goddamn business, hoss," he said in tones indicating that this should be the end of the conversation.

Riley wasn't having any of that, though. "Hell with ye. I've been in your employ—more or less—for more'n fifteen years now dammit. I've stood side by side with ye in starvin' times and good. I've worked for your company as if it were my own, pulled your nuts out of danger more than once, and I've run your own goddamn tradin' post for ye, whilst ye was back east romancin' politicians and other such scurrilous shit piles. Yeah, I got a goddamn right to know what that son of a bitch was doin' here."

"You're still in my employ, hoss," Bridger said harshly, "and I'll tell ye what is and what ain't your business."

Riley felt as if he had been slapped across the face. He said nothing for a while, certain his voice wouldn't work very well. When he decided he had it back, he pushed to his feet, and leaned across the table. "No, I ain't. Not no more." He turned and walked toward the door.

Bridger let him get the door open before he called him. A hurt, angry Riley looked back reluctantly. "Hickman brought me an offer from Young to buy the tradin' post and all the land I own," Bridger said, no apology in his voice. "I'm considerin' takin' it."

"Ye were right," Riley said tightly, barely controlling his anger. "It ain't none of my business."

"Ye don't care that I might decide to sell out?" Bridger asked, surprised.

"It's your post, your land, your business." He decided there was no need for him to hold back. "But if ye was to ask me, I'd say ye were a goddamn fool to sell out, especially to them shit piles."

"Why? They're close by, they're interested, and they've got the money in hand."

"They've coveted this land since they first come through here back in '47. Nobody'd listen to me when I tried to tell ye that. Nor all the other times I tried to warn ye. But that don't make no difference now. I will say one thing to ye, though—ye ought to think of others before ye sell out."

"Like who?" Bridger's demeanor hadn't softened a bit.

"Like the men who work here. Like the ol' mountain boys who're runnin' the ferries over on the Seeds-Kee-Dee. Ye sell out to the Mormons, there ain't a one of 'em who's gonna make a livin' here. What ones don't leave on their own account're gonna be run out by the goddamn Saints as soon as can be done.''

"They're all big boys," Bridger said roughly. "They'll find other work."

"I reckon they will," Riley allowed. "But it won't be the same."

"Nothin's the same, hoss," Bridger snapped. "We had to make do when beaver didn't shine no more."

"I expect. But what I can't understand is how ye can think of sellin' to Young, after what those pustulant shit piles've done to us over the years."

"Like I said, One-Eye, things change. I don't like the Mormons no more now than I did when they come here to arrest me." He paused. "Come and sit down again, hoss, so we can talk like men."

Riley hesitated only a moment, then shrugged, shut the door, returned and sat. Bridger remained stone-faced, but Riley thought he could see a flicker of humanity in the watery blue eyes.

Bridger's pipe had gone cold, so he set it down, and shoved some tobacco in his mouth. He chewed a bit. "Jist what do ye think'll happen if I was to tell Young to go hump a mule over this deal?"

Riley had never thought of that. He did now, but couldn't come up with much. All he could see is that things would go along as they always had. He knew life changed constantly, but he was not astute enough to see beforehand just how it would. "I cain't predict things, Jim, ye ought to know that," he finally said.

"It ain't hard to do, One-Eye," Bridger said. "What'll happen if I don't sell out is that Young'll form his own goddamn militia and send it this way. Ye think the hand-ful of us boys'll be able to hold off four or five hundred Mormon militiamen? When they'll be led by men like Hickman and that other lunatic . . ."

"Porter Rockwell."

"That's him. How long ye think we could hold 'em off?"

"A spell," Riley said, though he knew he was wrong.

"A spell my ass. They'd overrun us in minutes. The more resistance we put up, the more of the old boys'll die. Once they've wrested the fort from us, they'll march on the ferries. We might take some of 'em out, hell, mayhap even a passel of 'em, but there ain't gonna be none of the old mountaineers left at all."

Riley felt a chill slither up his backbone. He knew immediately that it was entirely possible, and the Mormons were certainly capable of pulling it off. More important, the Saints had the *will* to do it.

"I never thought of it that way."

"Neither did I, till Hickman come in here today. He thought he could scare me into sellin' the fort with his stories and sich. Well, that didn't work, but he sure made it easier for me to consider makin' a hard business decision." For the first time, Bridger looked a little sad. "Still, it don't shine with this ol' chil' to have to do it." He spit tobacco juice on the floor. "Well, I ain't made up my mind yet," he added, "and I told Hickman I'd need some time to cogitate on it. Mayhap I can figure somethin' out."

"Yeah, mayhap," Riley said, knowing that it was not at all likely. In fact, Riley realized with some dread, it was virtually impossible.

"I'd be obliged if ye didn't tell any of the others about this, One-Eye. Leastways until I make a decision."

"I'll keep quiet about it, Jim," Riley promised, not sure if he could. He rose and headed out. There was nothing left to say. He found it hard to keep a cheerful face on when he got to McGinnis's lodge, but he thought he succeeded. As the small feast among the friends and their wives and children continued, it got a little easier for him to get into the mood of it.

But that night, when he and Spirit Grass were alone in the small bed in Vasquez's old quarters, Spirit Grass said to him, "Somethin's botherin' ye, One-Eye. I could see it in ye all night."

"You're havin' visions, woman," Riley growled, and he turned his back to her.

Spirit Grass was not about to accept that. She placed a small hand on one of Riley's big shoulders and tugged. He resisted, so Spirit Grass reached down with her hand and pinched Riley's buttocks with strong fingers.

Riley jumped and half turned. "What the hell do ye think you're doin', woman?" he asked roughly.

"Now that you're lookin' at me again," Spirit Grass said, nonplussed, "tell me what's botherin' ye."

"It's not your concern," he said, but even as the words came out he knew they were lies. He smiled a little. "All right, it is your concern." He placed an arm around her shoulders and pulled her to him. She lay on her side, her front pressing along his side. He liked the feeling.

Without any more hesitation, he told her what Bridger had said. When he finished, she said, "And so, this makes ye unhappy?"

"Well, it means we've got to leave here."

"So?"

"So, I don't know where to go or what to do. We can go to Black Iron's village, I suppose, but I don't know how long I can stay there."

"Why not? I thought ye liked the People." She began running her left hand in circles through the hair on Riley's big chest.

"I do. But . . ." He wasn't sure how to explain this, and he certainly didn't want to upset her. "Well, it jist ain't right for me to not be doin' anything."

"Ye would hunt, and care for me and the children, and steal horses with the warriors, and go to war and . . ."

Riley placed a finger to Spirit Grass's lips. "Those things're fine, Spirit Grass," he said quietly. "But as much as I like the People, I ain't really one of 'em. A man like me's got to have work to do. White man's work. Like I been doin' here at the fort all these years now."

Spirit Grass had been afraid he was going to say something like that. She had known in her heart that he would have some need deep inside him, but had always thought it would not have to be revealed. She kissed him lightly, enjoying the tickling of the thick mustache he had grown a few years ago. It had taken her some time to get used to, but now she liked it. "Are there villages of your own people where ye could do such things?"

"Lots of 'em. Places like Salt Lake City, which I wouldn't go to. Trouble is, most of 'em are far to the east. Or in Californy."

"We could go to one of 'em," Spirit Grass said simply.

"It'd take ye miles and miles from the People, Spirit Grass. And you'd be alone there—alone in not havin' any friends or anything around."

"Maybe Paddy and Praises the Sky'd come with us." It came out as a question.

"I suppose that's true. But what if they don't?"

Spirit Grass shrugged, making her breasts move a little against her husband's skin. They both enjoyed the sensation. "Then I won't have no friends. Maybe I'll make friends there. If not, I have ye, and the children. Life'll be good."

"You're too optimistic, woman," Riley said gruffly, but he felt somewhat better.

"About more than one thing," she said with a smile, encircling his rigidity with her hand.

"Oh, so ye think ye want some of that, do ye?" he asked, kissing her forehead, nose, lips.

"Well, if ye ain't willin' . . ." she said playfully, removing her hand.

"Ye lookin' for a lodgepolin'?" he countered.

"Of one kind or another," Spirit Grass rejoined, replacing her hand. A moment later, she enthusiastically allowed herself to be pulled atop Riley.

It was the best news Riley had gotten since he had left the old trading post just over two years ago. The army was about to head west to retake the old post, as well as to restore federal control over Utah Territory. President Buchanan had finally concluded that the LDS Church and its ambitious leader, Brigham Young, had overstepped their authority, and were becoming an affront to the American people.

As soon as he had heard, Riley had gone to Fort Riley and spoken to the commander. He had no trouble in being hired on as a guide and interpreter. He knew in advance he would take a fair amount of joshing, since his name was the same as the fort's.

When he had left Bridger's fort up on Black's Fork— several days before Bridger was to make final the deal selling the place to the Mormons—he took the family to Black Iron's village. They wintered there, but right after the Shoshonis held their large spring buffalo hunt, he decided it was time to leave there and head for the Settlements.

He explained it to Spirit Grass that night in their lodge. She offered no objections, but Riley could see the disappointment and hurt in her eyes. That, in turn, made him feel guilty, and so he offered the only other alternative he could think of: "I can leave ye and the young'ns here, if ye want that," he said quietly.

If anything, there was even more hurt in her eyes now, and he felt like the worst man who had ever walked the earth.

"That what ye want?" Spirit Grass asked tensely.

"I'd rather have a hundred buffler use my nuts for a pawin' ground than leave ye here. I jist offered in case that's what ye wanted. I know ye really don't want to leave your family and friends."

"You and the young'ns're my family," she said simply. "But I . . ."

"It's true, I'd rather stay here with the People," Spirit Grass said. "But you're my husband, and I'll go where ye go. If that wasn't important to me, I would've thrown your possibles out of the lodge a long time ago." Her English had vastly improved in the twelve years or so they had been married.

"Ye certain?" Riley asked.

"Yep. Now let me go to sleep. There's much to do before we leave."

The next morning, Riley walked over to McGinnis's lodge—the young Irishman and his family had, of course, come along, too—and called for entrance. Inside, Riley wasted little time. "I'm leavin' out for the Settlements as soon as we can get ready, Paddy. I'd be proud to have ye come along."

"Without yer fam'ly?" McGinnis asked, shocked.

" 'Course not."

"That's a relief," McGinnis said with a laugh. "Fer a moment there, I thought ye'd gone and lost yer reason."

"There's been many a man before ye who's thought the same. I expect ye won't be the last one neither." He paused as Little Pony, McGinnis's three-year-old, tottered over to him and began hanging off his neck. The big blacksmith growled fiercely and pulled the toddler over his shoulder and onto his lap. He bent, slapped his lips on the boy's belly and "buzzed" him. The child erupted into shrieks of laughter.

Riley gave that up after a few minutes, set Little Pony

upright and sent him on his way. "Anyway, it'd suit this chil' if ye and your family was to ride along with us."

"That's a hell of a generous offer, One-Eye," McGinnis said truthfully. "I'll have to think on it some, though, and talk with Praises the Sky about it."

"Ye gonna let your wife make such decisions?" Riley asked, grinning to cover his embarrassment.

"Shit," McGinnis snorted. "Listen to ye. Like ye ne'er talked with Spirit Grass about all this. Ye're gettin' to be a damn poor liar in your old age."

Riley laughed. "Must be, if even some young snot like ye can find me out so easy." He paused. "I'm figurin' to ride out in about a week. That ought to be long enough for Spirit Grass to git ready. Whenever ye make up your mind, ye let me know."

"I will."

But his decision was not the one Riley had expected.

"I think I'm gonna head to Oregon, One-Eye," McGinnis said. "Seek out me mam, see me sisters."

Riley was disappointed and a little saddened that his friend wouldn't be traveling with him, but he could understand. "Well, boy, ye watch your topknot. There's many a hostile who'll raise hair on a lone white man." He smiled a bit ruefully.

"I'll watch out. Ye do the same."

Riley, Spirit Grass and their three children left soon after, traveling slowly, in no real hurry.

Riley was a little shocked when he reached Missouri. There were a lot more people than there had been when he had left so long ago. It was not much to his liking, so he moved around some, looking for a place where he and his family might be comfortable. He finally settled for a small farm near Fort Riley. He set up a blacksmith shop right off, but soon after went to the fort and got hired on as a scout.

He was glad that he had found a place outside of any town. Though Spirit Grass and the children had taken to wearing white people's clothing, they found out quickly that even in the frontier towns, Indian women and half-breed children were no longer welcome. And with Riley being gone so often, distance gave his family at least minimal protection from rabid Indian haters.

His frequent absences bothered him more than anything else, but he saw little he could do about them. He considered heading back to Black Iron's village, but that was unsatisfactory. He was the kind of man who needed work—real work—to do. And he could not find that in a Shoshoni village. So he decided to stick it out a while and see what happened.

Time dragged on and with it, Riley's annoyance and frustration grew. He drank more, although not to excess. He usually did so by himself, though he was generally in a town or at Fort Riley. It occasionally led to trouble, when someone who had gotten drunk thought to annoy an already irritated Riley, and found himself pounded to pulp.

So it was with great relief that Riley learned that a large force of soldiers was being sent to Fort Bridger and then on to Salt Lake City to return control of Utah Territory to the American government. He also learned that the fort was to be reopened as an Army post.

Seeing a chance for some revenge, as well as an opportunity to take his family home, Riley quickly and with no trouble at all got himself signed on.

Two weeks before the scheduled departure, Riley was standing outside his small house, watching the blazing sunset, and dreaming of being back along Black's Fork, when he saw some riders coming toward the house. ''Spirit Grass,'' he called over his shoulder, ''bring my guns.''

''Trouble?'' Spirit Grass asked as she handed him the Colt Walkers that Bridger had given him.

''Somebody's comin' this way. Until I find out who it is, I'll figure it's trouble. Take care of the kids.''

The figures out on the horizon shimmied and wiggled in the heat waves, but seemed to make little forward progress. Riley went in, got a drink of water, told his family that they didn't have to worry for a while, and then went back outside.

Finally the figures began to coalesce, and Riley decided it was either a small group of Indians, or perhaps some of the old mountain men. Another half-hour passed before the oncoming party became truly distinguishable.

"Spirit Grass!" Riley called excitedly. "C'mon out here, woman. Hurry!"

Spirit Grass hurried out the door, worry written over her face. Her children warily followed her.

"Look," Riley said, pointing to the approaching party. He was grinning hugely.

"Is it . . . ?"

"Hell, yes. It's Paddy, Praises the Sky and their young'ns. Goddamn!" He jumped off the porch, whooping, waving and in general acting like he was twelve years old again. Spirit Grass was more reserved, standing quietly on the edge of the porch, but her joy was evident in her beaming smile and fidgeting hands.

McGinnis stood in his stirrups and waved crazily when he saw Riley. Then he settled back into the saddle, jerked off his hat and swatted his horse's rump with it. He raced ahead, and with a flourish, pulled to a stop in a cloud of dust. He tumbled off his horse and practically jumped into Riley's arms.

The two men thumped each other and danced an impromptu jig, whooping and hollering, much to Spirit Grass's delight. Riley and McGinnis finally stopped their foolishness when Praises the Sky and the three children trotted up. Another small celebration took place among the two women and six children.

The men led all the horses to the small corral around the side of the house, while the women went inside, taking the youngest children with them, to prepare some food. The older children stayed outside, playing. It had been a long time since any of them had playmates other than their siblings.

It was well past dark by the time everyone was sitting

around the table, eating, talking and catching up on everything from the past two years. The kids made a lot of noise, which the adults ignored the best they could.

Finally, though, the children were sent off to their beds in the loft, and the adults could talk in peace. Coffee was poured, pipes lit and the four settled back at the table.

"So, my friend," Riley said, "what brings ye to these parts?" They really hadn't gotten around to talking about that—they had been occupied with what they had been doing this past year or so.

"Well, to tell ye, One-Eye," McGinnis said with a grin, "I plumb got sick of rain. Begorrah! It rained e'ery day out there, I swear. Christ, moss and bushes started growin' out of me." They all laughed, and when that welcome, and, they all realized, much-missed sound dwindled, he said, "Anyway's I was so sick of the rain, and me mam and sisters were all doin' well and so I . . ."

"What about your ma's husband?" Riley interjected.

A grim look flickered on McGinnis's face, and then faded. "Dumb bastard got drunk one night, fell in the river and drowned," McGinnis said, with something approaching pleasure in his voice. "Serves him right, the bug-humpin' son of a bitch." He sighed. "Well, that was a few years ago. Me mam remarried six months later to a man who seems to treat her well enough." He finished his coffee.

"Anyway, I figured I'd mosey on this way to try'n find ye," McGinnis continued, "see if maybe ye didn't want to go back to the mountains."

"And do what?"

"Damned if I know," McGinnis said somewhat defensively. He really didn't know. All he knew for sure was that he wanted to go back there.

Riley could see his own pain reflected in McGinnis's eyes. There was a longing in both of them. Riley's only real happiness had been in the mountains, whether running trap lines with Bridger back in the late thirties or working at the fort. He could see that McGinnis had the same general feelings.

"Well," Riley said slowly, "I cain't see ridin' all the way back there jist to wander around doin' nothin', boy."

McGinnis nodded, looking down, as a defeated air settled on his shoulders.

"Of course, was there a reason to do so," Riley said, trying to keep the grin off his face, "a reason like maybe the army headin' to Black's Fork, plannin' to reclaim the area for the country and reopenin' the old tradin' post as an army post, well, then I jist might consider such a thing."

McGinnis's head popped up, his eyes snapping with wonder and question. "Ye ain't jist joshin' me are ye, One-Eye?" he asked eagerly. "If ye are, I'll kill ye. I swear."

Riley laughed. "No, I ain't lyin' to ye, boy. Goddamn if that ain't somethin'. I jist hear a couple weeks ago of the army's plans, and I got me signed on to guide them boys out there. Ye showin' up is jist the icin' on the cake."

"Ye think I could go?" McGinnis's eyes sparkled with the possibility.

"Hell, yes. I been doin' a lot of work for the army since I been here, and I know the commanders pretty well. I got no uncertainty they'll be happy to hire a good man like ye. And if they don't, they can hire another guide. Me and ye can tag along with them for protection and see what we can set up once we git there."

"Ye that willin' to help me?" McGinnis asked, not too surprised. Nothing had been said, but he had felt for a long time that Riley considered him more than just a friend.

"Yep," Riley said seriously. "And it ain't jist 'cause I want to git back to the mountains myself somethin' awful."

McGinnis nodded. "When's this takin' place?"

"A few more weeks is all."

* * *

It was with growing anticipation that Riley and McGinnis finally rode out, minutes before the large army column left Fort Riley. They rode together, figuring to keep a half-mile or so ahead of the troops. It was early, and even if the Sioux, Pawnee and other tribes might still be on the prowl, there was no worry. With an army force this large, no Indians in the world would dare attack.

It was still fairly hot, so the two Irishmen set a leisurely pace on the trail. There was no need to wear down the horses, and there was no rush, if the army's commander —Colonel Albert Sydney Johnston—was to be believed.

Occasionally, Riley and McGinnis would stop on one of the interminable hillocks and let their horses breathe a little. Whenever they did, it was easy to see the long line of the column on their back trail, with the double line of mounted infantry and a seemingly endless line of supply wagons, including many civilian supply wagons for the outposts of various companies. They were along for the protection the army offered them. Bringing up the rear were the families of the civilians—Riley, McGinnis, several hunters, and the men who drove the wagons. Many of the wives along were Indians of various tribes, though a few were white.

At nights, Riley and McGinnis would set up camp with their families, off a little way from the rest of the civilians, preferring their own company. The two families were generally up before anyone else, the men fed and on the trail about the time the soldiers and the others were just getting ready to leave.

After a week or so, Riley and McGinnis began to chafe. They were used to traveling alone, or with just their families, and could make good time. But with this many soldiers, wagons and even hangers-on, the pace was almost painfully slow to the two free spirits. Still, across the open plains, they made fairly good time as they headed up the Republican River to the Platte.

Adding to the boredom of the trip was its uneventfulness. There were too many men along for Indians to attack, and animals fled before their advance. There were no wagon trains heading west at this time of year, though they did occasionally come on just a few families traveling together, heading east, giving up their dream of finding a new life in the west. The army generally would feed such people, allow them to sleep with the column that night and send them on their way in the morning with a warning to watch out for Indians.

A little over a month after leaving Kansas Territory, they reached Fort Laramie. The column spent a few days there. Riley met a few old mountaineers, and they spent some time yarning and such. He heard, too, that Bridger had been there not long before, and was a frequent visitor. Riley wasn't sure how he felt about Bridger these days, though with the passing of time, his anger and frustration with his old friend had lessened. He sort of wished he hadn't missed Bridger at the fort.

A couple of weeks later, they reached the eastern edges of Utah Territory, and the men—especially Riley and McGinnis, who were, as always, out front—became more wary. They had had reports from travelers heading east, as well as from men at Fort Laramie, that Brigham Young had organized a sizable militia and was planning to resist unto death the "invasion" of the American army.

Knowing what he did of Young, and the determination of the Mormons in general, Riley had told Johnston that the tales probably were true; thus the heightened wariness, as well as increased patrols and guards.

{ 32 }

The wariness of the troop was not misplaced. Almost as soon as they crossed the border into Utah Territory, guerrilla attacks started. They weren't much at first—a couple of men trying to run off some horses, some occasional sniping, strange sounds in the night to spook the animals and men. But the farther into Utah Territory the column proceeded, the more daring, desperate and deadly the Mormon attacks became.

The raids were fast, and directed at the lagging civilian wagons. By the time the army could mount any real kind of pursuit, the Saints, plunder in hand, would be long gone, leaving behind burning wagons and often some bodies. Riley and McGinnis finally went to Colonel Johnston.

"What can I do for you, men?" Johnston asked. He was a gruff but not unpleasant man, a tough but not harsh commander.

"Ye know, don't ye, that we're gonna be skeeter bit by those Mormons ever' step of the way?"

"The thought had crossed my mind," Johnston said dryly. "What's your point?"

"Me'n Paddy know this country better'n anyone here, but we ain't doin' ye much good as guides right now. Hell, a baby could foller this train now."

"Get to the point, Riley," Johnston warned. He could

be quite reasonable, but he was not a man who liked wasting time or effort.

"Relieve us of that duty, and let us mosey 'round the area, playin' the Mormons' game with 'em."

"Just the two of you?"

"Well, I don't know most of the other civilians, and I don't trust nobody but Paddy here."

"A few of my soldiers?"

"They'd cause more trouble than help, Colonel."

"You don't think United States soldiers are any good?"

"I ain't makin' light of your blue coats, Colonel," Riley said evenly. "It's jist that what I'm talkin' about ain't the kind of fightin' your boys know about. Your boys'll git a chance to show their stuff, I reckon. But these doin's ought to be left to boys like me'n Paddy." He didn't think it necessary to say that McGinnis really had little experience in this kind of fighting either.

"How much good do you think you can do—just the two of you?" Johnston asked.

Riley shrugged. "Maybe not too much, but I'll be damned if I'll jist sit here playin' target for them pot-shootin' shit piles."

Johnston's eyebrows rose in amusement, before he grew serious again. He took only a few moments to think it over. Then he nodded. "Will you two need anything?" He looked from Riley to McGinnis.

"Jist a couple boxes of paper cartridges. And that your boys keep a watch over our families whilst we're out there."

"It'll be done," Johnston said firmly. "Well, my good wishes go with you. If you two are successful, it'll make our endeavor considerably easier."

"We'll do what we can," Riley answered for himself and McGinnis, before they headed off to their own camp.

The two men were up and gone before dawn the next day. They had covered the hooves of their horses with sacking to muffle the sound. They were well-armed,

with two .44-caliber Colt revolvers in their waistbands
and two others in saddle holsters. Each also carried a
small, .36-caliber, four-shot pepperbox pistol secreted
under his shirt, and a single-shot, breach-loading rifle in
a saddle scabbard. Riley carried his large knife, and he
had brought out his old tomahawk. McGinnis had no
use for the latter, but he sported a long dagger. They
had enough food—jerky, some parched corn, hardtack,
coffee—for several days, though they did not plan to be
out that long at any one time.

They rode in a generally northeasterly direction, moving slowly, ever alert. Over the next several days, they
had a couple of small skirmishes. They didn't do much
damage, but they did scare off a couple of guerrilla
parties, including one led by a fierce-looking man with a
long, black beard. The Danites managed to burn two
more wagons, run off a dozen more horses and steal
some food and other supplies. Riley thought he and
McGinnis were doing some good, however. So did Colonel Johnston. They returned to the column each night,
staying with their families and heading out again before
dawn the next day.

As the sun reached its zenith on the fifth day of their
patrols, they stopped amid some rocks about a quarter-
mile from the main trail. They unsaddled their horses
and broke out their meager provender. The wind whistled and clacked off the rocks around them, bringing a
scattering of dust. It was a cold, brittle November wind,
and in it, Riley could feel a touch of the winter which
was to arrive soon.

The two men talked quietly while they ate. There
wasn't much that needed to be said, really. They had
talked much on the journey out here. Still, neither was a
man who liked to be silent, so they found things to chat
about, and Riley mentioned more than once that they
were only a day's travel or so from the fort. He would be
glad to get there, since it was about the only home he
knew any longer.

While McGinnis was responding to something Riley

had said, the older man suddenly held up a hand, indicating that McGinnis should shut up. The younger man did so immediately, knowing that Riley must have heard something. To McGinnis, Riley's hearing was uncanny, as was his eyesight, though he had only the one eye.

Riley cocked his head to the wind, trying to pick up whatever it was that had caught his attention in the first place. He had no idea what it was; he just knew there was something out there moving around. He was more than half certain it was just an animal, but he could not afford not to be suspicious.

Then he heard it again. It sounded like a hoof clacking on rock.

He pulled his rifle to him and rose until he was on one knee. With hand signals, he told McGinnis to move toward some high rocks a few yards south of where they sat. Riley scrambled up another pile of boulders more to the west. Once settled on his stomach across a mostly flat rock, he spotted eight white men riding at an angle from his position, toward a break in the rocks that would place them right on the road the army column would be using. The group was led by Porter Rockwell.

Riley considered dropping Rockwell then and there, but he could not bring himself to do it. It was possible that they were on perfectly legitimate business. Even if they weren't, they had done nothing wrong as far as Riley could tell. He might dislike Mormons—even hate some individuals among them—but he was not a cold-blooded killer. Besides, he could admit to himself a grudging admiration for Rockwell.

The point became moot moments later when the group rode around a rock-strewn hill off to Riley's left, and were lost to his sight. He remained where he was for a few more minutes, waiting to make sure no one else was coming, and to be certain the group did not return. Finally he stood and climbed down from his perch.

He went back to eating, waiting for McGinnis to return, which he did a few minutes later.

"Ye saw?" McGinnis asked as he sat in the dirt.

Riley nodded. "How far'd ye see 'em go?"

"Not too far, but almost to the road. They Mormons?"

"Yep. Porter Rockwell's leadin' 'em."

"What're we gonna do about 'em?"

"Foller 'em. See if we can find out what they're up to."

McGinnis nodded. "Shouldn't we get movin' then, before they get too far ahead of us?" he asked.

"Hell," Riley responded with a snort, "I ain't plannin' to ride right up their asses. They jist might discover us."

"Seems doubtful," McGinnis said with a chuckle. "But ye never can tell."

They took their time saddling their horses, but finally pulled out. They moved cautiously along the group's back trail, not wanting to be found out, and not wanting to learn too late that the group had stopped.

When they were within sight of the road, Riley pulled into the trees and rocks nearby and stopped. "Wait here and watch over the horses, boy," he said. "I'm gonna climb up yonder rock pile and see what I can see." When he got to the top, he lay there, scanning up and down the road, but mostly across it. Patiently he waited, watching. He was certain he would see the group.

After a bit, he could hear the soldiers and wagons coming. He shook his head. Such a group would never be able to sneak up on anything. He recalled what it was like when he was trapping with Bridger's brigade up in Blackfoot land. Even though those Indians had been pretty well decimated by smallpox, they were still formidable warriors. Yet a brigade of forty or fifty men, plus horses, mules and gear, could make it through such country without being discovered. With the noise the blue coats were making, a whole village could fold its lodges, pack their goods, round up all the horses and be miles away by the time the army got to the village. If they were ever going to gain a real foothold out in this great wide west, Riley figured, they were going to have to learn to move a lot more silently than this.

But that was not for him to judge. He didn't think the army would ever move into the mountains and plains in any real big way. There were simply too many Indians, and every tribe would be downright hostile to them. They would . . .

He cut off the thought when he spotted a movement deep in the trees and rocks across the road. Focusing, he could make out individual men moving into position behind or on boulders. He wondered at first why they had chosen to go on that side of the road, when he had a higher vantage point. Then he realized that from the other side, the men would have a much clearer and longer view of the road in both directions.

The army column was just beginning to pass beneath him, and he knew he must hurry. He slithered backward on the rocks until he thought himself safe from view, then half rose and clambered down to the ground.

"That ye, One-Eye?" McGinnis called softly.

"Yes, it's me, goddammit," Riley growled quietly, but he was proud of McGinnis for having been alert and wary.

McGinnis materialized from behind a tree, grinning a little. "I did all right?" he asked. He seemed almost shy, something he wasn't, in most cases.

"Yep. Now tie them horses off and let's go."

"Trouble?"

"Yep. The Mormons're settin' jist across the road all ready to do the devil's work." He wished now that he had shot at least Rockwell before, but he knew in his heart that he had done the right thing.

Rifles in hand, the two climbed back up to the rough aerie. Lying there, Riley pointed out where the Mormons were. They were hard to spot, since they blended in well with the surrounding landscape, but their subtle movements marked them for McGinnis.

"Why don't we take out a couple of 'em now?" Mc-

Ginnis asked nervously as the first of the soldiers moved between the two small groups of men.

"Ye got a clear shot at any a one of 'em?" Riley countered.

"Well, no, but . . ."

"Look, we know they ain't gonna attack the soldiers. Them shit piles'll wait till the wagons come along. And I'd wager a heap that they'll wait till the last wagon or two. They'll hit hard and fast jist like they've done all along, grab some plunder, run off a couple horses and set a wagon or two on fire. Then they'll run like hell."

"Got it all figured out, have ye?" McGinnis asked, not surprised.

"Well, they seem to be critters of habit. But do ye know why they'll wait till the last of the wagons?"

"No."

"So's they can't be follered easy. They'll have one wagon that the driver is tryin' to control because his horses're actin' up, and another wagon behind that, on fire. Both'll be blockin' the road and causin' so much consternation that they can make their escape without gittin' caught."

"So what're we gonna do?"

"Wait till they're jist about ready to attack and give 'em a goddamn surprise," Riley said harshly.

The wait was a fairly lengthy one, as the long army column dragged on and on. Then came the wagons, first the army's, then the civilian ones. The women and children walked or rode alongside or in between the wagons for the most part.

"Where's Praises the Sky and Spirit Grass and the kids?" McGinnis asked, beginning to get worried when he didn't see the two families for some time.

"Probably bringin' up the rear again—like usual," Riley growled. He, too, was worried, but he didn't want to show it.

"That could be trouble, eh?"

"Could be," Riley replied evenly. "But Spirit Grass's

got enough sense to know she and the others should
cache as soon as the shootin' starts. She'll see to 'em.''

"Still, One-Eye, if shootin' starts, there's no tellin'
what could happen down there. Any one of them
could . . .''

"Don't ye dare say it, boy. Don't ye even goddamn
think it,'' Riley hissed, his one eye glaring hotly at his
companion.

McGinnis gulped hard and nodded.

More wagons lurched along the road, creaking and
rattling. Finally Riley said, "By my count, there ain't but
four, five wagons left, boy. Best git ready. And pay attention to them boys over yonder, not the wagons or your
woman. With all this dust, it's gonna be damned hard to
see them shit piles at best.''

McGinnis nodded again, not figuring that needed a
reply.

After a couple more wagons rolled past their spot,
Riley and McGinnis noticed some movement across the
dusty road. "Git set, boy,'' Riley said urgently. "Ye take
anyone left of that one peaked rock over there. The one
with the notch about halfway down. Ye see which one I
mean?''

"Yeah. You'll handle anyone on the other side?''

"Yep.''

33

Riley and McGinnis fired at almost the same moment, and across the road, two men fell. One bounced down the pile of jumbled boulders until he stopped about halfway down against a short dead tree sticking out of a rock.

As Riley rolled onto his side to reload, he glanced down. As he expected, Spirit Grass was already shepherding Praises the Sky and all the children into the trees and rocks on his side of the road. "The women and kids've cached," Riley said, as he rolled back onto his stomach. He pulled back the hammer and tried to find someone to sight on. He caught a fleeting glimpse of a man, and he fired, but he didn't hit anything.

Neither did McGinnis on his second shot. Both swore and reloaded. Several balls whined as they ricocheted on the rocks where the two were lying.

Suddenly Riley jumped up. "C'mon, boy," he said as he ran recklessly down the rocky barricade.

McGinnis was only moments behind. He slipped at one point, falling on his buttocks and bouncing down several rocks, each landing on his seat or side hurting a bit more than the last. In the process, he lost his rifle, and one of his pistols fell out of his belt. He managed to stop the fall and right himself, then resumed his headlong flight down the boulders.

Riley had already hit the ground and was racing

toward where he and McGinnis had left the horses. He was certain that Spirit Grass would've looked for the animals and taken shelter there. He was right, but the Mormons were already infiltrating the area. One was moving toward Praises the Sky, who was crouched over her three children, trying to protect them.

The woman didn't look frightened, just resigned. She had considered getting up and fighting, but that would have left her children completely unprotected. She had no weapons, except for the rather small knife in her belt, but that would do little against the pistol the man was carrying.

Riley put on a burst of speed, which he didn't know he had in him, and slammed into the Mormon. They both tumbled over and over for a few yards before halting. Both lost their weapons—the Saint his pistol, Riley his rifle.

Riley, having been the aggressor, was up first. He stomped the few steps toward the man, who was on hands and knees, trying to get up. Riley grabbed him by the shirt collar and the seat of the pants, lifted him with relative ease, and pitched him forward. The Mormon's head slammed into a boulder, and he groaned. Still, he was not out, and he struggled to get up again.

Riley grabbed him by the shoulders and hauled him to his feet. "Ought not to go tryin' to pull your wickedness on women and children, shit pile," Riley growled, breathing hard. He snapped his big right paw on the back of the man's neck and smashed his face into the boulder again and again. He could hear bones splintering and cracking; blood splashed all over the large rock.

Finally he dropped the damaged, dying thing and turned toward his right to see where his friend was.

McGinnis had not been too far behind Riley getting to the bottom of the boulder pile, but when he saw that the big man was taking care of the Saint who had tried to molest his wife and children, and that there seemed to be no other Mormons in the immediate vicinity, he stopped at his family's side. All were fine, and he breathed a sigh of relief. He looked up, over at Riley, and his face drained to a sickly white. A Saint was about to shoot Riley in the heart from only five feet behind and off to his left side. He yelled, but it was too late already.

The shout did, however, startle the Mormon. His arm jerked as he fired, and the ball punched at an angle high into the meat of Riley's back, about halfway between the shoulder and the neck.

The power of the ball from so close knocked Riley to the ground. He rolled onto his back right away, reaching for one of the pistols in his belt. He heard Spirit Grass scream, and glanced back. She was charging the Mormon like a demon. "Sweet Christ," he murmured as he frantically jerked at his pistol. The Mormon was swinging his gun toward Spirit Grass, and she would be dead in seconds.

McGinnis came flying into the picture, which seemed to Riley to be unfolding, somewhat dreamlike, at a fantastically slow pace. McGinnis tackled the Saint, whose pistol fired. The ball screamed off a rock, and the two men grappled on the ground. McGinnis gained the upper hand, sitting on top of the Mormon and keeping a tight grip on the Saint's gun hand. He ignored the punches the man threw at his side for the moment. He glanced down, wanting to make sure his other pistol was there before letting go of the Mormon even for a moment. It, too, had been lost when he crashed into the Saint. "Begorrah!" he muttered.

Riley had finally gotten a revolver out. Seeing that McGinnis seemed to have control of his situation, he got to his feet, testing his wounded shoulder a little. Spirit Grass reached him and placed her arms around his waist, looking up at him with concerned eyes.

"I'm all right, woman," he said. "Now let go of me so I can help Paddy." He turned toward McGinnis and the Mormon just in time to see a glint of steel, that a moment later sank into the side of McGinnis's abdomen, just below the ribs.

McGinnis gasped, and his eyes widened. "Fuckin' Limey bastard," he cursed, as he pulled one hand free and punched the Saint in the face. The force of it loosened his other hand on the Mormon's wrist. The Saint shoved McGinnis off him, and stood. He aimed his pistol at the Irishman and said, "Atone in blood, damn you." Then he fired.

Shocked by the bullet wound, and by the sight before him, Riley's reactions were slow. But he was galvanized now. He lifted his revolver, cocked it and fired, cocked it and fired. Nothing happened. "Goddamn gun," he growled, throwing the Colt away. He had never had a gun misfire on him twice in a row. The powder must have gotten wet somehow, he figured, or the caps had fallen off in the melee.

Riley began stalking toward the Mormon, jerking out his other Colt. But just before he fired, he decided this was one killing that needed doing by hand, close up. He tossed the gun away.

The Saint had turned toward him, and noticed the action. He grinned evilly, and raised his own six-shot Colt. "You, too, shall atone in blood, damn you." He pulled the trigger. The gun clicked. Again and again.

Focused as he was on the man in front of him, Riley was only vaguely aware of someone a little ways off yelling, "Flee, men. Flee!"

"Even a toad-suckin' shit pile like ye should be able to count to six," Riley said as he stopped in front of the Mormon and snatched the pistol out of the man's hands. He threw it aside and reached behind his back to pull out his tomahawk. "I ain't 'hawked me a feller in some time, so forgive me if I'm a bit rusty at it."

The Mormon suddenly punched Riley in the jaw. He was surprised it had no effect on the former mountain man. Not hesitating, though, he hit Riley hard on the bloody hole where the lead ball had come out the upper chest.

That had some impact, and Riley staggered back a step. The Saint moved up and kicked him in the leg, and Riley started to list to the side. At the same time, he swung the tomahawk. The sharp blade sliced into the side of the Mormon's hip, hit bone, and slid down, eventually tearing out a chunk of flesh about four inches square. Blood began to flow freely down his leg.

"How's them apples, shit pile," Riley growled. He had reached a point where he was absolutely calm, yet singularly deadly. All his being was focused on the job at hand. Everything else was secondary. He felt no pain, saw no one but the Mormon in front of him. He had only been like this a few times in his life, but it felt comfortable to him, like an old friend who had come to visit. He realized the man looked familiar, but he could not place him. It didn't matter now.

Riley suddenly raised the tomahawk in both hands and swung it down. The weapon hit the Saint on the top of the left shoulder, plowing its way through the clavicle and several inches of flesh. The power of the blow drove the Mormon to his knees. Riley did the same to the Saint's other side, but his aim was a little off this time, and the powerfully driven weapon sliced through shoulder and armpit, hacking the man's arm clean off. Blood spurted from the severed brachial artery.

"Ye kilt a good man there, shit pile," Riley spat out in short, choppy syllables, "and ye deserve to suffer plenty for such a wicked deed."

"I . . . I . . ."

Riley dropped his bloody tomahawk and grabbed the Saint. Gripping the sides of the man's head with his fingers, he set his big thumbs on his eyes and exerted a relentless, steady pressure.

The Mormon screamed.

Then someone was pulling on Riley's hands. He seemed to awake from a trancelike state, and looked around dumbly.

"Let him be now, One-Eye," Sergeant Wally Dirmyer kept repeating. He was a big man, larger by a fair amount than Riley, but he was having difficulty pulling Riley's hands free of the Saint's head.

When Riley realized who it was trying to stop him, he relented. He released the man, who fell in a pool of his own blood. His screaming had stopped, and he was on death's door.

"Don't worry about him, One-Eye," Dirmyer said. "He won't last another two minutes." His voice dropped. "Go see to your friend."

Riley looked blankly at Dirmyer for a few moments, then nodded and turned. He was surprised to see that McGinnis was still alive. Praises the Sky was kneeling beside him already, her children being watched by Spirit Grass for the moment. Riley squatted.

"Took ye long enough to put that Limey scum under, One-Eye," McGinnis said weakly. He tried to smile, but couldn't. "I was waitin' till ye finished that, so I could say me goodbyes to ye. I didn't think I was gonna make it, seein' as how ye seemed set on makin' the killin' of that Limey prick yer life's work."

"Shut up," Riley said gruffly. "Quit wastin' your energies. You'll need 'em to git better. The surgeon ought to be here soon."

"Eat shit." McGinnis had to stop to cough, and when he was done, he was even weaker and paler. "Ain't no one gonna be able to help me now." His hand reached out, flailing feebly, until Riley caught it in his own two large hands. That seemed to strengthen McGinnis just a bit.

"I ain't ever had a brother," Riley admitted. "Nor even a real close friend. Ol' Ed there was a good friend fer sure, but not to say my closest one. Not like he was a partner or some such. That was all true till ye came along." Riley knew he was babbling but he didn't care. "If I'd have been given a pick sometime to choose whoever I wanted for a brother—or a friend—you'd have been it. No doubt."

Riley paused, trying to get his emotions under control, but he did not have the power, or the desire, it seemed, to do so. Tears ran down his cheeks and dripped on McGinnis's shirt. He sobbed once or twice.

"Why the hell did ye have to go and git yourself kilt for, ye goddamn idiot?"

"Wasn't my intent," McGinnis said, his voice barely audible. He managed to look up at Praises the Sky and ordered, "Kiss me." After she did, he used just about every ounce of strength he had left to half smile at Riley. He tried to say something, but could not.

And then he was dead.

Riley sat there for some time, just holding onto McGinnis's hand. Praises the Sky stroked her husband's head. Riley didn't feel the afternoon's cold, nor would he have cared if he had. Finally, he placed McGinnis's hand gently over his chest. He rose, and then forced Praises the Sky to do so, too. He led the woman to Spirit Grass and the children, knowing that his wife would take care of the new widow. It was doubly difficult for Praises the Sky because she had no real outlet for her grief. Riley knew she wanted to wail and screech and hack at herself, but she would not do those things in the presence of so many white men. For now, she would keep it bottled up.

Colonel Johnston strode up with a couple of fawning lieutenants in tow. "I'm sorry to hear about your friend, Mister Riley," Johnston said, seeming to mean it.

Riley nodded.

"I'll have the men prepare a grave for him, and we'll lay him to rest as best we can," the colonel continued.

"No," Riley said flatly, surprising Johnston. "I aim to take him back and bury him in the tradin' post's ol' cemetery."

"Not to be crude, One-Eye," Johnston said in discomfit, "but do you think he'll keep?"

Riley nodded. "We git a move on and make a bit more mileage today, we should be at the ol' place around noon tomorrow."

"Is there anything we can do to help?"

"Let me have a couple army issue blankets. And make some room in one of the wagons for the body."

"See to it, Lieutenant Larson."

One of the sycophants nodded.

"Anything else, One-Eye?" Johnston asked.

"Let me have one of your men for a bit. I need a small task done. It's menial to you and your men, really, but important to me."

"Anyone in particular?"

Riley shrugged. He really knew few of the soldiers at all. "Sergeant Dirmyer'd be all right, if he doesn't think my task is beneath him," Riley said.

"Get the sergeant, Lieutenant Dutton." Johnston pointed to Riley's shoulder. "Make sure you have the surgeon take a look at that soon."

The colonel left and a few moments later Dirmyer showed up, looking confused. "Lieutenant said for me to report to you, One-Eye," he said.

Riley silently cursed himself for that physical deformity. If he had had both his eyes, none of this would have happened. It was because he had no peripheral vision on his left side that the Mormon was able to sneak up on him, precipitating the entire episode.

"I need something small done, Sergeant," Riley said wearily. "And you're about the only one of the blue coats here I really know. However, ye don't have to do it. Ye don't like what it is, or if ye think it's beneath your position, jist say the word, and we can find us some private ye ain't too keen on."

"Hell, it might help if you'd tell me jist what it was you wanted me to do, One-Eye."

"I dropped my rifle somewhere along in here today, and tossed away my two pistols. Colt Walkers they were."

"No problem, One-Eye."

"There's something else," Riley said, embarrassed now to ask. "Paddy lost his weapons, too. I think he dropped his rifle when we come tumblin' down the rocks over yonder. I don't know about his revolvers."

"What're you aimin' to do with his weapons, if you don't mind my askin'?" Dirmyer said, curious.

"I ain't sure," Riley answered thoughtfully. "I jist know either I—or he—ought to have 'em."

"Those guns're as good as found," Dirmyer said. He could understand the sentiments Riley had. He had felt the same himself when he had lost a close friend in battle. "You just take a seat and let Doctor Arbegast see to your wound."

{ 34 }

Riley sat there looking at the island between the two branches of Black's Fork. He swore, several times. He turned his horse and rode back toward the army column, which was still a half-mile or so down the road.

"Ye ain't gonna believe this, Colonel," he said, stopping next to Johnston, but facing in the opposite direction. "There ain't a damn thing left of Bridger's ol' post except a block wall around most of it, which the Mormons must've built, 'cause it weren't there before they took over the place. Them shit piles must've jist burned it, too, since the thing's still smolderin'."

"Damn, that's unfortunate," Johnston snapped. "There's nothing we can use left?"

"Nope."

"What're we going to do about the winter, which is fast approaching?"

"I hope ye brought along your tents, Colonel," Riley said flatly. "If not, your boys best be the fastest damn builders the mountains've ever seen." He turned and trotted off, not really wanting anyone's company. He made it back to the old trading post site quickly, and again sat and looked over the place. It brought back a flood of remembrances: marrying Spirit Grass, the birth of Laughing Swan, meeting and helping McGinnis, the fights with raiding Blackfeet and Sioux, the coming of the Saints, the celebrations the men had had in the small square, the fight with the Mormons there, the humiliation of leaving.

But mostly, right now, he remembered Paddy McGinnis, his friend and companion for a fair many years. He was bitter and sick at heart at having caused McGinnis's death. And now all he could think of were the good times the two of them had had together. The only thing worse he could imagine would be Spirit Grass dying. That was the only thing he could think of that would make him grieve more deeply.

The soldiers began arriving at the site, but Riley stayed where he was—alone and out of the way. Only when the wagon bearing McGinnis's body arrived did he move, heading down to direct the driver where to take the body. There, in the old cemetery, he and the driver removed the blanket-wrapped corpse from the wagon and laid it gently on the ground. The driver got two shovels and dropped them nearby, assuming he would have to help dig the grave. He was not keen on the idea.

"Obliged," Riley said curtly to the driver, surprising the man.

Before Riley could change his mind, the driver climbed back onto his seat and drove the wagon away.

Riley was somewhat surprised to see the cemetery in such good shape. He figured the Mormons must have kept it nice while they had run the fort. Riley grudgingly had to acknowledge that, at least.

With a sigh, he pulled off his coat and picked up a shovel. Then he began digging. He had been at it perhaps twenty minutes and was making steady but mighty slow progress, when all of a sudden, Sergeant Dirmyer was beside him, a shovel in his hands.

Bent over, the blade of his shovel in the earth, Riley looked at the soldier. "This ain't necessary, ye know," he said.

"I know," Dirmyer acknowledged.

Riley nodded, and they both went back to digging. When they finished, they wiped off their hands and carefully laid McGinnis in the fresh grave. Then Dirmyer stood back, watching respectfully as Praises the Sky and Riley placed several items in the hole with McGinnis—a knife, a buckskin shirt Praises the Sky had made for him, eagle feathers to speed him on his journey, a little jerky and biscuit and the few treasured letters McGinnis had received over the years from his mother and sisters.

Spirit Grass brought up McGinnis's favorite horse, a strong, prepossessing piebald. Riley unsaddled it and placed the saddle—with the two Walkers in the holsters there—into the grave. Then he walked the horse close to the grave, and calmly shot the animal in the head, making Dirmyer jump. Several soldiers came running toward them, fear stamped on their faces, but Dirmyer waved them away.

When the horse quit kicking, Riley sliced off its tail and gently set that in the grave, too. Then he grabbed a shovel. "Goodbye, ol' friend," he whispered before pitching the first shovelful of dirt in the grave.

Dirmyer swiftly joined in, and between the two strong men it did not take long before the grave was filled in and the slightly rounded mound of dirt packed tightly down. All the while, Praises the Sky and Spirit Grass had been praying in Shoshoni for McGinnis's safe and rapid journey to the afterlife.

As Riley gave the grave dirt one last smack with the shovel, Johnston said from behind him, "Would you like me to say some words over your friend, Mister Riley?"

The blacksmith turned and nodded. He was pleased to see that Johnston also had been thoughtful enough to have his men make a cross for the grave. It was made of boards from one of the wagons, and words printed on it said: *Here lies Paddy McGinnis, a good man, died Nov. 1858.*

The service, which was how Riley saw it, was brief, and full of laudatory phrases for the deceased. When it was over, the soldiers went back to their work. Riley got his wagon and pulled it up to where he and the other fort workers used to have their tiny village. There Spirit Grass and Praises the Sky put up the two lodges, just like in the old days. Riley set up shop, as it were, right there by his lodge and the wagon of his tools.

Riley worked for almost a week, getting done everything the army needed him to do for the time being. He was glad for the work, mostly, since it kept his thoughts off McGinnis, at least part of the time. But after that week, he was ready to get away from this place. He went to see Johnston. "I'm leavin' out in the mornin'," he announced.

"Where?" the colonel asked, surprised. "Why?"

"From the signs I've been seein', this is gonna be a hell of a winter, Colonel. I'd recommend ye have your boys start gittin' some log shelters built. There's a little time before winter really gits here. And ye best git a bunch of 'em out huntin' so's ye got enough meat to last ye."

"I'll do that," Johnston said solemnly. "But what's that have to do with your leaving?"

"I can provide for my family, Colonel, and for Paddy's family," Riley said. It seemed to Johnston that the one-time mountain man hadn't heard him. "But the way I figured it, you're gonna be hard-pressed to keep your men fed and sheltered. I don't need none of your men come sneakin' around my lodge lookin' to see what they can pick up. Besides, I want to git Praises the Sky back to her people. It's where she belongs, especially at a time like this. So I'm gonna head to one of the Shoshoni villages."

"And then return, of course?"

"Nope. I aim to winter in Black Iron's village myself. I'll be back come spring."

"We could use you here, One-Eye." Johnston said. He was pretty certain he was going to get nowhere with his request, but he had to try.

"Ye don't need me for much, Colonel. Like I said, I'll be back."

"Can I take that as a promise?" Johnston pressed.

"If I don't go under somewhere between here and Black Iron's, I'll be back."

Johnston nodded. "Who's this Black Iron? I assume he's chief of the Shoshonis."

"He's a chief. One of many. Most Indians out here don't have any concept of a big chief and a bunch of little chiefs. They have civil chiefs, who sort of keep an eye on the way things're goin' in the village. But ain't no one has to listen to 'em. There's also war chiefs. Each one's in absolute charge for the duration of the war party he's leadin'. That's about it. Lots of both types git more important status from a lifetime of honor and wisdom, courage and action. Then they become real leaders, since the People willingly want to follow 'em."

"And is Black Iron one of these men?"

Riley nodded.

"Do you know him well?"

"He's my father-in-law."

Johnston's eyes widened in surprise.

"Well, ye mind what I told ye, Colonel," Riley said, rising. "Even if ye cain't git any shelters built, it'd be wise to make sure ye had a heap of meat put up. And ye might want to git some lumber cut and let it season some. Then ye can git an early start on buildin' when spring comes. *Adios.*"

There were still some weeks to go before spring arrived when Sharp Hawk brought Riley back into Black Iron's village. The one-time mountain man was half frozen and more than half starved, and he looked more dead than alive. His walk was an old man's shuffling gait, and he had trouble recognizing people.

"Damn fool," Spirit Grass muttered at her husband when her brother brought Riley into her lodge and placed him on the bed of buffalo robes.

When Riley had gotten to the village late in the fall, he decided he could not stay there. He craved solitude, so he had ridden off, alone and with little in the way of supplies. When winter hit, it did so with a fury, turning far worse than even Riley had imagined. He had managed to hunt for a while, but as the snow deepened and the cold worsened, the game disappeared. He had faced starvin' times before, but none quite this bad. He managed to survive on the leavings of scavengers, and the occasional old or crippled animal he stumbled on.

He had lived in a dismal, small cave for the winter. He had trouble keeping a fire going, since fuel for it was also sparse. Eventually he began to have visions, but not the kind he or his Shoshoni friends would look for. They were brought on by hunger and cold—and even fear.

In one of his rapidly dwindling periods of lucidity, he decided he had to try to make it back to Black Iron's village. If he didn't, he would surely die. There were times when that thought was a good one. He had caused death to others, including some, like McGinnis, who had not deserved it. It would be only fitting for him to die out here like an animal. But then he remembered Spirit Grass, Flat Nose, Arrives With Trouble and Laughing Swan. He knew he was selfish, but he wanted to see his wife and children again. That, plus an innate survival instinct, would not allow him to just sit and die.

He scavenged up some meat from a couple of old kills and ate as much as he could. There was precious little left by then, but he packed it away and finally left the cave. Six days later, two days since he had had anything to eat at all, he grew delirious again, alternating with periods of regretful awareness of his desperate situation.

Then things got blurry for him, and he had no idea how long he had traveled or where he was at any given time. Not until he awoke in his own lodge, with Spirit Grass and Sharp Hawk looking worriedly down on him. "Good goddamn," he mumbled, "there is an afterlife, and it's like the Shoshonis told me."

"This isn't the afterlife," Spirit Grass said, relieved. She knew Riley was still in danger, but if he was awake and lucid, she was fairly certain he would recover.

"It ain't?" he asked, bewildered. "Ye mean I'm home?"

Spirit Grass nodded, her joy growing.

Riley sighed. He should have known better. After being responsible for McGinnis's death, there would be no way the Great Spirit would welcome him into the afterlife. No, his spirit probably would be left to wander alone in nothingness for all eternity. But he was silent, figuring that if he was going to face such a life after death, he might as well live a little longer in this world.

With his iron constitution and equally strong will, plus Spirit Grass's care, it was not long before Riley was back on his feet. It was just about spring, though, when he really felt that he was fully recovered. The months had lessened his guilt over McGinnis's death a little, and he almost looked forward to heading back to the site of the old trading post. He wondered how the soldiers had fared. Still, after the harsh winter that had gripped the land, he did not want to leave too early.

Patience growing thin three weeks later, he finally decided it was time. Spirit Grass and Sharp Hawk lobbied to have him leave the children in the village—"so they can be raised properly," Spirit Grass had said—but Riley refused. "I want 'em to git a book education," he said adamantly. "The boys started it back in Kansas, and I want 'em to continue it here, as best they can."

"But that's useless," Sharp Hawk said. "They'll learn everything they need to know from me and the others." Riley's brother-in-law was quite angry about it. As Flat Nose's uncle, the training of the boy should have fallen to him. He had looked forward to that role.

"I ain't changin' my mind," Riley said. And when he and Spirit Grass rode out two days later, the three children were with them.

He was quite surprised to see how much work had gone on at the fort site, although spring had really just arrived. No buildings were up yet, but a number of them had been started and seemed to be progressing quickly, and two lunettes had been finished. He also learned that the army had suffered considerably.

"It got so bad," Johnston said, "that I had to send Captain Marcy and a detachment to Fort Massachusetts to try to get some supplies. A bunch of your old mountain friends showed up here at one point, and decided to go with the troops I was sending. I'm afraid, though," he added sadly, "that their fate was not good."

Riley said nothing. His own loss was still too fresh.

Johnston shook off the gloom somewhat. There was always a chance that Marcy and his troop had survived. "Well, as you can see, One-Eye," he finally said, "things're picking up around here. Come, I want to show you something."

They rode to the spot a few yards from Black's Fork, almost exactly where Riley had generally set up his lodge. Next to his wagon of tools was a pile of unplaned lumber. "I thought this'd be a good spot for your cabin, One-Eye," he said.

"Ye want me to stay on?"

"If you're of a mind to. We'll need a good blacksmith."

Riley nodded.

A few weeks later, a rider came into camp, bearing a message from Brigham Young. In the letter, which Johnston showed to Riley, the Mormon leader announced he would not resist the army as he had promised all along he would. With that, Johnston made plans for leaving, but it gave him more freedom. He decided that he would leave a sizable detachment here to continue erecting buildings and otherwise developing a military post.

Less than a month after that, Marcy and most of his detachment, including Sergeant Dirmyer, arrived. Though the supplies were not needed nearly as desperately as they had been during the winter, the men still celebrated their arrival.

Johnston finally left, taking most of the soldiers and

wagon drivers with him. Marcy went along with his company. Johnston named Major William Hoffman commander of the fort-to-be. When the first building—the post commander's quarters—was raised, Hoffman "christened" the fort, naming it for the man who had been such a large part of the history of the area, Jim Bridger. Riley felt rather proud of that, having gotten over his anger at his old friend.

With the advent of summer, work on the fort picked up steam, moving along rapidly. Riley built his cabin with the help of several soldiers, and directed the building of his blacksmith shop, this one with a real forge and bellows. By mid-June, he was at work in the shop, and relatively happy about it.

New troops arrived in mid-August, including a new fort commander, one Major Edward Canby, and a Lieutenant Irwin Keyes. Also along were the wives of several officers, including Canby, plus Judge Carter's wife. It made the unfinished fort seem almost homey in some ways.

Riley waited for what he thought was a reasonable enough time for Canby to get settled in, and then he asked to speak with the new commander. He introduced himself and said, "Colonel Johnston hired me as the fort's blacksmith, but I ain't one to force myself where I ain't welcome. Ye prefer someone else for the job, I'll not stand in the way."

Canby looked the big blacksmith over and decided he was satisfied with what he had seen, and heard. "I assume Colonel Johnston chose you for a reason, Mister Riley. I see no reason as yet to change that. If I ever think you're not doing a good enough job, I'll let you know."

"Obliged, Major."

PART 3

PART 3

"That's a hell of a story, One-Eye," Canby said. He felt sad yet exhilarated. "I reckon you have a heap of reason to hate the Mormons."

"Glad ye think so," Riley said sarcastically. He refilled his glass with whiskey. "Does it mean you've changed your mind?"

"About the court-martial, and arresting those Saints? No. I'm sorry, One-Eye, but those things're impossible."

Riley had liked Canby since the officer had taken over command of the fort a year or so ago. Canby was a fair, reasonable man, one not given over to making rash or foolish decisions. Until now, Riley thought. Canby was not an Indian hater like so many other military men out this way, and he generally did not take sides with ones like Keyes. It perplexed the former mountain man. As much as he knew about Canby, he couldn't figure out why the officer would reject out of hand his entreaties to have Halsey, Gudde and the others brought to trial, and to have Private Chuck Latimer court-martialed, the way he had. The reason Canby had given seemed specious to the former mountain man, so Riley figured there must be something deeper, but he had no idea what that could be.

Riley also spent a heap of time trying to figure out if there really could be a plot afoot, or if—as Canby had argued—he was just imagining one because of his dislike for the Mormons. He never could decide on that, though it kept plaguing him.

The blacksmith stewed about it for a couple of days, anger increasing. Empty Horn had not been his best friend among the Shoshonis, but he knew the warrior well and would miss him. He didn't know the three Shoshonis who had been killed by the raid on the small village, but he was enraged that anyone would kill a baby for no reason. It continued to bother him, until he thought he would burst from the strain of it.

Then he made up his mind. He was not given over much to pondering everything. He was a man of action; a man who lived by his wits and his instincts. That's what had driven him to the brink recently, he finally realized —he had been trying to figure out others' actions and motivations, when what he really needed was to let his instincts take over. When he let them, he knew what he had to do.

The wagon train, with Gudde, Halsey and the three others, was out of his reach, but Latimer was not. And now that he had made up his mind, he could bide his time.

One day, just before dark, he spotted the private walking alone nearby. "Hey, Private," he called.

Latimer strolled warily over to him. He knew Riley hated him for killing Empty Horn, and he had avoided the blacksmith since then because of it. Still, Riley didn't seem too angry right now. As he neared the wide doors of the old wooden blacksmith shop, situated in a corner of the large corral, he asked, "What do you want, Riley?"

"Ye still havin' trouble with that horse of yours?"

"Yeah," Latimer said, still suspicious. "Damn thing's got a gait like a goddamn buffalo. Why?"

"Got some new ones in yesterday. There's one I think might suit ye better."

"Where'd you get 'em?" Latimer asked. His suspicions grew. "I ain't seen no new horses come in here."

"Don't ask," Riley said conspiratorially.

Latimer's eyes widened, then he nodded. "Your Injin friends?"

"Yep."

"Keyes ain't gonna let me ride no damn Injin pony."

"They ain't Indian ponies."

Latimer thought it over, then nodded. "Sure. I'm interested. Long as it ain't gonna cost me nothin'."

"Hell, if I cain't figure out a way to charge it to the army, I don't deserve this job," Riley responded with a little chuckle. "Go on and check it out. Last stall on the left."

Latimer hesitated only a moment, then shrugged and went inside.

Riley waited a little, then turned and followed Latimer silently.

"Hey, there ain't no fuckin' horse here," Latimer said angrily as he turned—and his face ran smack into Riley's huge right fist. The soldier went down on his rump, his nose and lower lip bleeding.

"What the hell was that for?" Latimer asked. He was groggy from the punch, and sounded it. He reached up to wipe the trickle of blood from his lip.

"I don't like fellers who kill my friends, shit pile," Riley said. Because he was doing something productive, his rage seeped away. He felt better now.

Latimer was recovering some. "That damn savage, you mean?" he asked incredulously.

"His name was Empty Horn, and he was a good man."

"He was a heathen, baby-killin' savage, and I don't give a damn what his name was."

"Then it's gonna be real hell for ye to die because of him, ain't it?" Riley asked rhetorically.

"Die?" Latimer was surprised. "You're fulla shit. I ain't gonna die."

"Oh, yes ye are, boy," Riley said chillingly.

Latimer pushed himself up. He was scared, but not too much. Riley had a hell of a reputation as a fighter, and the blacksmith was obviously a strong man, but Latimer was no slouch himself when it came to brawling. He was shorter than Riley, but just as stocky. He was hard and unforgiving in battle. He also had a lot of confidence in himself. His only fright came because he was still a little groggy from the punch Riley had landed. "I don't think so, ol' man." Latimer spit on his hands, rubbed them together a few seconds, and then jumped forward, swinging a big fist.

Riley easily blocked the punch and then hammered Latimer square on the forehead with the pinky side of his right fist.

Latimer groaned and staggered back a step before sinking to his knees. He had taken some hard punches in his days as a brawler, but never one like this one. He could hear the blood rushing in his body; his head thumped with the crescendo. Speckles of light darted before his eyes, and he swore he could feel the fresh bump on his head swelling.

As soon as Latimer had fallen, Riley had turned and gone to the shop's door. He pulled it closed and locked it with a chain. Then he walked back to where Latimer lay. It was plenty dark in the big shop now, despite the several lanterns.

After what seemed like an eternity, Latimer managed to stagger to his feet. As his awareness returned, the pain came with it. His head ached worse than it had with any hangover he had ever experienced. Still, he was not about to give up yet. He considered drawing his pistol, but with it being in a flap holster, and as wavering as he was, he figured he'd have no chance to shoot Riley before the blacksmith pulled his own Colt and shot him down.

It also irritated the private that Riley was just standing there waiting for him, almost as if toying with him. "That's two lucky punches you got, Riley," Latimer said with groggy bravado. "You won't get another."

"Wasn't no luck involved, shit pile. But if it'll make ye feel better, ye can take one of your own for free."

"That'll be the end of you," Latimer boasted.

"I'll take my chances."

Latimer edged up carefully, then suddenly hauled off and pasted Riley in the face as hard as he could.

Riley's head moved back an inch or so, but he gave no other sign of having been hit. When Latimer backed off a little, Riley reached up and touched his flattish nose. "Goddamn, you're one lucky bastard," he said. "If ye had broke my nose, I would've been some irritated."

Latimer looked at Riley's hard face, noticing the blood that snaked out of the left nostril. Then he looked down at his own hand. The skin over two knuckles was split, and the hand was already swelling. He began to suspect he was in just a little bit of trouble here, though he still did not believe Riley was going to kill him. Whup him good, maybe, but kill him? That wouldn't make any sense. Not over one dead Indian, even if that Indian was Riley's friend. That was his hope now, and he fiercely clung to it.

The soldier suddenly swung his fist at Riley again, but the blacksmith was ready. Riley caught Latimer's wrist with his left hand. As he slowly bent and twisted the arm until at least one bone broke, his right clamped on the trooper's throat and squeezed enough to keep him from screaming.

Riley let Latimer's arm fall, though he kept his grip on the soldier's throat. Swooping, he grabbed Latimer's crotch in his other hand and lifted Latimer over his head. The trooper still could not utter a sound with his windpipe clogged off. Riley threw him several feet.

Latimer's back slammed into a post and cracked. The soldier moaned feebly—it was all he was capable of—and he hung on the verge of unconsciousness.

Riley walked up and kneeled next to him. "Goddamn fool," he muttered. "Did Keyes order ye to kill Empty Horn?" he asked more loudly. When he got no response from Latimer, he slapped the soldier hard in the face. "Don't ye fade out on me yet, shit pile," he growled. "Did Keyes order ye to kill Empty Horn—or any of the other Shoshonis—that day?"

"No," Latimer whispered.

"Ye jist did it on your own?" Riley didn't believe someone like Latimer would do such a thing.

"Yep," the soldier replied, sucking in a deep breath against the pain. "I knew the lieutenant was mad because of you and the Injins. I thought it might boost his spirits some was I to . . . to . . ."

"So ye made him a sort of present, is that it?" Riley asked. He was disgusted with the very thought.

"Yep."

"Ye should've thought about what ye were gonna do before ye did it, shit pile. See what it's all come down to."

"The army'll get you back for this, Riley."

"I have my doubts, but I'm willin' to take the chance on it."

"All this over one dead Injin?" Latimer was losing his battle with consciousness—and life.

"Yep." Riley paused a moment. "Anything else ye want to tell me before ye die?"

"Jist one thing." Latimer licked his dry lips. "Fuck you."

Grim-faced, Riley grabbed the soldier's throat again and squeezed. Latimer was dead in seconds. Riley rose. He felt neither joy nor regret. He went to a stall on the other side of the large livery and saddled up the big, rangy horse there. That done, he pitched Latimer's corpse across the saddle and then mounted, shoving the body up over the saddle horn. He checked outside through the small door to make sure no one was watching. Then he rode out, locking the door again without dismounting.

It was dark now, and the temperature was dropping a little, making it almost bearable. Riley rode slowly, keeping to the shadows of the buildings, until he was out of the fort. He rode another half-hour, roughly following Black's Fork toward where Muddy Creek joined it. Finally stopping, he lifted Latimer's body off the saddle horn and let it fall to the ground. Then he moved closer to the water and dismounted.

He loosened the saddle and let the horse drink its fill from the stream. He liked it out here—here being just about anywhere away from a town or fort. But this was a particularly pleasant spot. There were trees and brush along the river, and the water ran cool and fast, even in the summer. A man could be comfortable and happy at a place like this. He didn't know how anyone could find true joy in the close confines of civilization. Cities, and even forts, had their uses, he well knew, but as for happiness, he'd as soon be up in the mountains, unfettered by the bounds of civilization, with Spirit Grass, his children, and maybe a few close friends.

He sighed. Such a life was not within his grasp right now. But maybe one of these days soon he would be able to live the free life of a mountain man again. He tightened the saddle, mounted up and rode off.

He slipped into the fort as he had left it, unseen. Instead of going to his shop, though, he went straight to his cabin. Spirit Grass came out, worried about him.

"I had some business to see to," he said tersely. "We'll talk about it later."

She nodded and took his horse around the back, where she unsaddled and tended it. When she got back inside, Riley was sitting at the table eating, having been served by five-year-old Laughing Swan.

Arrives With Trouble, who was almost twelve, was sitting near his father and reading from his McGuffey primer. All three Riley children took lessons from Judge Carter's wife. They were taught separately from the children of the soldiers, since so many of the troopers, and more often their wives, objected to having Indian children in the makeshift classroom with the white children.

Later, when the children had been sent to bed in one of the two bedrooms at the back of the cabin, Riley explained to Spirit Grass what he had done.

"Are ye in danger from the army?" she asked, worried.

Riley shrugged. "I doubt they'll find the body too soon, if at all. If they do, there's a good chance the animals will have been at it. And if they come for me anyway, I'll deal with it then."

"I don't like that idea," Spirit Grass said bluntly.

"Haven't I always gotten out of scrapes, woman?" he said with a laugh.

"One day ye won't, damn ye," Spirit Grass said seriously. "And where'll that leave me and the young'ns?"

"You'll be took care of," Riley growled. He didn't like to think of such possibilities. "Now, suppose ye jist hush up and let's go to the robes."

Spirit Grass had no objection to that.

{ 36 }

The soldiers came for Riley three days later, just about the time he was thinking he was in the clear. Lieutenant Irwin Keyes led the small troop into Riley's cabin as he was having a noon meal, shoving Spirit Grass out of the way when she opened the door.

"You're under arrest, Riley," Keyes said, gloating.

"They teach ye such good manners at West Point, shit pile?" Riley asked harshly.

"I knocked," the officer responded defensively.

Riley nodded. "I heard. Then ye damn near knocked my wife down when ye come bargin' in here."

"But she's only . . ." He stopped in a hurry. "Like I said, you're under arrest, Riley."

"Git the hell out of my home," Riley growled.

"I'll do no such thing." Keyes was about to say more when he heard a clicking noise that he recognized right off as a pistol being cocked. "You have a gun under the table?" he asked.

"What do ye think?" Riley grinned insolently.

"We can't leave without you," Keyes insisted. "And you can't get us all."

"Ye have the balls to test it?"

"I walk out of here now, I'll be back with a larger force soon. And then you'll be dragged out of here in irons. I came here like this to show you some respect."

"Bullshit. Ye come here like this to shame me in front

of my family and the whole goddamn post.'' He could tell by the look on Keyes's face that he had hit the mark. ''Now git out of here. Come back in half an hour and I'll go along peaceably.''

''I will not,'' Keyes insisted.

Riley grinned. ''Fine. Then sit down whilst I finish my meal. Ye and your men can join me.''

''I will not eat slop prepared by a savage,'' Keyes snapped.

''Beggin' your pardon, Lieutenant,'' Sergeant Karl Wurtzmann interjected.

''What is it?'' Keyes asked in annoyance.

''Missus One-Eye is one of the best cooks on the post, Lieutenant,'' Wurtzmann said. ''And if that there's venison stew, which it appears to be, most of the boys here'd be plumb grateful to have some.''

Keyes whirled and looked at the noncom as if the man had gone mad. But he could see that the others were interested. ''I cannot believe this,'' he breathed, shaking his head at the wonder of it. ''I surely can't.'' As much as he hated Riley and wanted to degrade him, Keyes had enough sense to know that getting a couple of his soldiers killed for no good reason would end his career, and quite possibly his life. He decided to assuage his anger by being magnanimous about all this. He would get back at Riley soon enough.

''All right, men,'' he said, trying not to sound too bitter or officious. ''Have at it.'' Keyes took the seat at the end of the long table opposite Riley, who had uncocked his pistol and set it down. ''None for me,'' Keyes said when Spirit Grass went to place a steaming wooden bowl of stew before him.

Spirit Grass made no sign that she was annoyed or upset. She simply went to Sergeant Wurtzmann, and set the bowl down before him. The noncom dug into the meal with gusto.

So did the others, Keyes noted right off. He began to wonder if it was as good as they seemed to think. But he was too proud and too stubborn to change his mind now. He even refused the coffee that little Laughing Swan tried to give him. He just sat stone-faced while his troops slurped up bowl after bowl of venison stew and hot, strong coffee.

"By the way, Keyes," Riley said, "what am I bein' arrested for?"

"The murder of Private Chuck Latimer."

"He's dead?" Riley asked, shock on his face.

"As if you didn't know."

"How'd he die?" Riley asked innocently.

"You killed him," Keyes answered impudently.

"That's interestin'. Tell me how I did it."

A soldier's quickly stifled guffaw drew an angry glance from the lieutenant. Keyes looked back at Riley and said, "I should think you know that a lot better than I."

"You've lost your reason, shit pile," Riley said evenly.

"Have I?" Keyes said, almost as if musing.

"Where'd I do this nefarious deed?" Riley asked.

"Up by where Black's Fork and Muddy Creek run together. That's where we found Latimer's body."

"A pity," Riley said with a decided lack of sincerity. "What makes ye think I had anything to do with him dyin'?"

"You were the only one who had a grudge against him."

"Ye ain't so dumb as to believe that, boy," Riley said. Then he added, "Or maybe ye are."

"It's going to be a real pleasure to command the firing squad that finally puts an end to you, Riley. Indeed, it will."

The two men fell into silence. The soldiers had paid attention to the exchange, but that did not slow down their feeding any.

Finally Riley rose. He picked up his pistol gingerly and tossed it to Keyes. The officer was surprised and fumbled the weapon getting a grip on it. Keyes was better prepared when Riley tossed him his second revolver.

The soldiers hastily stood, trying to grab a last spoonful of food or sip of coffee.

Riley kissed his wife and Laughing Swan. Then he headed for the door, grabbing his hat from the peg next to it. He was walking swiftly toward the guardhouse and was almost halfway there before all the soldiers had gotten out of his cabin.

Once Riley was locked up, Keyes felt relaxed enough to gloat some more. "Don't get too comfortable in there, you Indian-loving son of a bitch. You won't be in there long."

"I'll survive," Riley said dryly, "since it ain't so bad here. I've been in worse places," he added. "Like your ma's place in Alabama." The lie was designed to get Keyes's goat, and it succeeded quite nicely.

Keyes was livid. In his rage he forgot where he was and who his antagonist was. He reached through the bars and grabbed Riley's shirt and tried to jerk him forward. It didn't work.

Instead, Riley took hold of Keyes's wrists and twisted them until Keyes had no choice but to let go of his shirt. Then the blacksmith twisted the wrists a little more and forced them up against the cell bars. "I can break 'em easy for ye, if you're of a mind to have it done," Riley said quietly.

"No, dammit," Keyes hissed.

"Then mind your manners around me and my family."

"Go to hell." A little more pressure and Keyes could feel his bones at the snapping point. "All right, all right, goddammit."

"Your word—for what little it's worth?" Riley questioned.

"Yes." Keyes was afraid to even breathe, lest that give the fraction of impetus needed to leave him with two shattered wrists.

"And keep away from me, shit pile," Riley said, giving the officer's wrists a shove.

Glaring hatefully at Riley, Keyes left the guardhouse. His thoughts were all on revenge. He wanted nothing more. Later, however, when he had calmed down some,

he realized that taking revenge—at least overt revenge
—against Riley would do more harm to his own career
than it would to Riley. He decided he would wait until
he could devise something subtle.

Soon after Keyes left, Lieutenant Browning came in.
"I heard they were going to arrest you, Pete," he said.
"I didn't like the idea, but there was nothing I could
do."

"I know that, boy."

"Anything I can get you? Or do for you?"

"I'd be obliged if you'd keep an eye on the family for
me. I don't trust Keyes." He felt no shame in asking for
help.

"Sure. As much as I can anyway. Anything else?"

"Tell Canby I want to see him." He grinned a little.
"And say it nice, like I know ye can."

Browning laughed. "I'll do so."

The two chatted about inconsequential matters for a
while, making almost a show of avoiding the reason
Riley was behind bars. Then Browning had to leave.

It was the next afternoon before Canby showed up.
Riley had begun to wonder if perhaps the fort commander had decided to let him languish here forever.
When the major walked in and sat on the camp stool an
aide had placed in front of Riley's cell, the blacksmith
said sarcastically, "Nice of ye to make it, Major."

Canby smiled and waved his aide and the jailer out.
When they were gone he looked at Riley. "I couldn't let
the men see me come running over here as soon as you
asked me to, One-Eye," he said. "It wouldn't look
good."

"I suppose not." Riley could see no reason for beating around the bush. "What am I doin' in here, Major?" he asked.

"I'm sure you know that, One-Eye," Canby said
bluntly.

"No, I sure don't. All I know is that Lieutenant Shit
Pile says I kilt Private Latimer."

"Didn't you?"

"That doesn't deserve an answer," Riley said sourly. "What really galls me, Major, is that ye got no more reason to arrest me for this than ye did to arrest Latimer for what we *know* he did."

"Lieutenant Keyes has reason to believe you're responsible," Canby said flatly, "and I think his reasoning is sound. You were the only one to have a motive for killing Latimer. You also have it easier than just about anyone else of getting off the post to do the deed."

"That ain't enough to convict a man on," Riley said seriously.

"Maybe not," Canby replied. "If it's not, you won't be bothered by it again, though." He looked pointedly at Riley. Then he stood and called for his aide. "I'll arrange for the court to convene soon, One-Eye. That way we can get it over with."

"Judge Carter gonna preside?"

"Yep." Canby strolled out, looking imperious, and comfortable with it.

When Canby was gone, Riley sat on his hard cot and thought about the visit. On the surface, it seemed terse and offhand. But there was more to it than the few words that had been said. Now Riley knew he had to try to figure out that deeper meaning.

It was obvious to Riley that Keyes was responsible for this. There could be no way he knew that Riley had killed Latimer. Riley was sure of that. Obviously, though, the lieutenant had assumed that Riley was responsible. That made sense. It also made sense that Keyes was trying to get back at him.

What was confusing to Riley was Canby's casualness about it all. Riley knew that Canby liked him and considered him a good worker. The blacksmith was sure the fort commander would not want him tried for murder and possibly executed. Not without a lot more proof than Keyes could offer.

What was it Canby said? Riley wondered, sitting there. He snapped his fingers when he recalled: Canby had seemed to agree with him when he said Keyes didn't have enough evidence to convict a man. Then the officer had said that if that were true, Riley wouldn't be bothered by it again. That could mean only one thing, Riley figured. According to the country's laws, a man couldn't be tried for the same crime twice. Which means that he would be found innocent because Keyes had no real evidence against him. And when he was found innocent, he would never have to face charges of killing Latimer again.

"That must be what he meant," Riley muttered.

There was more to it, though. Riley remembered Canby's parting words: "I'll arrange for the court to convene soon, One-Eye. That way we can get it over with." A trial right away would mean that Keyes would have no time to dig up any evidence, if any was to be had.

Riley smiled. Canby had practically guaranteed him a not-guilty verdict with the knowledge that he would be free from further prosecution. He settled back, prepared to have a few days' rest.

By the next day, he was not nearly so certain. With the patience gained in many an Indian council, he forced himself to wait, seemingly unconcerned. He told himself he would make no move for three days if nothing happened. After that, he would decide what he would do to get out of this situation.

37

Three days after Riley had been arrested, a solitary Shoshoni rode fearlessly into the fort. No one made any effort to stop him. The soldiers had seen plenty of Shoshonis before, but somehow this one seemed different to them, and they watched in interest as the warrior made his way across the parade ground.

The Shoshoni halted near the commander's office. There he waited, his lance held in his right hand, point skyward. Two dozen eagle feathers on the lance haft flapped in the wind. On his left arm was a painted bullhide shield, two eagle feathers and two Blackfoot scalps dangling from it. He wore a tall, colorful headdress, a decorated buckskin warshirt, fringed leggings, breechcloth and moccasins. His pony—a sturdy, short, brown prairie mustang—also was marked with paint. To those few who could read the signs on the horse, they understood that the rider had stolen plenty of horses in his lifetime, had killed several enemies, and had counted plenty of coup.

The soldier on duty just outside Canby's door was almost dumbstruck at the sight. But after a few seconds, he turned, poked his head inside the door and said, "Major, there's an Injin out here."

"What's he doing?" Canby asked, annoyed. He had barely gotten into his chair.

"Just settin' there. I expect he wants to speak to you, sir."

"Go see what he wants, Lieutenant," Canby said to Keyes, who was leaning against the wall.

"Yes, sir," Keyes said. He stepped outside and moved to the edge of the porch. "You want something here, boy?" he asked.

"I am Black Iron," the Shoshoni said in a deep, powerful voice, using English. "I want to speak to the soldier chief."

"He ain't interested in talking to the likes of you, boy," Keyes said smugly.

"Tell him!" Black Iron thundered.

Keyes was taken aback by the power and authority in the voice. It also rankled him to be spoken to in such a manner by an Indian, even if he was a chief. "Wait there," he said tightly. He spun and went back into the office.

"Well?" Canby asked.

"Son of a bitch says he wants to talk to you, sir," Keyes responded flatly.

"Tell him I'm too busy."

"I did so, sir. He either doesn't understand or doesn't want to understand."

"You know who it is?"

"He said his name's Black Iron."

Canby's eyes widened. "That's odd. Black Iron's a peaceable fellow for the most part. He usually doesn't make much of a show when he comes to the fort." He paused, then nodded. "Go tell him I'm busy and that you're acting in my stead. See if you can find out what he wants."

"Yessir," Keyes said with a distinct lack of enthusiasm. He went back outside and stopped on the porch again. "The soldier chief," Keyes said, feeling like an idiot using the term, "is a mighty busy man. He has many things to do, and so doesn't have the time to speak to an ignorant savage like you." He wondered how much of this Black Iron was getting. "If you really need to talk to somebody, I'm here in his stead." He smiled in self-satisfaction.

"Canby won't talk to me?" Black Iron asked. His flat, dark face had a look of chilling finality.

"No," Keyes said flatly.

"Stupid thing," the Shoshoni muttered. He raised his lance straight up and then shook it a few times.

Keyes's smugness faded rapidly as Shoshoni warriors suddenly began appearing around the fort, looking eerie in the morning's rising mist. He looked around. As far as he could see, ringing the inside of the fort perimeter, there were Shoshonis.

Shouts of "Injins here" or "Warriors in sight!" drifted on the wind to smack on Keyes's ears. He estimated that they were facing two hundred Shoshoni warriors, all of them looking ready for war.

"Ye, shit pile," Black Iron ordered, pointing his lance point at Keyes, "tell Canby I want to talk to him!"

Keyes now knew where Black Iron had learned his English, and that irked him even more. He was about to retort when he realized with a sudden sense of dread that the warriors were prepared to attack at any moment. "Jesus Christ," he breathed. He spun and hurried back into Canby's office. "You better get out there right this minute, sir," he said nervously.

"What?" Canby roared.

"There's maybe two hundred Shoshonis out there, and not a one of them looks disposed toward peace, Major," Keyes said hastily. "Black Iron demands to talk to you."

"You sure about how many Indians're out there, Lieutenant?" Canby asked skeptically.

"No, sir. That's just a guess as to the number. But I can tell you that they've ringed the fort."

Canby quickly realized the danger, and nodded. He slapped on his hat. "Well, then, Keyes, let's go." He stepped outside into the new day's sun and stopped on the porch just about where Keyes had been before. Keyes was just behind him to his right.

"What can I do for you, Black Iron?" Canby asked. He looked cool and composed.

"Parley."

"All right. Tell your boys to go on home and we'll talk."

"No. They stay."

"All right, Chief," Canby said easily. "Have it your way. You want to parley here, or would you rather get out of the sun and do it in my office?"

"Here. And I want One-Eye to translate."

"You speak English well enough not to need a translator."

"I want my son-in-law here," Black Iron insisted. The knowledge shocked Keyes.

"He's in the guardhouse," Canby said.

"I don't give a damn. Git him."

Canby knew when he was beaten. He turned to Keyes. "Go get Riley," he ordered. "And make it quick. I don't know how long the Shoshonis'll hold off attacking if they think we're trying to trick them."

"Yessir," Keyes said sourly. He pointed at two privates and commanded them to come with him.

Canby stood in the shade of the portico, but he was still sweating. He didn't know what Black Iron and the Shoshonis wanted, but he hoped that Riley's presence could stave off the war that appeared imminent.

"Let's go, Riley," Keyes bellowed as he and the jailer hurried down the stone corridor to the blacksmith's cell.

"Go where?" Riley asked when the men arrived at the cell and began working the key in the lock. They were in a mighty big hurry, and that didn't bode well for him, Riley thought.

"Don't ask questions, Riley," Keyes snapped. "Just get moving."

"I ain't goin' one goddamn step, shit pile, until ye tell me what's goin' on."

"There's a whole gaggle of goddamn savages out

there threatening to attack the fort. They want a parley with Major Canby, and they insist that you be there.''

Riley burst out the door and charged up the corridor, the soldiers struggling to catch up. Riley didn't much care about the parley; he just wanted to make sure no more Shoshonis were killed.

''Hey, Black Iron,'' Riley said as he stopped next to the war chief's pony. He had taken in all the Shoshonis around the fort on his run over here. ''What brings you to these parts?'' He tried to sound light-hearted.

''We came for ye,'' Black Iron said in Shoshoni.

''How'd ye know?'' Riley asked in kind.

''Spirit Grass sent Flat Nose to the village. He told us what happened.''

''Ye can't do anything for me here, Black Iron. This'll do nothing but bring trouble to the People.''

''The People've taken too much, my son,'' Black Iron said. ''You're not the only reason we're here. We want the men who killed the three people in the village to pay for what they did. And we want the blue coat who killed Empty Horn punished.''

Riley smiled grimly. ''He's been taken care of already,'' he said, still in Shoshoni. ''That's why I'm in the guardhouse.''

''Did ye kill him?''

Riley nodded. ''I promised Sharp Hawk that I'd see he was punished. When the blue coats didn't take care of it, I did.''

''This is good. But are ye in danger?'' Black Iron was concerned.

''Not too much. The blue coats don't know for certain that I did it, but they sure suspect it. I think I'll be all right.''

''What the hell're you two gabbing about?'' Canby asked in irritation.

''Family,'' Riley responded innocently.

''If Black Iron wants to parley, let's get on with it, One-Eye,'' Canby said. ''All those Shoshonis out there are making me—and everyone else—nervous.''

"As well they should, Major."

"Don't lecture me, One-Eye. I know the danger here. And I don't want bloodshed any more than you do."

Riley nodded.

The war chief had dismounted and was sitting cross-legged on the porch. Riley took a seat next to him. "What're your demands, my father?" Riley asked. Black Iron spoke to him briefly in Shoshoni.

Riley looked up at Canby. "Might be wise to take a seat, Major," he said.

"Of course, of course," Canby said, sitting with little grace. "Lieutenant Keyes, Lieutenant Browning, join us."

Browning had arrived while Keyes was getting Riley from the guardhouse. He sat, looking forward to the parley. It would be his first. Keyes was more reluctant, but he knew he had no choice.

"Well, One-Eye, what does Chief Black Iron want?" Canby asked.

"Well, Major, the first one's somewhat of an embarrassment," Riley said.

"I suppose it has something to do with you," Canby said astutely.

"Yep. The Shoshonis want me released and your promise that I'll not face trial in Latimer's death now or anytime in the future."

Canby kept his face expressionless. "The other demands?" he asked evenly.

"The Shoshonis want Lieutenant Keyes court-martialed for ignoring them and their complaints about the attack on the village. And they want Halsey, Gudde and the others involved in that attack to be arrested and tried."

Canby sat silently for a while, thinking the demands over. He was outraged at what was being asked. For some reason, he was particularly annoyed by the first one. He had always liked Riley until the blacksmith had gone and killed Latimer. And Canby had no doubt whatsoever that Riley had done the deed. Not that he objected to Latimer's demise all that much. It was just that the murder had put him in a tight spot. More galling was the fact that Canby had given Riley an easy and virtually foolproof way out of the fix. Now this.

Canby didn't like being dictated to by anyone, even an Indian war chief. When he looked around and saw the determined Shoshoni warriors just waiting for an excuse to attack, however, he knew Black Iron had him by the short hairs.

Lieutenant Browning, who had been watching silently, as had been his wont since he had arrived at the fort, finally found the courage to speak. "Excuse me, Major," he said in a quiet but firm voice, "if I might say a word."

Still annoyed, Canby nonetheless was grateful for the interruption. "If you have something to say, Lieutenant, speak up."

"I recommend that you agree to the demands, sir."

"Without resistance or negotiation?"

"Yes, sir."

"Why?"

Browning ignored Keyes's derisive snort. "Because the Shoshonis aren't demanding anything more than simple justice, sir. They earlier requested that the men from the wagon train be tried for what they claim were crimes against their people. But they didn't demand that the apparent offenders be given to them for punishment. No, they asked that those suspected in the killings be tried in our courts, knowing full well that they would most likely go free anyway."

"Commendable sentiments, Lieutenant," Canby said evenly. He agreed, but he was not quite willing to give up without some kind of fight. He looked at the Shoshoni leader. "You understood what Lieutenant Browning said, Black Iron?" he asked.

Black Iron nodded.

"He's got a point. At least on the last one. But there's no way I will court-martial one of my officers for a judgment made in the field. Whether that judgment is right or wrong isn't important. Officers are called upon to make such decisions at a moment's notice.''

''But why're those damn judgments always against my People?'' Black Iron asked bluntly.

''They're not, Chief. Though maybe sometimes it seems that way. But I remain adamant about not giving up one of my officers for court-martial.''

The fort commander and the Shoshoni leader negotiated a while longer, but there was really little more that could be said. Black Iron and Canby finally agreed that the first and third demands would be met, but not the second.

The two smoked briefly from Black Iron's ceremonial pipe to sanctify the pact. Then Black Iron rode off, still in solitary splendor. Minutes later he was gone, along with the rest of the warriors who had surrounded the fort.

A troop under Lieutenants Keyes and Browning, with Riley along, of course, headed after the wagon train the next day. Keyes moseyed along in no hurry to get anywhere—not if it would help Riley in any way.

Riley put up with it for a few miles, then rode up alongside the lieutenant. "Ye don't git a move on, shit pile," he growled, "we ain't ever gonna git anywhere."

"What's your hurry, Riley?" Keyes countered. "We're not gonna find 'em anyway. They're in Salt Lake City by now. Or close to it."

"Somehow, I jist don't believe that. Now, pick up the pace, shit pile."

"Or what?" Keyes sneered.

"Or I'll twist off your goddamn head and shove it up your ass where it belongs."

Keyes suddenly realized that Riley meant what he said. He set a quicker pace.

They came on the wagon train just before nightfall, much to Keyes's surprise and annoyance. He had been certain the emigrants would have been in Salt Lake City after this much time had passed, but the wagons were hardly more than a few miles beyond where they were several days ago. He wondered why. So much so that he asked about it straight off when he met with the wagon master, Augustus Gudde.

"Ve've had a little trouble vit' some of the vagons," Gudde said, "und a few people are too sick to travel."

The wagon master's face held no expression, so Keyes was not sure whether the man was lying or not. Since he couldn't prove it either way, he decided to accept Gudde at his word. "Anything we can do to help?" he asked.

"*Nein.* Ve haff sent to Salt Lake City for help from other Saints."

Riley knew Gudde was lying, but he could not prove it, so he said nothing.

"Is there some reason vhy you haff come here again, Lieutenant?" Gudde asked.

"Unfortunately, yes," Keyes said sourly. "Some people"—his eyes rolled in Riley's direction, a gesture that was acknowledged with an almost imperceptible nod from Gudde—"don't believe that your men were attacked by the Shoshonis. They seem to think there's some kind of conspiracy goin' on amongst your people. Personally, I think they're mad, but the major told me to come on out here to see if I could find you and ask you again just what happened."

Gudde repeated the story he had told Keyes the last time. "Und," Gudde added when he had finished his narrative, "I am very angry vit' you for renewink these accusations. If I vasn't a Saint, and used to such persecution, I'd challenge any und all accusers to fight over this."

"I can understand that, Mister Gudde," Keyes said smoothly. "It was not my desire to offer offense. In fact, it was not my desire to come here, but those who have made the accusations managed to exert undue influence on Major Canby."

"Vell, you haff asked your qvestions und gotten the truth," Gudde said, his anger evident in his tone. "Now, vhy don't you go back to your fort vhere you belong und leave decent people alone."

Keyes smiled a little, attempting to calm Gudde. "It's night, Mister Gudde," he said simply.

"Then go in the mornink."

"We should be able to do that," Keyes said evenly. He looked at Riley. "I told you this was a waste of time."

"Ye know, boy," Riley said calmly, despite his rising ire, "for a man with two good eyes, ye sure are one blind son of a bitch. Ol' lard ass over there," he added, pointing to Gudde, "wouldn't know the goddamn truth if it come up and bit his nuts off."

Gudde spit into the fire. "I challenge you," he said in a tight voice.

"Suits me, shit pile."

Keyes glared at Riley for a moment, then looked back to Gudde. "Stop it, the both of you," he ordered, "or I'll have you both put in irons." The lieutenant was not happy about any of this. He still believed Gudde—indeed, he'd believe just about anyone except for Riley, and Indians—and was inclined to just head back. But the thought of several hundred Shoshonis surrounding the fort was still fresh in his mind, as was Canby's taut face. What he needed was a little time to figure a way to get out of this without causing himself any trouble. He decided to wait until morning before he made any decisions.

That night Riley decided to prowl through the Mormon camp, as he had before. He had spotted Hyram Jenkins, one of the people who had spoken to him last time, and it seemed to him that Jenkins wanted to talk with him again.

Skirting the firelight, and sticking to the shadows to avoid the moonlight, Riley prowled the camp, surreptitiously examining each wagon. He finally found Jenkins's and quietly made himself known.

"Git in," Jenkins said out of the corner of his mouth as he walked by the bulky shadow in the darkness.

Riley was silent and unseen as a phantom as he moved into the back of the wagon. A few minutes later, Jenkins joined him, lit a very small candle and set it on the floor. It threw barely enough light for the two men to see each other.

"Again, I can't afford to be found out talking to you, Mister Riley," Jenkins said quietly. "But I'm more determined than ever to leave this infernal church as soon as I can." He paused, wondering how much he should say, then decided he shouldn't hold anything back, though he was really sure of very little.

"There's somethin' mighty suspicious goin' on with this wagon train, Mister Riley," Jenkins said tentatively. "I ain't fer sure what. It's jist a feelin' mostly." He shrugged in apology for not having anything better to say.

"Ye know why this wagon train ain't made more'n a few miles progress in near a week?" Riley interrupted.

"We were told some of the wagons weren't in shape for going on."

"That's what Gudde said. Ye believe it?"

"I ain't seen no evidence of it," Jenkins said. "And nobody I've talked to has a broke wagon."

"So I thought. Gudde also said there were a few folks too sick to travel. That got any truth to it?"

"Not much that I can see," Jenkins said, a look of puzzlement on his face. "Sure, we got sick folks. Ain't ever been a wagon train come out this way that didn't have a heap of illness of one sort or another. But folks bein' too sick to travel? That's ridiculous."

"My thoughts exactly. There might be some folks stove up so bad they cain't travel," Riley commented. "But too sick to travel? Shit."

"I don't have much more to say to you, Mister Riley," Jenkins offered. "Jist one thing, really. But I think it's important."

"Tell it."

"There's another of us who's disgruntled with what he's seen of the Mormons on our journey. Like me and Willard and Orson, he's fixin' to leave the church as soon as the wagons reach Salt Lake City. He's not said anything about it publicly, of course."

"What's this got to do with me?" Riley questioned.

"He wants to talk to ya, Mister Riley. He says he's got some information for you that's real important."

"What is it?"

"I don't know," Jenkins said with a shake of the head. "He won't tell me, or anyone else that I know of. Says it's too dangerous to spout off around here."

"What's this feller's name and where can I find him?"

"Eli Higgins is his name. I'll go git him and bring him here. That'd be best."

Riley nodded. "Do so," he commanded softly.

It wasn't long before Jenkins was back with another man, and the three of them were huddled around the sputtering candle in the cramped, loaded wagon.

"Mister Jenkins tells me ye got information that might help me, Mister Higgins. That true?"

"Damn right it is." Higgins was a man of medium height and somewhat disreputable look. He was thin almost to the point of scrawniness, but Riley could see a lot of corded muscle in his arms. "Gudde, Halsey and a few other men approached me jist the other night. They told me there was a plot afoot—one supposedly concocted by Brigham Young himself—to regain control of the fort, and thus open the Green River Valley to Mormon settlement."

"And jist how was they to accomplish this great feat?" Riley asked skeptically.

"Well, from what they said, Young hatched the plot and sent word back east. By the by, I don't really believe Brother Young'd plot such intrigue."

"I do," Riley said flatly.

Higgins shrugged. "Whatever. Gudde, Halsey and the others got the letter—a letter; they told me it was from Brother Young—jist before leavin' on this trip. They were supposed to foment as much trouble as possible, at the fort, and among the Indians."

"So that's why this caravan stopped at the fort," Riley said with a nod. That would explain things, he thought. They saw almost none of the Mormon travelers at the fort these days; hadn't since the Mormons had settled Fort Supply. Though that settlement had been burned down by the Mormons when the army arrived, the Saints had had neither need nor inclination to stop at the new Fort Bridger since it was created last year.

"Yep. And they were supposed to cause you whatever pain they could, Mister Riley, even kill you if necessary," Higgins said.

"Why?" Riley asked, not too surprised.

"Well, sir, they hold you in large part responsible for the many troubles the Saints have faced in these parts. You've had several set-tos with the Saints, from what I've heard. The brethren tell many tales of your plots against the church and its leaders . . ."

"My what?" Riley demanded, though in soft tones. He was surprised this time.

"Brother Young's letter was full of information about the plots you conceived against him and the church," Higgins said. "Or so I was told. Halsey also tells of your many machinations."

"Halsey's a lyin' shit pile," Riley growled low.

Higgins shrugged. "I only know what I hear, Mister Riley. I ain't accusin' you of none of this, jist tellin' you what the others said."

Riley nodded, calming down a little. "Any other reasons they're against me?" he asked. "And call me One-Eye."

"Yessir. You were against Mister Bridger selling the fort; and you were the one responsible for holdin' the fort while he was gone. In effect, One-Eye, they consider you the leader of all the former mountain men, who have caused the church so much trouble in these parts." He paused, then added quietly, "In fact, they wanted me to pretend I wasn't interested in the church no longer and ride back to the fort and kill you."

"I'm honored," Riley said sarcastically. "But that's doin' some assumptin' that ought not to be done. Like what'n hell makes 'em think some scrawny-ass feller like ye could kill me?" There was a note of bragging in his voice.

Higgins shrugged again. "Anyone can be killed if it's done right, One-Eye. Especially by a man like me."

Riley thought that over for a moment and then nodded. No one would fear Eli Higgins, not as unprepossessing as he looked. He had the appearance of a man whom life had whipped down to the ground. Most folks wouldn't even look twice at him, and he could fire a bullet or jam a knife into a man without really being noticed. "But what good would that do?" he finally asked.

"Well, since Halsey's attack on the Shoshonis didn't stir them up, and Latimer's killing that other one—oh, yes, we knew about that—didn't do it either, they thought maybe killing you would, since you're on such good terms with them." He seemed ashamed of having this knowledge, as if he had been a part of it all.

Riley knew that his being killed would pit the army against the Shoshonis. Once that bloodbath ended, it just might be possible for the Mormons to move back in, remove what was left from either side and rule the whole region. It was, Riley thought, typical of the Mormon leadership. Still, something didn't ring quite true to him. "Then why would Halsey attack me at the fort, before he tried to stir up trouble with the Shoshonis?" he asked.

"That was personal, Halsey told me."

"Personal?" Riley questioned. "I don't know him from Adam. What's he got against me?"

"He said you killed his brother. Hacked him into bits, was the way he put it."

"When?" Riley asked tightly.

"When the army was headin' out here. The Danites were raidin' the column, and apparently you come on him somewhere and chopped him up without givin' him a chance to fight back."

Riley sat absolutely still as a blinding flash of rage pounded in his temples. The vein on his neck throbbed powerfully, like a snake writhing in a sausage casing. It took nearly two full minutes before Riley thought it safe to say something. "I'll tell ye the truth of it, boy," he said, throat still constricted by rage, "that toad-suckin' shit pile shot me in the back, tried to shoot my wife down, and then killed my best friend. He was fuckin' lucky I treated him as fuckin' well as I did, goddamn his fuckin' putrid soul to hell three times over."

Higgins was taken aback by the raw emotion that seemed to spill out of every pore of Riley's body. "I . . . I didn't know, One . . . Mister Riley. I was jist . . ."

"I know, boy," Riley said quietly, though the fury still throbbed inside of him. He fell silent again, except for the ragged sound of his deep breathing. Finally he thought he could speak again. "Why ye?" he asked. "Why did they ask ye to join them this late in their connivance?"

"Same reason they thought I could kill you," Higgins said with a combination of shame and evenness. "They knew me as a loyal member of the church, and a man who could pass anywhere without drawin' attention."

Riley nodded. It made sense. Still, he was not entirely convinced. "What're ye supposed to git out of this?" he asked.

"They offered me a spot on the Council of Elders," Higgins said simply.

"Sounds like an exalted position," Riley said, trying to contain the sarcasm he felt.

"It is."

"Then why turn on them and talk to me?" He had thought right from Higgins's first statement that this could be a way of setting him up for something. He wasn't sure what, but the possibilities were numerous. He suspected there was at least some truth to what Higgins had told him. It was a matter of determining how much.

"I know this is all hard to believe, Mister Riley. But I swear on the Lord's grace that it's the truth. I don't know where they got the idea that I'd be willin' to walk in a door and jist kill a man in cold blood. And I don't know where they got the notion that I'd be interested in their connivances. When I learned that Halsey and the others had attacked those innocent Lamanites, my feelings for the church, and the people who populate it, began to shift. As more and more of this deceitfulness came to light, I turned against the church entirely. So here I am, talkin' to you, at great risk to my life."

"Why?" Riley was still not convinced.

"It's the best way I can think of to try to halt what's goin' on," Higgins said simply. "My leavin' the church when we hit Salt Lake City wouldn't accomplish anything, though I admit, it'd be a hell of a lot safer for me and my family."

Riley didn't know what to think. He still suspected a trap, though Higgins certainly seemed to be telling the truth. "I'd like to believe ye, Mister Higgins, but I'm havin' a bit of trouble doin' so."

"I don't know how to convince you, Mister Riley. All I can do is tell you what I've been told. I wish I had something I could give you to prove my truthfulness, but I don't."

"Does anyone else know about this grand conspiracy?" Riley asked.

"Nope. No one on this wagon train anyway, other than the ones involved, and now Brother Jenkins." He paused. "There is one other thing about all this," he said. "I almost forgot. Apparently another reason why Halsey and the others attacked those Shoshonis is that some of the Saints wanted to punish the Shoshonis for having snubbed the church's missionary efforts a few years ago. I think that one of the reasons we've been goin' nowhere is so that Halsey and his fellers can continue causin' trouble with the Indians. And to see what other kind of deviltry they can stir up."

Riley sat there a bit, thinking it over. He had no reason to believe this man had told him all this out of altruism. It had all the earmarkings of a trap. But for some reason he could not fathom, Riley decided he would take Higgins at face value. "I'm obliged for what you've told me, Mister Higgins," he said. "Now ye best git back to your wagon before someone takes notice that you're gone."

In a virtual re-enactment of the last time they had come out here to confront the Mormon wagon train, Riley strode up to Keyes's fire, poured himself some coffee and then looked at Keyes. After a mouthful of coffee, Riley said flatly, "I want Gudde, Halsey, Bob Sprague, Dan Hyde and Billy Kimball arrested."

"You've got to be out of your mind, Riley."

"I might be crazy enough to kill ye here and now," Riley snapped.

"What the hell's got into you, Riley?" Keyes asked. He didn't like the look in the former mountain man's eyes.

"None of your goddamn business. Jist do what I said. And I want to be on the trail in thirty minutes."

Keyes didn't like this one bit, but it seemed he had little choice. He did not want to precipitate a fight with Riley. Reluctantly, he said, "Lieutenant Browning, take a few of the men and go arrest Gudde, Halsey, and the three others."

"With pleasure," Browning said evenly.

Keyes soothed his conscience by telling himself that there was no way that the five Mormons would be convicted of attacking Indians. He told the "suspects" just that, and kept them calm by telling them he had to go through the motions to keep the peace.

He also told Riley, frequently, on the ride back to the fort that it was plain that the Saints would not be convicted. He looked smug, and his troopers—except for Browning—sneered. The smirking prisoners added to the chorus.

Riley put up with it for a while, then shrugged. He looked at Halsey and said with a smugness that equaled that of any of the others, "Ask Keyes what happened to Private Latimer."

Halsey looked at Riley with wonder and a little worry in his eyes, but he said nothing.

They rode into the fort a couple of hours before dark. The prisoners were placed in the guardhouse, where they immediately began demanding to see Major Canby. The fort commander acquiesced, mainly to shut the prisoners up. Riley tagged along, at Canby's invitation.

"Let's get this farce over with, Major," Halsey snapped. "We have important church business to tend to, and this is wastin' our time."

"You keep making this much noise, you'll rot in here," Canby retorted. "You keep your peace, we might be able to have this over and done with in a few days. Of course, considering why you're here, I can't understand why you're in such a rush."

"Because we ain't done anything wrong. What I can't understand is why we're here in the first place." He was still arrogant, but he was also somewhat unnerved by Riley's glare.

"We'll find out about that," Canby said. "Now, keep quiet."

The trial was held three days later, Judge William Carter presiding. Lieutenant Keyes received permission to represent the defendants. Lieutenant Browning acted as prosecutor. It was a strange arrangement, but there was no one else available.

As Riley had known in his heart it would, Keyes's sneering prediction proved true. Judge Carter, a fair and even-handed man, listened patiently as Riley explained the conspiracy. He listened just as patiently when the five defendants, one after the other, gave identical stories.

Carter took only a few minutes to deliberate. Since there was no jury—an unprejudiced one could not be found among the soldiers and mountain men around the fort—there was no reason to delay. Carter pronounced all five men innocent of the charges leveled against them.

Riley jumped up and roared, "How can ye let these shit piles git away with these doin's, Judge?"

"Shut up, One-Eye," Carter said sternly. He was not angry, but he was determined to keep control here. "All we got is your word, Pete. Without someone to corroborate what you said here today, I just cannot in good conscience convict those men." He was sad about that, though he didn't show it. He was almost certain that the Saints were guilty of killing a couple of Shoshonis, if not conspiring to take over the Green River Valley, though Carter also suspected even that was at least partly true.

Casting dark glances at the celebrating defendants, Riley stomped outside and waited, leaning against the log wall of the makeshift courtroom.

When the gloating victors emerged from the court, Riley challenged them.

The men laughed at him as they moved away from the building. "You got balls, I'll say that," Halsey commented. "Hell, we outnumber you five to one. Besides, the army ain't gonna let you do anything to us. Ain't that right, Major?"

Canby, standing nearby, had had his fill of these men and the troubles they had brought. He, too, thought that Riley had told the truth, at least in large part. Still, there was no evidence, really, and he could not fault Carter for rendering the verdict he had. On the other hand, he did not have to suffer fools on his post. "Well, no, Mister Halsey, it isn't right," he said calmly. "You and your friends aren't soldiers, Mister Halsey, and I am entirely unconcerned about your welfare."

"You ain't kiddin', are ya?" Halsey asked, eyes wide.

"Not a bit."

"And you don't mind if we go ahead and kill your fat friend there?"

"I'm not so sure that's the way it'll turn out. Mister Riley can be a mighty formidable opponent."

"He ain't anything to worry about."

"If you're that eager to get killed, you have my blessing." Canby folded his arms across his chest. He was not as cocky as he seemed. He liked Riley, it was true, but the blacksmith had a knack for having trouble find him. Or causing it himself, as in the Latimer case. Still, he had seen little of the Mormons, or at least these five, to recommend them. They, too, were troublemakers, ones whose impact would be more widely felt if they had their way.

A little surprised, the Saints turned to face Riley, quite ready to do him in. "You have us at a disadvantage, Riley," Halsey said. "Since we've just been in the guardhouse for a few days, and on trial, we have no weapons."

"That all that's worryin' ye?" Riley said sarcastically. With deliberate slowness, he pulled out his Colt revolvers and set them on the ground. His tomahawk followed, but he kept his knife. "That better?"

"Infinitely," Halsey said. "Now, suppose you get your at ass down here and let us commence this fight."

Riley moved up as the Saints shifted until they circled him. Riley stood, looking patient, almost bored. "Well, since y'all're so eager to git this goin', one of ye best start it," he said with a sneer.

Billy Kimball made the first move. The young, baby-faced man charged, arms wide. He wasn't sure what he wanted to do exactly. He just wanted to get in the first licks, show the others he was as tough as they were.

Riley locked his hands together and swung the two meaty appendages as one unit. The flesh club caught Kimball on the left side of the jaw, splintering it and sending some of the young man's teeth flying. Kimball fell sideways in a lump on the ground.

Riley straightened and looked around at the four

men still facing him. "Which one of ye shit piles is next?" he asked. His rage was building now, peaking when he needed it most. Though he was yet big and brawny, his muscles kept rock hard by long hours of pounding hot iron, he wasn't nearly as young as he used to be. Still, he could use the controlled rage inside him now. It would give him a little more power and stamina.

"Ah, that Billy vas only a boy," Gudde snapped. "Let's see how you do against a real man." He hitched his pants up, then advanced, his hands making small, wavy grabbing motions in the air.

Riley figured Gudde to be the second most dangerous of the men he faced—Halsey being number one. Gudde was short, with a huge neck, wide chest, a big, hard stomach turning to fat. His arms looked powerful, as did the short, stubby fingers.

Both men locked their hands on each other's biceps. They strained, each trying to gain an advantage and throw his opponent. Their hands slipped off at times, and there was a little flurry of slapping until they regained their holds.

Finally Riley managed to get his right heel behind Gudde's left leg and trip him. As Gudde fell backward, he got his other foot up and planted it in Riley's stomach as his back hit the ground. With a shove, and the momentum Riley had, the Mormon flipped the mountain man back over him.

Riley landed with a thud, angry that he had been outfoxed. He got up and faced Gudde, who, like Riley, was breathing heavily. The two men circled warily for a while, trying to get their breath back. Then Gudde charged, but he fell just before reaching Riley. Too late the mountain man realized he had been fooled again. The Saint kicked Riley's legs out from him, and Riley fell in a heap.

The Mormon jumped up with a cry of victory. He lifted his foot to stomp on Riley, but the blacksmith grabbed the leg and jerked Gudde onto his back. Riley rolled, shoving the Mormon's leg up toward his chest a hard as it would go. Gudde roared in pain as muscles tore.

Riley let go of the leg and stood, his breath coming hard. Then he knelt, grabbed Gudde by crotch and shirt and lifted the two hundred forty pound Mormon over his head. Then he dropped him. Gudde's neck snapped when he hit the hard, dry ground.

Riley bent over, hands on knees, trying to catch his breath, thinking again that perhaps he was a little old for such activity. Finally he straightened and looked at Halsey. "Your turn," he said coldly, and began walking toward the Mormon.

Dan Hyde suddenly rushed at Riley's right side. Without even looking, Riley lashed out with his right arm. The forearm cracked across the bridge of Hyde's nose, and the Mormon dropped to the ground. Riley continued walking.

"It's about time we got to this," Halsey said as he wiped his hands on his pants. "I've waited a long time to kill you."

"For your brother?" Riley asked. When Halsey nodded, Riley said, "If he wasn't such a toad-fuckin', back-shootin', scabrous shit pile, he'd still be alive."

With a scream of anger, Halsey swung a fist at Riley. The mountain man brushed it aside as he would a gnat, and kept advancing. Halsey continued to swing punches at Riley's head. None connected.

The Mormon was constantly moving backward away from the relentless blacksmith. Without warning, Riley dropped to one knee. As a surprised Halsey reared back to drive a punch at Riley's head, the blacksmith drove his right fist upward, with all the strength in his mighty arm, shoulder and back. The fist hit Halsey in the solar plexus, rupturing the diaphragm and making his heart burst.

Halsey hung there for some moments, blood running out of his mouth. His face had taken on a strangled look. Unaware, he urinated in his pants. Then he collapsed.

Riley spit on the body, and then pushed to his feet. Suddenly he heard Browning shout. He looked around to see Bob Sprague, knife in hand, fall dead, two arrows in his back, just a few feet away.

Riley smiled harshly when he saw eight Shoshonis, led by Black Iron and Sharp Hawk, stride into the camp on foot, bows ready, guns cocked. The soldiers suddenly became nervous. They didn't wonder whether there were more Shoshonis just outside the fort. What they wondered was how many.

The Shoshonis stopped and waited. Their faces were painted, but expressionless. "Hey, ho, One-Eye," Sharp Hawk said by way of greeting.

Riley nodded and turned to see if any foes remained. Kimball was dead, having strangled on his own tongue. So were the others, except for Dan Hyde. Riley headed for the young man. He knelt and grabbed a handful of shirt in his left hand. He raised his right fist. "Ye know any prayers, shit pile, ye got ten seconds to say 'em."

"Wait!" the cowering Hyde screamed. "Wait, please. Don't kill me," he begged.

"Why shouldn't I?"

"I'll talk! I'll tell ya everything."

"There ain't no reason for me to trust a lyin' shit pile like ye, boy."

"Let him go, One-Eye," Canby ordered.

Riley looked at the major, still enraged, but dropped his fist. He rose, jerking Hyde up with him. He shoved the Mormon toward the fort commander.

Canby glared at Hyde for a moment. Then he said harshly, "Tell me the truth, boy. All of it. You'll get only one chance, and it's your only hope of staying alive."

In fits and starts, Hyde babbled out the tale. It was a little disjointed, but it was pretty much what Higgins had told Riley, and what Riley had told the court. Finally Hyde stumbled to a halt, looking ashamed that he had ever been involved in such activities.

"Jist one question," Riley said. "Did Brigham Young initiate this wickedness?" He just had to know.

"No. Bill Hickman come up with it and sent the letter to us back east. I don't think Brother Young even knew of it."

Riley nodded. It wasn't what he had wanted to hear, really, since it would boost Young in his estimation, ever so slightly. But he was satisfied that he knew the truth.

"Lock Mister Hyde up," Canby ordered. "You will, of course, be tried again, Mister Hyde—on new charges—and I can assure you that the verdict will be different this time."

As several soldiers led Hyde away, Riley turned his attention to Keyes. "It's about time me and ye settled our differences, shit pile. You've had a hell of a spree at my expense, but now it's time to pay up."

The lieutenant sneered. "Go to hell, Riley," he snapped. "You wouldn't dare kill an army officer on the post, right in front of the commanding officer."

"I'm afraid I have to agree with him, One-Eye," said Canby, who was still standing nearby.

Riley shrugged. He knew what he had to do, and he was willing to accept the consequences. As Canby turned to head toward his office, Riley moved in on Keyes.

The haughtiness dissipated fast from Keyes's face when he saw the fearsome look in Riley's eye and suddenly realized how little support he had among the men. Nervous, he prepared to fight Riley.

The former mountain man threw three swift punches, starting to pound Keyes to mush.

Canby jerked around when he heard the sound of fist on flesh. "Goddammit," he muttered. He looked at Lieutenant Dwight Browning next to him and said, "Get some troops and put a stop to that immediately. I want Riley arrested, too. Move it, man, before One-Eye kills the dumb bastard."

"I suggest, sir," Browning said nervously, "that we let them continue."

Canby raised his eyebrows, then shrugged. He had no love of Keyes, never had. Keyes was an annoyance at best and a threat at worst. Canby knew that Riley would have no trouble disposing of Keyes, and on reflection, he figured that might even work to his advantage. He would be rid of the troublesome lieutenant, and then he'd have the bothersome Riley arrested. That way, he'd be shed of two thorns in his side. He sort of hated to see it happen, since he liked Riley, but the man was trouble, and Canby had had his fill of that.

He stood and watched, face tight. And when Keyes was little more than a dying lump on the ground, Canby ordered Riley arrested. As some reluctant soldiers moved toward the blacksmith, who looked as if he was ready to take on the entire fort, about two hundred Shoshonis rushed in through the gate. A number of them swiftly surrounded Riley protectively.

Tensions were high, and Riley began to worry. He knew the Shoshonis would win the battle that seemed imminent, but many of them would die in the process. "Major," he said urgently, "call off your soldiers. Jist tell 'em to back off."

"And your friends, what about them?" Canby was angry at having been boxed into such a tight position.

"I'll keep the Shoshonis in check if ye do the same with your soldiers."

Canby didn't have to think about it. He was no more interested in further bloodshed here than Riley was. He nodded, but then said sharply, "You'll have to leave the fort and not come back, though, One-Eye."

Riley defiantly began to protest, but Canby cut him off. "Listen, damn you, I'll have to deal with a lot of Saints at this fort," he said tightly. "I can't have someone as antagonistic toward those people as you are working here. Not after what's gone on today. Nor can I continue to harbor a man who killed one of my officers as disagreeable as Lieutenant Keyes might've been."

Riley nodded sadly. He knew that if he stayed, he would constantly be fending off trouble, since the Mormons felt about him the way he felt about them. "What about the plot against the fort, though?" he asked.

"I'll be sending a courier to the wagon train and then on to Salt Lake City. He'll be carrying two letters—one for those with the wagons still out there, the other for Brigham Young. Despite Mister Hyde's swearing that Mister Young wasn't involved in all this, he could have been an unseen hand behind it all. Regardless, he will be warned."

Riley nodded again. Surrounded by Shoshoni warriors, he headed to his cabin. With the help of Spirit Grass, Flat Nose, and Arrives With Trouble, the blacksmith hurriedly prepared to leave. Outside, the warriors waited, keeping watch.

When Browning showed up a little while later, Riley told the Shoshonis to let him in. "What're you going to do, One-Eye?" Browning asked.

"Live with the Shoshonis maybe," Riley said with a shrug. "Or head to the mountains. The high country's the only place I was ever really comfortable."

Browning nodded. He wasn't sure of what else to say, but he couldn't just let Riley leave like this. His eyes strayed to the fireplace and to the weapons hanging above it—a rifle placed at a diagonal, with one big Colt pistol above it and one below. "Those're Paddy's guns, aren't they?" he asked, pointing.

Riley nodded. He was almost proud of Browning for having figured it out.

"You're taking them with you?"

"Of course."

The knowledge somehow strengthened Browning. "I'll try to carry on your ways here," he said a little bashedly. "You've taught me a lot about dealing with Indians. And a hell of a lot more about life. I hope I can live up to your legacy here."

Riley smiled and shook Browning's hand. As he slapped him on the shoulder, he said, "You'll do jist fine, Lieutenant. I figure I'm leavin' the fort in good hands."

Soon after, Riley and his family, with the warriors still guarding them, left the fort. Riley was astride his horse.

Flat Nose drove the wagon, with Riley's tools and the family's goods in it. Spirit Grass rode on the seat next to her oldest child. In the back, the two younger children sat amid the belongings.

A short way off, Riley stopped and looked back, somewhat wistfully. He had had the best times of his life here, and he would miss it.

Sharp Hawk stopped alongside him. "Forget this goddamn place," he said. "Ain't nothin' but trouble here."

"I suppose you're right, my brother," Riley said with a grin. He really didn't feel too bad about leaving. And he knew that while his only real success had come here, he could now succeed elsewhere. He turned his horse and rode on.

AUTHOR'S NOTE

For a small trading post and later a small army post, Fort Bridger has a rather convoluted history, some of it still in dispute.

In 1841, when even Jim Bridger knew that the beaver trade was over for good, he partnered up with Henry Fraeb (pronounced "Frapp") with the idea of building a small trading post along the Oregon-California Trail. Bridger and Fraeb had been partners before, in the Rocky Mountain Fur Company. They chose a spot along Black's Fork of the Green River. By most accounts, this "fort" was a single small cabin. But before it even got into use, Fraeb was killed in a battle with a large force of Sioux, Cheyenne and Arapaho. Some accounts have this battle happen within a few miles of the fort; others (including the official Wyoming state map) place it a considerable distance east, near present Encampment, Wyoming. I used the former for the purposes of the novel.

After Fraeb was killed, Bridger roamed, as he was prone to do, but sometime in 1842, he and Louis Vasquez formed a company with the intent of building a trading post in the same region as the earlier one. This fort was operating by 1843 and was to continue almost unchanged until the Mormons bought it and occupied it in 1855.

This trading post was on an "island" formed by the

two branches of Black's Fork, and was only a few miles from the original. This unprepossessing outpost was to become, for a time, an important stop on the Oregon and California Trails, as well as the Mormon Trail. It later was used as a stage waystation, and the mail and Pony Express stopped at the fort.

The first Mormons, led by Brigham Young, who was bedridden with Rocky Mountain spotted fever, arrived at the fort in the spring of 1847. Relations, apparently, were cordial at first, though not overly so. With the history of persecution the Church of Jesus Christ of Latter-day Saints had suffered, it was no wonder that the Mormon people were rather reticent to deal with Gentiles. Also because of the persecution they had suffered, the Saints did form a group called the Danites, back when they were still in the east. Men like William Hickman and Porter Rockwell were members, and they carried out many violent tasks in defense of their church.

Some accounts say that the Danites did not exist once the Mormons reached the Salt Lake; others say they did. Whether these "Avenging Angels" existed under the name Danites or not is moot. The Mormons fielded large posses and even armies at various times over the years.

There seems to be little definitive reason for the beginning of the trouble between the Mormons and the mountain men. Certainly there were plenty of reasons, but what sparked it seems cloudy.

There is no doubt that Brigham Young and Jim Bridger hated each other, and there's no doubt that each did things that heightened tensions between the two groups. Young did covet the Green River Valley, and particularly the lucrative Green River ferrying business. Bridger and his fellow mountain men did stir up the Indians of the area, urging them to raid Mormon settlements; they lied to the Mormons about the Indians and to the Indians about the Mormons.

Whatever the root causes, things were not the same in the area from Salt Lake City to the Green River within a

few years of the Mormons' arrival. As early as 1848—
only a year after the Saints' arrival—Young wrote to
Bridger asking him to control the Indians of the area.
No action was taken, though when Bridger heard that
Wakara and Old Elk were planning to raid Mormon
settlements, he did warn Young.

In the early 1900s, Bridger's daughter, Virginia
Bridger Hahn, told a reporter that Bridger did have a
Mormon wife sometime back in the old days, and had
had two sons—James and John—with her. There is no
credible evidence of this, though, and the remark, made
by Virginia when she was in her late sixties, is given no
credence by most experts. I have used the incident (as
well as the one about hiding the gold) to lend tension to
the story. Virginia Bridger Hahn is buried in Fort
Bridger's cemetery.

By the early 1850s, tensions between the two factions
were quite high. Young created the state of Deseret and
applied for admission to the Union. Worried about
Young's growing power and daring, the federal government established Utah Territory instead, though Young
was appointed governor.

Also during this time period, the territorial Legislature, under Young's direction, began imposing taxes on
the fort's business as well as the ferrying business. It also
granted rights to ferries to Mormons, though the mountain men had been running them for years. This caused
friction, and several small battles.

In 1853, Young, acting as governor, issued a warrant
for Bridger's arrest. A posse of one hundred fifty men
headed toward his fort to arrest him. Getting word of it,
Bridger disappeared. It is assumed by most authorities
that he hid nearby and waited it out. During the "occu-
pation" of the fort, there were more skirmishes with
mountain men over the ferries.

Bridger did head east after the short takeover, and
tried to get reparations. He sought astounding amounts
of money, far beyond what was reasonable, and spread
some pretty tall tales around Washington about what

had happened in Utah Territory. Most sources show, however, that the Mormon posse made a good accounting of everything that they confiscated or used, and paid for it, though not immediately, since the situation was in such flux.

A small group of mountain men did hold the fort for almost two years between the time the Mormon posse left and the LDS Church bought the fort in 1855.

The fort's purchase also has been in dispute, though it seems to be fairly certain now that there was indeed a sale. Bridger always claimed that he never sold the fort; that the Mormons just took it over, not paying for it. But letters in the LDS archives show that Bridger agreed to the sale of the fort in 1855 for eight thousand dollars. Four thousand dollars was paid then; the other four thousand was signed for by Louis Vasquez in 1858—a year after the army retook the fort.

The Saints occupied the fort for almost two more years, building a wall around it, and making plans to enlarge it.

But in 1857, President Buchanan sent an army of twenty-five hundred men—between one-sixth and one-fifth of the standing American army at the time—to restore federal control over Utah Territory. The army arrived in the territory in November and were immediately hit by guerrilla raids, many led by Rockwell, as well as Lot Smith. The raids were mainly to heckle the army, but also to give the Mormon settlers in the vicinity time to pack up and flee for Salt Lake City, which they did.

Just before the last of the Saints pulled out, they burned to the ground the settlement at Fort Supply, as well as Bridger's old post. When the army arrived at the old fort site in late November, they found the Mormon-built wall and ashes.

The army spent a hellacious winter at the site. It was bitter cold, and they had only tents to protect them. With the loss of supplies to raiders during the march out there, Captain Marcy, a troop of soldiers and some mountain men who had shown up were sent to Fort

Massachusetts—in present Colorado, near Fort Garland, about one hundred miles or so from Taos, New Mexico. That troop was almost wiped out by the winter as they struggled through mountain passes and such. The men did make it, then went to Taos before eventually returning to Fort Bridger in the spring. By then the army had managed to build only two lunettes—stone guard towers—at the fort.

In the spring, the army got word from Brigham Young that the Saints would not resist the army, and the major part of the force headed to Salt Lake City. The Mormons had also evacuated the city, just in case the army planned to sack it. The official transfer of power, though, to a non-Mormon governor was made without trouble. The LDS Church, however, remained the major power in reality.

Construction at the fort picked up rapidly in the spring and by the end of 1858, quite a bit of it was finished. When the Civil War started, the post was drained of troops for the fighting back east. At one point, the garrison consisted of a sergeant and two privates. Because of that, Judge William A. Carter—who had come out with the army in 1857 and became the fort's sutler and trader—formed a militia of sorts from former mountain men living in the region. It was nominally under the control of the California militia until late summer 1865, when the fort was manned by a Nevada militia company. The military returned in 1866. Nothing much untoward happened while the fort was "unoccupied."

The fort was officially abandoned by the army on November 6, 1890. In April 1929, the fort remains were acquired by the Wyoming State Historical Society, which runs it as a state park today. The state park is on State Route 308, a few miles of Interstate 80 in the southwest corner of Wyoming. The nearest cities are Evanston to the west and Green River to the east. It is open to the public, free, from April until October. A replica of the old fort has been built, and many of the army buildings remain—including much of officers' row and many of the buildings built by Judge Carter (his store in a museum now).

Excavations on the original fort (which lies just about squarely under the fort museum) have shown that the blacksmith shop was in the southwest corner, at the "rear" of the fort. For the purposes of this novel, however, I have placed it in the northwest corner.

Real characters appearing in *Blood at Fort Bridger:* Jim Bridger, Captain Robert Burton, Major Edward S. Canby, Judge William A. Carter (sometimes known as "Mr. Fort Bridger" because of his importance), Sheriff Sam Ferguson, Tom Fitzpatrick, Henry Fraeb, William Hickman, Colonel Albert Sydney Johnston, John Nebecker, Old Elk, Jack Robinson, Lewis Robison, Orrin Porter Rockwell, Elisha Ryan, Louis Vasquez, Narcissa Vasquez, Wakara, and Brigham Young.

The major resources I used in the writing of *Blood at Fort Bridger* were "Fort Bridger: Island in the Wilderness," by Fred Gowans and Eugene E. Campbell; "In Mormon Circles: Gentiles, Jack Mormons and Latter-Day Saints," by James Coates; "Fort Bridger: A Brief History," by R. S. Ellison; and " 'Wild Bill' Hickman and the Mormon Frontier," by Hope A. Hilton.

And my thanks to the folks at Fort Bridger State Historical Site.

THE TRAIL DRIVE SERIES
by Ralph Compton
From St. Martin's Paperbacks

The only riches Texas had left after the Civil War were five million maverick longhorns and the brains, brawn and boldness to drive them north to where the money was. Now, Ralph Compton brings this violent and magnificent time to life in an extraordinary epic series based on the history-blazing trail drives.

THE GOODNIGHT TRAIL (BOOK 1)
———— 92815-7 $4.99 U.S./$5.99 Can.
THE WESTERN TRAIL (BOOK 2)
———— 92901-3 $4.99 U.S./$5.99 Can.
THE CHISOLM TRAIL (BOOK 3)
———— 92953-6 $4.99 U.S./$5.99 Can.
THE BANDERA TRAIL (BOOK 4)
———— 95143-4 $4.99 U.S./$5.99 Can.
THE CALIFORNIA TRAIL (BOOK 5)
———— 95169-8 $4.99 U.S./$5.99 Can.
THE SHAWNEE TRAIL (BOOK 6)
———— 95241-4 $4.99 U.S./$5.99 Can.
THE VIRGINIA CITY TRAIL (BOOK 7)
———— 95306-2 $4.99 U.S./$5.99 Can.

Coming in January 1995
THE DODGE CITY TRAIL